THE REJUVENATION PROJECT

THE REJUVENATION PROJECT

SHARON STARR

UNITED WRITERS
Cornwall

UNITED WRITERS PUBLICATIONS LTD
Ailsa, Castle Gate, Penzance, Cornwall.
www.unitedwriters.co.uk

British Library Cataloguing in Publication Data:
A catalogue record for this book is
available from the British Library.

ISBN 9781852001704

Printed and bound in Great Britain by
United Writers Publications Ltd.,
Cornwall.

To Mum and Dad:
'We still love you.'

Chapter One

It was hailed as the greatest advance for mankind since the 'big bang'. Newspaper editors saw it as the opportunity of a lifetime and made no attempt to restrain their creativity. Instead, headlines such as 'Frankenstein Lives!', 'From Here to Eternity' and even 'Spawn of the Dead' were splattered across the tabloids. The broadsheets tried to remain detached and dignified but headlines including 'Scientist Solves the Mystery of Immortality' could not disguise the boiling excitement.

Of course, the breakthrough was not quite as reported but, nevertheless, news that someone had succeeded in reviving a cryogenically-frozen corpse hit the Western world like the second coming.

Helen was driving to work when the news hissed over the radio. At first she thought she had misheard; the newsreader was always stumbling over his words, using inappropriate inflection and generally making mistakes, and she had just driven through a dip which always knocked a hole in the reception. But the radio presenter's subsequent comment reaffirmed the news. Helen felt cold. Then she checked the date – 1st April. A chuckle escaped from between her lips and she grinned at herself. The whiteness of her teeth flashed in the rear-view mirror and she watched briefly as her cheeks returned to their usual pink veneer. 'What a trick!' she thought, surprised at how frightened she had felt. The puzzle made her uneasy for a moment. Then she shrugged her shoulders, glanced again in the rear-view mirror and, wishing the man in the van behind would not drive so close, accelerated towards her office.

The Reverend Philip Mouland had just begun morning prayers at St. Nonna's Priory – 8am until 8.30am every day except Saturday. Sometimes he felt guilty about Saturday. Faith was a full-time vocation so how could he justify taking Saturdays off? What if someone in spiritual need was turned away just because it was Saturday? On the other hand, he enjoyed his lie-in once a week – he needed it.

As a result of the early prayer session and the hectic day swinging into action as usual, Reverend Mouland did not hear the news that morning. That is not to say that he did not hear any news; on the contrary, there was always at least a nugget of wrong-doing broadcast by one member of the congregation to the detriment of another, but the vicar usually missed any national news until one o'clock. Then he would sit in the worn armchair in his tiny, but well-organised, office, drink tea, try not to eat too much and listen to the news on the radio. The programme was broadcast from across the road, the radio station being housed in a glass tower, typical of city architecture, which had been designed to gleam in the setting sun, dwarfing the tiny spire above the ancient priory.

Due to the close proximity of the studio, Reverend Mouland had occasionally been invited to appear on one of the programmes to comment on topical features when more sought-after, higher members of the clergy proved unavailable. His forthright, 'no nonsense', committed views had begun to develop him a small following. He usually enjoyed these opportunities in contrast to the trivial concerns of his congregation. Today was no different. Mouland conducted the short, sincere service to a handful of sinners. Mrs Wainscott always came. She never failed to attend every service, every day, but she never mixed with anyone else. It wasn't as if she was unpleasant or even strange in some way – just very insular. She appeared to have a profound need for the services but no need of the peripheral supporting act. 'For most of the other members of the congregation the reverse seemed to apply,' Mouland thought, moodily. He rarely found a chance to speak to her despite contriving to manipulate a casual word or two. Mrs Wainscott was always one of the last to arrive and the first to leave.

This morning there were two tramps in attendance. There was always at least one – sometimes half a dozen, depending on the weather. Mouland used to find it difficult when dealing with people such as these. He had believed it to be his Christian duty to help them and try to provide them with some warmth, shelter, comfort and food. He soon found that in the majority of cases this was unwelcome – they seemed to want only to destroy themselves. He could not leave the church unlocked anymore. If he did, the lady chapel became a social club for drunks or drug addicts who would lie there, radios blaring, dogs whining and their curses bouncing off the rafters. One morning he arrived for prayers to find a fire burning, fuelled by torn hymn books and pieces of wood prised from one of the ancient pews. Mouland, himself, blazed in fury and went on an offensive for his faith. Suddenly he realised that he was tired of Christianity being seen as weak and insipid. 'Why should his sacred place be abused?' The offenders were dragged to their senses unceremoniously, their stinking blankets torn away, before they were forced, blinking, out into the frosty sunshine. From then on the large vestibule at the entrance was the only part of the priory accessible during the hours of darkness. Beggars were offered a voucher for fish and chips at a local take-away and the vicar truly believed that he was doing all that was possible under the circumstances.

Some refused the vouchers contemptuously: "What am I supposed to do with that?" rasped one recipient, angrily. "I want cash!" he growled, clenching and unclenching his large, dirty palm. Mouland picked up the torn pieces from the floor and silently moved towards the next man who, in contrast, seemed pleased, even grateful for it. Mouland understood how difficult it was to help people who could not help themselves. He could not give away cash – if he did the word would soon spread and tens, if not hundreds, of beggars would descend on the small band of disciples, swamping them and their efforts and probably defiling the sanctity of the building.

This morning, the two vagrants in attendance were not causing any trouble. Reverend Mouland glanced at them warily from time to time but they remained quiet, almost peaceful, as they slumbered – one leaning against the fat Portland stone pillar, the other slumped forward supporting his head in both hands as if praying devoutly. Perhaps he was. Mouland hoped that his sonorous tone would seep into them and his measured words, delivered in the style of a chant, would provide whatever it was they sought.

A further sweep of his eyes encompassed the remainder of his flock. That morning, Julian Devereux, one of the churchwardens and his good friend, whose turn it had been to unlock the priory, fulfilled his duty. Dressed smartly in fawn, cavalry twill trousers (with a dangerously sharp crease in each leg), matching jacket covering a red lambswool jumper, a check shirt and finished off with a green woollen tie, he positioned his angular body as far away as possible – diagonally opposite – the two 'men of the road'. Devereux was the sort of man who smelled strongly of soap – never aftershave. His hair, grey but plentiful, was carefully arranged with a severe parting of mathematical precision on the left side from which his thick mop had been trained to emerge and settle obediently at a right-angle. No hair was ever out of place. Sixty years of life and distinguished military service had lined Major Devereux's thin face but his faded blue eyes still possessed a laser-like quality. He was the sort of man who instantly dissected an image or impression, stored it and then assessed it. No one, with the exception of his wife, Felicity, dared to oppose him. Next to him were two foreign students obviously unsure of the required responses and in awe of their magnificent surroundings. Finally, there was Mick Pettifer, the market trader, who often attended the service 'for a bit of peace and quiet', as he explained to his friends, and whose emphatic vocal participation could be heard as clearly as when he was advertising his wares out in the street.

Reverend Mouland blessed them all and retired to the vestry to remove his robe. For some reason he felt more depressed than usual. The number of people in the congregation was pathetic. Yet again, he pondered the question, 'why'? 'Why are we no longer able to reach them?' he thought. It seemed that spiritual awareness was generally inversely proportional to material well-being. Immediately he remembered the two homeless men who had attended the service. They had nothing, but he doubted that they were very spiritually aware. Perhaps that was because they were on the periphery of society – his theory was a general one, applicable to society as a whole. For the poor, religion had always

10

promised desperate salvation, for those embroiled in materialism it was an ignominy. Mouland felt sure that it would remain that way only until the cycle had been completed and then people would reap what they had sown. Then, although gorged on possessions, services and every imaginable, tangible thing possible, they would eventually realise that they were still unsatisfied, that they felt empty. All Mouland could do in the meantime was to ensure that there was still something for them to seek and find when that time came.

Helen swung her car into its usual parking space, gathered her belongings from the back seat and after glancing at her watch, entered the office building. The security guard nodded to her before continuing to munch at an apple and study something in his crumpled newspaper. Helen still felt a little wary. April Fool's Day. There was always someone who found it amusing, rather than irritating, to play a juvenile practical joke and the office contained several likely candidates at present – two youngsters, fresh from university, and David Jones, the middle-aged sales manager, who should know better. Last year she had spent the entire morning desperately trying to locate an apparently urgent bogus order set up by him. Consequently she had had to stay late and had missed a planned evening out with her fiancé, Peter. The thought of Jones' plump, sweating face and its satisfied grin repulsed her. The corners of her mouth curled and the thought that she wished he would die passed through her mind.

Guiltily, Helen began to arrange her desk for the day whilst mentally preparing the list of tasks left over from yesterday. She was the first to arrive, as usual. Ten minutes later an excited chattering charged the sterile atmosphere and the two graduates – Ruth, a trainee web manager, and Darren, a trainee salesman, arrived. Smiling and agitated, they exuded the impression that it was the last day of term. Helen looked up from her work, 'It's only Thursday,' she thought, frowning.

"Helen, have you heard the news?" demanded Ruth. "Obviously you haven't or you wouldn't be sitting there so calmly as if nothing's happened," she continued, without waiting for a reply.

"Looks like she's already lived forever," Darren whispered too loudly. Ruth giggled.

"What news?" Helen asked in a bored voice, without deflecting her eyes from her computer screen.

"Only the news that's on the television, radio and all the newspapers," replied Darren, rolling his eyes at Ruth who giggled again.

"Only the news that we can all live forever!" he announced dramatically.

"Oh, that." Helen dismissed this particular Holy Grail as though it were no more than a prediction of rain in November. "You do know that it's April Fool's Day?" She enquired rhetorically, whilst clicking the mouse.

"Yes. But this is true!" Ruth sounded almost in pain.

"Trust you not to believe it!" Darren retorted with hostility. "It's being announced everywhere, all the television programmes are full of it – they've suspended the normal schedules and the prime minister's going to make a statement at twelve o'clock. Turn on the radio or look on the internet!"

The childish intensity in his voice worried Helen. Something must have happened. The atmosphere and reaction of those around her teemed with an incongruous mixture of bereavement and elation. People trembled and a veil of nervous energy cloaked the room. Reluctantly, she clicked the internet into life. At the same time, Darren pressed the switch on the new digital office radio, instantly flooding the room with 'the news'. He turned round triumphantly, "I told you. . ." he began.

"Shhh!" hissed Helen, "I'm trying to listen."

The rest of the day was very odd. 'The news' was confirmed over and over again until it became in danger of losing its impact. Nevertheless, no one (including Helen) could concentrate and very little work was accomplished. A festive atmosphere reigned. Strangers on the telephone joked amiably – even the woman for Directory Enquiries made an excited comment.

David Jones arrived at work late, which was not unusual, and disappeared soon after. He lumbered in, already perspiring slightly, his suit crumpled in its familiar condition and the twisted knot of his sticky tie resting on his chubby chest.

"Morning all. Morning all. Busy day," he panted. "Things to do – people to see and all that. Darren, can you look up prices and availability etc., of a virtual website? I'll need the info by first thing tomorrow morning."

12

Darren rolled his eyes at Ruth who hid a smile. 'Now I'll have to do some work,' he thought begrudgingly. "What do you think about living forever, then, Dave?" he called across.

"Oh that. I'm far too busy to think about it," David replied, shoving a bundle of paper into his briefcase and avoiding Darren's eye. "Got to go. Don't forget those figures."

After David Jones had safely disappeared Darren turned to Ruth and Helen. "How can anyone be 'too busy'? he mused. "Where's he gone, anyhow?"

Helen snorted involuntarily. "Off on a jolly, no doubt – to celebrate his eternal youth. . ." she stopped suddenly, interrupted by the radio – the presenter had just mentioned her father's name – Professor Marcus Deighton. Then his own familiar nasal tone filtered across the airwaves,

"Yes. I'm absolutely delighted to announce that after years of intense research, and may I add, frustration, our, er, my efforts have finally come to fruition. We have, indeed, succeeded in rejuvenating a cryogenically preserved human being. I'm not prepared to go into further details at this stage but would like to report that the patient is doing well, and I'd also like to extend my thanks to my team who have supported my work over the last few years."

"Can you give us the name of your patient, where he or she is and what happens next?" The reporter could not refrain from interrogating the professor whose smile was obvious to those who listened.

"No. As I've previously stated, I'm not able to divulge more detail. Suffice it to say that the patient is doing well and has a small number of observations and tests to undergo before being given an absolutely clean bill of health, but we're confident that we will be able to do that very soon. Thank you."

"Thank you, Professor Deighton," returned the interviewer humbly, emphasising the word 'you' so that it unmistakeably elevated the professor's status to a realm far above the ordinary.

"Isn't that your dad?" Ruth recalled Helen's father being a scientist or something.

"You're crafty, aren't you?" accused Darren, aggressively. "Pretending you knew nothing about it, pretending you thought it was an April Fool's joke. I suppose you had it all planned."

"I did know nothing," Helen snapped. "Do you think my father discusses his work with me? Didn't David give you a task to do?" she added, reminding him of her authority.

It was true. Her father never discussed his research with anyone outside a very small clique of colleagues. She would not have understood it if he had. She was not particularly interested – he was a research biologist, whatever that entailed, that was all. Everything would change now. He would probably be awarded the 'Nobel Prize' and other great honours. Helen tried to concentrate on the screen in front of her; she scrolled down the screen without reading anything. The knowledge that her father was responsible for the earth-shattering announcement which had so aroused everyone made her wary and uncertain. Cold crept over her body and her skin prickled. She fought a compulsion to sob. It was ridiculous, she never did that.

Chapter Two

The frenzy that the announcement caused was almost indescribable. The media was as excited by the newsworthy opportunity which had arrived as with the actual news itself. Editors and producers invoked the full extent of their self-importance. Orders were issued in harsh, staccato barks and each subservient individual was reminded, very acutely, of his own insignificance. Underlings rushed to and fro with confused purpose – one minute being ordered to do one thing and the next moment the opposite. Adrenaline flowed.

There were several casualties. One senior producer of a well-known and much loved daytime television chat show suffered a fatal heart attack moments before transmission. The warning signs had been apparent but he had ignored them in his determination to deliver the best show and capture the highest audience figure. A colleague had briefly become aware of his ashen, perspiring face but had not bothered to enquire whether he felt all right or to suggest that he took a break – time was tight and the programme far too important.

A young reporter was run over by a car in Butcher's Row. Apparently he was dashing to join the mêlée of reporters who were interviewing Professor Deighton outside his laboratory. A female studio technician, responding to a demand to start work early, slipped from the platform at Embankment and was crushed beneath the wheels of the arriving 7am train. It was not an accident. A surreptitious hand had given her a firm push – just enough to ensure that she tumbled over the edge of the platform.

The hand's owner slipped away, his urge fulfilled for the time being. The dead technician was unlucky: had she caught her usual train someone else would have laid mangled on the track. She would merely have been late for work.

Despite the manic activity there was a danger, from the media's point of view, that the story's impact would evaporate too quickly – the announcement had been made and everyone had heard it (so they believed) and therefore something had to be done to keep the story running. Interview after interview took place but not with anyone who knew intimate details of the process. Anyone with even a hint of a qualification in anything loosely scientific, was given the opportunity to speculate on the procedure and its likelihood of success. The ensuing meaningless comments were no more relevant than the musing of two cleaners from Professor Deighton's laboratory, who were mistakenly thought to be members of his research team and who were interviewed at length, twice, on national television.

Reverend Mouland unlocked the door to his small office in the crypt of St. Nonna's to the sound of the telephone ringing. Its red light flashed angrily – the memory was full of messages – and the ring assumed an urgent, frustrated tone. The vicar stared at it with an air of concern. It was still early to receive telephone calls – usually all but the most impatient of his congregation waited until after nine o'clock, when they had cleared away their breakfast things. Sighing he picked up the receiver:

"Good morning, Reverend Mouland speaking," he answered automatically.

"Hello!" a hurried, breathless voice filtered through; "Thank God I've got you at last!" it snapped in unmistakeable admonishment. "It's Tara Golesworthy – researcher for National Prime Time Radio. I've been given your name by a colleague. I believe you've been interviewed on our 'London Calling' show a few times?"

"Yes. That's correct," Mouland confirmed.

"We need someone! Can you come at once?"

The vicar understood that this was a command rather than a request; Tara was verging on hysteria.

"Yes. Certainly, I'll come," Mouland replied soothingly, "but in what capacity? Is there something wrong?"

It had not occurred to him that he was required to be

16

interviewed, instead Tara's tumbling words and urgency had made him suspect that someone had been taken ill or was in distress. He had often noticed how at such times even the most confirmed atheist chose to enlist his help rather than cope with a crisis alone.

Miss Golesworthy was shocked into uncharacteristic silence, for almost three seconds, while she assessed the man's sanity.

"Of course something's happened!" she finally retorted. "It's the news, isn't it? And we need someone to comment from the 'God slot' angle – I mean religious, Christian, perspective. You must come right away!"

The reverend floundered for a moment whilst feeling, quite correctly, that he had missed something.

"What news?" he enquired timidly, sensing that he was about to be engulfed.

The young researcher was stunned for longer this time.

"I am speaking to Reverend Moundland – I mean Mouland – aren't I?" she asked at last, full of doubt and hysteria rising in her voice again. She wondered whether it had been wise to contact this man who seemed so ignorant of the great, good news. What possible use could he be? He was probably the wrong person. That idiot, Charles, must have given her the wrong contact details.

"You are the vicar from across the road, from St. Nanny's?" she continued anxiously.

"Yes. Yes. Definitely. But tell me what has happened. I've been very busy this morning and haven't had time to stick my head above the parapet, as it were, yet." Mouland coughed apologetically.

"We can all live forever!" Tara squealed, gleefully. "Nothing can stop us now – what is it they said? I know, 'The ascent of man has reached its pinnacle,' she continued gloriously. "There are no boundaries, no death, no end, no time, no need for religion."

Mouland correctly imagined a far away look in her eyes.

"We need you to comment, though," Tara added.

Mouland wondered whether she was mad. "Tell me a little more about it," he enquired cautiously.

Tara complied eagerly and furnished him with what she knew, which was as much as anyone else outside Professor Deighton's close circle. She revealed the information in a matter of fact way,

17

in the manner of reading a shopping list. After all, it was factual now. The vicar was as shocked as everyone else. He trembled. Then he asked himself, 'Why? Why should a person want to live forever?' The whole idea seemed ridiculous and improbable. He suspected that Tara was playing her part in a hoax which had been planned at his expense.

"Are you sure you're from 'London Calling'?" he asked. "I am aware that certain persons find practical jokes very amusing – I'm afraid that I am not one of them – and I really haven't the time to play childish games."

"Of course I'm from 'London Calling'!" Tara howled, as though it was inconceivable that she might not be. "Are you coming or not? Oh, my God, we're actually on air now!" Her frustration suddenly evaporated as she abandoned all hope: "OK," she whispered resignedly, "if you're not interested can you please, please, suggest someone else – a colleague, perhaps?"

Mouland, fearing that the young woman was about to burst into tears and thinking that it would be unfair to involve another, busy colleague in the charade (although he was tempted to suggest Devereux, who still lurked somewhere within the building) finally agreed.

"Don't worry. I'll come at once. . ."

"I'll meet you in reception," Miss Golesworthy interrupted and flung down the telephone receiver in relief before he had time to finish.

Mouland was still puzzled and full of disbelief – the young researcher had seemed very anxious, though. 'Oh well,' he thought, 'the sooner I go across to the radio station, the sooner it will be over.' It couldn't be true, of course. The media, desperate for a story and determined to out-do each other, could always be relied upon to come up with something bizarre. He was about to slip out of the side door when he glimpsed Devereux, hard at work, manically polishing one of the large, brass candlesticks. The vicar considered speaking to him for a moment about 'the news' but decided against it. The church warden was so engrossed in his task and Mouland did not want to risk appearing foolish, so he stepped into the strangely quiet road and approached the glinting tower opposite.

Tara Golesworthy pounced on him before he had the chance to announce his arrival to the receptionist. He sensed a nervous atmosphere; it reminded him of young children on Christmas Day.

"The interview will be quite simple," Tara burbled. "Jason will just ask you what you think about rejuvenation. It won't really matter what you say – we just need to be seen to be reporting without bias."

Mouland followed her to the studio full of dread. Either there was something in this 'news' or he was about to become a huge laughing stock.

Tara glanced at him impatiently wondering why he was taking so long to trundle down the corridor. Then she realised. "You really hadn't heard, had you?" she asked him incredulously, before continuing: "It must be a shock. It's been a shock to us all – but especially to someone like you."

She focused on his dog-collar as she spoke. As they entered the ante-room to the studio, Tara grabbed some newspapers from a desk and thrust them at him,

"Have a quick glance at these – they'll put you in the picture," she suggested before bustling away full of importance, her task successfully completed.

The priest did as he was told. 'It was true, then.' After passing his eyes over some of the more lurid headlines, he chose a broadsheet and hastily read the front page. Trembling, a myriad of questions began to form in his opened mind. Most were not allowed to develop before they were elbowed away by yet more which rose to the surface of his consciousness until bursting like delicate bubbles. Tara breezed back into the room, jolting him into physical presence.

"Right, you're on next. Jason will play a recording of Professor Deighton's statement and then it's your turn."

She found it necessary to manoeuvre the shocked man into the studio, where she directed him to his seat. Jason waved a hand in acknowledgement and pointed to the headphones. Mouland, with Tara's help, put them on. The professor's voice repeated his previous interview.

"That was the great Professor Deighton," chimed Jason, "the man some people are already nick-naming 'God'. But we have a man of God here ourselves, who has agreed to share his views with us. Let me welcome Reverend Mouland from St. Nonna's Priory. Reverend Mouland, what do you think of that?"

"Hmm," the clergyman stuttered, "I expect I'm as surprised as everyone else. It seems incredible. . ."

"Incredible is certainly the right word," sang Jason, easily, "but what are the implications for you as a Christian? Surely religion is redundant now? He used his matter-of-fact broadcaster's voice but Mouland felt his directness as a personal, steely blow.

"Of course there will be implications for Christianity, indeed for all of the world's faiths," snapped the vicar, having begun to recover and adopting the fight rather than flight response. "But we need to know more – much more – about the professor's claims. One, unproven, rather vague, statement is hardly enough to shake the foundations of belief which have held firm for countless centuries."

"But what if it is exactly as Professor Deighton claims?" Jason continued to attack with relish. "What if we now hold the key to eternity? Surely there will be no need for a god?"

Mouland felt his face glow red.

"There will always be a need for God," he countered. "Note I said 'God' not 'a god'. Mark my words – if the professor can perform as he claims then we are in need of God more than at any time in mankind's history. The idea that anyone should wish to live forever physically illustrates to me just how much of a Godless society we have become. Ultimately, no good will come of this."

"Thank you, Reverend Mouland." Jason cut him off before continuing, "Strong words there from a man of the cloth but what do you think? Phone, email or send us a text with your views. How many of you would like to live forever and what's wrong with that? Let us know now. . ." Jason's voice melted away as he recited the radio station's telephone number and email address.

Tara re-appeared and ushered the vicar through the ante-room. Mouland, feeling dazed and frustrated, allowed himself to be propelled back to the reception. He wished that he had been allowed to say more – the short, superficial interrogation had been worthless and he understood bitterly that he had been used.

"Right, Mr Moundland," Tara announced cheerfully as she consulted a note attached to the obligatory clipboard, "we'll make the usual donation to St. Nanny's."

"St. Nonna's," Mouland attempted to correct her.

Tara looked at him curiously, still oblivious to her error.

20

"As I said, we'll make the usual contribution. Thank you." Without waiting for a reply she hurried away busily. Mouland wryly wondered whether she would manage to fill every moment of an eternity on Earth with such vigour and with so many important tasks.

The reverend had hoped to sneak back to his office, listen to the responses to his interview and reflect on Deighton's announcement in peace. Unfortunately, Devereux had progressed to polishing the huge brass eagle which hovered at the top of the lectern. Mouland was unable to avoid him.

"Morning, Julian." His short greeting contained an unmistakeable note of weariness. "We certainly live in strange times, don't we?"

Devereux, apparently familiar with 'the news', nodded and rubbed the eagle's body harder. "It's the devil's work, in my opinion. I have never condoned all this interfering with nature – no good will come of it. Darwin has a lot to answer for," he added inexplicably.

Mouland steered the conversation away from evolution: "I wonder whether it really is true. I mean that they have actually 'rejuvenated' a human being. Perhaps their patient is only a mouse or an amoeba or something?"

"It does seem rather fanciful," Devereux agreed, still polishing vigorously. "But all the reports are adamant – some even say it's a man from Cheshire. I really don't see how they could make such a definite statement and then back-track. They certainly think they've done it – or want us to think so," he continued cryptically.

"I have a feeling that we're going to be very busy," Mouland sounded weary again.

"You never know – it might be just what we, that is, the church, needs." Devereux flicked his duster at the eagle's head with a theatrical flourish. "Something to galvanise us. A reason to unite us. An opportunity to put our point across. It's an unprecedented chance for publicity; God does, indeed, work in mysterious ways."

The thought that, perhaps, it wasn't 'the devil's work' after all filtered through his mind.

Mouland suddenly felt better. A warm glow of energy emanated from an unidentified source deep within his body. He knew what he had to do. No longer questioning his role, he understood that the time for insipid faith was over. He would willingly grasp this opportunity to bring Christianity to the forefront of society's conscience. His realisation that this would be the final battle invigorated him, causing his flesh to tingle in the manner of a warrior on the eve of war.

"I do believe you're right, Julian!" he exclaimed. "This is what we have been waiting for!"

"It won't be easy," Devereux warned, his voice trailing away as he turned his attention to the brass rails.

"There's much to be done," Mouland muttered to himself, rather than to the church warden. "We must present a united front!" He needed to consult with his colleagues but something was far more important than that; "I must phone my wife," he said.

Chapter Three

Helen was the last to leave the office, as usual, although she had accomplished very little that day. Darren had left early in a state of annoyance having realised too late that the task David had assigned to him was an April Fool's joke. After several humiliating telephone conversations with website providers, who could not understand his request, he became angry.

"Jones is going to get it," he growled, "wasting my time like that and making me look stupid."

"That's a thought!" cried Ruth suddenly. "There'd be no point doing something to somebody anymore – like killing them for revenge – they'd just be rejuvenated!"

Darren observed her coldly.

"I wasn't going to kill him," he sneered contemptuously. Ruth could be very stupid sometimes – he wondered how she had managed to obtain a first class degree while he had only been awarded a third.

"Now then, children," Helen intervened facetiously, "I know it's been an exciting day but you're all grumpy and tired now. It's time to calm down."

"I'm going," retorted Darren, even more annoyed and starting to clear his desk.

Ruth started to follow him before turning back to explain guiltily: "I think I'll go too, if you don't mind, I have some flexi-hours owing. . ."

"See you tomorrow," Helen assented, her eyes already re-fixed uselessly on her computer screen.

She had tried to contact her father several times during the day but had only succeeded in reaching his messaging service. Disappointed but unsurprised, she attempted to relegate her thoughts, which mostly consisted of questions, to the back of her mind. Finally, she slipped out of the building, pausing only to speak to the security guard, who had swapped his newspaper for an evening edition and his apple for a dank-looking mug of coffee. By the time she reached home, Helen felt miserable. She unlocked the door to her flat wishing that she did not live there. Her apartment was small, practical and functional but it was also lifeless. No matter how she tried to liven it up it always exuded drabness. Helen thought it too square, too angular and too lonely.

How different everything would have been had Peter not died. Even the flat had improved with the sound of his laughter. Rejuvenation had come too late for him, she thought with deep bitterness whilst scuffing the meagre pile of mail to one side. They would have been married by now. The drunk driver had put an end to that and all their dreams. Now she was alone, stuck in this horrible little box, whilst others would be rejuvenated and live happily ever after. Thirty-five was not old. That's what her friends never ceased to tell her (all in happy relationships) but she felt very old at times. Sometimes she felt as though she had already lived a lifetime and now she was just passing time – her chance of living the normal, comfortable dream had been taken from her and Peter. Instead, she was imprisoned in this horrible flat – the best that she could afford – with not even a cat for company (no pets allowed).

Helen sighed and tried to shake the negative thoughts from her mind. She dumped her briefcase on the floor, switched the kettle on and settled herself in front of the television. Predictably, all the channels were still devoted to 'the news'. Even the children's channel was broadcasting a badly-made, junior cartoon version of 'Frankenstein' in which the monster had a feisty American-speaking dog as a companion. Helen quickly flicked to another channel. Her father's face filled the screen and his voice drifted into her room, repeating, yet again, his previous statement. Helen's thoughts drifted to her mother. 'What would she have made of all this?' she wondered. 'Would she have been pleased and proud of her husband's success or more cautious – hostile even?' Her mother had always had definite views regarding what

24

was right or wrong, about everything, really, and was never afraid to voice them. She had certainly not been in awe of her academically-gifted husband, but had often kept some of his more fanatical ideas in check. Helen was not sure that she would have approved. Not that it mattered anymore, her mother was another for whom it was too late, having succumbed to cancer ten years ago.

The telephone rang. Helen jumped, turned the volume down on the television and picked up the receiver cautiously, hoping that it was a friend. There was silence for a few seconds and then the unmistakeable sound of office rumblings in the background. Annoyed, she flung down the receiver and stomped into the kitchen to make some tea. The telephone rang again. Helen responded, ready to attack the potential salesman.

"Can I speak to Helen Deighton?" a man's voice enquired.

"Speaking," she replied, curtly.

"I'm from 'Glamorous Gossip' magazine," continued the unwelcome voice. "Can you give me your reaction to your father's announcement?"

"No!" Helen yelled and replaced the receiver instantaneously.

The telephone rang again, immediately. She pulled the plug from the socket and made her cup of tea. Annoyed by the television programmes and already slightly bored by the day's 'news', she sank back into her chair, closed her eyes and tried to listen to her favourite piece of calming music. *The Lark Ascending* transported her to the grassy banks of the old Roman fort where she had spent happy childhood days. She could see the bird hovering, smell the thick scent of summer and feel the comforting beating of the afternoon sun. She watched as the long blades of grass rippled like green waves in a churning sea and the sound of grasshoppers infiltrated and complemented the evocative notes of the violin. The experience did not last. A cloud blotted out the sun and chilled the air. Helen's dream became fitful and, after trying for some time to recapture her innocent memories, she gave up and reached for her mobile phone.

She had to talk to someone. After pressing only three digits of Anna's number she stopped. Although Anna was her best friend she could not face discussing the 'news' even with her, knowing that she would expect answers to unfathomable questions. Helen could not discuss rejuvenation with anyone – except her father.

b

She tried his number again, without much hope but this time he answered.

"Helen?" he began cautiously, not sounding at all as he had during his broadcast.

"Yes. It's me," she replied. "I've been trying to reach you since this morning."

"I'm sorry. I had to switch the phone off. I've been so busy – it has been rather an eventful day." The professor regained some of his swagger.

"I gathered that," Helen replied flatly.

"You've heard about my discovery, of course?" her father asked uncertainly and then, unable to wait for her affirmation, continued, "The fruition of my life's work, truly the greatest discovery mankind has ever made. . ."

"Yes," Helen interrupted quickly, not liking the inexpressive tone he had lapsed into. "Why have you done it?"

Deighton was taken aback and could not reply at once – no one had asked him this. Everyone else had been full of praise, excitement and congratulations – the Nobel Prize had been mentioned several times already. It was agreed by all that he had achieved an undeniably great thing. No one had asked 'why'?

"I should have thought it was obvious," he finally retorted, tetchily. "Hasn't eternal life been the quest of man since the beginning of time? No more fear, no more sorrow, no more grief. I'm sure you can relate to that. We are about to enter a new era – creation was just the first phase – rejuvenation is the next."

"So it is true? You really can bring people back from the dead?" Helen continued in the same matter-of-fact way.

"Yes. It's exactly as I have announced!" the professor exclaimed impatiently. "That's what the whole world's been talking about today. Why are you being so negative? I would have expected more support and enthusiasm from my own daughter!"

"So now that everyone will, apparently, live forever have you thought of the implications?"

Helen's critical probing continued to irritate the great scientist.

"We're not quite at that stage yet. (But do not repeat anything I say – it will be misrepresented.) It depends on the cause of death and how and when the body is preserved. Obviously, we are still working on improvements to the process but it's only a matter of a very short time. The important thing is that we have made the breakthrough, crossed the threshold and rejuvenated a body from cryostasis. We will soon be able to widen the net and apply our techniques to more circumstances. Give us two or three more years and it will be commonplace. Everyone will have it done."

"But have you considered the implications?" Helen repeated, having inherited a stubborn trait from her father, who replied vaguely:

"The implications? Oh yes. My breakthrough will change our personal lives. I will be in great demand both here and abroad. There are bound to be huge demands on my time – you know, television, radio lecturing etc. as well as carrying out the technique and further research. You might actually find that the media show an interest in you. Please do not respond in any way. I can't allow my work or reputation to be misinterpreted."

"I meant the implications for society," Helen explained, soberly.

Her father's attitude worried her. He was so immersed in his quest that he could see no danger. His blinkered fanaticism was frightening.

"It's the answer to everyone's prayers," Deighton sounded irritable again. "Ask the man in the street – they'll all say the same. As for society – I can't concern myself with that – I'm a scientist not a sociologist. My only regret is that I hadn't made the discovery before your mother died."

Helen knew better than to argue further. In any case, he had done it now – it was never possible to recapture the genie. She wondered what her father's legacy would be – would he be credited with man's salvation or would he be remembered as the fiend who had destroyed nature's delicate balance?

"Just be careful," she warned. "Nothing will ever be the same again."

"Oh, I know that!" Her father chuckled, unable to conceal his self-satisfaction. "I've done it!" he murmured. "I've found the elixir of life."

Helen felt empty and very vulnerable.

"Bye, then. I'll speak to you soon," she ended the call abruptly, unable to listen to his self-satisfied chant any more, and tried Anna's number once again.

*   *   *   *

Mary Fields changed the television channel for the umpteenth time and scrutinised the professor's performance yet again. She had watched all the news programmes that day, since the first bulletin at 6am. On the floor lay discarded newspapers, each having had the reports of today's announcement neatly cut from them. The cuttings were piled up on the table, ready to be stuck into her scrapbook. Mary watched silently and impassively, gazing intently at the hallowed man as though she wished to drain all the knowledge of his features from his face. She would certainly recognise him in the street now. Then, prompted by a thought, she removed herself from in front of the screen and scrabbled amongst a pile of bulging scrapbooks until she found the telephone directory. Deighton was not a particularly common name so it was worth a try. There was no one listed as a professor which was disappointing; Mary was sure that he would wish to advertise his status, as he was the type of man who would consider being addressed as 'mister' a great insult. Undeterred, she went through the list methodically and called all the numbers. Most times someone answered and replied wearily that no, it was not Professor Deighton's residence. After noting carefully the numbers and addresses from which she had no reply, in the early hours of the morning Mary finally went to bed.

She had to take the following week off work; there was so much to do, so many newspaper and magazine articles to collect and file, so many television programmes to watch and so many radio reports to listen to. Many hours were spent attempting, unsuccessfully, to participate in radio 'phone-ins'. Finally she was allowed to address the professor on Jason's 'London Calling' show. She had told them that she wished to congratulate him on his pioneering work and ask when he thought the procedure would be generally available, but when her turn came she had only been allowed to croak, "You are the Anti-Christ. . ." before being cut off and YMCA sung by The Village People blared out cutting short her rant. Mary frowned. Then, remembering the meeting planned for that evening, felt better.

The meeting was arranged for 7.30pm at Mary's flat. It would be attended by a small number of like-minded people – six or seven at most – all of whom fanatically opposed 'Western interventionist medicine' whilst maintaining that all ills could be cured by meditation and, at most, the inhalation of an infusion of a select group of herbs. Despite a glaring failure in the use of these remedies (the original founder having succumbed to pneumonia and passed away last winter) the group's disciples aligned their beliefs strictly to his teachings. He had named the movement 'Man Against Doctors' – conveniently abbreviated to MAD. Some of the female members had objected, being unsure whether or not 'man' included themselves. The founder had reassured them that, of course, it did – 'man' being merely a term to define all human beings.

Mary had been his first recruit and was regarded by the others as the mother of the movement. She had succeeded him naturally and now led the largest local group or 'cell' as they liked to be called. MAD's adherents insisted that the movement was national, if not international, based on the existence of a cell consisting of three family members in Birmingham (although this could have been a student spoof) and a potter who survived on a small Scottish island who sometimes sent Mary a rambling letter. The internet could, of course, be relied upon to tease out individuals with similar views – America being the greatest source, closely followed by Japan – but these people encompassed a variety of interests and ideas within their own groups none of which were officially affiliated with MAD.

Mary looked forward to the weekly gathering with great pleasure. The evening always began with a 'cleansing session' in the form of group meditation led by herself. Then there would be a round up of members' campaign activities since the previous meeting, a discussion of the week's newsworthy events followed by a 'campaign trail' in which new campaigns would be identified and, finally, a plan of action for each campaign with individuals being assigned a task for the week. Mary prepared her flat for the meeting. It was naturally devoid of much light due to the two large conifers which stood, as if on sentry duty, on either side of the bay window, their dark green leaves brushing constantly against the sticky, unwashed pane. The room was made even darker by the thick, faded velvet curtains which were never fully open – mostly they remained completely drawn but occasionally Mary allowed a chink of summer sun to enter through an exact twelve inch gap between the two.

One advantage for visitors was that the lack of light made the thick layers of dust and dead potted plants less noticeable. Not that Mary cared. After clearing enough space for seven people to be seated, which entailed moving piles of newspapers and hiding an empty take-away tray behind the settee, she arranged the scrapbooks on the scratched and stained coffee table. Then she looked around – they would have candles tonight. The three sticks of half-burnt white wax would do. She distributed them haphazardly on the pieces of old furniture. Then she searched through the video tapes she had recorded of the professor and, settling herself on the damp, sagging settee, hummed happily to herself and rocked gently to and fro as the television screen flashed into life.

Chapter Four

Reverend Mouland had been extremely busy. He had consulted with colleagues and taken direction from his superiors – which he had decided to ignore. A disappointing number of his fellow clerics, including his bishop, had urged caution. Mouland could not understand why.

"This is both the greatest threat to Christianity and perhaps its greatest opportunity!" he raged to his wife, for the thousandth time. "Why can't they see it? If we sit back cautiously and take what is thrown, yet again, it could be the end of us. From what I can tell, there's a very worrying number of people out there who see rejuvenation as the opportunity of a lifetime. I mean, an opportunity to divest themselves of all responsibility," he corrected himself quickly, annoyed at his unintentional pun, before resuming his tirade. "Rejuvenation will be seen as a very attractive option if we don't stand up and countermand it. We must provide people with an alternative, but why is it always so difficult to get the message across?"

Mouland strode up and down the room fuelled by anxiety and pain. His wife, Caroline, watched him without attempting to intervene. His passion and devotion to his causes had been one of the things that had attracted her to him in the first place. A flame certainly burned within him to which he never failed to respond. He was simply incapable of ignoring or fighting against it.

Caroline smiled slightly. "It does seem as though it's up to you. You will have to take the lead, surround yourself with colleagues who believe as you do and become the mouthpiece for the church.

See it as an opportunity for yourself, personally. Perhaps this is what you were called to do." She sipped the last dregs of her coffee before adding, "You know I'll help in any way that I can."

Philip looked at her gratefully. "Thank you. You're right, of course, again. You always are. I couldn't do anything without your support, you know."

Caroline laughed. "Oh yes you could. You just think you couldn't, sometimes."

"I suppose we must approach this like a political campaign?" Philip suggested, already beginning to plan a long-term course of action. "The services in church are like the hustings, where I presume I am preaching to the converted. We must reach out. A leaflet drop's the thing! If one person bothers to read it and stops to think it will be worthwhile."

"And plenty of media exposure," his wife added. "Favourable exposure, of course – they will try to make a fool of you."

"Oh, I'm used to that!" Philip glanced at her slyly before breaking into a grin and continuing hastily, "Only joking, dear!"

Caroline chose to ignore his last remarks.

"You'll need to write letters or emails," she commanded. "Lots of them to the national and local press and to any television or radio programmes you can think of. And there's the internet – perhaps you could do a blog or something. Don't hold back – be controversial, then at least you'll be noticed."

"You should write too. In fact, all our supporters should join in. We need to get a debate going. Hostile responses will serve us just as well, as long as we can respond and reinforce our point of view. After all, our argument is unassailable in the end; we are putting forward the truth."

"The truth is only what one believes," Caroline murmured to herself, not wanting to discourage her husband.

"I'll start with Sunday's sermon," Philip decided. "As you're well aware, I've mentioned the issue before but I was waiting for leadership from the boss before launching into a full-blown attack. Afterwards, I can make an appeal for help with the campaign."

"There are bound to be lots of volunteers," Caroline observed. "Julian and Felicity, for a start."

"Yes," her husband agreed nonchalantly, "I must say I owe him a debt of gratitude, he was the first one to see this whole despicable scenario as an opportunity. You, of course, have made me realise that it's why I was called to serve the church. Heaven knows, I have often wondered until now."

Caroline knew as well. She could always tell when he was wrestling with an inner conflict, even when he had tried his best to conceal it. She knew that he often felt inadequate and overwhelmed. Sometimes he convinced himself that he was not the right sort of person to be a cleric – that he was not good enough. Instead he was too unforgiving and too much of a sinner to lead and guide others. He also felt from time to time that he was too aware of the delicate balance between a spiritual pathway and the practical consequences of modern life. He still felt guilty about his treatment of the tramps. Caroline's role was one of constant reassurance.

"For Heaven's sake, you're not a saint. You're just a man who's trying to do his best! No one, no thing, can ask more than that!" she would cajole.

Philip would groan in reply, partly sincerely but also in the unconscious hope of wringing more sympathy from his wife. "But is my best enough? My best always seems to result in upset and conflict, especially when I speak out and act with conviction."

"You're doing what you were meant to do. Let others play different roles. There's a place for everyone. You probably reach those that others cannot."

Caroline's sensible words would placate the crisis-stricken vicar temporarily. Although, she did speak the truth: her husband was the right man, in the right time and place to lead the defence against man's greatest assault against himself to date.

Helen spoke to Anna for a long time on the telephone until she eventually replaced the receiver thoughtfully. Naturally, they had devoted most of their conversation to discussing rejuvenation. Helen was surprised and more than a little disappointed at her friend's unbounded enthusiasm, bordering on joy, for the development. Anna had been equally surprised at Helen's reticence and cautious comments.

"You don't seem very pleased," she observed in puzzlement. "Everyone else is so excited. People have been celebrating all day. No one's going to work tomorrow – we're having a party instead. You should come. Actually, you'd be the centre of attention – the professor's daughter – everyone would want to meet you. You could be the guest of honour."

"In that case I certainly won't come. Thanks for the offer but I don't want to have to talk to lots of strangers. I know nothing about the process and wouldn't be able to answer any of their questions."

"Are you sure?" Anna sounded very disappointed.

Helen confirmed her decision, and instead promised to meet Anna, alone, soon.

How she wished that someone other than her father had made the discovery – if it had had to have been made at all. She wanted to be able to congratulate and support him and to share his great moment. She felt that she ought to be proud of his achievement, but she was not. The memory of her mother rested gently on each of her senses and the persistent feeling of doubt intensified. Helen decided that the best she could do would be to remain neutral and play no part in the grotesque charade as it unfolded. She would neither condemn nor condone her father's work in public but would nurse her unease privately. Her discomfort was compounded by confusion – she wished that both her mother and fiancé were still alive but she still questioned whether it would have been right to rejuvenate them at the time of their deaths had it been possible then. Peter's happy, infectious smile flashed in front of her face – how could anyone truly recreate that and the surging, pure energy which lay behind it? It was impossible, but her father had apparently done it. Helen suddenly felt exhausted. In an instant all her energy had drained away, leaving her with heavy, aching limbs and overwhelming fatigue. Defeated, she climbed slowly into bed where she slept motionlessly until she awoke the next morning feeling unrefreshed.

Mary Fields was very pleased. MAD's meeting had gone very well. There had been no absences and an unusual, but vibrant, air of nervous urgency had driven the meeting. Members spoke to each other in hushed tones, bursting with the 'news' but unwilling to broach the subject directly. It reminded Mary of the aftermath of a funeral and the discomfort of a wake. After the mutual preliminary greetings between individuals and the occasional unguarded outburst of jollity, Mary called the meeting to order. Whilst enjoying a deep sense of satisfaction, she observed the expectant faces which surrounded her and could not resist toying with them for a while.

"Right," she began, "welcome to another MAD meeting. Thanks for coming everyone." Then she cast her eyes round the group and took an unnecessary sip of water from a cloudy, plastic tumbler before continuing, "A full house tonight, brilliant! As usual, we've lots of things to discuss."

Each member focused directly on Mary's faded, blue eyes willing her to mention the 'news'. Some fidgeted, others leaned forward, while a couple of members could not bear it and switched their gazes as Mary caught their anxious eyes.

"We'll start, as usual, with the cleansing session, followed by last meeting's minutes and a round up of what you've all achieved since then."

Mary's announcement was automatic; she was observing reactions in infinitesimal detail. Disappointment was palpable. Joe, a man in his sixties, who had been desirous of the leadership of the group and had suffered rejection in favour of Mary, clenched his jaw sideways, raised his head and sighed. Mary took a mental note and read his thoughts accurately; he would be of the opinion that the 'news' was far more important and urgent than the group's vigorous adherence to their weekly routine. Joe liked to think of himself as a man of action but in reality his activities manifested themselves in having a lot to say at meetings and belligerently advising other members about what they should be doing and how they should be doing it. He was not popular. There always seemed to have been a difficulty or problem with each of the tasks assigned to him – his computer had been out of order, no one had answered any of his telephone calls, his bicycle had had two punctures – the list was endless and always imaginative. Everyone knew that he had little to offer but tolerated his membership. Sometimes his ridiculous behaviour unintentionally enlivened a dreary meeting and provided a source of amusement. Joe had no chance of ever becoming leader but remained oblivious to this indisputable law and believed that he would succeed Mary.

Mary tossed her head back against the grubby armchair and

breathed in and out noisily. The other members reluctantly copied, although more quietly, like well-behaved children. After only a few seconds had passed, Mary opened her eyes – not obviously, just enough to be able to see, fuzzily, through quivering eyelashes. She examined each group member in turn beginning with Sonja. Sonja was young (aged about nineteen), enthusiastic and had a penchant for 'causes'. Mary could envisage her becoming a threat in the future. She continued to scrutinise the younger woman whose features had unconsciously twisted themselves into a frown as a result of her determination to meditate as instructed. Mary noticed Sonja's suede pixie boots, knitted cardigan and braided plaits. She had been like that a long time ago. Now she no longer cared.

Ricky, sitting on the lumpy, damp sofa, next to Sonja, coughed, swallowed and shook himself. Fearful that he was about to notice her watching him, Mary shut her eyes tightly. However, no one moved and silence dominated. Mary felt it safe to open one eye and directed it at Ricky, or Mr Trago, as he was known to his pupils. She was well aware that Ricky and his pupils disliked each other in equal measure. Ricky did not like the staff or the school in general, either. Mary wondered why he stayed in the job. She looked at his well-kempt beard, leather jacket and expensive shoes. She presumed he was well-paid. He was the deputy head at a large, failing comprehensive school and generally within the profession it was considered that he had done well at the age of thirty-one but would go no further. His wife had achieved slightly more, having become a head teacher at the same age, and was destined for further ascent up the ladder of success. Ricky did not mind. Instead, he enjoyed the trappings of their joint salaries and became adept at delegating. He likened himself to a ship's captain (probably erroneously) – a man who retained overall control but who ensured others carried out the work. Ricky was fond of reports, the contents of which he assimilated with ease and then ordered action by someone else. His methods had proved very successful as far as he was concerned. Mary was puzzled by Ricky's membership of MAD. He had never revealed his reason for joining to anyone. Even his wife was unaware of his involvement. Mary watched his mouth fall open and listened to his gentle snore. She wanted to laugh. Instead, she quickly turned her attention to Rose.

Rose could meditate, relax or fall asleep on command. She was the mother of five children. Mary looked at the large, jolly woman and considered her a threat. Rose was everything that Mary was not: highly organised, jovial, popular and maternal. One of her greatest assets was humour – she could make anyone laugh, even Mary on occasions. Some of the others had begged her to try for the group's leadership but she had refused on account of being too busy at home. Her motivation was her children, whom she wanted to be free of chemical pollution. MAD was just one cause to merit her worthy support and anyway, she joked, it gave her a night off from the kids!

The two students, who were the group's most recent recruits, were sitting cross-legged on the dusty carpet. Mary did not think that they would last long. She knew that Carly only attended as an appendage to Will whom she was desperate to impress. For some time Carly really had believed that their interests were identical. Mary had noticed that Will had contrived to steal the seat on the sofa, next to Sonja, but had been beaten to it by Ricky who had plonked himself down, unceremoniously and oblivious to Will's thwarted manoeuvre.

Finally, completing the circle was Howard. Although sitting quietly he fidgeted and frowned constantly as if in physical discomfort. Howard never meditated and told everyone that he did not believe in that sort of nonsense! He also did not believe in "Big business, and being brainwashed into accepting invasive techniques and poisoning ourselves, either." So he joined MAD and was determined to see the movement grow. Howard was a very popular member, although Sonja was slightly afraid of him and thought he ought to be a bit more open-minded about meditation.

Mary closed her eyes and breathed in loudly, sucking a gasp of air noisily through her nasal passages and exhaling with quick relief. The group members responded to her warning and each person (with the exception of Howard) waggled a limb, rotated their shoulders or sighed in unison.

"And, ten, nine, eight. . !" Mary counted down to the order to relax. Everyone obeyed. Even Howard visibly relaxed as a result of the meditation session at last being at an end. Sonja looked surprised and blinked several times as though she had suddenly been thrust into daylight, although the flat remained dingy.

"Thank God for that!" retorted Howard, loudly. "I thought it was going to last forever. Let's get down to business and discuss this rejuvenation thing."

"Good idea," agreed Ricky. "That's what I've been waiting for."

The dam burst and for the first time Mary had difficulty in controlling the group's mass enthusiasm. Each person recounted how they had heard the 'news' and their subsequent reaction of horror. They chatted like excited infants, their words tumbling over each other's as they abandoned social convention in their eagerness to be heard.

"I was sitting on the bus," squeaked Sonja, twitching characteristically, "and I saw a newspaper headline that the man opposite was reading. Actually, he was diagonally opposite, three rows in front, I think," she added hurriedly, as if fearful that she would not be believed and must corroborate her story.

"Really?" Rose replied tactfully before revealing; "I was in the garden, just putting some washing out, when my neighbour popped her head over the fence and told me. I didn't really take it in at first, a pair of tights had twisted round some of the clothes and I was trying to untangle them – it's surprising how tightly they wind themselves round things – isn't it?"

Mary glowered with impatience, anger mounting inside, until she snapped loudly, "We must keep to the agenda!" Glaring at each member in turn, she continued, inflexibly, "We'll have the individual reports – of what you have done – next."

"That's all very well, but considering the importance of the recent developments, I should have thought that our time would be better spent discussing that." Howard was not afraid to argue. Joe and Ricky shifted themselves in support and expectation. Sonja looked afraid. Will sniffed and assumed a non-committal façade at the same time hoping that Mary would bend to Howard's suggestion. Carly copied him. Rose was about to speak when Mary cut in ignoring Howard's comment completely:

"Sonja, how have you got on with the 'Awareness Event'?"

Sonja swallowed, glanced quickly around the room and responded timidly, "Not very well, I'm afraid. I'm still waiting for people to phone me back or leave a text or something." She gave a nervous, apologetic giggle. "Sorry, nothing to report, really."

Howard looked very pleased and tried to give her a surreptitious wink that Mary saw.

Each group member, except Will, followed Sonja's inadvertent cue – apparently, none of them had achieved anything worth reporting since last week's meeting. Will, however, announced that he had designed a 'great' poster for the 'Awareness Event' but had unfortunately forgotten to bring it with him.

"I can put loads up around the uni," he added, proudly.

"I'll help," Carly volunteered at once, prompting everyone to offer to display some.

"I'll take at least a dozen," Rose declared. "I can put them up all over the place, there's the Scout hut, playgroup, Women's Institute, library. . ."

"They'll have to be approved first," Mary warned. "Is there anything else anyone wants to bring up?"

"Yes. Rejuven–bloody–ation!" Howard demanded, aggressively. "I can't believe we've wasted all this time meditating and talking about posters while other people are bringing back the dead all around us."

"Dead lucky – some would say!" joked Rose, directing her remark at Joe who wanted to laugh, but thought better of it. Instead, the combination of preventing a smile and assuming a grave expression resulted in him sucking both cheeks inwards, giving him the appearance of having tasted something bitter. Mary threw Rose a disdainful look. Then, despite growing bored and deciding that she had almost finished toying with them all, she could not resist a further display of authority:

"Right, the next item on the agenda is 'Current Developments'."

"About time – although we've taken so long it can hardly be called current," muttered Howard, rolling his eyes.

"Does anyone wish to discuss something other than rejuvenation?" Mary continued.

No one moved or made a sound. The expectant silence heightened all their senses and the flat suddenly smelled more musty, and appeared more grey and dirty than before. Ricky realised that he was sitting on a damp patch and wriggled with displeasure.

"In that case, as I'm sure you're all aware, an extremely evil person has used interventionist medicine to the extent that he claims to have brought a dead body back to life." Mary paused in the belief that she had made a dramatic announcement but Howard responded impatiently:

"Yes, we know that. The point is, what are we going to do about it? I assume that we are all of the same mind, i.e. opposed to it. We have to act before it's too late, before it goes too far, before it's considered normal. Once that happens we won't be able to do a thing to stop it."

Joe cleared his throat in warning that he was about to speak and expected everyone to listen. "We certainly need to take action," he agreed. "Someone ought to organise a protest rally. Will, you could make some placards and banners. . ."

"I'll help him," Carly volunteered predictably.

"Where's the best place?" Joe asked himself.

"Obviously, we must take action," Mary snapped again, coldly, annoyed that control of the discussion had been so easily snatched from her and that Joe seemed to be taking the lead. "We need a clear, intensive plan. What do you think, Ricky?"

"I agree," he assented simply, wondering whether the seat of his trousers looked damp. "There must be others who would join us, if only for the one occasion. If we arrange a rally it's got to be big – anything else would be a disaster."

"We need to make more use of the internet," suggested Rose. "I'm not allowed on it at home – the twins are always using it – but I'm sure Will and Carly, and you too, Sonja, are experts."

Carly smiled at Rose, pleased to have been included in the same sentence as Will. Mary stiffened, paled and clenched her jaw – she hated modern technology and used the internet very sparingly. Sonja was the only person who noticed, but added her support – the cause was more important than anything else.

"I think you're right, Rose," she agreed. "Some of us may not be too keen but we have to use every tool to our advantage – our enemies will. The end will justify the means."

A general murmur of assent rose from the group and even Mary felt her self in agreement.

The discussion continued for several hours. Each member was assigned several tasks. Finally, Mary drew the meeting to a close:

"I think we should end with a small reminder. Something that will inspire each one of us to do the utmost to defeat this devil which has sprung himself upon us, who has revealed himself to be our greatest challenger to date. Can you all see?"

She pressed a switch on the television remote control and one of her video recordings wavered onto the screen. Professor Deighton appeared in front of them at one of his many press conferences, bathed in a halo of studio lights and flashing cameras which exploded like a storm of dying stars. The recording re-ignited and concentrated the group's hatred for the man, his achievement and the onward, unchallenged march of science in general.

Each member of MAD returned home uncomfortably agitated, desperate to take action.

Chapter Five

Both MAD and Reverend Mouland, along with any other opponents of rejuvenation, soon found themselves in a very small minority. The tantalising prospect of eternal life ingrained itself on the psyche of society as a whole and turned the most sober of individuals into reckless, shallow adventurers. The first and most obvious effect was a huge drop in followers of all religions – spirituality certainly appeared to have been cast aside, no longer relevant in this reborn, exciting, technological world. One or two scientists, who had previously made a name for themselves by writing populist books purporting to prove the non-existence of a creator or even life-force, could not help gloating and appeared on television with permanent grins engraved on their arrogant faces.

The general status of science and technology was elevated speedily and spectacularly and members of the profession slipped too easily into the role previously occupied by 'rock gods'. Professor Deighton embarked on a huge international tour during which he was fêted by fans and believers. At his packed lectures he presided over an incongruous mix of rock concert atmosphere and evangelism. Deighton soon mastered, and did not hesitate to use, every trick at his disposal to heighten the effect: music, lighting, unbearable anticipation and crowd manipulation. Many of his colleagues could not resist copying, desperate to grab this opportunity for fame, wealth and adulation unreserved for them before. Many had no knowledge of the process of rejuvenation but that did not stop them from making it up. Topics previously on the periphery of science, such as time-travel and the concept of multiple universes, surged in popularity and provided fodder for yet more lectures, interviews and media exposure.

Mathematics, physics, chemistry and biology became the most popular subjects at junior school level. Students enthusiastically enrolled for the subjects at senior level as well, only for the majority to give up in despair and boredom having found the monotony of the basic mechanics of the subjects infinitely less interesting than learning the secrets of rejuvenation.

Philip Mouland despaired. During the first few months which followed the announcement, he, his colleagues and representatives from all faiths had been in demand as the media felt obliged to present the case against rejuvenation as well as enthusiastically celebrating its discovery. Mouland repeated his mantra endlessly. He tried to warn of the consequences but was painfully aware that his weapons were subjective, invisible and unproven. Faith and spirituality could be tested but not seen. For the increasingly materialistic inhabitants of the modern world, this was not enough. Evidence was required, and Professor Deighton had plenty of that. His research gathered pace, fuelled by unprecedented funding, and within twelve months he was able to announce that the process had been perfected.

"I am now able to rejuvenate any body which has been correctly stored with a ninety-nine-point-nine percent success rate," he told the waiting world, happily. "Remember this date as the day that man conquered death and time!"

After this the broadcasters and newspapers did not bother to seek a balanced argument. Rejuvenation was a popular, indisputable fact – those who disapproved were just best ignored as cranks.

Phillip Mouland was opening his post whilst complaining dolefully to Caroline: "No one comes to morning prayers anymore – except Julian and sometimes Felicity. Since Deighton perfected his 'wonderful' technique the church has been empty. Of course, you already know that," he sighed. "That last television interview was disastrous."

"They had already closed their minds. You had no chance," Caroline consoled him. "The presenter was so uninterested he didn't even look you in the eye – it was obvious. He gabbled each question at you and couldn't be bothered to listen to your responses – it was a very poor piece of journalism."

"Do you know that my view has always been that mankind in general, and man as an individual, has been, or at least should be, progressing along a spiritual path to some form of enlightenment?"

Caroline glanced at her husband sympathetically. After twenty-five years of marriage she was intricately aware of his religious philosophy, but acknowledging his need to voice his thoughts, she allowed him to continue.

"Our physical presence is only part of that – it's just a stage in our development. It shouldn't last forever. Why can't people see that?"

"They're frightened," Caroline replied simply.

"I suppose so. Frightened of the unknown and too frightened to have faith."

"I don't quite agree with you. Yes, they're frightened of the unknown – isn't everyone? But I wouldn't say that people are frightened to have faith, rather that too many people haven't acquired faith."

"That's fairly obvious," her husband retorted, tossing an electricity bill onto a pile of similar documents. "Why? Why? Why? – that's the question we've been asking ourselves for approximately the last one hundred years."

"I watched a television programme a long time ago (you weren't here – at a PCC meeting, I expect) about the existence of God and the presenter asked why he had not been given faith whilst others had. I can't remember the response but it was something typically inadequate. I would have told him that he had been given the capacity to have faith and only he could choose to use that capacity based on his own experiences, thoughts and free will," Caroline snapped the ironing board into position.

Philip listened attentively. "A type of 'seek and ye shall find' situation?"

"After all," Caroline continued, simultaneously selecting a creased white shirt from the oval, wicker basket, "apparently, neurologists (I think – some branch of science, anyway) have identified an area in the brain which governs the ability to embrace spirituality or religious experience. Why would we have that capacity if there's no foundation for it?"

"To give false hope – they'd say," Philip replied despondently.

"But why should that be correct? It's still only one side of the

44

coin. Actually, I'm getting side-tracked, what I wanted to suggest is that people need opportunities to discover faith and perhaps we, as the church, and society in general – you know schools, parents, the media and all kinds of institutions have stopped supplying those opportunities. If children grow up oblivious to Christian values on the one hand and bombarded by materialism and the 'me-first' culture on the other, how will they ever find faith?"

Philip listened, reliving the familiar argument and adding, "It certainly seems to be the case that the more wealthy and comfortable people become, the less they acknowledge, or are even aware of their critical spiritual needs. I'm sure this is what Jesus meant when he talked about it being easier for a camel to pass through the eye of a needle than it is for a rich man to enter Heaven."

"Luke 18:25," Caroline murmured.

"I should have written a sermon about it – actually I did – lots of them but I was preaching to the wrong people. Too late now," the vicar broke off.

"It probably would be too late in a packed church, but you have to reach out to people who are ignorant or too easily dismissive of our beliefs for one reason or another. Your congregation have already been reeled in."

"Even so, look how fragile their faith is. Look at my empty church. Materialism and physicality is much stronger. It's an addiction which feeds upon itself." Philip jabbed the letter-knife into another envelope.

"It's bound to have an advantage. After all, everyone can see themselves and what's all around us. If you inhabited a spiritual world would you believe that the Earth existed?" Caroline continued but her husband was no longer listening. His eyes were fixed on a parchment-like letter, an expression of horrified surprise embedded in his features.

"I don't believe it!" he whispered, shaking his head. "Can't believe it. The bishop's resigned! He says he's lost his conviction and can no longer lead an archaic institution pitted against the knowledge that science has given us. Instead, he's to take up the post of Chancellor of 'The City University of Technology."

Caroline's eyes widened in horror as she outstretched her hand to take the letter.

"This is dreadful," she agreed, quietly, her eyes flicking across the piece of paper. "A man like that, someone we had all looked to for leadership."

Her husband was completely deflated. A physical blow could not have damaged him more.

"What if the bishop's right?" he quavered, momentarily losing his faith.

"Don't be ridiculous!" Caroline snapped, aggressively. "Of course he's not right – what have we just been talking about?"

"No. No. You're right – he's not," Philip agreed, having regained his composure. "It's just a shock, that's all. Nevertheless, it's a huge blow to our credibility."

"At least we're in no doubt about what we're up against," Caroline continued. "The press will have a field day."

The sound of the telephone interrupted her. Although she had little else to say, the bishop's resignation having shaken her almost as much as her husband.

"I bet that's Julian," Philip groaned, reaching out for the receiver.

"Reverend Mouland," he answered, mechanically.

"Hi there, Mr Moundland. It's Tara – Tara Golesworthy from National Prime Time Radio. Would you be available for a slot on 'London Calling' today?"

"Yes," Mouland replied wearily, acutely aware what had prompted the invitation.

"Great. I'll meet you in the foyer, as usual. Say, twelve o'clock?"

Mouland reluctantly agreed to the assignation.

"I have a feeling I'm stepping into the lion's den," he told Caroline after informing her of the impending appointment.

"Someone's got to do it!" was her rather unfeeling reply. She glanced at her husband's pale, subdued face and added hurriedly, "And you're the best person I could possibly think of."

Reverend Mouland sat in the studio listening to Jason's introduction and awaiting the inevitable attack. The presenter turned to him at last.

"We've now all heard the sensational news that the bishop has resigned and thrown his lot in with rejuvenation. Surely, that must be the final nail in the coffin for Christianity?"

Mouland detected an unmistakeable tone of glee in Jason's voice.

"Not at all!" he countered vehemently. "The bishop has demonstrated uncharacteristic weakness and failing but ultimately his actions are merely those of one man. . ."

"One man who is your figurehead, though," interrupted Jason. "Surely, if he has given up on his religion, that's it? You're absolutely haemorrhaging support. Isn't it all over for you now?"

"No. Many people, be they bishops or the most ordinary of all of us, experience the testing of their faith and often they come out of it stronger and with greater conviction. . ."

"So the bishop has failed the test?"

"Temporarily, perhaps, but there's still time for him to reassess and return. He will be welcomed back to the fold. Nevertheless, his actions do not define nor alter the basic tenets which I have reiterated many times to you – rejuvenation has not diminished God in any way, only ourselves. On the contrary, the advent of this knowledge should act as a catalyst to encourage us to examine ourselves, what we value and how we live our lives and also to embrace, more fully, the spiritual aspect of our being."

"But what's the point? Any 'spiritual aspect' has been firmly relegated to bottom place now that we can live forever. People will say, and are saying very loudly, that they are no longer interested in mystical mumbo jumbo anymore." Jason sat back, emphatically, in his seat.

Mouland gave a short laugh: "You know I don't agree. . ."

"But the bishop does!" Jason cut in triumphantly.

"That's his prerogative. There are plenty of us who think he is misguided." Mouland tried to sound casual and unworried.

"Plenty of people?" Jason queried. "Aren't congregations dwindling more dramatically than ever before? Aren't hundreds of churches becoming redundant and being sold? More junior members of the clergy than the bishop are resigning in their thousands. I've heard that your own church, St. Nonna's, is to be turned into a store for cryostasis."

"That's just rubbish!" Mouland exclaimed, turning red with anger. "Mark my words, far from Christianity being outmoded and unnecessary we have reached an era when we need its values, possibly, more than at any time in our history!"

"But that's obviously not your bishop's view – or should I say ex-bishop," Jason continued, nastily. "The man in the street will have got the message loud and clear – your organisation's imploding. Why can't you accept that?"

"I agree that we are definitely facing a challenge. But the challenge is to get our message across. It's not a challenge to our raison d'etre," Mouland responded, weakly, in the knowledge that he was losing the debate.

"On the contrary. Rejuvenation has shaken – no, destroyed – your 'raison d'etre', as you put it." Jason adopted a mocking tone. "There's no reason to fear death anymore – it's been conquered – so consequently there's no call for your religion."

"Christianity is based on more than the simple fear of death." Mouland tried to assume an aura of calmness.

"But no one's going to believe that after the bishop's resignation – instead, they'll see it as a green light for rejuvenation – its ultimate vindication," Jason argued, logically.

"I agree that the bishop's actions will cause confusion, and that's very regrettable, but I implore everyone to stop and think before they rush headlong towards rejuvenation. We have all been side-tracked at times in the past. We've always had questions but we must keep our faith, or at the very least an open mind. Remember that 'all that glistens is not gold'.."

"Well, it's glittering enough for me – and millions of others, I might add." Jason brought the discussion to an end. "Thank you for giving us your views, Reverend Mouland, we're always pleased to have you on the show. Let's have a piece of topical music." He pressed something on the computer console and *Three Steps to Heaven* blared across the airwaves.

Reverend Mouland made the short trip back to St. Nonna's in a state of depression. A feeling of helplessness pressed itself down upon him from above and he feared that he was the wrong man in the wrong place at the wrong time. Fortunately, he did not bother to listen to the predictable comments aired by the programme's audience; these would have darkened his mood even more.

"Why won't religion die gracefully?" demanded Charles from Egham before adding in an attempt at humour, "It's the one thing which will never be rejuvenated!"

"It's time the church dragged itself into the twenty-first century. Perhaps it served a purpose a long time ago, but now it should make way for reason, science and technology," agreed Kyle from Sunderland.

"The church is an institution society no longer needs. In the past it was used as a capitalist tool of repression – good riddance to it!" thundered Olivia from Monmouthshire.

Jules from Notting Hill added a similar comment: "Religion has been the cause of innumerable wars and much pain and suffering throughout all societies. I welcome the day when it has been lost in the annuls of time completely. We can well do without it!"

Anne, from Liverpool, voiced reservations: "Religion, and Christianity in particular, whilst admitting it has faults, has provided us with a code of moral values which, if everyone followed, would be hugely beneficial to society. What will happen now?"

"People can still have values," retorted Paul from Ipswich. "I'm a good person. I've got a conscience but I'm putting my money on rejuvenation."

"It's very simple," argued Scott from Walsall, "we can live forever. We've got eternal life here and now. We don't need Heaven or Hell anymore."

Sally from St. Austell agreed, "We don't have to take the risk of believing in an afterlife or not. Personally, I'd rather stay alive forever, here. At least I know it's real."

A lone voice, Steve from Glasgow, dissented ineffectively against the majority: "Religion is not a commodity to be thrown away or recycled until it comes to represent just what you want it to. It's integral to each of us, whether we like it or not, or whether we acknowledge it or not. The truth is out there and one day will reveal itself. We can try to ignore it but it won't go away."

Finally, Mary from London added her comment: "Whether religion has had its day or not is a side issue. The real issue, and the thing that we should be most frightened of, is man's continual and extreme intervention against himself. We should abandon medicine as we know it and, of course, rejuvenation, in favour of self-healing and nature."

To be fair to 'National Prime Time Radio', the station would have broadcast an equal number of opposing views in respect of 'balanced journalism' but an overwhelming majority (ninety-nine percent, at least) were hostile to any form of religion and greatly in favour of the new order. 'National Prime Time Radio' felt that it was its public duty to reflect this.

c

Reverend Mouland pushed at the heavy, main entrance door to his church. It opened slowly. The vicar walked in through the ancient, weather-worn, stone porch, passed through a further oak door (a little lighter than the first) and sat for a moment on a pew just in front of the font. Taking his head in his hands, he prayed silently. After a few moments he raised his head and observed the distant altar. It was one of his favourite scenes. At this time of the day, the sun would sometimes blaze through the mediaeval stained glass window in the Lady Chapel and light up the altar and magnificent leaded light behind it. Today was one of those days. The light beam, filled with specks of dust, appeared as a solid mass. Mouland remembered Einstein's comment about 'riding on a beam of light'. This one certainly looked capable of taking his weight.

Then he identified the unmistakeable smell of furniture polish mixed with the age-old fabric and atmosphere of the building. Almost at once, Devereux appeared from the vestry, bright yellow duster in hand, and turned his attention to the brass eagle. 'The man's obsessed with that thing,' Mouland thought uncharitably. Then sticking his hands in his pockets in a very un-vicar-like manner, shoulders hunched and eyes cast to the ground, he wandered deliberately along the nave. Devereux polished Mouland's reflection in the eagle's smooth breast.

"Bad day, eh, Mouland?" he enquired without turning round.

"I've known better," was the resigned response.

"Cheer up, old chap. We knew it would be like this. It's got to get worse before it gets better."

It suddenly occurred to Mouland that as long as Devereux was able to polish the eagle he would remain cheerfully oblivious to the seriousness of the situation. As if to confirm this theory, the churchwarden turned and questioned him anxiously:

"I say, there's no truth in the rumour that St. Nonna's is to be sold and turned into one of those rejuvenation mortuary-type things, is there?"

Mouland gave a short, reassuring laugh: "Of course not! You'd be one of the first to know if it was – being on the PCC."

"That's a relief!" Devereux took opposing sides of the duster in each hand and performed an energetic sawing motion on the eagle's beak. "The radio chap was just trying to wind you up, then!" He hesitated for a moment, before adding, "I have heard, though, that planning applications have been put in, in various parts of the country, for that purpose. Apparently, old stone buildings are ideal – nice and cool, etc."

Mouland had been aware of this development but so feared St. Nonna's succumbing to a similar fate that he had forced it to the back of his mind and refused to contemplate it.

"We're losing the battle, Julian," he stated with quiet conviction. "The congregation's down to you, Felicity and Caroline, plus one or two others who are wavering – even Mrs Wainscott hardly appears now. If anything, it's worse elsewhere with half – well, more than half – of the clergy resigning. At least I'm still here, but for how long I really don't know. Perhaps they're right, the bishop's resignation could be the end of us."

Devereux actually stopped polishing, momentarily. "We should change tactics," he declared. "So far, we've appealed to the general public (who, incidentally, we've failed to reach with spectacular success, for decades) and looked within our own dwindling ranks. We've yet to join forces with all opponents of rejuvenation, despite our original intention, regardless of their motives and core beliefs. If we all worked together we could present a constant overall opposition. It happens all the time in politics (as we all know) – the most unlikely alliances are forged with one consensual aim in mind. Once that's achieved they go their separate ways again."

Mouland knew that Devereux's plan made sense. To date, he had been reluctant to consider associating the church's values with a diverse range of secular groups whose intentions could, perhaps, be extreme and dangerous in his view. Now it seemed to be the only option left.

Chapter Six

Helen had been forced to resign. Working in the office had become intolerable as a result of the media's attention. Reporters would trick their way through the telephonic maze and constantly interrupt her if there had been the slightest newsworthy development. Even if there had been no such pretexts she would be hounded by researchers demanding that she appear on the latest reality television show. At times a gaggle of journalists would congregate outside the entrance to the building hoping to waylay her. The final straw was when a tabloid newspaper trained a video camera on the office from across the road. Helen felt violated.

Her employers were sorry to lose a conscientious worker but, at the same time, secretly relieved. She had become a liability, through no fault of her own, but they had feared bad publicity and, probably, an industrial tribunal if she had been dismissed.

Helen met her father in the laboratory's canteen, where she felt reasonably safe, and gave him the news.

"I quite understand," he agreed, before adding proudly, "I'm hounded too."

'As the result of your own actions,' thought Helen, bitterly, unable to dare to voice her thoughts.

"What do you intend to do?" enquired her father whilst trying, unsuccessfully, to capture an olive on his fork.

"I don't know," she replied, blankly. "Obviously, I'll have to find something. I must support myself somehow. But it won't be any different anywhere else once the media tracks me down."

"Perhaps I could find you something here?" the professor offered, not noticing Helen's eyes widen in horror. "Of course," he continued, "you don't have to work at all." He lowered his voice and glanced furtively around the room. "I'm worth millions now, and everyday it's growing more and more, ridiculous really." He laughed with false modesty, obviously very pleased with himself.

Helen felt uncomfortable. She certainly did not wish to work for her father; it would be a disaster! They did not get on well enough and she knew that deep down she did not agree with his work. Furthermore, her principles and conscience prevented her from agreeing easily to his financial support. For the moment she could think of no alternative.

"It's kind of you to offer," she replied, "but I don't think I'm suited to the scientific environment. . ." 'Even this canteen looks like a laboratory,' she thought, noticing the staff in their white uniforms and the stainless steel counter and appliances. She sniffed, imagining that she could smell the pungent aroma of formaldehyde – was it real?

"Really?" Her father sounded genuinely surprised, unable to contemplate that not everyone could share his enthusiastic obsession. "Just let me support you, in that case. I've already put in motion the most tax efficient trust fund I could find. That's been a complete headache!" he announced with a kind of emphatic weariness.

Helen was still unsure that she could accept the proceeds of his discovery but quickly made a decision. "Perhaps if you could tide me over in the short term. It would give me time to work out an alternative."

"Fine. I'll give you a cheque now." Her father reached into his pocket. "How much do you want?"

Helen did not know.

"Here's ten thousand to be going on with." The professor scribbled quickly before catching a glimpse of his watch. "Goodness!" he cried. "Look at the time! I must go! They'll be waiting for me in the lab."

Helen stared at the cheque. It seemed unreal. The whole situation felt like a muffled dream driven by emptiness. Apprehension stabbed at her. What would she do now? At least her job had provided a structure to the day and social opportunities. Helen, deep in thought, recognised loneliness with distaste. She feared isolation. After contemplating the dissatisfying situation for some time an opportunity presented itself and a surge of excitement lifted her spirits. She would accept her father's offer of financial support and put her talents to use by immersing herself in voluntary work. She would not feel guilty then. A desire to do some good, make her mark and use her life productively had always been present in her psyche. Perhaps she was more like her father than she could ever accept. Now was her chance. It was ironic, she felt, that her father's work — something to which she could not reconcile herself — had led her to this. Perhaps something positive could be gleaned from any situation? she mused, still buoyed by elation before telling herself 'no' she did not quite believe this.

Helen was not the only person to resign from her post. Darren had left too, having quickly recognised an opportunity for advancement and, he believed, great wealth by becoming a salesman for an insurance company offering cover for the storage of bodies whilst awaiting rejuvenation. Hundreds of such plans were available matched by millions of potential clients; people did not need much persuasion. Companies vied with each other for business resulting in several television advertisements remarkable only for their tackiness. One of which in particular, always caused Reverend Mouland to curl his nose as though he had encountered an unpleasant smell, featured a cartoon skeleton dancing on a grave singing 'Don't be late — rejuvenate!'

Television game shows abounded offering free rejuvenation as first prize. Not to be outdone, one reality programme offered the winner the chance to be killed, or as they euphemistically called it, put to sleep and rejuvenated by Professor Deighton himself. Millions of people applied to take part and tens of millions watched the entire process live on television. Helen did not. Reverend Mouland ensconced himself in St. Nonna's at the time of the broadcast, prayed fervently and drank the communion wine.

Eventually, the crazy enthusiasm for the process, which had swept at least the Western world, abated as the procedure became accepted as an ordinary (not to say mundane) fact of everyday life. The questions that remained were glibly pushed aside in case delving too deeply spoilt everything. At first, socially minded individuals argued that it was unfair that only the rich could afford the procedure and several 'days of action' were organised by some of the more militant trade unions. The government responded by hastily announcing a government-backed, means-tested insurance scheme. Only a few worried about the potential effects of the inevitable population explosion. Eminent scientists smoothly replied that we would 'soon' be able to colonise neighbouring planets.

A scientific byproduct of the rejuvenation technique was the increased research into the use of human embryos to provide new body parts for diseased rejuvenates. Soon embryos were farmed specifically and solely for this purpose. Predictably there was an outcry from a minority of society, Reverend Mouland and the small core of quaintly religious believers which remained, and MAD amongst them. The prevailing argument against their opposition was that 'embryos can't feel anything, therefore it's perfectly ethical to use them' coupled with 'embryos are not human beings'.

"If they're not human beings, what in God's name are they?" raged Mouland desperately. The next evening a brick smashed through the Vicarage window. Mouland felt obliged to report the incident to the police in deference to the much vaulted statement that 'if we don't know we can't do anything'. He also thought that it was necessary if they were to compile accurate crime statistics. When he finally got through, after using three different recommended numbers, listening to the dialling tone for ten minutes and being transferred twice, he was met by casual indifference.

"Would you say it was an accident, sir," enquired the officer, "or done on purpose?"

"How do you hurl a brick through a window by accident?" Mouland demanded tetchily.

"Did you see it happen?" the officer went on, ignoring the other man's response.

"No. It was dark at 10pm. My wife and I were inside with the curtains drawn."

"So it could have been an accident." The officer's bland tone caused Mouland to imagine him sucking a pencil and filling in a scruffy form. (He was actually completing a form on a computer, clicking boxes and typing laboriously using only two fingers.) Mouland was aware of his temperature rising rapidly and evenly from his chin to the top of his scalp.

"Were there any witnesses?" The officer made no attempt to sound interested.

"No, not as far as I know."

"Did you go and look?"

"Yes, of course. As soon as we realised what had happened, after the shock, I ran outside but there was no one to be seen anywhere. Then I wondered whether it was safe. You never know nowadays – someone could have been lying in wait for me with a knife of something."

"What do you want us to do, sir?" the officer asked, to Mouland's surprise.

"Find out who did it, of course!" he exclaimed, indignantly.

"I'm afraid we're very unlikely to do that, sir," the officer admitted carelessly. "No evidence, no witnesses. It could have been anyone. Could have been an accident. . ."

"What's the matter with you? It's obvious it wasn't an accident!" Mouland fumed venomously.

"Now then, sir. I know you're upset but there's no need to be rude – we take a dim view of that. If you insist, we can send someone round but not until the end of the week. Otherwise, I can give you a crime number so you can claim against your insurance. Which would you prefer? I expect you want the window repaired as soon as possible?"

"Just give me the crime number," Mouland requested, completely defeated.

"Fine, sir." The officer's relief was apparent. Then he added in a more friendly, confidential tone, "To tell the truth, there have been lots of minor incidents like this, lots of vandalism to churches and church buildings. It's because people don't like the opposition to rejuvenation. We haven't got the manpower to investigate petty, low level crimes like these, especially with the rise of more serious violence which has gone through the roof this year, I might add!"

Mouland, although already aware of this, was astonished to listen to the officer admitting so readily to the shortcomings of his profession, having become used, instead, to official figures flaunting any reduction in the percentage increase in criminal activity rather than admitting to the annual overall increase. The officer, seemingly reading his thoughts, jerked himself back into the well practised official tone demanded of him:

"I've logged the call, sir. Your crime number is ZX3104. If you need to contact us again, please quote that reference. Thank you for calling." The line went dead.

Mouland held the telephone receiver in front of him and stared at it momentarily, a strange mixture of emotions jostling for prominence. He did not know whether to feel angry, surprised or sad. Weariness was the eventual winner. The priest knew that the brick incident would be categorised as a very low level crime – quite rightly in the scheme of things – but the accelerating rise of all types of incidents from vandalism to violence worried him. The authorities worked overtime to massage the figures and to try to convince the population that 'fear of crime' was greater than levels of crime itself. No one was fooled. The Orwellian attempt at brainwashing failed but as long as the authorities peddled their lies the man in the street was powerless.

Of course Mouland had always pondered about such things – not because it was part of his job but because it was part of his nature, which in turn had led him to his vocation. In the last few months he had detected a chill in society. Arrogance and supreme confidence had swept away man's finely tuned sense of reciprocal dependence on each other and nature. The thread of morality and conscience which had previously held mankind together in the most adverse circumstances had been severed. Mouland was not sure why. It would be easy to attribute society's moral demise to the discovery of rejuvenation and Mouland maintained that it was, of course, a factor but he felt that something else was at work too. He was unable to identify it though – even his long discussions with Caroline concerning the subject were of no help.

"Perhaps the acceleration of criminal activity is self perpetuating," she mused.

"How do you mean?" Philip responded, his interest making his words sound unintentionally sharp.

"Like the slippery slope," she continued. "The further you go, the faster you go. I expect mathematicians have a word for it –

57

you know – a curve on a graph or something, and then it becomes the norm."

"It's not only crime, you know. That's just a reflection of what's going on which can be relatively easily measured. There's something else. The way people speak to each other, interact with each other, on a microscopic level. . . the bond between individuals, even between families, seems to have been damaged. People have become insular. We're not the only ones to have suffered; I mean the church when I say 'we'. I was reading a report the other day and charities and voluntary bodies of all kinds are suffering terribly. Subscriptions and donations have plummeted – one excuse is that people have to use their spare cash to pay for rejuvenation insurance – but that doesn't explain the dearth of volunteers. The Charity Commission has announced that there has been a fall of thirty percent in the number of registered charities compared to twelve months ago. People seem to have lost the will to live outside themselves."

"It seems as if we can live forever, but what kind of lives?" Caroline posed the rhetorical question quietly and further depressed her husband.

Later that week Mouland received an email from Mary Fields. The vicar generally considered emails to be a time consuming nuisance as he trawled his way through the daily junk which appeared on his computer screen. Lately the task had been made even more unpleasant as he became the target for an increasing number of hostile messages from people unknown to him. Mary had entitled hers, 'Challenge Rejuvenation' which made Mouland interested and hopeful that it was not yet another aggressive affront.

Mary had controlled herself admirably and merely written: 'My organisation is sympathetic with your views concerning rejuvenation. Please contact me if you would like to discuss further.'

Mouland typed his reply rapidly, buoyed by a surge of hope: 'Very interested. Would like to discuss further. Please send information re your organisation.'

It was the first positive communication that he had received for a long time. It always seemed to be his responsibility to seek out potential allies – no one approached him and his efforts had resulted in very little support. The vicar pressed himself back against the chair and wondered about Mary Fields and her organisation idly. Little did he imagine the pungent aroma of the fousty flat and Mary bent over the coffee stained, grubby computer keyboard, typing. It was hard work. How many times had she written something, then peered unseeing into the corner in front of her, her eyes furtively examining her own mind, before deleting the message and beginning again? Eventually, she had been able to pare her message to Mouland so that it resembled a businesslike, measured communication devoid of hysteria and emotive nouns and adjectives such as evil, Anti-Christ, wicked and Armageddon. The self-control required was exhausting but Mary was well versed in the finer points of manipulation. She sent a further message, 'I'm part of an organisation – we like to call ourselves MAD! – which tries to warn people of the dangers of too much medical intervention. Naturally, rejuvenation is the most extreme example of this. We concern ourselves with natural, physical and spiritual wellbeing. I believe our aims are very similar to yours and it would be mutually beneficial if we joined forces to promote our cause.' Mary successfully projected a measured, businesslike tone laced with a touch of self deprecating humour. Mouland was fooled. A meeting at the vicarage was quickly arranged for the following day.

The vicar's buoyant mood disappeared instantly on reading his next email. It was from the diocese office and contained a list of churches and church buildings to be disposed of. St. Nonna's was on the list. Further details revealed that St. Nonna's (and the vicarage) were to be sold to B-Stored UK Limited – a company specialising in body storage prior to rejuvenation. For a moment, Mouland felt as dead as one of the company's clients. Unable to prevent himself exhaling deeply and slumping forward, he closed his eyes and supported his forehead against his whitened right hand. A dense black fog obstructed the light from his eyes, shrouded the atmosphere and enveloped him in a cloak of despair. Mouland was bereft.

The closure of St. Nonna's was symbolic. Although it would obviously affect Mouland personally, he feared more the unrelenting march towards secularism and un-enlightenment which it represented – the assault against selflessness and harmony in favour of short term physical gain. He remained in a childlike huddle for some time whilst absorbing, and becoming used to, the shock, horror and disappointment. Loneliness and an agonising sensation of impotence mingled in his well of negative thoughts. An unwelcome mantra pierced his head:

"It's over. It's over," he muttered, devoid of any hope, energy or vitality. The vicar could have remained in that state forever – the descent into great despair often being a one way spiral – had the telephone not rung.

At first Mouland did not hear it. Then he ignored it. Eventually its persistent tone began to irritate and he imagined that it resembled the piteous cry of a child. Angrily he grabbed the receiver. "Who is it?" he snapped.

"Julian," came the deadpan reply, "you've heard, obviously?"

"Yes," Mouland still sounded aggressive.

"I'm very sorry. . ." Devereux began before realising he had nothing adequate to say.

"Sorry! Sorry's hardly the word! We'll all be a lot more than 'sorry' before it's all over," Mouland began to rant. "It's only the end of civilisation as we know it but you're 'sorry'. The culmination of thousands of years of teaching and attempted development, the sacrifices millions of people have made and it comes to this – all over in a few short months – and you're 'sorry'. I'm beside myself with fear, despair, sorrow and everything else but it won't change anything."

Devereux listened silently. He had known that his friend would take the news badly but even so was surprised at Mouland's personal attack.

"You're right, of course," he interjected at the first opportunity, when Mouland was forced to take a breath, in an attempt to placate. "The significance of all this is overwhelming and desperately disappointing – even dangerous. Let's hope you are not affected personally too much."

"What do you mean – personally affected? Of course I'll be personally affected. . ." Mouland sounded hysterical again.

"I meant, I hope your clerical position is safe, in one form or another, at least the email mentioned 'consolidation' and redundancies, didn't it?"

Mouland's anger dissipated as a result of this second blow. He had not read all the communication. Devereux guessed from the vicar's abrupt silence that he was the harbinger of this piece of bad news.

"Erm – you hadn't read that far, obviously," he added delicately before resisting the temptation to deliver a platitude of false hope.

Mouland pulled himself together.

"No, I hadn't. But it's a fairly logical, expected step. If the church is sold, I'll be out of a job. I should have seen it coming. I had really, but chose to ignore it in the hope that it would never happen. Now it has I'll just have to deal with it."

"Quite right. Quite right," Devereux responded quickly, full of relief. "It's not the end of the world. You'll find a way to use your talents and we can still fight against rejuvenation – you'll have more time, perhaps."

Chapter Seven

As the months passed and the initial excitement and impact caused by the perfection of the rejuvenation technique lessened, people became used to the idea and accepted it as the norm and even as their right. Consequently, the media's interest in Helen waned, helped by her noncompliance and avoidance of potential traps. Several prominent agents attempted to engage her with promises of appearances on television game shows and 'possibly, her own chat show,' but Helen remained unmoved and unimpressed. Eventually, her pursuers, puzzled by her obstinacy, gave up, decided she was odd and ungrateful, made uncomplimentary remarks about her and turned their attentions to some other vulnerable prey who they believed could be manipulated and humiliated into lining their already bulging pockets.

Helen had taken a long holiday with Anna. They had travelled to Eastern Europe and Asia, specifically to where rejuvenation had made little impact, being only the preserve of a very small, wealthy minority. Helen observed and absorbed the intricacies of these foreign cultures, both good and bad, and could not help but compare them to the rampant, shallow, materialism which had convulsed the Western world. 'In time, with industrialisation, these peoples would probably emulate their first world counterparts.' She thought with an air of resigned dejection.

Helen had been very careful to remain incognito wherever possible, having noticed a dramatic increase in her popularity amongst those to whom her identity and connections were revealed. This sickened her. She would rather be lonely.

One evening, Helen and Anna had been enjoying a quiet meal when two men sidled up to them.

"Excuse me," began the first man, flashing a wide grin. The two women looked at him politely, their deadpan expressions hinting at the deflation within.

"We couldn't help overhearing. I'm Matthew and this is Dave, by the way," he continued, waving a chubby finger at his accomplice who smiled unconvincingly. "You're not that science bloke's daughter are you? The one who's invented rejuvenation?"

"No," Helen replied shortly, before Anna could speak.

"Are you sure?" Matthew probed, whilst Dave looked on, his fixed smile becoming increasingly macabre.

"Yes," Helen indicated that the conversation was at an end by resuming her meal.

Matthew was not to be dismissed so easily. "Don't say much, do you?" He glanced at Anna to ensure that she understood she was included in his criticism. In the absence of a reply or a contribution from Dave who was momentarily resting from smiling, Matthew felt obliged to change tact. "I think that professor's a great bloke. Now I can do anything – forever. No worries. He's like the new messiah, isn't he? Did you see that film once? He's certainly given us what everyone's always wanted. I'd be the first one to admit it if he was my father. . ." He waited for a moment, expecting confirmation of his suspicions. None was forthcoming, instead Anna found her voice:

"We'd like to finish our meal please. . ."

Dave began to move away but Matthew hovered beside the table with an irritating persistency. "Mind if we join you?" He directed his request at Anna suspecting that she would weaken. He was wrong.

"Yes," she replied firmly.

"Come on Matt," Dave called and beckoned to his friend.

"Suit yourselves, ladies." Matthew shrugged his shoulders, obviously annoyed and uncomprehending as to why his advances were unwelcome. The two men wandered back to the bar muttering together and throwing an occasional hostile glance in the direction of the women.

Now Helen was suffering from post-holiday depression and still searching for a meaningful role as she wandered aimlessly along the busy street. She felt more isolated than ever. It was as if she was travelling in a huge, thick bubble – able to observe all that went on around but unable to be part of it. Then a group of youths bounded past her, jostling and shouting. Helen felt afraid. The bubble disappeared, leaving her physically vulnerable. One of the group stopped, suddenly:

"Hey, look at this!" he cried to his mates, before tearing at a poster and chucking it to the ground. Several members of the gang took it in turns to take flying leaps at the old, wooden notice board (erected in memory of C.J. Harleyson 'a true servant of this borough') until cracked and splintered it lay dead and useless on the pavement. The gang marched on. Helen, pretending to study a bus timetable, watched from a safe distance as they shouted obscenities, pushed and shoved at each other and stuck their fingers up at anyone who they decided was taking too much of an interest in their behaviour.

Helen made her way slowly to the broken notice board and, bending down, pulled the torn piece of paper from beneath the split timber. Smoothing it out, she easily pieced the two large fragments together. (The gang's attention span, even for acts of vandalism, was pathetically short.) It was one of Will's posters advertising MAD's open meeting which was planned for the next day. Will had made some modifications following Deighton's announcement and the poster consisted of a large black missile on a yellow background with the words 'Don't detonate – don't rejuvenate' blaring from it, in bold black letters. Underneath, in smaller print, readers were invited to 'come to the rally, speak to us – see what it's all about.'

A flicker of interest stirred inside Helen which was immediately interrupted by a woman pushing a pushchair and chattering loudly on a mobile phone. The child in the pushchair gazed blankly ahead, her mouth covered in chocolate and her cold, white hand clinging to a dirty soft toy. A little boy, clutching the side of the pushchair trotted precariously next to his mother who attempted to wheel the buggy over the remains of the broken notice board. The pushchair lurched and came to an abrupt stop almost catapulting the younger child, who cried with fright, into the road. The woman's son tripped, lurched into Helen and fell forward onto his face, scraping his delicate skin on the pavement and piercing his hand with a large splinter of wood. He screamed. Helen immediately started to pick up and comfort the distressed child.

"It's alright. I'll do it," his mother snapped ungratefully, before elbowing Helen out of the way and unceremoniously standing her son on his feet with an unsympathetic jolt.

"I've got some tissues if you like. . ." Helen offered, beginning to open her bag and looking at the pinpricks of blood, oozing from the boy's grazed forehead.

"There's no need. I've got one." His mother pulled a crumbling, piece of well worn tissue from her pocket and looked at Helen suspiciously. "I can manage," she continued. "Anyway, he should have been looking where he was going." She wiped at her son's nose and then gave the graze a flick with the damp, soiled tissue.

"Come on, Taylor," she commanded the blubbering child, whilst simultaneously sending a text message. "Be careful this time."

Helen watched incredulously as the mother and children resumed their unhappy journey. Taylor's wet, red face turning back every few seconds staring into Helen's gaze in equal puzzlement.

Both incidents disturbed her. Then she saw the connection; in ten years time Taylor would be an unthinking vandal full of misplaced aggression and pride but lacking self-respect. It was an unpleasant thought. It did not seem right that his future was so determined at such a young age. Helen felt unaccountably guilty. Then, feeling annoyed with herself, picked up the torn poster again, which she had dropped in her eagerness to assist the tragic boy.

The rally was to be held at the Corn Exchange. She could go. It would be interesting to hear a different perspective on rejuvenation. Helen had not dared to voice her reservations in detail to anyone – not even Anna. She did not wish to betray her father and had tried to bury the persistent misgivings, but instead of subsiding, her distaste for rejuvenation grew steadily as did her sense of isolation. She would go! Pity about the acronym, though – MAD – what did it stand for? Perhaps she shouldn't go? Perhaps it was a joke or some kind of student spoof? The paper fluttered in her hand. The meeting was tomorrow. After that it would be too late. She had nothing else planned except a day of isolation. She need not join in the open day. No. She definitely would not take an active part but it would do no harm to watch – and listen. She would go! She would not feel guilty either!

65

Helen shoved the torn poster into her pocket, knowing that she would need to check the date, time and venue a thousand times before becoming confident enough to remember them. Turning to go, she noticed an elderly man hurrying, agitatedly towards her, muttering loudly.

He stopped next to Helen and began to pick up the pieces of the destroyed notice board.

"Bloody hooligans!" he fumed, tossing the board and splinters into a small pile. "Old Charlie would have been so disappointed. – turning in his grave. He did a lot for people round here – housing, facilities for the youngsters, all that sort of thing. Used to put on a big Christmas party for all the children. All of 'em! And they had a present from Father Christmas, a magician, everything and see how they pay him back for it!"

"I know," Helen agreed. "It is awful."

"Charlie wasn't a rich man either," his friend continued. "Brought up in an orphanage, he was, and that was a strict upbringing in those days. Had nothing – pushed from pillar to post, not like nowadays. And he always said that that was what first started him off wanting to make things better for people who didn't have much. Now look at 'em with their fancy trainers, mobile phones, computers and I dunno what. Got everything haven't they?" Stopping his tidying for a moment he stared into Helen's eyes. She could think of nothing soothing to say to ease the pain, disillusionment and resignation from his sagging features.

"Got everything," he repeated, more quietly, "and they're never satisfied. The more they've got the less content they are. They're only happy if they're breaking something or destroying someone's hard work. They never do any work. Look at them! How come they're marching about the high street at 11 o'clock in the morning? Why aren't they at work?"

Helen shrugged her shoulders. "I don't know – jobs are hard to find. . ." was all she could think to say, annoyed with herself for such a lame response.

The old man's agitation and physical exertion had made him breathless. Steadying himself against one of the sheared, upright notice board posts and panting, to Helen's alarm he ignored her last remark and continued, "I could do with a sit down. There used to be a seat here, of course – dedicated to Charlie but they tore that to pieces and set fire to it. We replaced it with a concrete one which wasn't as nice but lasted a bit longer, until they stole a car and rammed into it. We gave up after that. Charlie would be spinning in his grave," he repeated sadly. "He just couldn't understand it. Wouldn't understand what's gone so wrong. And it's not just the youngsters, there's something wrong with the whole of society – it's like it's got cancer and it's growing and spreading and we can't do anything about it. There are more and more vicious, violent crimes going on everyday – not that the powers that be will admit it. But we know it. They can lie and falsify their figures, and treat us like dirt all they like, but we know it. We're not as stupid as they like to think."

The old man stared again at Helen, whilst catching his breath. It made her feel uncomfortable as though she should have an answer. She did not. Charlie's friend misinterpreted her silence.

"Ah, you probably think I'm just a stupid, moaning old man," he began, resuming his collection of the spoilt timber. "Someone who thinks everything was better years ago and looks back fondly to the war years. . ."

"No. No. I don't. You're quite wrong," Helen interrupted him hastily. "I agree, this wanton destruction is awful and I know it's getting worse. I don't believe the well practised mantra that 'fear of crime is more prevalent than crime itself'. I can see it all around. The papers and the news on television are full of it. What are you going to do with that?" she asked suddenly, pointing at the bundle of timber under his arm and the remains of the board at his feet.

"Oh, I'll chuck it in the skip at the back of the community centre. The caretaker won't mind, he's a mate of mine."

"Let me help you," Helen offered, surprising herself with the note of determination in her voice and simultaneously grabbing the notice board.

"Thank you very much," her companion beamed. "I'm not quite as fit as I used to be."

They walked the two hundred yards to the community centre at a slow pace, during which time Helen discovered that her new acquaintance was Freddie Meredith, aged seventy-nine, who lived nearby with his wife, Ada. They had been married for more than fifty-five years.

"Ada doesn't get out as much as she used to," Freddie confided. "Her health's not so good nowadays – nothing like as good as mine!" he added cheerfully, before shaking like a rattle and coughing deeply into a large, sharply creased handkerchief. They deposited the debris in the skip and Freddie began to pant again.

"Would you like to get a cup of tea?" Helen suggested, nervously, noticing the colour rising in his otherwise creamy-tinged cheeks. "This has all been quite an exertion and there's a very nice café, just up the road. . ."

"Do you know what? I don't mind if I do. A cup of tea would be lovely just now." Freddie grinned. "Of course, we could have gone in there," he added, nodding in the direction of the community centre, "but it's closed today."

They made their way to 'Miriam's' where Freddie, exhibiting immaculate manners, succeeded in making Helen feel special. He placed her order and when the bill arrived insisted on paying for both. During their assignation, Freddie revealed a little more about himself and Ada.

"Wait 'til I tell Ada I've been out to tea with a young lady!" he announced with a grin, his eyes twinkling mischievously. Helen smiled politely. " 'Freddie Meredith,' she'll say, 'you'll be the death of me! Out gallivanting and leaving me at home all by myself!' " Freddie glanced at his watch before murmuring to himself almost inaudibly, "Mustn't be long."

"Don't let me keep you. . ." Helen interjected, hurriedly.

"No. It's alright," he replied easily. "Ada would only be joking. It's me that don't like leaving her too long. She can't see so well and the damp weather plays her rheumatism up. I've been a lucky man – I am a lucky man," he emphasised before continuing. "It was the best day of my life when we got married." Freddie seemed to be focussing on something in the distance, far behind Helen's bent head, something resigned to time, nearly fifty-six years ago – a warm, bright day in May. Freddie remembered the excitement coupled with a strange hollow sensation, signalling apprehension, the tightness of his shirt collar and his towering reflection in the new pair of highly polished shoes – all of this permeated by the sickly smell of hair oil. His parents, brothers and sisters flitted into view, smiling, happy and brimming with vitality. He remembered his elder brother, Joe, at his side, reeking of tobacco and alcohol (although he swore he'd only had one) and them both turning at the sound of the organ, warming the church with its sonorous announcement, and snatching the first glimpses of Ada as she and her father made their way steadily up the aisle.

Helen remained silent, allowing Freddie to enjoy his memories.

"We've always lived round here," he revealed suddenly, signalling his return to the present. "It used to be a lovely area but now. . ." He shook his head sadly. "I won't start on all that again but suffice it to say I'm glad I haven't got grandchildren or great grandchildren being brought up."

"Do you have any children nearby?" Helen enquired with genuine curiosity.

"No. No. We haven't got any. Never had any children – not lucky in that department. That's partly why we spend so much time helping out 'in the community' as they'd call it now. Charlie used to call me his right hand man and Ada helped out in the charity shop for years, as well as doing her own job, you know. She was so active, that's why she finds ill health and getting old hard to adjust to. Do you know what? She's even interested in this new rejuvenation thing. It worries me a bit."

Helen pricked up her ears. "Is that what she wants? Do you think she'd go through with it?"

"I think she would," Freddie replied mournfully, "but I'm not sure about it at all. I think when your time comes, your time has come and that's it. It's dangerous to go messing about with nature. It's natural to live and die and we should accept it. The trouble is, people get desperate, don't they. And scared. I suppose we've always been searching for an elixir of life." He smiled self-consciously. "Here I go again, you're bound to think I'm batty. Everyone else is as pleased as punch now they can be rejuvenated – especially young people, like yourself – soon they'll think it's normal. I don't want to pour cold water on everything – I should make myself move more with the times." He smiled falsely, as if everything was all right.

"Actually I have huge reservations about rejuvenation," Helen told him. "In fact, I don't agree with it, something's not right about it, but it's almost impossible to get this across as ninety-nine percent of the population seem to be completely in agreement with it."

Two women sitting at the table opposite, glared aggressively at Helen and Freddie, before whispering to each other and erupting into cold, hostile laughter.

"You surprise me," Freddie admitted, with a hint of relief. "I thought it was just me. I don't usually mention it anymore – I get such a bad reaction. People think you're mad and won't listen to anything you say. I've fallen out quite badly with people I've known for years, who I thought were good friends. I soon learnt that it was better to keep quiet."

"There are a few people who are against it," Helen replied, fishing in her bag for the remnants of the torn poster. "Look, this was what was on the noticeboard."

Freddie studied the wrinkled notice through his heavy, slightly smeared glasses.

"I'm not surprised they tore it down and wrecked the notice board. This is just the sort of thing that enflames 'em – if they can read."

"I'm thinking of going," Helen revealed, shortly.

"You're right. Ada will be looking for me," Freddie answered misunderstanding, and beginning to ease himself to his feet.

"No. No," Helen corrected him, before a surge of embarrassment could stop her. "I meant I'm thinking of going to the meeting. I don't know anything about this MAD group though, but it might be worth finding out."

"Good for you!" approved Freddie. "Don't take it lying down, go and see what it's all about. We might not be as daft as everyone thinks. You never know – I might even go myself – it depends, I probably won't mention it to Ada – no need to upset her."

The two new acquaintances parted company. Freddie shook Helen by the hand solemnly in front of the café door and thanked her for her help and company.

"Come round and see us, one day," he invited. "Ada would like to meet you – number twelve Keats' Meadow."

"Thank you, it's been nice talking to you." Helen responded before they both turned and walked away in opposite directions. Freddie ambled along, his large frame occasionally lurching to the left, a soft whistle emanating from his lips and thoughts of Ada occupying his mind. Helen hurried purposefully, propelled by a feeling of nervousness brought on by her declaration that she would attend MAD's meeting. 'It would be much easier to stay at home' she mused, 'but what if Freddie went expecting me to be there? He might think that I had been humouring him or worse still, lying.' Now she would have to go.

Chapter Eight

Mary prepared gleefully for her meeting with Reverend Mouland. She washed her thick, unkempt hair and donned her most recently purchased clothes: a calf length voluminous, purple, corduroy skirt; bottle green silk blouse; a heavy green, cream and purple, mottled, woollen cardigan and knee length, black leather boots. After several attempts, and concentrating hard in her greasy looking glass, she at last fixed to her satisfaction, two silver slides in her nest of mousey hair. Staring into the mirror again, in passport photograph style pose, an idea enlivened her face and produced a sly grin. Mary delved into the central drawer of the dressing table, scrabbling through dust, elastic bands and broken pieces of cheap, old fashioned jewellery. After several moments, and stopping two or three times to look at long forgotten treasures, she found it and grasping a long piece of dusty, black cord in her fingers, pulled out a large metal Celtic cross. This would do perfectly! After staring at it for a moment and allowing herself to become mesmerised by its distinctive shape and converging patterns, she closed her fist and absorbed its cool indentation cutting into the palm of her hand. Eventually she fastened it around her neck and feeling it dangle pleasingly, considered herself prepared.

Reverend Mouland welcomed her at the door of the vicarage. He had been tempted to cancel the meeting during a moment of deep despair when he had temporarily yielded to his depressed belief that everything was hopeless, it was all too late and the rampant popularity of rejuvenation had made it unassailable.

Caroline had, once again, supplied support, encouragement and guidance.

"Of course you shouldn't cancel the meeting!" she exclaimed, horrified. "It's a light at the end of the tunnel; someone else –an organisation – opposes rejuvenation and they've contacted you – you haven't had to search them out. This could be the beginning of the fight-back!"

"I suppose you're right," her husband responded, sounding unconvinced. "But I've been down so many dead ends, been humiliated on the radio, betrayed by the bishop, even our home has been attacked and now St. Nonna's is being made redundant. Sometimes I do feel like giving up."

"Well you can't!" snapped Caroline firmly. "Or if you did, you'd spend the rest of your life regretting it," she added as an afterthought. "Anyway, I won't let you! Your role is to fight back and you must accept the mantle. You need fulfilment and you're not going to get it from a congregation that has dwindled to nothing and a redundant church. Our faith has faced obliteration throughout history but there have always been a few stalwarts who have kept it going and it's survived and flourished over time. Think of yourself as privileged. You've retained your belief and trust in God and because of that you have been chosen to lead. Not in a cosy way, preaching to the converted in a warm church surrounded by passivity, but in an arduous, wearing struggle. A struggle which will relentlessly seep your energy, make you despair and sometimes reduce you to nothing – but you have to do it. Someone has to keep the flame alight and your reward will be peace of mind, which is unfathomable."

Mouland listened silently. He had been on the receiving end of numerous oratories from his wife during his married life (and some before) and they never failed to lift and inspire him. That was her gift. She was the catalyst for his talents.

"You're absolutely right," he agreed quickly, as Caroline took a badly needed breath. "I don't know why I allow myself to become so despondent at times. It's a good job I've got you here to keep me going and to get things into perspective. Of course the meeting should go ahead – I'm quite looking forward to it now. Perhaps these people will enable us to get a foothold and to start getting our message heard."

Caroline smiled, trying not to reveal the deep sense of relief exploding inside. She always feared that one day her persuasive skills would fail and she would be unable to rouse her husband from his self doubt and feelings of failure.

"I'd like to be present at the meeting. Do you think that will be alright?" she asked.

"Certainly," her husband beamed. "After all, it's not a private meeting, it doesn't concern personal matters. Miss Fields will be representing her organisation, MAD."

"Mmm. It's an unfortunate acronym," Caroline mused. "Quite likely to put people off, I should think."

"I shouldn't worry about that. I get the impression it's meant to be humorous – the woman sounded quite sane on the phone. People like to have quirky names for nearly everything nowadays."

Mary arrived dead on time. Reverend Mouland welcomed her warmly and invited her into the small room he used as an office. Caroline appeared instantly, offering tea, coffee and biscuits. Mouland introduced his wife, who scurried uncharacteristically to the kitchen to make the drinks as quickly as possible, then he asked Mary to tell him a little about MAD.

"We're a small, but growing, organisation. Our original aim was to make people aware that there are better alternatives to modern medicine and its procedures. . ."

"Such as?" the Reverend enquired.

"All the usual therapies – which I'm sure you've heard of – homeopathy, massage, aromatherapy, herbal remedies, etc."

Mouland nodded, encouragingly, whilst remarking, "These things have shown to be effective in many cases but they're well known – surely your organisation doesn't need to promote them?"

Mary had prepared for this question and was about to reply when Caroline reappeared with a tray of tea and coffee.

"Shall we go into the other room?" she suggested. "It's much more comfortable in there." The vicar and his visitor followed Caroline into the sitting room where Mary perched on the edge of the deep, soft, sofa and sipped her black tea. Mouland and his wife looked at her expectantly.

"As I was about to say," Mary took her cue obediently, "you'd be surprised at how many people have no knowledge of alternative therapies – often the underprivileged – and the

73

founders of M A D (she spelled out the letters) felt they had a duty to make such people aware of the choices they have. That's partly why they chose such a silly name." She gave a deprecating giggle. "But it was calculated to draw attention to the group and I think it has worked – we have members in other countries. Also M A D (she spelled the letters, again) was set up several years ago before the alternatives were so well known. Their increased popularity has been a sign of our success."

"So much so that MAD could find itself redundant?" enquired Caroline.

Mary turned to her, battling to disguise the sense of dislike for this woman which was rising inside her. "No. Not at all. There are many less well known approaches which need exploring and promoting, such as self healing, metal therapy, prayer – all of which can offer successful, non invasive treatment. People are rediscovering remedies all the time."

"But now they can be rejuvenated they won't need any of these," Caroline stated with more hostility than her husband would have liked.

Mary smiled ruefully and, following a condescending glance at the vicar's wife, turned her attention to the man himself. "That's why I'm here. Rejuvenation represents the greatest form of invasive therapy imaginable. Needless to say, it's the most serious assault on our principles that we have ever faced."

"We're certainly agreed that it's an unprecedented assault on our principles," Mouland admitted, "but does your group believe that death is preferable to life? This is where the opposition lies. From those that consider death is the end – those without hope, you might say. We would say, without faith. People prefer to put their trust in what they know or can see – anything else is an unacceptable gamble."

"Obviously our views are not identical to your own," Mary replied with ease, clenching her teacup, "but we have a similar outlook based on the cycle of life – we believe that rejuvenation already happens but in a natural, non-invasive way. We feel that scientific rejuvenation (for want of a better phrase) removes us from our place in that cycle, diminishes us and will upset the delicate balance of nature."

"Are you saying that you believe in reincarnation?" Caroline quizzed her aggressively, but before she could obtain a reply her

74

husband interrupted hurriedly:

"I don't think it really matters – we don't have to delve that far. It's enough that our main principle is the same." 'And we need all the support we can get,' he thought, conveying this message to his wife with an almost imperceptible flicker of his eyes in her direction.

"No doubt you've encountered much opposition to your views," he continued, turning once again to Mary. "Which will increase from some quarters, perhaps in a very hostile way. Are you prepared for that?"

"Oh yes," Mary laughed, unconcerned, "we are quite used to being insulted, called cranks, insane and even spat upon – quite literally – but we are committed to our cause. We won't give up – in fact, we're determined to be successful, that's why we want to work with others who have similar views. We need to raise awareness that rejuvenation is dangerous, that it is not the panacea people think it is. We hope that you will agree to join us, but if not we will carry on – we will never give in." She stopped abruptly, realising that her tone had developed a monotonous edge and her gaze was about to drill into the minds of the vicar and his wife. Luckily, she had controlled herself in time and neither of them appeared to have noticed.

"We've, naturally, been attempting to galvanise support for our view since the whole thing exploded – but not very successfully, I'm afraid," Mouland admitted whilst dunking his chocolate biscuit into his tea and immediately experiencing an annoying spasm of guilt. "It's about time to join forces and begin the fight-back. It's very encouraging to have been approached by your organisation – we were beginning to think that we were alone."

"Have you a campaign plan?" Caroline asked. "Any ideas or projects in the pipeline?"

"Yes. We have an open meeting planned for next week at the Charlie Harleyson Community Centre, which will be an informal question and answer session, when we will try to get our point across on a personal level and where we can debate with people. Following that, we hope to organise a protest rally with other groups and interested individuals – hopefully some of whom will have attended the meeting and been converted – I mean educated or persuaded – perhaps enlightened is a better word."

For a moment Caroline briefly sensed Mary's true nature but

the revelation was too fleeting to impress itself. Like the sense of déjà vu or an interrupted dream, the action of attempting to grasp and retain it merely caused it to dissipate and float away forever. Philip noticed nothing.

"Can we take part in the meeting – on your side as it were – answer questions etc? If we're going to join forces, we might as well do so at once. There's no time to waste and the meeting will be an ideal opportunity," he asked.

Mary looked pleased and smiled encouragingly. "I don't see why not," she replied, "but we'll have to vote on it at our next MAD meeting, which is on Monday. I'm sure you'll be most welcome. I'll let you know." She rose, placed her cup and saucer carefully on a coaster depicting Truro Cathedral and left the clerical couple wondering whether they had done the right thing.

"What do you think?" Philip asked his wife quietly, after watching Mary disappear safely round the corner at the end of the gravel path.

"I think we have no choice," she replied deliberately. "We knew from the beginning that MAD would probably be a slightly strange organisation; unconventional, not very well known or popular, but at least they have the strength of their convictions. So far we've got nowhere on our own, we're going backwards, look at St. Nonna's."

Philip had temporarily forgotten about the closure of St. Nonna's. His wife's reminder made him angry – not with her but with the situation – and he felt pleased, in a belligerent sort of way, that he had joined forces with MAD and that at long last he would be doing something.

"You're right," he agreed briskly. "The decision's made as far as we're concerned and I can't wait to get on with it! I'm tired of being trodden on, ridiculed and feeling depressed, I'm ready for the next phase. I know why I'm here!" Caroline could feel the fire reigniting inside her husband and remembered why she had married him. She knew that he would not falter now.

Mary waited at the bus stop, feeling pleased. Deep in thought she replayed the meeting in her mind, her lips involuntarily expanding into a thin smile. It was the first time that any recognised organisation had shown a serious, sympathetic, interest in MAD. She had been treated as an equal, which rarely happened in any aspect of her life. Despite her pleasure, she could

76

not prevent a gurgle of contempt for Mouland and his wife, popping into the mixture of emotions which filled her head. These were, indeed, desperate times.

The bus arrived and Mary boarded it and paid her fare to the silent driver. Selecting one of the few vacant seats, next to an expensively casually dressed, well-kempt man, aged somewhere in his thirties, she detected a hint of disappointment as her fellow traveller turned his head and focused intently through the steamed up, rain splattered, grimy window pane for the remainder of his journey.

On her return to the musty flat, Mary prepared for the open meeting. First she read through her tattered collection of press cuttings, then she watched the video recording of Deighton's hallowed announcement. Due to frequent use, the tape had become worn and slightly twisted resulting in a jumpy, incomplete picture with a thick, black grainy band at the bottom. Finally, Mary began to imagine, and rehearse aloud, prospective conversations with attendees at the meeting. With effort she managed to control herself during most of these fantastic debates but occasionally could not prevent breaking into the hysterical, accelerating monotone which simultaneously energised and exhausted her. As a result, she flopped heavily on the lumpy bed and dreamed of success, prestige and respect.

Reverend Mouland, in the meantime, sought out Julian Devereux in St. Nonna's. The heavy sound of the organ, ploughing through *Eternal Father Strong To Save*, signalled the church warden's presence. Devereux was an enthusiastic, if untalented organist, who reached a standard which was just acceptable for services, in the absence of an alternative, through bloody minded determination and hours of practice. "At least it keeps the Alzheimer's at bay," he used to joke, well aware of his limitations.

Mouland slipped through the main door unnoticed and took a seat at the back of the ancient building, just outside Devereux's range of vision. The organ's deep, rich tone filled the building bringing warmth with each magnificent chord. The vicar leant backwards against the hard wooden pew, folded his arms, raised his closed eyes to the pink and cream lime-washed ceiling and allowed himself to melt into the music, atmosphere and fabric of the building. The past memories, his faith and the present merged into one. The only element missing was the future which, refusing to be included, stood outside Mouland's moment waiting to pounce.

Devereux played a wrong note. The reverend heard him exclaim angrily and mutter an unidentified oath. Mouland smiled and thought he should reveal himself. Devereux began to play again and Mouland made his way up the central aisle, like a reluctant bride, to the organ's accompaniment. Eventually Devereux spied his friend in the mirror strategically placed above the manual and stopped playing,

"Don't stop on my account," Philip told him.

"There's a tricky bit I'm trying to get right in time for Sunday," revealed the hapless organist. "I keep on forgetting there's a sharp. . ."

"I'm afraid there is actually no need to practise for Sunday," Mouland announced with a tone of finality.

Devereux, who was just about to resume his playing, turned round looking puzzled. "What do you mean? Why not? We have two services planned. I know the congregation will be small, miniscule is probably a better word, but we have to carry on as normal and do the thing properly."

"The services are cancelled. We've had the last one, although we didn't know it, last Sunday. I've had another email from the diocese – St. Nonna's is to close with immediate effect. They've had an offer they can't refuse from one of these storage companies who want the building ASAP. I'm being allowed to stay on and co-ordinate the dispersal of the contents and arrange access for the new owners."

Devereux was visibly shocked. "I'm flabbergasted, can't believe it, so soon," was all he could say.

"It's a huge job to do in such a short time," Mouland continued with a strange lack of emotion. "I wondered whether I could count on your help?"

"Of course, of course," Devereux replied hastily, returning to his senses. "What are you supposed to do with it all?" he asked while taking a sweeping glance at the building's interior.

"Some of the artefacts – as they like to call them – are to be sold at auction and the rest – a small number I assure you – are to be kept and exhibited in a new museum they're planning called 'The People's Museum of Christianity'. I believe that items of special interest from all the redundant churches are to be housed there. They've applied for a lottery grant."

Devereux's eyes widened in horror as Mouland revealed the plans in a brisk, automatic manner. "How can they decide this without asking us?" Devereux demanded angrily. "The PCC has not been consulted or even informed. The haste is almost indecent!"

"I'm afraid our views are unimportant now," Mouland replied quietly. "We have no voice anymore – at least not through our usual channels. I think we have to accept that the church as we know it has finally disintegrated. We've been forced to take a tremendous step backwards – to our roots, or beyond. All we can do now is keep the flame alive, nurture it and be prepared for when the world finally comes to its senses."

"If it comes to its senses," the church warden interjected miserably.

"Do you know, Julian – I am convinced that it will – eventually. There's something so wrong, so unnatural, about rejuvenation that I really believe it can't last," Mouland responded thoughtfully.

"I hope you're right." Devereux still sounded grumpy. "But in the meantime everything's being destroyed in its wake."

"Looking on the bright side, I've met the woman from that group MAD. She seems quite keen to join forces and they're organising a public meeting which, hopefully, we can take part in with them. Caroline and I want to go – perhaps you would like to as well?" Mouland suggested.

"I'll think about it." Devereux sounded like a sullen, sulky, schoolboy, but his friend knew him well enough to understand that nothing would keep him from the meeting.

"Good. That's settled then," he replied without thinking. Devereux's response was to snort as a result of a mixture of puzzlement and annoyance. 'Why did Philip think it was settled then' – when he had just said that he would merely think about it? 'Sometimes no one takes me seriously,' he moaned internally, whilst staring morosely at the eagle lectern.

Mary prepared for Monday's MAD meeting in her usual methodological manner which served to disguise the quivering excitement which simultaneously weakened and energised her. Although the meeting was scheduled to begin at 8pm, Mary knew that the society's members would arrive up to half an hour early or an hour late. She could also predict with ninety percent accuracy who would arrive when. At 7.30pm she spied Sonja loitering behind the laurel hedge which almost met the crumbling gate pier. Sonja would wait there until approximately 7.50pm when, deeming it was an acceptable time to arrive, she would knock on the door, apologise for being early, explain that the next bus would get her there at 7.55pm and it might be late and she didn't want to risk it. Mary would allow her into the dingy flat and they would wait in uncomfortable silence for the next arrival.

This would be Joe who would turn up puffing a couple of minutes later, and insist on parking his bicycle in the narrow hallway, forcing the others to squeeze past. Ricky, arriving next, always complained about the state of Joe's bike and worried that he would get oil on his tan, leather jacket. Once, whilst negotiating a path round the offending machine, Ricky had leaned too heavily into the wall and had snagged his previous jacket on a rusty protruding nail which tore an almost perfect square of soft, Italian leather from the sleeve. Ricky had then rowed with Joe throughout the ensuing meeting, opposed everything he suggested and argued with all his comments.

Carly and Will always arrived a few minutes late – sometimes together if Carly could contrive it. Howard had recently begun to arrive ten minutes after he calculated that the meeting would have begun. This was solely to avoid the compulsory period of meditation with which Mary insisted on starting the meeting. The final straw had been at the first meeting following the announce-ment of rejuvenation when Howard felt vehemently that the development should have been discussed at once. He disagreed with meditation especially if it was compulsory and vowed never to be forced to take part in it again.

Rose had never yet managed to arrive on time although she had once turned up at 8.10pm. Sometimes she had been an hour late. She had insisted that actually she was naturally a good time keeper but her maternal duties invariably interfered. One of her five children could be relied upon to invoke some sort of crisis which she would have to deal with before leaving home, or the babysitter would be late, or something. Occasionally, when all else had failed, she would be accompanied by a sullen, bored looking child, clutching an electronic game.

80

Tonight everyone arrived on cue (even Rose made it by 8.20pm) except Will. Carly rushed in expectantly, returning greetings mechanically whilst looking round for him. She positioned herself at one end of the lumpy sofa which gave her an uninterrupted view of the path to the front door. During the meditation session she managed to take surreptitious glances out of the window but Will did not appear.

Eventually, at about half way through the meeting, Sonja received a text.

"Sorry," she squirmed but was unable to resist reading it. "Oh, it's from Will. He's not coming. . . anymore," she revealed hesitatingly.

Mary grabbed the mobile phone and peered at the screen angrily. "I see. This is the kind of person we can rely on," she announced before reading the message aloud in a facetious style: " 'Sorry guys, can't support you anymore. Gone over to rejuvenation.' "

Carly turned white and wondered why she was there.

"I'm not surprised. You can hardly blame him – there's so much pressure on young people nowadays," said Rose, full of understanding.

"You seem to know him better than we realised. Did he say anything to you?" Mary snapped at Sonja before hissing "traitor" to herself.

Sonja flushed, embarrassed and fearful could only stutter, "No. Nothing. I only ever saw him here. . ."

"Why did he have your number then?" Carly joined the assault eagerly, an awareness growing rapidly that she did not like Sonja.

"He asked for it in case we needed to discuss anything. . ."

"And did you need to discuss anything?" Carly continued between clenched teeth.

Sonja shook like a frightened rabbit. "No," was all she could bleat.

"I thought young Carly was his mate," Howard joined in perceptively. "It's no good having a go at current members. It's bound to happen – you win some and you lose some. We need to concentrate on winning some and hopefully the open meeting will do that. Are we all ready?"

Sonja pressed herself back into her chair wishing to be invisible, grateful for Howard's support and wounded by Mary and Carly's aggression. Rose gave her a comforting wink. Mary noticed but managed to regain her self-control.

"Thank you, Howard. The meeting will take place if everyone's pulled their weight and completed their assigned task. I'll run through a quick check list. Community Centre booked?"

"Yes and paid for, plus the deposit. I've got the receipt here somewhere. . ." Rose began to rummage in her large, floral cotton bag.

"Advertising?"

"Yes," Carly responded, still sounding annoyed, "Will and I produced loads of posters."

"And I placed the adverts in the local paper and the free one," Sonja confirmed timidly in the hope of redemption.

"Did everyone manage to put up their designated number of posters, in the agreed locations?" Mary enquired, still reading from her list.

There was a general nodding of heads and murmurs of assent until Carly, invigorated by anger and disappointment, suddenly asked loudly:

"What about you, Joe? Did you put all yours up?"

"Yes. Of course I did," he replied with finality.

"Well I don't know how. Your pile is still in my room. You never collected them."

Howard snorted, drummed his fingers on the wooden armrest and stared at the ceiling. Ricky gave him a sympathetic, backwards nod and Rose looked at Joe with great disappointment. Sonja melted away even more, feeling both pleased and guilty that someone else was to be the focus of Mary and Carly's ire. Joe looked startled and cleared his throat.

"Oh you mean those posters! I thought you were talking about some we put up before," he lied ludicrously. "I was about to apologise. I've had a crisis at work – one of the machines broke down and we couldn't get the part (it has to come from Holland apparently) and I've had to do lots of overtime. To top it all, my mother's been ill – you know, worse than usual – so I'm sorry but this time I just haven't been able to do my task. You know that's not like me – I always work damn hard – probably harder than anyone else." Smiling ruefully he looked at each member in turn, alienating them all. Howard emitted a huge guffaw and swore loudly.

"Surely you don't expect us to believe that?" Ricky asked contemptuously.

"I'm not asking you. I'm telling you. It's the truth!" Joe shouted, thumping the nearest piece of furniture, having by now convinced himself that his story was undeniable fact. "I'm the only one who ever does anything around here. If it wasn't for me MAD would have been finished long ago. What have you lot done lately?"

"Quite a lot, actually." Mary took control, addressing Joe in a deliberate, staccato style and staring at him through half lowered eyelids. "I think we can all identify dead wood when we see it," she continued menacingly, emphasising the word 'dead', causing Sonja's blood to run cold and the others to feel uncomfortable. "But on a happier, more positive note, I have some good news." Mary smiled widely but sounded far from happy, the combination of her frozen grin and hard impassive grey eyes chilled everyone else to the bone. Mary was at her most dangerous when she effected to be pleasant. "I have been in contact with a small group of people who would like to join us. Initially, it will only be one or two of them but they have the potential to bring more in. They wish to take part in the open meeting with us. . ."

"As members of the public or with us answering questions etc, do you mean?" asked Rose.

"With us. That's why we need to vote on it," Mary replied.

"What sort of group are they?" enquired Ricky.

"They're Christians – Church of England."

"Oh my God!" groaned Joe putting a huge amount of effort into his despair. "That's all we need 'happy clappers' trying to force their nonsense down our throats. Haven't we got enough problems?"

"You're quite right, Joe," Mary responded sweetly, causing him to smirk contentedly until she added, "We have immense problems with some members showing a pitiful lack of commitment and downright dishonesty. This serves only to illustrate our weakness and emphasise how we desperately need to increase our numbers and general support."

"I'm all for joining forces but we have to make sure that anyone else is subsidiary to ourselves – they have to become part of MAD rather than the other way round," suggested Howard.

"I think Howard's right," agreed Rose, "but I also think it's too good an opportunity to miss. The C of E has a much bigger profile than we do – to allow them in would benefit us hugely."

"The only reason they're interested in us is because they're dying on their feet," Joe continued with his negative argument. "They could do us more harm than good – everyone will think we're like them – they're generally a laughing stock now."

"Unfortunately, we've barely moved beyond that stage ourselves," argued Ricky. Mary clenched her teeth but allowed him to continue, guessing correctly that he would be supportive. "I'm of the opinion that they should be allowed to take part."

"Hear, hear!" Howard agreed with enthusiasm. "Let 'em in, I say. Our main objective is to get rid of this rejuvenation rubbish – we can worry about the nitty gritty later."

"Yes – I think you're right," Rose murmured.

"Me too." Sonja allowed herself to speak, pleased to be able to join in again.

Mary looked at Carly.

"I'm not really bothered," the young woman announced childishly, in a bored voice.

"Typical!" Joe thundered, then added, "They'd better make sure they don't try any of their preaching on me or they'll regret it. They're the cause of all the trouble in this world. . ."

"Right, let's vote," Mary decided firmly. The motion was carried with only Carly abstaining. Joe, exhaling loudly, voted in favour, lacking the courage to do otherwise.

Chapter Nine

The day of the open meeting arrived and the members of MAD sprang into action. Ricky arrived at The Charlie Harleyson Community Centre in his open topped BMW sports car with a variety of display stands, borrowed from school, spilling out from the rear compartment. Mary had brought a video tape of Deighton's hallowed announcements and was engrossed in setting up the video player in preparation for her presentations. Rose, accompanied by her two youngest children, busied herself in the small kitchen, preparing plastic cups of tea and coffee and fighting a losing battle over disappearing chocolate biscuits. Howard and Sonja arrived together (Howard having given the younger member a lift) whilst there remained no sign of Carly or Joe.

"That's no surprise," Howard commented as he started moving the furniture around. "Could you bring some chairs down from the stage, please Sonja? I knew Joe would be late. He'll turn up once all the work's done with some lame excuse. And Carly, mark my words, won't turn up at all!"

"Don't you think so?" Sonja was genuinely surprised, if not relieved.

"Nah. She only came because of Will. Now he's left we won't see her again."

"Oh," Sonja mumbled, not daring to believe him.

"That should just about do it," Howard panted as he pulled the last table into position. "Hey Ricky, have you got a stand to go here?"

A blast of loud music hurtled through the public address system. Everyone jumped, including Mary who was fiddling with the controls.

"I'm trying to get it to play 'Earthwaves'," she explained unapologetically. "We need some background music."

"She's right there," Howard whispered. "Otherwise it'll be like a morgue in here. People will think it's one of those rejuvenate stores!"

"How do you think it will go today?" Sonja, after giggling guiltily at Howard's remark, asked Rose, who had temporarily left her post by the teapot.

"Who knows?" she responded. "I hope someone turns up – it will be a disaster otherwise. We don't want too many though, there aren't as many cups as I thought and my naughty boys have eaten most of the biscuits – all the nice ones, of course!"

Mary had succeeded in adjusting the volume to an acceptable level. "Right everyone, gather round please," she ordered.

"Here goes," whispered Ricky and was about to add a further comment when a hammering at the locked door startled everyone. For a moment Rose thought it was a keen, early arrival.

"We're not ready yet," she hissed.

"It's Joe, isn't it? Just as I predicted!" announced Howard triumphantly, as Ricky let him in.

"You lot here already!" Joe sounded surprised as he looked at the displays, arranged furniture and plastic cups waiting to be filled. "I thought you said 10.30am," he lied.

Howard rolled his eyes.

"That's the time it starts," Rose told him, a note of exasperation in her voice. "We obviously had to get here early to set everything up."

"Don't even bother," Howard muttered.

Mary clapped her hands. "Everyone, gather round please. We've just got time for a quick meditation before we finalise everything and open the doors."

"Oh gawd!" moaned Howard as if in real pain. "I might have known she would fit one of those in – I'm off to the little boys' room."

Everyone else formed a circle and meditated obediently until they were disturbed by a discreet knock at the unlocked door, an introductory cough and the sound of footsteps. Reverend

Mouland, Caroline and Devereux stood politely and hesitatingly just inside the hall.

"Here comes the God squad," announced Joe rudely, pulling himself upright in his plastic chair. "I'll give 'em five minutes until they start."

Devereux, who had hearing akin to a bat's, heard both comments and glared at the foolish perpetrator.

Mary jumped up and spread her arms in an uncharacteristic, warm greeting. "Ah, Reverend and Mrs Mouland, welcome, welcome," she beamed. "And you have brought an accomplice, how wonderful. Please come and join our group. We were just indulging in a little meditation – prior to the fray." Mary allowed herself a little chuckle which she was certain would put the visitors at ease. The MAD members knew her well enough to look aghast.

"Thank you," Mouland replied, ushering his wife ahead. "We're very pleased to be here."

Devereux, looking anything but pleased, scowled at the group and at Joe in particular.

"Please take a seat," Mary ordered, still trying to sound friendly. "We're just about to have a quick run through, prior to opening the doors. But I'd better introduce you first."

"Hello!" boomed Howard, marching across the empty hall with his hand outstretched, as she stopped momentarily to draw a breath. "Pleased to meet you," he continued whilst pumping Devereux's arm violently.

"Likewise," the church warden murmured unenthusiastically.

Mary completed the introductions and the three newcomers took their seats. Devereux had to take the vacant place next to Joe who folded his arms across his chest and grunted moodily. Devereux responded by pointedly turning his back on Joe and appeared to concentrate with great interest on Mary's instructions.

"What exactly do we have to say to people when they come in?" asked Sonja nervously.

"Just be welcoming," advised Rose. "I'm going to offer them all a cup of tea or coffee and a biscuit – if we've got any left!" she added threateningly, whilst casting her eyes round to the two young boys who responded with an air of guilt combined with nonchalance.

"We must be sure to be non-threatening," added Ricky. "People must feel able to come in, ask questions, if they want, look at the literature etc, have a cup of tea and go home. If we jump down their throats we'll be sure to put them off. If we can get just a few people to start thinking, that's all, the day will have been a success."

"The last thing we want is people spouting a lot of nonsense," said Joe addressing Devereux's back.

"The idea is that people browse, watch the presentations, hopefully ask questions, see what we're about – in general. I mean not just regarding rejuvenation – and come over to our side," Mary explained.

"Yeah. Make 'em understand that we're not all complete loonies," Howard agreed darkly, before addressing Mouland: "What do you say, vicar?"

"Oh I quite agree. We just want an opportunity to engage with people, perhaps sow a seed of doubt in their minds that what they perceive as progress could be just the opposite. I certainly don't want to deliver a sermon or anything!"

"Thank God for that," Joe replied, unable to stop himself, oblivious to the irony of his remark. "That'd be sure to put them off," he continued in his blinkered fashion. "The whole day'd be a complete waste of time. . ."

"Thank you, Joe." Mary cut him off and he winced as Devereux manoeuvred his chair just enough to pinch a wedge of skin from Joe's ample thigh between the two seats.

"Right!" continued Mary briskly, after glancing at her watch, "10:30 exactly. It's time to open the doors!"

After a general scraping and clatter of chairs, everyone took up their positions. The three Christians attached themselves to Rose's refreshment table and Mary flung open the doors expectantly. There was no one waiting outside. The group relaxed and began chatting amongst themselves. Rose offered the Christian contingent, or 'God squad' as Joe insisted on calling them, a cup of tea, which they all accepted gratefully.

"It's early days yet," Mouland remarked soothingly. "People like to relax on a Saturday – they'll be out and about later."

"Oh yes," Rose agreed. "Take my teenage daughters, for example, they lie in bed until well after midday at the weekend – and even then I have to prise them off their mattresses!"

Caroline laughed politely.

"I think I'll take a wander round, have a look at your leaflets etc.," Devereux decided.

"Yes, by all means," Rose responded encouragingly, before adding as an aside, "Howard and Ricky are the best people to talk to."

Devereux tried to saunter across to the table manned by Rose's suggested members, but his true stiffness of gait resulted in him lurching awkwardly and appearing to have one leg shorter than the other.

"Here he comes," sneered Joe with predictable satisfaction. "What's the matter with him?" he added quizzically, peering through his thick glasses at the unfortunate church warden. "That's all we need – a bloody cripple!"

"Shut up!" Mary hissed angrily, whilst simultaneously elbowing him hard in the ribs. "I don't know what's the matter with you. Why are you being so rude and so 'anti'? We need more people like these to join us. We don't need you putting them off!"

"Do we really need people like these Christians?" Joe replied laconically. "Actually, I think he's drunk."

"Don't be so ridiculous," Mary snapped again, whilst curiously wondering how easy it would be to dispose of Joe's body. The main doors slammed shut. "Go and wedge them open," Mary ordered, pleased to divert Joe's attention. Joe obeyed and in an attempt to imitate Devereux, who was by now flicking through some pamphlets, limped across the hall, smirking childishly.

"Do you know much about us?" Howard asked.

"Can't say I do really," Devereux replied. "Philip – Reverend Mouland over there – said he thought we might have a common aim in opposing rejuvenation. I've come along today to see what you're all about, really."

"Good idea." Howard nodded in friendly agreement before continuing quietly, "The first thing you should know is don't be put off by our name. Several of us don't like it. Do we Ricky? We think people will discount us as being really mad – we don't think it does us any favours but Mary likes it, she thinks it's light-hearted and humorous."

"So you're opposed to all forms of medical intervention – are you?" Devereux enquired, scanning a leaflet.

"Not entirely," Ricky answered this time, before glancing at

Mary and lowering his voice. "Some of the group have more. . . let me say, definite views than others. We all agree that more natural approaches should be used and are open to alternative remedies, which we feel are debunked out of hand. We try to avoid chemical contamination. But having said that, Howard and I both think that Western-style medicine has its advantages in acute cases."

"Yes," Howard interrupted, "but I'm against being forced down a road which has been decided on by someone else (one of these corrupt, dictatorial politicians who rule over us). I want to make my own choice and I want alternatives to be promoted (or debunked if necessary, after proper, non-biased investigation) rather than being given no choice as a result of alternative practitioners being hounded out by aggressive EU legislation."

"I quite see your point," Devereux agreed warming to the two men. "Your views seem moderate and sensible but you imply others are more extreme."

"Yes. Mary for one," Howard confided, uncomfortably catching her eye and suspecting that she was listening to his heretical views. "But you're bound to get that in any organisation and it's usually the extremists who keep it going."

"Oh yes, Mary's certainly dedicated, but for her the group would have folded several times," Ricky added his support.

"And naturally, as an extension of your ideals, you are opposed to rejuvenation?" Devereux probed.

"Yes, of course," Ricky explained. "We consider it to be the most extreme form of interventionist medicine – something totally unnatural."

"That's where we're in definite agreement," Devereux continued. "Although, I would say it's unnatural from a spiritual point of view rather than purely physical as you do."

"Oh no! There is a spiritual element to our stance, as well," Ricky maintained. "Mary's very keen on the meditative aspect – she believes that it enhances physical well being."

"That's where I beg to differ," interjected Howard. "That sort of mumbo jumbo doesn't work for me."

Devereux smiled faintly.

"That doesn't mean to say the others can't do it if they want to – they should have the choice," Howard added hurriedly, before changing the subject abruptly; "Look out! We've got our first visitors."

90

Everyone turned their attention to the open doors, at first expectantly and then nervously; a small group of young, teenage boys entered noisily. One of them carried a dirty football which he bounced loudly on the wooden floor. Mary increased the volume of the CD player and 'Earthwaves' flooded the room. One of the boys laughed and jiggled his hips in time to the music. Several of the others made a beeline to Rose's table.

"Can we have a cup of tea? Is it free?" asked a short, pale faced boy.

"Yes, of course," Rose replied, unable to resist her maternal instinct. "Or there's squash, if you like?"

"Nah. Tea'll do," the boy replied, helping himself to a handful of biscuits.

"You'd better get rid of them," Joe instructed Mary, "before they start causing trouble. They'll be kicking that ball about in here in a minute."

"They haven't done anything yet," Mary replied. "And I don't want to antagonise them. Let them have some drinks and hopefully they'll get bored and disappear."

"Just as you like, but don't blame me if they get out of hand. I still say you should do something and turf 'em out." Joe was used to giving ineffectual orders.

The boys ate and drank noisily, joking amongst themselves and pocketing a good proportion of the biscuits.

"You'd better leave some for other people," Rose warned to a general murmur of disappointment.

"What other people?" asked a large, plump boy looking round.

"They haven't arrived yet," Rose replied firmly.

Then the boy spied Ricky. "Hey, it's Mr Trago!" he exclaimed before skidding across the polished floor in the teacher's direction. "Do you remember me, sir? You used to teach me at Beechwood."

Ricky was soon surrounded by the boy's friends, all of whom were anxious to interrogate and inspect their friend's ex-teacher in the unnatural, non-school environment.

"Yes, I do," Ricky answered. "Let me see, whose class were you in. . ?"

"Mr Shipley's," the boy replied at once, ignoring a giggle from one of his mates and the comment:

"What, Mr Shitley?"

"Oh yes, of course. And I remember your friend – what was his name?"

"Kyle Rodden."

"Mmm, I remember you both got up to a certain amount of mischief."

"Yes, we did," the boy answered, confessing unnecessarily proudly. "It was us who let off stink bombs in the library and Kyle got caught smoking in the changing rooms." His companions laughed enviously, wishing it had been them who had committed these offences.

"I see." Ricky forced himself to adopt a stern tone; "I hope your behaviour has improved at your new school."

"It hasn't!" the boy confirmed airily. "What are you doing here anyway, sir?" he continued, glancing round the largely empty hall. Ricky explained briefly and invited the boys to take some leaflets. One or two grabbed a handful whilst the others stared at the pamphlets and sheets with determined disinterest.

"Rejuvenation's just for old people," the boy with the football declared before throwing the ball in the air and catching it deftly between his shoulder blades. "I don't want to read about it – it's like being at school. Come on!" He let the ball roll down his back, dribbled it skilfully towards the door and could not resist belting the ball against the end wall before collecting his ricochet and running outside, closely followed by the remainder of his group.

"I told you they'd start kicking that thing about in here, didn't I?" Joe addressed Mary, moodily. "You should've chucked 'em out in the first place, when I said so."

"They hardly played football in here," Mary replied acidly. "And anyway, they've gone now so you've got nothing to worry about."

"Oh dear," Rose moaned, "they've cleared me out of all the biscuits. You two, go to the shop and get some more." She beckoned her sons down from the stage where they had watched their contemporaries from a safe distance.

"Let's hope our next visitors are a little more interested," observed Devereux.

"I hope there are some more visitors. It'll be so disappointing otherwise and we've gone to all this effort," Sonja gesticulated sadly at the carefully arranged displays.

"I'm sure there will be. This sort of thing always takes a while to get started," Mouland responded encouragingly, sounding much more confident than he felt.

"Give us a cuppa, Rose," Joe requested, whilst slumping onto a chair next to her, before noticing the return of her sons: "Good, the cavalry's arrived – more biscuits. I'll have a couple of those chocolate ones."

"They're for the visitors," Mary interjected sternly.

Joe rolled his eyes. "What visitors?" he replied and scenting rare victory plunged his forbidden biscuit into his drink.

Mouland, Caroline and Devereux exchanged glances whilst Mary imagined lowering Joe's plump, twisting body into a vat of boiling oil.

The tension was broken by the arrival of a group of shoppers whose real motivation was the opportunity to rest their weary arms and legs and take advantage of a free cup of coffee. The group consisted of about half a dozen women, one of whom announced in a loud voice that she was in complete agreement with rejuvenation and couldn't wait for her turn. She couldn't understand what all the fuss was about. After the group had spent some time discussing and showing each other their purchases Mouland thought that he ought to try to engage with them.

"Can I interest you in any of our leaflets or a video presentation, perhaps?" he enquired, politely.

"No thanks," replied the loud woman, "we're busy." Then she turned to Mary, "Excuse me, love – could you turn that music down – it's getting on our nerves? I can't be doing with that whale sort of music – give me Elvis any day." Her friends laughed in agreement. Mary, white faced and stricken, turned the music off completely, much to the amazement of the other MAD members who were all holding their breath. In an act of revenge, she switched on the video player at full volume and Deighton jerked to life on the screen. The loud woman began to give Mary a disapproving stare until something unsettled her and she looked away, concentrated on her coffee and became strangely subdued.

Howard shrugged his shoulders and Ricky became engrossed in his laptop. Finally the women, re-laden, wandered out of the hall leaving a table littered with empty plastic cups and biscuit crumbs. Rose rushed to clear away the detritus.

"Shopping – the opium of the masses," declared Devereux.

"Don't, Julian," Caroline warned him. "We have enough to worry about as it is."

As the day passed, MAD played host to a dozen or so genuine visitors, most of whom were confirmed supporters of rejuvenation and came to espouse their entrenched views with absolutely no chance of changing them. Predictably, some were angry and aggressive and seemed determined to row. Unfortunately for Mouland his dog collar exuded magnetic properties as far as the more hostile visitors were concerned; they were drawn to him as a symbol of opposition. Mouland provided a model of patience, replying calmly to each of them.

"All we're suggesting is that you take a moment to stop, think and examine your beliefs. Consider the consequences of rejuvenation very carefully, from all angles, and finally listen to your conscience. Seek out your inner voice – which all of us have, somewhere deep down inside, and listen. Is there a seed of doubt?"

Invariably the reply was an obstinate 'no' coupled with insults such as, "You're nothing but a bunch of loonies" or "Trust the church to try and spoil everything. Now we can really have eternal life (which you've always promised) they don't want us to!" Most of the vocal opponents confined their comments to loud mutterings amongst themselves and their companions but one thick set, shaven headed male, who looked about forty-five years old, but could have been younger, was particularly aggressive.

"You make me sick!" he spat at the vicar venomously. "What have you ever done for me? Nothing! All you do is stand in front of your wet believers and talk a lot of crap! All your goodness and 'turn the other cheek' nonsense makes me want to vomit and now you're telling me that I can't be rejuvenated, if I want to. What's it got to do with you?" He pushed his sagging, angry face as close to Mouland's as the intervening table would allow.

Mouland, ignoring the warm, damp breath which billowed onto his cheeks, stood firm and stared back into the aggressor's pale blue, bloodshot eyes, unable to stop himself from wondering vaguely why someone so full of anger would wish to prolong his unhappy life indefinitely. At the same time he felt Devereux trying to manoeuvre in front of him, stepping painfully on his right foot as he did so. Howard smoothly appeared on his left.

"All we're trying to do is put across an alternative point of view. There has been so much coverage of the positive, er perceived positive, aspects of rejuvenation but very little of the dangers. We just want people to be able to make an informed choice," Mouland responded calmly but determinedly. He would not deny his belief.

"You just don't get it, do you?" The man swept a small pile of leaflets to the floor. "Who do you think you are? What gives you the right to tell me what to think and what I can do. . ?"

"We're not trying to make you do anything – we want to give you a choice. . ." Devereux replied before being interrupted rudely.

"I'm not talking to the monkey – I'm talking to him," the man shouted and pointed at Mouland. Caroline bit her lip angrily. Mary decided to intervene:

"Would you like to watch a short presentation about MAD's work?" she enquired. "It's not all concerned with rejuvenation. I'm sure you'll find it interesting and we have some free 'Earthwaves' CDs – people find them very soothing."

The angry man responded by narrowing his eyes, parting his lips and staring unflinchingly at Mary in an attempt to intimidate and humiliate her. He failed. In spite of his most concerted effort to convey contemptuously and silently, that Mary was truly insane and worthless she held his gaze. The man thought he could decipher the shadow of a smile contorting her expression and revealing a little of her character. He looked away first. Mary remained focussed upon him watching but not seeing, as he stamped out of the building mouthing obscenities.

"I'm glad he's gone," Sonja remarked with relief, quivering slightly. "We don't want too many visitors like that! I thought he was going to hit someone."

"You'll have to get used to such people," Mary called from over her shoulder. "The opposition can be quite fanatical, I've become hardened to it."

"He met his match in Mary," Caroline whispered to her husband. "It was as though she put a spell on him!"

"Quite." Mouland cleared his throat and felt uncomfortable. Rose abandoned her refreshment post and unnecessarily helped Sonja rearrange the leaflets. Whilst her back was turned her sons took the opportunity to help themselves surreptitiously to more biscuits.

The next arrivals were Helen and Freddie, who had met by chance outside the community centre. Helen had spent a restless night deciding whether to attend the meeting or not. Her internal discussion disrupted her dreams constantly, stabbing its way to the forefront of her conscience, leaving her unrefreshed on waking.

"Why do I have to make such an issue out of it?" she wondered, angry with herself. "It's only a very small, insignificant meeting. No one will really care if I go or not. Except, perhaps Freddie. . . and even he's probably forgotten already."

On the other hand, why shouldn't she go? Finally the nagging, small voice inside her, which refused to be stilled, won the debate and Helen, having checked that her appearance remained substantially altered from 'the announcement days', ventured out to the 'Charlie Harleyson Community Centre'.

Freddie was delighted to see her. "Hello," he called cheerily, "that's a bit of luck meeting you here. I knew you'd come but thought I'd missed you. I'm later than I intended – Ada's not feeling very well today so I stayed in for a while. She says she's feeling a bit better now. I told her I won't be long."

"I'm pleased you could come," Helen replied warmly whilst shaking Freddie's formally offered hand. "Let's go in and find out what it's all about!"

They entered the hall to the sound of 'Earthwaves' and the smell of scented candles which Sonja had only just remembered and had lit anxiously, afraid that naked flames were contrary to the hiring conditions of the establishment.

"Just light the bloody things!" Howard had urged irreverently.

A couple of people were sitting at a table drinking tea and scanning leaflets in silence and Helen discerned the flicker of the video presentation taking place in the small committee room at the side. Freddie marched up to Mouland as if they were friends of old:

"Morning vicar," he announced briskly. "What's all this about then?"

Mouland began his well rehearsed patter in reply whilst Caroline and Devereux eyed the old man suspiciously. Helen hovered next to Freddie's right elbow taking in every word but attempting to assume a casual air. The video presentation ended, three weary looking attendees emerged, blinking in the reinvigorating brightness of the room, and Mary.

Mary recognised Helen at once, despite her coloured hair and restyled cut, and layers of misshapen, old clothes.

"Anyone else for the final presentation?" she called.

Sonja almost volunteered.

"Might as well, might'n we?" Freddie nudged Helen encouragingly,

"Yes – as we're here. . ."

Helen felt as though she was committing treason as she sat in the darkened room and watched images of her father jump across the screen. She could take in nothing of the commentary. Freddie, in contrast, enjoyed the performance enormously. Mary watched Helen through the darkness.

"Any questions?" she demanded at the end, wondering when Helen would reveal her identity and intentions.

"No. It all seems quite clear to me," Freddie replied unnecessarily; silence would have sufficed. "I quite agree with all you say. I thought I would. It's nice to hear that someone else is against all this coming-back-to-life nonsense. What do you think, Helen?"

"No, I haven't any questions," she responded, to Mary's surprise. Freddie wheezed loudly and scraped his chair along the highly polished, wooden floor as he heaved himself to his feet. Luckily, the sound of his cumbersome movement masked Mary's guttural utterance which she aimed aggressively and involuntarily at Helen:

"Think you know all the answers, do you?" she hissed, her washed out eyes fixed on Helen's retreating back.

"Let's have a nice cup of tea," suggested Freddie, precipitating Rose springing into action at once.

"Yes, go ahead. I'm just going to choose some leaflets," Helen decided.

Freddie had been served with the rather over-brewed, tepid, plastic cups of tea and had secured two seats at one of the empty tables, when the insipid atmosphere was rudely destroyed by the intrusion of the boy with the football. His entry, having been preceded by several ominous bounces and beatings of the ball against the exterior wall, consisted of the ball being booted through the open doors, knocking a chair over and belting the

e

wall opposite before rebounding awkwardly into a diagonally opposed corner. The boy followed closely, his cheeks tinged with the teenage embarrassment of being compelled to expose himself to this room of strange adults. Flicking the ball deftly onto his instep, he retrieved it from its resting place, jiggled it a couple of times before sprinting outside to the audible, teasing laughter of his friends.

"Bloody kids!" moaned Joe predictably. "I said someone should have thrown them out."

The others ignored him.

"It's just high spirits," Freddie began. "They're not intent on doing any harm. . ."

But he was interrupted by the crash of splintering glass as the remnants of a large window pane showered both him and Helen and a crude lump of angry flint and concrete landed between them on the table. Freddie gasped, spluttered into the plastic cup and jumped backwards involuntarily, spilling tea on Helen who had been equally startled.

Joe strode angrily across the polished floor. "That's it! I've had enough of these little hooligans. Let me sort 'em out!" he yelled, his white hand turning a weird shade of blotchy red and purple.

Devereux, Mouland, Ricky and Howard, started to follow him. Mary merely watched as though observing an experiment.

"Aw gawd, what's he going to do now?" lamented Howard.

"Hold on a minute, Joe!" Mouland called anxiously. There was no need. No sooner had Joe marched manfully through the open main doors than he suddenly reappeared at a trot, his previously puce features now ashen. In pursuit was the angry man, who had visited earlier in the day, accompanied by two rough looking accomplices. Shouting and swearing they threw flour bombs around the hall, kicked chairs over and finally overturned the tables of leaflets and remaining, forlorn, cups of tea. On the way out one of them triumphantly let off a fire extinguisher.

The assault took place in seconds although it seemed as if time had stood still and the hostile, pantomime had been enacted in slow, deliberate motion. None of the MAD members, nor Mouland's group, were able to react for several seconds. Finally, Joe emerged from behind Sonja where he had taken refuge, unashamedly and ungallantly. After jogging, deceptively slowly, to the door (putting a lot of effort into little more than jogging on

98

the spot) he announced, with an air of disappointment, "Damn! Missed them. They've gone!" Whilst judiciously choosing to ignore the fact that the three attackers had merely reached the edge of the car park and were sauntering merrily on their way, pleased with their actions.

The remainder of the group slowly came back to life.

"Why do people have to be so horrible?" Sonja cried miserably, tears welling in her large, dreamy eyes. "We're not doing any harm. We only want to help people. . ." she sobbed.

"Never mind. Don't take it personally – some people just can't understand," replied Rose comfortingly, to murmurs of general agreement.

"I'm not entirely surprised," whispered Caroline to her husband. "Remember that brick through our window?"

Before the vicar could reply Mary's voice boomed sonorously and deliberately across the hall,

"You have to remember that we are pioneers. We are leaders, we have the knowledge and are bound to show others the way. Throughout history those who have brought a message, contrary to what the mob want to hear, have been vilified. It will always be so. The reactions we have encountered make me more certain that we are right. Our detractors will, one day, regret that they did not listen."

Mary's sermon was originally directed at Sonja, who quivered at the thought of the awesome responsibility she was assuming and her quest for a potential place in history. The others (except Joe who paid no attention to the leader) listened with mixed emotions. Devereux raised his eyebrows and Caroline glanced knowingly at Mouland's impassive face. Ricky, Howard and Rose accepted the truth behind Mary's statement but felt it with a less harsh intensity. Mary, however, had been invigorated by the attack and continued manically, "Nothing will deflect us from our cause. They are angry because deep down they know that we are right and they are frightened. They lash out unintelligibly like frightened animals. They are reduced to physical violence because there are no words with which to beat us. Their arguments are futile and infantile and they know it. But they fear. They fear everything. They fear death because they are not ready for it and because of this they fear life itself. But they remain oblivious. By wrapping themselves in materialism they manage to hide from it, but it's always there – lurking outside their pathetic cocoons."

Mary's speech would have continued indefinitely had she not been interrupted by the boy with the football. At first he appeared inquisitively into the room, the ball tucked snugly under his right arm.

"Cool!" he breathed incredulously, before stepping over the threshold, his wide eyes absorbing the scene of disruption. "What's happened, sir?"

"Just a minor difference of opinion," Ricky replied briskly. "Perhaps you and your mates would like to help us clear up?"

"Yeah, OK," yelled one of the boys, all of whom were by then in the hall, as he skidded through a small pile of flour.

"Flour bombs!" he stated approvingly, before whispering to a companion. "We could make those!"

With the boys and Helen and Freddie's help it did not take long to clean and tidy the room. The boys' sense of fun and enthusiasm was matched in equal and opposite measure by the adults' sombre deflation.

"It's a bit depressing really," Sonja, having regained her composure, confided to Rose. "The whole day's been a waste of time."

"No it hasn't, dear. Just because one or two people over reacted it doesn't mean the day hasn't been successful. Lots of people seemed very interested in our work. Take those two, for example," she nodded secretively in the direction of Freddie and Helen, "I'm sure we'll see more of them."

Freddie, with typical enthusiasm, was sweeping flour into a large pile until he was overcome with an alarming fit of coughing and had to sit outside in the fresh air. Helen, who had been cleaning flour from the tables and chairs, joined him in the weakening sunshine.

"Are you feeling better now?" she enquired anxiously, noticing that the redness had faded from Freddie's features and he was now back to his usual blue tinged hue.

"Yes, yes. I'm fine now," he assured her whilst gratefully accepting the cup of water she offered. "I forget that I should take things easy sometimes, that's all. Ada's always reminding me. 'Freddie Meredith,' she says, 'you're not a spring chicken anymore – you should slow down!' The thing is, she's right," he added, a note of depression creeping into his voice.

"That was interesting – in more ways than one." Helen pointed into the hall.

"Yeah," Freddie chuckled mischievously, his good humour returning. "I shouldn't laugh but I think they got more than they bargained for. That Joe's a bit of a twit isn't he?"

"Yes. Did you see him hide behind the young girl? Sonja, I think her name is. He wasn't embarrassed at all!" Helen whispered incredulously.

"They're a bit of a funny lot. I was surprised to see a vicar here, but it makes sense I suppose. They're all opposed to rejuvenation and I'm definitely with 'em on that score – how about you?"

Helen, feeling treacherous, took a deep breath. "So am I," she declared with trepidation.

A car stopped in the queue of traffic at the end of the path, its radio blaring out the pips denoting the hourly news bulletin.

"Oops!" Freddie stumbled to his feet. "That time already! I must be off – Ada will be waiting. Come round and see us – do you remember the address? Ada would love to meet you."

"Yes, I will. Bye Freddie."

Helen watched him hurry, as quickly as his health and age would allow, down the path and along the pavement. Then she slipped, unnoticed by all except Mary, into the Community Centre, returned the cup and went home.

Chapter Ten

"What did you think of it all?" Caroline asked her husband, as they drove away from the community centre.

"A bit depressing really," the vicar admitted with a sigh. "I'm still not sure that we're doing the right thing by joining forces with a group such as MAD. I detect a definite undercurrent of fanaticism there somewhere, which makes me feel uncomfortable. We're still concerned with far more than rejuvenation and not at all with medical intervention. I'm worried that we'll become subsumed by MAD and all their policies and people will lose sight of our complete message. At the same time, the general lack of positive interest from people serves to emphasise our isolation and the desperate times in which we live."

"You're right about one thing – Mary's certainly barking," observed Caroline bluntly. Devereux remained silent in the back of the car, moodily staring out of the window. Caroline continued, "We had some interest from the couple who helped us clear up – what were their names? Freddie and. . . I didn't catch the woman's."

"I think they had already made up their minds. That's the problem – the issue has polarised everyone – the majority, of course, in favour of rejuvenation and against us. There don't seem to be any 'floating voters' as it were. I don't think debate and rational argument will be enough – something needs to happen – we need an event, I don't know what, but an occurrence to shake people out of their stupors," Philip replied.

"If rationality is not needed then perhaps Mary is just the right person," Caroline barbed. "What do you think, Julian?"

"Eh, what?" Devereux slowly came to his senses.

"What's your opinion about MAD and Mary and today's meeting?"

"None of it was my sort of thing I'm afraid. I knew it wouldn't be. I feel as if I've spent the day in a lunatic asylum and Mary's not the worst one – that Joe fellow was particularly irritating."

Caroline laughed. "I noticed you battling it out with him – it was a no-contest though, I almost began to feel sorry for him."

Devereux sniffed appreciatively and was about to comment further when he and Caroline were hurled forward in their seats as Mouland braked violently.

"Idiot," was the politest name that the irate clergyman yelled at the hapless driver who had pulled out in front of them. Several more obscenities poured from Mouland's mouth and he gesticulated rudely and aggressively from the side window before screeching away.

"Really, Philip – there was no need for that!" Caroline admonished him, embarrassed but more familiar with these sudden outbursts than she would care to admit. Devereux remained silent at the back, pretending not to have noticed. Mouland ignored his wife and they made their way home in an atmosphere akin to physical pain.

The next few days felt like an anti-climax, the open meeting having taken place unproductively as far as Mouland, Caroline and Devereux were concerned and nothing planned to take their campaign further. Mouland's sense of hopelessness was compounded by an email from his diocesan superiors urging him to dispose of the contents of St. Nonna's at once. Apparently, the deal with 'B-Stored UK Limited' was due to be finalised imminently and St. Nonna's should be cleared as a prerequisite to the signing of the sale.

"How am I supposed to do this in one week?" Mouland panicked. "You'll have to help me Caroline, and Julian. How am I to know what's to be saved for 'The People's Museum of Christianity' (how I hate that name) and what should be sold? I'm no expert. I thought they'd send a specialist to sort things out."

"Calm down, Philip. Of course I'll help and I'm sure Julian will too. Why don't you give them a ring to clarify what they want? Perhaps they are going to send someone?" Caroline purred in soothing mode. Her husband took her advice and made the telephone call with frustrating results,

"Look, to put it bluntly," the anonymous voice on the other end of the line declared with more than a hint of impatience, "we haven't the time to go through all the stuff. We're getting a good price for the building as long as the contracts are signed by early next week. Just sort out a few things that you think will do for the museum and sell off the rest. I don't think you'll get much for it – history's a thing of the past now, if you'll excuse the pun." The voice laughed, pleased with its own wit, before continuing, "People are no longer interested in harking back – they're all looking to the future." Then as an afterthought the voice added, "I'll give you my name and number. If you come across anything of real value – you know, precious metal or anything – let me know and I'll take it off your hands and sort it out. Ask for me personally. Otherwise just send most of it to auction."

"I don't think I can bring myself to do it. I can't desecrate my own church," the despairing vicar confided to Caroline. "How can they ask me to destroy everything in which I believe?"

His wife, ever practical, took a more pragmatic view: "I know how you feel Philip, but it could be worse."

"How?" Her husband replied incredulously, his tone assuming an unnaturally high pitch and his eyes widening, before his whole face sagged.

"At least you're being given the chance to retrieve some of the more precious items. They seem mercenary enough to get rid of the lot, at the best price. And by precious, I don't mean the most valuable in monetary terms, I mean most iconic, most valuable to our faith. Ultimately, we don't need much. This sort of thing has been played out time and time again throughout history – think of the puritans, for example. We like our man-made artefacts etc., but they're not crucial to our beliefs – they're aids, that's all. Nice things."

Mouland remained silent for a few moments. Caroline looked at him anxiously. Eventually, he responded.

"You're right, again. We are living through a strange time – through a tsunami of change – perhaps even 'the end of days'. People have felt and feared this before, throughout the ages, but Christianity has pulled through and survived and it will do so

104

again. I suppose that's why I want to save the contents of the church – the tools of my trade – for when they are required again. I know they will be, and it would be a pity to lose these artefacts so steeped in prayer and worship – timeless, even."

"We have to make the best of a bad job," Caroline urged. "Save what you can for the revolting museum – at least it will be safe there – and the rest will have to go."

Mouland, Caroline and Devereux began the unwelcome task later that day. They intended to put aside one example of each item for the museum but soon realised there were too many.

"It's the fabric of the building I fear for most. What will they do to the stained glass windows and the mediaeval wall paintings? The stonework and timber carvings – are they to be desecrated?" Philip mourned.

"What about the organ?" asked Devereux suddenly. "What are we to do with that?"

"Nothing, apparently," replied the vicar. "It's included in the sale as part of the fixtures and fittings – no doubt the cryogenically-stored will have fun with it."

Devereux finished sorting through a pile of hymn books and, hands on hips, cast his eyes high into the innermost recesses of the vaulted ceiling.

"It feels different already – more like a warehouse or something – as though it's lost its soul. The atmosphere's changed. The light still streams through the glass but for no purpose. It no longer reflects God's glory – it's gone already."

"I can't help but to agree." Caroline stood upright having been bent over a box in the act of cramming in one last pair of brass candlesticks. "It's strange, isn't it? I think it shows how a building becomes imbued with emotional investment and turns into what you want it to be – in this case a spiritual place, but now 'God has left the building' as it were."

"There's no need to be trite!" the vicar snapped. " 'God has left the building', indeed. Surely you don't need reminding of the basics?"

Julian raised his eyebrows, grimaced and gave Caroline a knowing glance. "I think we've done enough here today," he suggested. "Time to give it a rest. We can start again, first thing tomorrow."

Caroline, having noticed Philip's ashen features, agreed

readily, "Yes. It will all be here tomorrow. We deserve a rest and something to eat. Come on Philip."

"Alright, I don't suppose any of it really matters anymore," he assented enigmatically.

The vicar toyed with his evening meal silently; eating very little and saying even less. Usually mealtimes in the Mouland household were animated and accompanied by discussion – sometimes jovial and happy, at others stricken with sombre sadness as the vicar examined a current parishioner's tragic tale through his wife. For once Caroline could think of nothing to say which would alleviate her husband's suffering. Finally, Mouland pushed the almost complete meal away, muttered something which sounded like 'sorry' and noisily pushed his chair back from the table. Then, after transferring himself to the living room and settling back into an armchair, he lifted his heavily closed eyes to the ceiling and absorbed the musical strains of *Tristis est anima mea* by Juan Gutiérrez de Padilla. For a short time he was removed to another world, formless and ethereal, concerned only with his senses and an emotive appreciation of the beauty of the anthem. Mouland's peace ended with the music and a further depressing thought gate crashed his mind.

"I suppose it's also the end of music like that," he announced to his wife who had crept into the room and seated herself next to him. "There will be no more need for it and no inspiration from which to compose it," he continued, before adding with a harsh laugh, "What a bland, simplistic world we find ourselves inhabiting!"

"You must believe that it's only temporary," Caroline urged him gently, managing just in time to prevent herself from adding that her husband should 'have faith'.

"I know what will replace it!" Mouland declared loudly, completely ignoring her attempt to improve his mood. "Computer games – the more violent and cruel the better. The entire population can numb their empty minds playing computer games. They can live forever in a virtual world! How ironic!" He laughed again, nastily. Caroline felt worried.

Mouland heaved himself out of the chair. "I think I'll take a wander round the garden," he declared, sounding more normal. "A breath of fresh air will do me good."

"Put a coat on," Caroline called maternally. "It's cold out tonight!"

Mouland grabbed a jacket and strode into the icy, black air. Shoving his hands deep into his trouser pockets for warmth and with the sound of rushing traffic whizzing through his ears he stared into the night sky. The stars glinted in their timeless fashion reminding him that some things never change and human activity is no more than a ripple on a pond. Then he turned his attention to the large, black outline to his right – St. Nonna's grotesque shape in the dark, devoid of spirit and meaning, redundant, useless. The moon projected a thin, insipid, beam of light onto the rose window serving only to accentuate the window's empty eyes which stared back unseeing, in marked contrast to the sun's earlier rays which had flooded the chancel with warmth, light and life.

A small, isolated cloud, passed in front of the pathetic beam with puffed up self importance and the church fell back into darkness. Then Mouland could have sworn that he saw a light passing by several of the windows, one by one. At first he could not be sure whether it was inside or out, it being more likely that someone would be in the grounds rather than actually inside the building. Then the light stopped moving and the rose window turned a shade of pale, quivering yellow. Mouland was in no doubt – someone was inside!

Feeling for the vestry key which was always in his pocket, he sprinted across the saturated lawn and surprised himself by vaulting easily over the low stone wall into the small, decaying churchyard. Then, with no regard for the ancient graves underfoot, he raced towards the vestry door. It was ajar. Mouland, hesitating outside, could hear a strange, heaving sound accompanied by puffing and panting, as though someone was dragging along a heavy, unwieldy object with great difficulty. Anger flooded through the vicar, destroying any fear or reluctance to intervene which might have tried to take root.

"This really is the final straw!" he snapped in an angry whisper to himself. Then he barged through the stumpy, oval vestry door and with one sweeping movement flicked on the rows of switches opposite. The entire interior lit up like a stage, revealing the unfortunate robber. It was Devereux.

"Julian! What on earth are you doing?" Mouland demanded.

The churchwarden was overcome by guilt, embarrassment and foolishness. For a moment he was unable to move, unable to retain his dignity and stood cradling the eagle's body part of the lectern against his chest. The long pillar on which it stood stretched out before him leading to a tramline of gouges along the oak floorboards. He stared at the vicar open mouthed.

"I thought we were being robbed!" Mouland continued in the absence of a response. "I thought you had gone home – finished for the day!" Then he realised. "Oh, I see. . ." he said, his words fading away awkwardly. Devereux continued with his impression of a startled rabbit until the weight of the lectern became too great and he was forced to drag it noisily a few steps further and rest the feathered creature against a pew.

"I thought it would be a pity to let that museum of heretics have it," he began with an air of aggression, solely caused by his acute embarrassment.

"What exactly do you intend to do with it?" Mouland asked.

"Take it home, of course!" the churchwarden replied tetchily, as though it was the most natural thing to have in one's front room. "I thought no one would care or even notice. The diocese isn't interested, unless there's money in it, and the museum's beyond words." Devereux perched on the pew, next to the bird without noticing, and mopped his brow with a crisply ironed, white handkerchief. "Oh, I suppose it will have to go there or auction," he conceded.

Mouland managed to prevent a smile forming. "Go and get your car," he said. "Bring it as close as you can to the door and I'll help you lug it out."

"Really?" Devereux brightened immeasurably. "Are you sure we hadn't better declare it?"

"I think it should be consigned to safe keeping in your very capable hands," Mouland responded, no longer able to keep a huge grin in check. "Does Felicity know about it?"

"She will soon." Julian sped off like an excited schoolboy to get his car and soon the two men were manhandling the heavy object into the back.

"Have you got a name for him?" Mouland asked slyly. The churchwarden was about to respond with an irritated rebuff when he caught a glimpse of his friend's smile in the watery moonlight and both men burst into a riot of rude laughter.

Mouland and his companions had not been the only ones to mull over the events of MAD's open meeting. Helen felt a strange sense of relief, tinged with apprehension, having openly declared that she opposed rejuvenation. Hardly anyone else had heard, and those that had, barely remembered; with the exception of Mary. Mary had stiffened with shock, having expected Helen to dramatically reveal her identity and support for her father's work. Then Mary's eyes had narrowed as she suspected that Helen's motive was to infiltrate her beloved society and destroy it from within. Mary chuckled inwardly; she would make sure that Helen would certainly regret any such attempt!

Helen also nursed a sense of let-down in the aftermath of the meeting. One morning, in an attempt to fill the void, she found herself making her way towards the address Freddie had pressed upon her. As usual she was racked with indecision but something drove her on and having come so far she refused to allow herself to hesitate before ringing the doorbell. It was some time before anyone appeared to open the door but Helen was sure that they were in; the strains of a radio filtered towards her. She glanced around the small, neat front garden which was kept with military, if unimaginative precision; a square of weedless lawn, enclosed with a border of earth completely bare, save for several vicious-looking gnarled rose bushes. The tarmac path, on which she stood, was freshly swept (there were traces of broom marks in the dust in the corners) and the little kingdom was encircled by a low, brick wall.

Eventually the front door was tugged open and a large, slightly breathless woman, clutching a walking frame, stared blankly at her for a second before asking briskly, "Hello. Can I help you?"

"Yes. I hope you don't mind. Is this where Mr Meredith lives?" Helen answered, wishing that she had not come.

"Who is it? Who is it?"

A familiar voice called from the little, Victorian house. Then Freddie appeared, bustling along the hallway behind his wife. "I told you, I'd go," he scolded, before catching sight of Helen who was relieved to see the old man. "Why, it's you Helen!" Freddie beamed. "Come on in, come on in. See Ada, this is the young lady I was telling you about. I knew she'd come to see us."

Freddie almost bounded ahead, whilst Helen followed his wife, who made her way slowly and with some discomfort into the small living room. A strong smell of vinegar and onions pervaded the air. Helen was instructed to take a seat while Freddie went out to put the kettle on and 'turn me onions down', he winked.

"You're the lady who helped Freddie with the notice board," Ada observed. "He told me all about it. I worry sometimes when he goes out – especially with all these yobs about. He's not as young as he used to be – despite what he thinks – and I worry that he'll get himself into trouble. It was very kind of you to help him."

"Oh, not at all." Helen dismissed her actions. "You don't mind me calling on you out of the blue, I hope? Freddie said it would be alright."

"No. It's lovely to see someone. We don't get many visitors – not having any family – and I can't get out much, so it's nice to see someone for a change." Ada repositioned her shapeless legs which were beginning to glow due to their close proximity to the ancient two barred electric heater. "That's better," she whispered to herself.

"You seem to have a nice comfortable home here," Helen observed from the sinking cushions in the armchair, which threatened to envelope her and suck her beneath their soft plumpness.

"Yes. We still like it here," Ada agreed. "We've been here over fifty years, now. Freddie always says an Englishman's home is his castle. It's cosy and doesn't cost too much to heat," she added with a smile.

A rattle of china preceded Freddie's reappearance carrying a wooden rectangular tray containing a large porcelain tea set and a plate of biscuits. Ada pushed the chrome wheeled, coffee table from by her side to further towards the centre of the fireplace. Freddie set the tray on the table and began the tea pouring ritual.

"Have you brought in any of my diabetic biscuits?" Ada asked scrutinising the tray.

"Yes, dear," replied her husband absentmindedly.

"Well where are they then?" Ada continued puzzledly.

Freddie handed a cup and saucer brimming with weak tea to Helen and stared at the tray. "Oh, I've left them on the side. Ada says I'd lose my head if it wasn't screwed on!" he joked with unoriginality. Freddie left the room once again to retrieve the errant biscuits. The two women waited in silence, listening to the remnants of the radio programme which still wafted through the building, until they heard Freddie curtly flick the switch, killing it abruptly.

"Turned me onions off and turned that racket off too," he announced, placing the plate of biscuits gently in his wife's hands. "They don't half talk some rubbish nowadays. Apparently, some new government idea or 'initiative' as they like to call it is 'going to have more impact on the economy and society than the industrial revolution'. I ask you! They think we're all daft!"

"Now don't let yourself get all aerated," Ada replied, whilst patting his arm. "Sit down and drink your tea."

Freddie obeyed, gradually losing the green tinge which had attached itself to the rims of his eye sockets and in front of each of his ears.

"The industrial revolution!" he muttered to himself in disgust.

"Don't take on so," Ada admonished him more sharply. "You never know. They might be right. Look how things have changed with this rejuvenation thing."

Freddie shot Helen a knowing glance. "You know I'm not sure about all that," he replied, hoping she would not continue with the subject but unable to resist voicing his reservations.

Ada was not to be censored, she turned to Helen. "What do you think about rejuvenation, my dear? I'm sure being young and more open to new, modern things you must think it's wonderful. I'm sure I do."

"Well. . ."

Helen hesitated and glanced desperately at Freddie. "Actually, I don't think it's a good thing. I can't help but feel it's not right. There's something extremely unnatural about it. Although I can understand why not everyone thinks like this." Helen added a conciliatory note.

"I must say I'm surprised." Ada dipped her biscuit in the delicate teacup and a soggy portion of it dropped into her lap. "Oh dear," she fussed, trying to pick the remnants from her blue, nylon overall. "I hope you don't mind me dunking my biscuit – I know it's not good manners – but otherwise they make my gums sore."

Helen laughed, thrusting her own biscuit into her tea. "No. I don't mind, as long as I can do it too!"

Ada chortled and Freddie smiled in silence, pleased that the two women were at ease.

"What was I saying?" Ada mused. "Oh, yes. I'm surprised that a young woman like yourself isn't all for rejuvenation. Perhaps it is because you are young and you've still got your life ahead of you. But time flies so fast and you become old and every day's full of aches and pains and worries. I worry about whether he'll be able to cope with looking after me, and I don't want to go into a home, and then I wonder how he'll cope when I'm gone. Sometimes I feel like I did when we were seventeen – just the same, in here, inside." She pointed to her head and then to her heart and Helen noticed her snatch a glance at the fading wedding photo which stood proudly on the sideboard. "I'm the same girl, the same person as I was then, but now I'm trapped in this old worn out body of mine. It doesn't matter how old you are, you still want to carry on, you know – you still grasp hold of this thing we call living and don't want to give it up. Now there's a glimmer of hope. When this silly body of mine gives up, I can sleep for a while, be stored somewhere and woken up again, and hopefully they'll be able to renew everything as well. Me and Freddie can be together forever."

Helen briefly thought of Peter; they had thought they would be together forever. For a second she wished that rejuvenation really was the answer – then all her doubts came flooding back and reaffirmed to her that it was not.

"I'm not ready to have my name eroding into nothing on an abandoned gravestone," Ada added with poignancy.

Freddie took offence. "I'd never let that happen," he retorted. "You know I'd look after it!"

Ada smiled and laughed and patting his arm again answered easily, "I know you would but that's not what I meant. How did we start talking about such maudlin things anyway? Especially when we've got a visitor. I'm sorry about the cooking smell." Ada lowered her voice in confidence despite Freddie's close proximity. "He's pickling onions, today. It's one of his hobbies."

"Oh, yes!" Freddie boomed, "and we make marmalade, don't we? I'll see if I can find a jar for you." He went off to find one of his pots of gold and the two women listened to the sound of opening and closing of doors and clattering and scraping.

"I know we've got some left," Ada assured Helen confidently

before bellowing at her husband, "Down beside the fridge – have you looked there?" There was no response. "Oh well, let him get on with it. He'll find some in a minute. He's always busy doing something or other. He's become really good at cooking since my hands seized up."

Helen looked at the elderly woman's twisted, misshapen, swollen fingers with pity she could not hide.

"Oh, they don't hurt too much now, my dear. Not since the doctor injected them – they just don't work very well. Anyway. . ." Ada forced a note of briskness into her voice, "tell me about yourself – have you a family of your own?"

"No, unfortunately," Helen replied. "Just my father now."

Ada sensed that Helen's brief response was all she was prepared to reveal and tactfully attempted to change the subject, "Ah. You're a career lady then, I suppose?"

"Not exactly. I'm in between jobs at the moment. I'm really just doing voluntary work until I find the right thing."

"Oh yes. I used to do a lot of charity work. I ran the local shop for years – before they had any paid staff. I really enjoyed it. I met lots of people and felt it was doing something really worthwhile. We had some laughs too – the stories I could tell you. . ." Ada chuckled, her eyes full of memories. She took a sip of her tea and looked at Helen mischievously. "Actually, there is a story I will tell you – before he comes back in, he doesn't like me repeating it."

Helen nodded encouragingly, with genuine curiosity.

"Well," Ada continued deliberately and quietly whilst projecting a knowing look, "we used to have a gentleman volunteer in the shop who used to take a particular interest in the clothes – the ladies' clothes, I mean. At first, we thought he took them home for his wife and felt a bit sorry for her because he always chose really fancy things – you know, silk or satin – once he found a bright pink feather boa and took that home – ever so pleased, he was. Then someone told us he didn't have a wife but was one of those people who like dressing up – I can't mind what you call them now."

"Transvestites or cross-dressers," answered Helen, helpfully.

"Yes, that's it. Eventually he became more confident and used to wear women's clothes all the time. I seem to remember he particularly liked to wear high necked, frilly blouses and tartan skirts when he was working in the shop. Well, we didn't mind, we used to tell him what looked best and help him choose things. I know some people don't agree with it but he was a nice boy. There was only one volunteer who was a bit funny about it and she used to pretend that she didn't know and hadn't noticed – I ask you! How could you not notice?"

Helen laughed. Freddie reappeared with the coveted jar of marmalade. Ada pressed her finger to her lips in subversive secrecy, behind his turned back, and changed the conversation to a discussion about the merits of homemade marmalade in preference to mass produced.

After an hour of lively chat, Helen thought it was time to leave. She had surprised herself at how much she had enjoyed the visit, having been treated to Ada's playful sense of humour, which had obviously not weakened over time. She had been struck by the interaction between the elderly couple who fitted together like an old worn pair of slippers – completely at ease with each other and completely dependent upon each other. Despite their frailties, there was a warmth and vigour in their household which was sadly lacking in homes whose occupants, on the surface, seemed to possess so much more. Helen could not help but to draw a comparison between her own sterile existence and that of the vital old couple. Instead of making her miserable, the revelation propelled her from the safety of a bland, unquestioning life to the desire to wring every drop of experience from every moment in the short time available. To wonder at creation and purpose, from each shaking leaf to the incessant roll of the thundering waves. To immerse her tiny spark into the sum of time and energy which marks out the universe. Most of all, not to waste her chance.

Chapter Eleven

Mary had returned to her grubby flat, following the public meeting, in a strange mood. The angry attack on her precious society and personal principles had elated rather than troubled her. She enjoyed upsetting people. She would bathe in the warmth of these troubled waters for some time. It wasn't that she particularly enjoyed attention – her satisfaction was derived from antagonising others – a surreptitious poke here or jab there – and then settling back and silently observing the outcome. Mary was capable of absorbing everything. She never missed the most imperceptible flicker of muscular facial movement, the lightest intake of breath or the slightest hint of missing eye contact. She was an expert at reading body language and could have put her talent to good, perhaps even lucrative, use had she been inclined to do so. She was not. Mary preferred to suck in all the information for herself. She would then live off it for sometime, calculating, planning and scheming. Hers was an isolated, oppressive world, rarely infiltrated by reality or living people. Only occasionally would a tentacle from the outside world reach in and deposit something real.

Mary not only had the violence to nurture, but was also intrigued by Helen, whose appearance she mulled over delightedly. What was Helen's raison d'être? She wondered. Was she a coiled snake, waiting for the right moment in which to pounce or was she really the nondescript, slightly nervous, undecided character she had portrayed with convincing ease?

Mary hoped that the truth would not be revealed too soon. It was so pleasurable to watch and watch and wait and see.

In the meantime, Mary looked forward to MAD's next meeting with a renewed sense of purpose and a subconscious, nagging feeling that it was time to propel MAD's activity to a higher level. Rousing herself eventually from her self contained reality, she checked her emails. Mixed in with the junk and the usual few abusive and vulgar communications was a greeting from MAD's exaggeratedly named USA Branch and a message from Joe which read, 'Sorry, but I'll have to miss the next meeting – problems with transport.'

Mary creased her face in annoyance. How typical. Trust Joe to send an email to avoid speaking to her. 'Transport problems' indeed! All that meant was that he was too lazy to get on his bike or too mean to catch the bus. He wouldn't get away with it that easily!

Quickly, she typed a message and sent it to Howard: 'Please can you give Joe a lift on Monday? Please let me know either way. Mary.' Then she sat back, brooding. Joe was obviously trying to find an excuse to miss the meeting – he could have easily arranged a lift for himself. What could she do to punish him? For the moment she could only thwart his plan to be absent. With a small measure of satisfaction, she responded to his message: 'Don't worry, I have arranged for Howard to pick you up. Look forward to seeing you on Monday.' Then she imagined his annoyance and disappointment on receiving her email and smiled slightly.

Mary fervently checked for a response from Howard, several times a day, until the day of the meeting arrived. She tried to reach him on the telephone but with no success. Finally, on the Monday afternoon, she telephoned Ricky and requested that he collect Joe.

"Yes, that's fine," he responded easily, wincing at her pinched staccato tone and imagining her clenched teeth and deathly countenance. "See you later." He added cheerfully in an attempt to counterbalance her fury, somehow, in the scheme of things.

The MAD members duly arrived, on time and one by one, with the exception of Howard and Joe who arrived together.

"Why didn't you respond to my message?" Mary demanded.

Howard looked surprised. "I did," he replied. "Didn't you get it?"

116

"No."

"Well I sent it two or three days ago. Anyway, no harm done – we're both here." He nodded in the direction of Joe who was not listening but was engrossed in choosing from the selection of slightly stale biscuits. He grabbed chocolate digestives greedily, ignoring the thin white film which coated the chocolate surface.

Howard had pulled up outside Joe's dilapidated bungalow as requested and had been surprised to see Joe waiting outside under the rotten porch canopy, despite the driving rain.

"You're keen," he remarked as Joe heaved himself into the front passenger seat of the car, spraying water droplets onto Howard and dampening the seat with his fousty raincoat.

"What d'ya mean?" Joe puffed.

"There was no need to wait outside in the rain. I could have knocked on the door," Howard explained, wishing that Joe was not transferring so much water to the interior of his vehicle.

"It's no bother and the doorbell doesn't always work."

"You want to get it fixed then."

The two men continued their journey generally discussing the forthcoming meeting, the recent public meeting and MAD's future campaign.

Joe made plenty of unveiled criticisms of Mary's leadership, finally announcing, "If we don't get some results soon I'm calling for another leadership election."

"Really?" Howard was genuinely surprised. "Who would you put forward?"

"Who do you think? Me, of course!" Joe pointed to his own chest. "We need someone strong and dynamic – with charisma. Someone with plenty of ideas who'll get things done. None of this pussy-footing around. I'd be perfect," he added imperviously.

Howard struggled hard not to laugh and had to pretend to have something caught in his throat. Joe took Howard's mangled silence as assent and puffed his chest outward as far as the restriction of his overly tight raincoat would allow.

Mary convened the meeting and began with the usual meditation session. Howard sighed predictably and wished he was in Ricky's place – the only member yet to arrive. 'I timed that wrong.' He thought, miserably. After ten minutes of compulsory relaxation, Mary counted the group back to wakefulness.

"I don't know where Ricky's got to," she wondered, irritably, drumming her fingers on the sticky, wooden arm of her chair.

"Mr Perfect's not so perfect now," sneered Joe with satisfaction, to the others' surprise.

"He was going to give you a lift," Mary addressed him pointedly.

"What. . ?" A look of panic seared across Joe's open mouthed face and he glanced at the door as if considering dashing out.

"I said, 'he was going to give you a lift'," Mary repeated with mock patience. "I asked him and Howard, and you came with Howard, didn't you? So it's OK. You're here. I only asked him if Howard couldn't."

"Oh, I see." Joe relaxed visibly, his plump body reposing and becoming one, once again, with the sinking armchair.

At about the same time that Mary was calling the meeting to order, Ricky was driving towards Joe's house. He was late. Never having been there before, he had miscalculated how long it would take. Then had been held up by roadworks and, finally, frustratingly, had taken two wrong turns – one into a long cul-de-sac. The rain lashed upon the windscreen and Ricky peered through, mentally lashing Joe too with ill-humoured thoughts. At last he drew up outside the bungalow at number seventy-one Goodwood Road, half expecting Joe to be visibly waiting for him. Both the garden and house appeared empty; there were no lights on. 'Damn!' thought Ricky, 'I'll have to get out and get wet now.'

Jumping from the vehicle and carelessly slamming the door, he jogged through the half open, rusty, metal gate and rang the doorbell. There was no response. He rang it again and immediately tried to look through one of the smeared windows but the foul weather, darkness and decaying net curtains revealed nothing.

"For God's sake!" Ricky muttered, angry at his wasted journey and the uncomfortable sensation of cold water seeping through one of his soft leather shoes. He was about to hurry back to the refuge of his car when he noticed that the front door was slightly ajar. Joe, in his determination not to miss Howard's arrival, had forgotten to close it properly. 'Perhaps, he is here.' Ricky hoped, and pushed the door open with one finger whilst gingerly waiting for his eyes to adjust to the even greater gloom inside.

"Joe!" he called out tentatively. "Joe! Are you there?" The

cloud overhead ruptured rapturously, hammering on the ubiquitous concrete and drilling into Ricky's ears. He took a couple of steps inside, wrinkling his nose involuntarily, as he breathed in the unclean, pungent air.

"Joe!" he called out more loudly. "Joe! It's Ricky. I've come to give you a lift to the meeting." There was no response – at least he could not hear one. Then, the raincloud moved on as quickly as it had arrived and Ricky thought he heard a reply. He called out again and this time was rewarded by a thin cry:

"Here. In here," the voice moaned.

Full of puzzlement, Ricky ventured to the end of the hallway and tried the handle of the door on the right. It was locked. The ethereal voice cried out again:

"In here. It's locked. The key's. . ." before fading into nothing. Ricky twisted the key violently, which turned easily in the well oiled lock, and wrenched the handle downwards. He had to kick at the bottom of the door to release it fully, at which point a vile stench overwhelmed him and he stumbled back into the hallway, gasping and retching, overcome with nausea.

"Please. . ." the voice wavered. "Don't go. Please – let me out."

Ricky, feeling as though he had entered a nightmare, clamped his silk handkerchief to his face and moving forward again, felt for the light switch in the room. He flicked the old fashioned bony knob to no avail.

"He takes the bulb out," the voice panted expressionlessly.

His mind in a whirl, Ricky grimaced and tried to gather his senses. Desperately, he patted the palm of his hand up and down the walls of the threshold and eventually, feeling a switch beneath his trembling fingers, pressed it down. A yellow light illuminated the hallway and crept through the open door to reveal a cell-like bedroom. Someone was lying beneath a couple of threadbare blankets on an old iron bedstead. Ricky was unsure whether the elderly creature was male or female until she turned her head from its apparent fixation on the ceiling directly above, and looked at him with vacant, hopeless eyes. Her long, grey, straggly hair obscuring one side of her face.

"Who are you? Why are you in here like this. . ?" Ricky asked inadequately, surveying the old woman's prison which consisted of a colourless, soiled carpet; closely drawn, dusty, heavy curtains; the bed and a stinking, metal bucket at its side.

119

"He keeps me here. My son. . ." she whispered.

"Who? Joe?" Ricky was astounded. The woman uttered an almost inaudible murmur in assent and closed her eyes, exhausted by the effort. Ricky felt a wave of schoolboy panic – fearing for a moment that she had died. He grasped one of the emaciated hands and shook it violently. "Mrs. . . Mrs. . . Wake up! Wake up! It's alright now! I'll get you out of here! Wake up!" He desperately tried to remember Joe's surname. What was it? Something unusual. . . Then it came to him. "Mrs Whittleburgh!" he called again. The warmth of his breath on her yellow face combined with the familiarity of her name succeeded in rousing the woman. Raising her sagging eyelids again she stared, motionless at her rescuer. Ricky was almost overwhelmed by pity, horror and outrage and unable to bear this glimpse into Hell, quickly averting his gaze from the stationary grey eyes.

"I'll get an ambulance," he said, speaking more to himself than to Joe's mother.

In seconds the paramedics were on their way. Ricky crouched next to the bed, in silence, clutching the old woman's hand. For some reason that he could not understand, he felt an overwhelming desire to breathe life into the decayed human being and a desperate wish that she would not die. Occasionally she opened her eyes and stared lifelessly at him. As soon as Ricky spoke, she closed them again as if defeated and failed to even attempt a reply. Ricky feared that he had stumbled into this personal Hades far too late. Feeling tainted by his association with Joe, he inexplicably and unjustifiably felt guilty.

The two participants re-enacted a scene which had been played millions of times throughout cultures and centuries. The prostration of the living next to the dying, illuminated only by twilight and surrounded by silence, save for the raging of emotion battling inside.

At last the eerie wailing of a siren and the pulsating flash of a blue light, signalled the arrival of the ambulance. Ricky leapt to his feet and ran to the open front door.

"Here! In here!" He shouted desperately through the rods of rain which still pelted the weed-ridden gravel below. Two paramedics, one male and one female, hurried in, heaving bags of medical equipment onto their backs. The first one to enter exhaled loudly, his face disfigured in disgust at the putrid atmosphere, and immediately slipped a mask on. Then they both began basic checks on Mrs Whittleburgh.

"Are you a relative?" asked the man sharply, as his colleague listened for a pulse.

"No. I found her by accident," Ricky replied, shaking his head.

"Did you know her then?"

"Not really. I know her son. I came to give him a lift. . ."

"So, she doesn't live here on her own – her son lives here as well?"

"Yes. I don't think there's anyone else. . ."

"What's his name?"

"Joe Whittleburgh."

"So this is Mrs Whittleburgh?"

"Yes – I believe so."

"Have you phoned the police?"

"No," Ricky replied surprised, his primary thought having been to call for medical assistance.

"They'll need to be informed. I expect they'll want to have a look at the place." The paramedic bent his head towards his radio and, pressing the button, gave a brief description of the scene and requested for police attendance.

The female paramedic had begun to prepare a saline drip, having already placed an oxygen mask over the elderly lady's wizened features.

"I've found a pulse," she announced briskly. "Fainter than I would have liked – but it's there. She's badly dehydrated," she continued professionally, before adding more warmly, "Poor old thing. I wonder who let her get in this sort of state?"

"Can we move her, do you think?" her colleague asked.

"Give it ten minutes and I think so. Let control know and warn A and E."

Ricky stood looking on, aware that his saviour's role had ended but not sure what he should do next.

"Where are you going to take her?" he enquired.

"St. Imelda's. You'd better wait here and talk to the police – they're on their way. What's your name and address – for our records?"

Ricky gave them the required information.

"And you're sure you're not a relative?" the ambulance man probed again, a hint of disbelief marring his voice.

f

"Of course I'm sure." Ricky fought irritation. "For Christ's sake – I wouldn't let a relative of mine live like this!"

"OK sir, don't get upset. Just checking for the records."

The paramedics put their well practised routine into action and began to prepare Mrs Whittleburgh for transfer to hospital. The old lady opened her eyes intermittently and stared at her rescuers for a few seconds in turn. Then they fell shut and she remained silent – too exhausted to whisper or even moan.

A car door slammed and the crunching of footsteps on the saturated gravel heralded the arrival of a police officer and a community support officer.

"Hi chaps," the female paramedic greeted them familiarly. "We're just off to St. Imelda's. This is Mr Trago – he found her and called us."

The police officer glanced at the bundle of bones about to be removed to the ambulance. "Phew. She's in a bad way. Do you know her name?"

The ambulance crew imparted the sparse information and departed into the storm. Ricky was left to be interrogated by the police officer. He repeated the story.

"We're obviously going to have to speak to Mr Whittleburgh. You say you had come to collect him for a meeting but he wasn't here. Any idea where he might be? Do you think he's gone to the meeting by his own means?"

"Perhaps. If so, he'll be back soon. I could phone them and find out if he's there, if you like?" Ricky offered, helpfully.

"Yes. Do that. But don't mention what's happened."

Ricky dialled Mary's number. He knew she would be annoyed – both with him being late and by the meeting being interrupted.

"MAD," she responded harshly, in business mode.

"Hi, it's Ricky. I'm sorry but I've been delayed. Is Joe there or do you still need me to pick him up?"

"He's here. So there's no need – which is just as well as you're so late." Mary metaphorically slammed down the receiver.

The other MAD members looked at her with a mixture of fear and expectation. Joe, exhibiting the most fear, had turned an unusual shade of white again. Rose, noticing, at once marvelled to herself how quickly the colour could drain from such a usually pink, puffy face.

"That was Ricky. Nice of him to let us know that he's going to be late. Late! I think we'd managed to glean that much."

Joe cleared his throat, "Did he mention me? My lift, I mean."

"You heard!" Mary glared at him. "I told him not to bother – despite your best efforts, you're actually here. Let's get on with the meeting."

In Goodwood Road, Ricky turned to the police officer, "Yes, he's there," he confirmed simply.

"Right. We'll send someone to pick him up. What's the address?"

Ricky gave him Mary's address, wincing internally as he imagined her rage at the invasion of her precious privacy. The community support officer wandered around the filthy room peering at its few contents in disgust.

"Don't touch anything!" his colleague warned. "We'll have to get CID in." He radioed to the police control accordingly. Then turning to Ricky again he asked, "Are you sure no one else is in? No one else lives here?"

"No. Only Joe – Mr Whittleburgh," he began, before stopping uncertainly and then adding, "Well, I assume so. . ."

"You wait down here," the police officer commanded, addressing the young community support officer, "I'll have a quick look around." Then he turned, once again, to Ricky. "I'd appreciate it if you waited here too, sir."

The policeman disappeared and Ricky and the CSO were left alone in awkward silence whilst the sound of heavy footsteps and the opening and closing of doors clattered above. The CSO, new to the job and wondering whether he had made the correct choice of career, thought he had better ask Ricky a few questions:

"What time did you arrive, sir?"

"About half an hour ago, I should think," Ricky replied before consulting his watch and adding; "Yes. It was about 7pm. I was running late – I got lost and the weather's so dreadful."

The CSO nodded his head and murmured in agreement, wondering whether he should start making notes. Luckily the return of his superior released him from the dilemma.

"There's no one else here," the officer announced, looking around the room, "This room's by far the worst – the rest of it's not too bad – a bit shabby but comfortable. One room's pristine though, the computer and tech room, I'd call it. I'm not surprised the old lady was in such a state."

The now familiar sound of growling gravel punctured the baying wind, headlights loomed and a car door slammed twice.

"CID, I expect," the CSO confirmed, unnecessarily.

"Make sure you don't touch anything," his colleague warned again as he disappeared into the dirty hallway. A pair of CID officers bustled in: the police officer confirmed briefly the evening's events.

"Right. I'm Detective Inspector Roux and this is Detective Sergeant Inch. We're going to need you to come down to the station and make a statement, please, Mr Trago. A car's on its way to pick up Mr Whittleburgh, I believe?" he addressed the police constable.

"Yes, sir," he confirmed with brisk efficiency.

"Right, we'll take a quick look around, you wait here constable until SOCO arrive. We'll take Mr Trago's statement and come back when they've had a chance to have a look. Keep the scene clean – we don't know the extent of the investigation yet – it depends on how the old lady gets on."

Shortly afterwards, Ricky found himself clasping a plastic cup of gut wrenching coffee whilst surveying the bland walls of interview room number one. He had never been inside a police station before and felt more akin to a small boy than a respected deputy headmaster. The all encompassing power of the state revealed itself and he understood his worthless value in the face of it.

His interviewers were courteous and superficially friendly.

"I see 'The Hammers' lived up to their name and took another hammering tonight," groaned Sergeant Inch as he slipped a tape into the recorder. "Do you follow football, Mr Trago?"

"Not really. I lost interest gradually."

Inspector Roux pulled up his chair which emitted an eerie, screeching sound, next to his colleague.

"Right, let's get on with it. Is the tape running, Inch?"

Inch nodded before announcing the date, time and the three men's names.

"OK, Mr Trago, start at the beginning and run through tonight's events, please," ordered the inspector.

"I was on my way to a meeting – a group called M A D. (Ricky was careful to spell the acronym) and. . ."

"I see, M A D," Inch interjected at once. "MAD. What's that – a comedy group or something?"

"No," Ricky admitted with a sigh, resigning himself to ridicule, 'It's Man Against Doctors'."

Inch rubbed his forehead as if in pain 'another bunch of loonies' written on his face, but he continued professionally, "Man Against Doctors, eh? Can you tell me what that's all about?" Inspector Roux stared at Ricky silently, who briefly explained.

"OK. There's no law against that," confirmed the sergeant. "You'd be surprised at the number of fringe groups and associations there are about. ('No, I wouldn't,' thought Roux.) Some of them, quite frankly, are completely barking, 'The Clone Your Own Pet Group' etc. There's even one raising money so people can have plastic surgery to make them look more like their pet. . . or the other way round – I can't remember which."

Roux leaned forward and cleared his throat, "If you'd continue please, Mr Trago. You were on your way to the meeting. . ."

"Yes. Mary – our leader – had asked me to give Joe a lift – his bike had a puncture or something. I agreed, and called for him at his house."

"Did you often give him a lift?"

"No, it was the first time and I lost my way."

"Had you ever been there before, for any reason?"

"No. If I had I don't suppose I would have taken a wrong turning."

"What did you do when you finally arrived?"

"I knocked on the door, waited for a bit but no one came."

"How come you went inside?"

"I realised that the door was ajar and thinking that Joe was probably somewhere inside, waiting in the dry, I went in. I walked along the hallway and called out, but there was no reply. I was just about to give up when I heard Mrs Whittleburgh."

"Did you know she lived there?"

"No, it was a complete shock – Joe had never mentioned her. I assumed he lived alone."

Roux mentally acknowledged Ricky's still pale expression.

"What do you know about Joe?"

"Very little. I only ever see him at MAD meetings."

"You've never socialised with him?"

"No. He's not my type of person."

"What type is he, would you say?"

125

"To be honest, I don't really like him. He's lazy and arrogant – always got a lot to say about how other people should be doing things but does nothing himself. He seems to think he should be the group's leader but no one else does."

"What about other members of your group? Do they like him?"

Ricky grunted and pursed his lips. "Not really," he replied with a shrug, feeling slightly disloyal. Then he remembered the pathetic Mrs Whittleburgh. "Everyone tolerates him, that's all. He's a bit of a figure of fun and besides, our membership is so small that we don't want to turn people away."

"Did he ever mention any other relatives?" Inch probed this time.

"No. I assumed – I think we all did – that he was alone. I remember once he mentioned that he had never married, adding some sort of derogatory comment about women and how lucky he was to have escaped the numerous attempts on his bachelorhood. Rose, one of the group, commented too loudly that she was surprised anyone would want him. Joe heard, made a dig at her about bringing too many children into the world and stomped off. That's typical of his interaction with the group."

"I see. So he's not the easiest type to get on with."

"No. He seems to have perfected the knack of making himself unpopular. He's a bit temperamental and bores everyone to death by droning on about money, or to be precise, his lack of it."

"A bit hard up, is he?" Inch enquired colloquially.

"Says he is, but he's such a fibber who can tell? He certainly doesn't have much to show for it – no car." Ricky glanced at his watermarked shoe. "Shabbily dressed, he certainly doesn't spend much on himself, and look at the house – that could do with a lick of paint or two."

"Right," Inch steered the conversation, "let's go back to when you found Mrs Whittleburgh and take it from there."

Ricky recounted the story once again.

Finally Roux concluded the interview: "Thank you Mr Trago. You've been very helpful. Let's hope you found the old lady in time. We'll get this typed up and ask you to sign it, then you can be off. Depending on how things pan out we may or may not be in touch. You should receive a courtesy call, at any rate, from our support team."

Ricky was guided through the maze of identical passageways

and numerous, swinging fire doors to the front exit. Feeling extremely relieved to escape the harsh, white, artificial lighting and recycled, unrefreshing air which dominated the interior of the building he stood for a moment on the characterless, smooth concrete steps and allowed the thick swelling wind, which now only contained a sprinkling of moisture, to blow through him. Had he been a smoker, he would have fumbled for a cigarette. As it was, he glanced at his watch and with surprise noted that it was too late to bother to attend the MAD meeting. It would be ended by the time he arrived. He made his way deliberately slowly across the car park, this time enjoying the wind and hint of rain, and thought that he would call in at The Bear and Swan for a nice pint of real ale. Inexplicably, he remembered Mrs Whittleburgh again and wondered how she was. It was far from certain that she would survive.

Ricky was in the process of sliding himself into the driver's seat of his car (an acquired feat) and was under the full illumination of the vehicle's interior light when a panda car swung through the entrance. Joe was sitting hunched up in the back, a police officer at his side. Catching sight of Ricky, his magenta-coloured, large, flabby cheeks turned white and in an instant appeared to blacken. He stared hard at Ricky. The school teacher could not fail to intercept the expression of undisguised hatred which was directed at him through Joe's cold, inhumane eyes. Their eyes met for less than a second but the effect was to unnerve Ricky, as a nightmare disturbs a young child. A sense of danger washed over him, sweeping away the warmth and vitality buried deep in his core. For a moment he trembled. The interior light extinguished itself and Ricky felt cold, alone and extremely vulnerable. Somehow he made himself turn the key in the ignition and the music which bounded in, dragged his mood to the surface and revived his spirit.

Joe's interception at MAD's meeting had provided its members with the most exciting evening they had ever witnessed. They had all expected the knock on the door to be Ricky arriving late and apologetic. Several snatched a surreptitious glance at their leader in anticipation of some form of humiliation at the expense of the tardy arrival. Mary uncoiled herself in preparation for her strike. Howard opened the door. An unfamiliar voice greeted him:

"Excuse me, sir, is this the right place for the MAD meeting?"

"Yes," Howard confirmed with puzzlement whilst staring quizzically at the two police officers who stood before him.

"Can we come in sir, please?"

"Yes," Howard replied again uncertainly and stood aside.

"After you, sir," the officer insisted before following him along the hallway and up the stairs into Mary's living room.

"We have some visitors," Howard announced unnecessarily.

The MAD members glanced at each other, silently, exchanging looks of bewilderment. All except Joe, who sank in his seat and gritted his teeth, seemingly having noticed something extremely interesting about a stain on the coffee table upon which he focused with unseeing eyes.

"Can I help you?" Mary enquired coolly, displeased at the interruption.

"Yes. We're looking for Joe Whittleburgh – is he here?"

Everyone turned their attention to Joe, who for a second remained silent and then uncharacteristically, suddenly burst into activity. To the astonishment of his peers, he leaped from his chair with unfamiliar speed.

"That's me. How can I help? Is everything alright?" he garbled.

"I have to inform you that your mother's been taken ill and we'd like you to come with us," the officer replied mechanically.

"Oh no! What's happened? Where is she?" Joe tried to sound concerned but he was no actor and there was a flatness in his tone which betrayed his intent.

"St. Imelda's."

"Oh dear! Shall I come with you, Joe?" Rose offered.

"That won't be necessary," the police officer snapped.

"Oh." Rose, deflated and disappointed, withered in her seat.

"Mr Whittleburgh – if you'd like to come with us," the officer continued, wrapping his unmistakeable command in the form of a question.

"Yes. You must go at once, Joe. Don't hang about here. Your poor mother. . ." Rose had found her voice again. Mary said nothing.

"I suppose I must," Joe agreed quietly, eyeing the second officer who had positioned himself directly in front of the yellowing door. The three men filed out of the room to the sound

128

of Rose calling out, helpfully, "I'll phone you tomorrow, to see how she is. I hope everything's alright. . ."

The atmosphere had tuned hollow and an eerie excitement had entered their souls. All except Mary's – she was merely irritated.

"Right, that's the second interruption out of the way, and what with Ricky letting us down and Joe marching out early, I suggest we try and get on with the meeting – which is, after all, what we are here for."

Rose, Howard and Sonja exchanged guilty glances.

"I wanted to plan the next stage of the campaign – the rally – but there seems to be a certain lack of interest," Mary continued coldly.

"I'm interested," Sonja confirmed, nervously and eager to please. Mary sighed and threw her a look which unmistakeably made it clear that Sonja's support was negligible at best.

"What no one seems to understand, is that we require solidarity and total commitment from each of you. One hundred percent attendance at all meetings – for the full duration of the meeting – and one hundred percent effort in between. Nothing less is good enough."

"On that note," Howard intervened, "and I must say I agree entirely with you Mary, why don't you call an adjournment and arrange another meeting as soon as possible, when Joe and Ricky can both attend? Then we can get down to business. I'm as keen as anyone to get this rally sorted out. Perhaps we can get Reverend Mouland and his merry men (and woman) to come, and maybe that other one who came to the public meeting? What was her name?"

"Helen," Rose replied before Mary had a chance. "I agree with you Howard, after all, it's not Ricky and Joe's fault that they're not here and we need their input."

"Joe's is debatable," Howard murmured to himself as Mary's voice rose above him,

"Excuse me! Just who exactly is chairing this meeting? I think I'm capable of deciding whether to adjourn or not, thank you, and it was going to be my next suggestion! It's a pity you're all not so forthcoming when we're looking for ideas or planning something!"

Howard sighed loudly and drummed his fingers angrily on the wooden arm of his chair. "So when's the next meeting?" he asked tetchily.

"Thursday," Mary replied before adding, with a hint of menace, "That's if everyone can make it, of course!"

"I can," Sonja confirmed, at once. Rose was just about to cast a doubt – two of her boys attended Scouts that evening – but thought better of it. Instead she nodded her head whilst frantically wondering how she could juggle the two commitments.

"I'm free," Howard declared moodily.

"Right. I'll contact the others and hopefully it'll take place," Mary conceded through gritted teeth.

So it was on that note of discord that she drew the meeting to a close and the depleted number of MAD members ventured out into the relentless buffeting of the autumn wind.

"I didn't know Joe still had a mother– he's never mentioned her – did you?" Rose asked both Howard and Sonja simultaneously.

"No. I thought he was too old," Sonja replied with youthful naïvety and a certain lack of tact.

"Perhaps she lives away and they don't have much contact," Howard mused. "As you say, it's a bit of a shock to be dragged away by the police like that, out of the blue. Old Joe certainly seemed shaken up."

"Well, he would do, wouldn't he? Poor thing. I hope his mum's alright. Like I said, I'll give him a ring tomorrow. See you on Thursday." Rose waved merrily at her two companions as she hurried away. Howard offered Sonja a lift home and Mary's net curtain flickered back into position.

Chapter Twelve

"That's it!" Mouland announced to his wife, with more conviction than she had heard him muster for a long time. "I'm throwing my lot in with MAD – whatever the consequences. You and Julian may do as you wish, but I've made up my mind – it's our only chance."

Caroline had been waiting anxiously for his return from the radio station, the vicar having undertaken (at short notice) his first interview since the bishop's resignation announcement. As they were both painfully aware, people had become progressively less interested in his views since then, but this morning Miss Golesworthy had been desperate, again. She had phoned him in a panic,

"Reverend Mouland? Thank God you're in! Would you mind coming across to do another little interview, a follow up from the last one. We wouldn't usually have bothered but we've been badly let down. Someone was coming from 'Corpses Unlimited' – one of the storage companies – to talk about their preservation methods, to put people's minds at ease, you know, and he's stuck in traffic. Could you pop over at once?"

Mouland, concealing his irritation, agreed and after informing Caroline, who immediately switched on the radio and located the correct station, made his way across the road, carrying a heavy burden of hopelessness.

Tara, bustling and flapping in her usual unproductive manner, met the vicar and conveyed him into the studio with an eventual semblance of uncharacteristic efficiency.

131

"Is it a phone-in?" Mouland asked dismally, an image of Daniel in the lion's den forming itself obstinately in his mind.

"No. We didn't want people asking 'Corpses Unlimited' awkward questions on air. It's more of a chat between you and Jason, with the audience just listening in."

Mouland's image of Daniel evaporated, prematurely. Thinking he could out-manoeuvre Jason with ease, he took his seat confidently and accepted the headpiece Tara offered.

"In a change to our programme, I'd like to welcome Reverend Mouland, who regular listeners will be familiar with, to tell us all why we shouldn't rejoice at rejuvenation and the amazing opportunity it represents."

'Hardly an auspicious introduction' Mouland thought grimly, whilst uttering a short, "Good morning."

"Reverend Mouland, it's some time since you've spoken to us," Jason continued in a tone coloured with a mixture of exasperation and boredom, unmistakeably portraying his view that he was revisiting a previously won argument. "How would you say things have moved on since then? Have you moved on at all or are you still hell-bent against eternal life?" Jason laid heavy emphasis both times on the word 'you'.

Mouland cleared his throat before beginning briskly, "You're right. Things have 'moved on' – in a most unfortunate way. No one can argue with the figures. Since the announcement and implementation of rejuvenation, society has plunged towards darkness. There has been an unprecedented rise in violent crimes, robbery and theft, a general lowering of morality and a rise in selfishness. People are giving less and taking more, in all things. My opinion, however, has not altered."

"How can you so confidently attribute these more negative events to rejuvenation? Crime statistics have risen year by year for decades."

"The rise in recent times has been huge – it's not a coincidence. If you take a step back you will identify a general malaise in society, a return to the laws of the jungle. We are becoming brutalised."

Jason adopted a chatty, almost jocular tone: "Some people might agree that there seems to have been a rise in robbery, etc., but could it not be because people need money more than ever now, for storage and the rejuvenation process? Surely they're just looking after themselves?"

"Exactly," Mouland retorted to Jason's obvious puzzlement, who continued erroneously:

"So you'd agree with our listeners who said – very aptly, I think – 'It's like a gold rush but ours will never end'?"

"No. I wouldn't agree at all. We may be rushing, but we're rushing away from all that humanity has striven for and achieved since the beginning of time. We're witnessing a far greater destruction of culture, history and art than that that took place during the reformation."

"But does that matter? How important can history be, now that we have eternity?"

"We should be able to learn from it." Mouland replied. "It gives us a foundation, a sense of collective identity and a feeling of belonging. It should make us wary of abnormal practices, be they political, social or otherwise. Societies based on evil have always floundered, ultimately, and we should remember that. Instead we are witnessing the rise of hedonism and self gratification but it will be short lived and there will be a price to pay."

"Despite that, which may or may not be true," Jason countered dismissively, "how can you justify depriving anyone of man's most sought after prize – eternal life?"

Mouland gave a short laugh; "I'm not depriving them of eternal life. It's always been there, through Christ, as Jesus said (Mark 15:36) 'Do not fear, only believe'. That's all it takes. By prolonging their physical existence people are depriving themselves of the true meaning of eternal life." Mouland condensed a lifetime of sermons into his short response.

"That's the weakness in your argument. We can't see, feel or hear what you are offering but we can see successful rejuvenates all around us – they can't even remember dying. People do not want to believe in what is probably a fairytale. Millions of people in the West, at least, are benefitting now. If we can lead a physical life forever why do we need some kind of spiritual eternity?"

"You've made some interesting points there," Mouland probed. "You speak of millions of people in the West – what about those in the Third World – should they not share your wonderful opportunity and how will the West cope with overpopulation, lack of jobs, resources and food etc?"

"Don't worry about the Third World – it will filter through to them eventually. Currently, most of them have nothing to live for anyway – there's not so much point in perpetuating a life of misery. As for population growth, it's all been taken care of, the European Union has been keen to extend social control measures for sometime, you know, things like strict limits on births, food rationing, designated housing etc. They're just going to bring forward a new directive that's been in the pipeline. They've been waiting until the conditions are right for public acceptance and now's probably the time."

Mouland's heart sank further and shrivelled a little more. For a moment he was lost for words, which suited Jason who, pouncing on his guest's hesitancy, and ensuring that he had no chance to respond, brought the discussion to an end:

"Thank you, Reverend Mouland, for sharing your thoughts with us, once again. Now let's have some music."

The vicar removed his headset slowly, having been unprepared for the abrupt ending of the session. A feeling of finality weighed heavily on his mind and body – a sense he recognised as being akin to bereavement. Jason's flippant comments and simplistic arguments in support of his deep seated conviction reminded him of the stark beliefs engendered by a twentieth century dictatorship. In this case the people had brainwashed themselves. There had been no compunction. They had chosen the way and charged towards oblivion. The veneer of spirituality has proven to be microscopically thin, Mouland concluded bitterly, perhaps non existent, merely an illusion blown away on the slightest breeze. Even he had not realised the extent to which the prospect of rejuvenation had emptied minds and then taken root like an obstinate, incurable, cancerous growth. Society had exchanged real life for an empty, fixed grin and staring eyes, mesmerised with misplaced joy on a fake future.

"Thanks, Vicar," Jason was saying, whilst the music played but Mouland could no longer hear. Tara stirred, in her usual fussy manner, and roused the depressed vicar.

"Thanks for stepping in at the last moment, Mr Mouland," she breezed. "I know the rejuvenation thing's really been done to death by now and no one's interested in the arguments against it, but you got us out of a hole. I'm sure we'll be able to reschedule 'Corpses Unlimited' very soon with a bit of imaginative juggling.

134

We've got to keep the audience happy, you know." She laughed.

Mouland, having involuntarily and unknowingly assumed the gait and bearing of a very old man, accompanied her silently to the foyer.

"We'll make our usual donation to. . . St. Nanny's," Tara continued after glancing at her clipboard, which she carried as a badge of office. Then she remembered, "Oh, I forgot. Hasn't St. Nanny's closed? Who should we pay – the new owners?"

"No, Heaven forbid," the vicar almost cried. "Make a donation to charity."

"Mmm – well I suppose we could. . ." Tara responded with uncertainty, as if the idea was highly unusual. "Any ideas which one?"

"If it's difficult, send a cheque to me, in my name, and I'll make sure it's put to good use," Mouland suggested wearily.

"Yes, that's better. I'm sure we can do that. Bye then, Mr Mouland."

The cold, bright sunshine and easterly wind revived the ailing vicar a little, as he made the short journey back to his home. Caroline had already prepared a strong cup of coffee for him.

"Actually, I think you did rather well," she announced.

"Really?" Mouland sounded incredulous.

"Yes. You made all the salient points, firmly but in a controlled manner, despite the presenter's hostile, lunatic remarks. No one could have done more. If Jesus Christ himself had reappeared it wouldn't have made any difference. These people are completely blinkered – it's as if they've been taken over by an alien force or something. They're completely irrational."

Mouland laughed at last. "I think, perhaps, we're the irrational ones. But I agree with your other thoughts – in fact, I had come to the same conclusion. It's impossible to argue logically against complete nonsense. The disease has spread even more quickly than I had imagined and more deeply. Hence my desperation and decision to work with MAD."

"I'm with you – any port in a storm, so they say."

Mouland smiled, gratefully. "I wonder if Julian will join us?"

"I hope so. I'm sure he would like to in spirit but I detected a certain frisson between him and one of MAD's members. You know, the bossy chap – Joe."

Philip chuckled involuntarily. "Julian's made of sterner stuff –

he won't be beaten by someone he doesn't respect. I wonder if he heard the broadcast?"

They discovered later that Devereux had not listened to Mouland's interview. He was only interested in an alternative station and, in any case, as he retorted, he would not have tuned into an interview with 'Corpses Unlimited' as advertised. Despite his antagonistic beginning with Joe, he too felt that their only option was to work with MAD and was keen to attend the next meeting. He would try to persuade Felicity to join them too.

Mary, however, had listened to the broadcast. She had recorded it as well for her collection, and had replayed it several times. Thoughts of the vicar crowded her mind and his now familiar, educated accent hammered into her subconscious, at last producing the desired, semi-hypnotic state. Mary knew he would contact her shortly. At once, all her thoughts merged into one and she implicitly understood. The little band of Christians had only one aim common to MAD's and many opposites. But they were desperate. More desperate than MAD and more desperate than even Mary herself. She would allow them to join. Her dream was to increase MAD's membership and thereby heighten her credibility as a leader of a serious force. Mouland's relatively high prominence would push MAD (and herself) into the public eye.

Then her thoughts turned to Helen. Helen Deighton – the secretive, poorly disguised, professor's daughter. What were her motives? Was she a mole, planted by her father, determined to destroy the group? Mary, oblivious to the exaggerated importance with which she credited MAD, could not allow that to happen.

The scent of danger roused her, and after flicking the switch on her tape deck and ending the hiss of the empty, twisting tape, she opened the greasy drawer of her cabinet and felt inside. Her fingers briefly met with several soft objects but she ignored these. Knowing exactly where the item she sought lay, she reached further inside, against the back of the drawer and in the right hand corner. Then she pulled out a small, mouse like object and held the little effigy of Helen, so carefully constructed, up to her eyes. Staring dispassionately at it for several happy minutes she perused every detail. Then she smiled.

Mary had always enjoyed inflicting pain, for as long as she could remember. From the first surreptitious pinch of her younger sister's chubby flesh to the cruel torment of their faithful puppy, she discovered a fascination with this unseen weapon. She marvelled at the effects of this invisible sensation in others and that however hard you tried, you could never really feel someone else's pain. Yet, just a tweak here and there could produce fantastic results. Mary enjoyed huge, clinical pleasure from instigating these tweaks and absorbing their effects.

Piercing tiny effigies with pins had been a natural progression for her. It was handy and equally satisfying to be able to torture from a distance. She was sure it worked one way or another. Sometimes a victim would not feel the discomfort at first, but the malevolent energy and intention would build up in time, after several applications, until the unfortunate recipient was brought to his or her knees by illness, injury or misfortune. Mary gained great comfort from this.

Swinging her right arm loosely to her side, still clutching the dreadful little doll, but this time in the manner of a crumbled rag, it having lost its precious detailed charm, Mary pushed the fingers of her free hand back into the drawer. Now she searched more carefully, her fingers brushing delicately over the worn, green, baize until she clasped a large dressmaker's pin decorated with rusty patches but retaining a sharp point. Then with a jolt, her caresses stopped and she rested the pin over the doll's heart. Mary had to fight the many demons within her, all urging her to pierce the soft felt – to 'stick it in' – to prevent herself from ever so gently, forcing the tip into the plump, soft chest area of the manikin. She teased herself. Then she drew back and whilst murmuring, "No, not yet. It's not time," and tossed both the doll and the pin back into the open drawer, her strange desire having evaporated in an instant.

Almost at once, the telephone rang forcing Mary back to her nearest form of normality. It was Reverend Mouland.

"Hello, Miss Fields," he began with polite formality, before introducing himself and making his request. "My little group, who you met at the open day, have come to a decision. We've decided we'd like to 'throw in our lot' with you, as it were, and wondered if that's acceptable and, if so, when we can come along again?"

137

Mary's eyes narrowed and she drew her lips back to form a thin, closed, smile.

"Yes, Reverend. It's perfectly acceptable," she agreed and then realising she had slipped into monotone, forced a note of easy friendliness into her welcoming response. "That's wonderful! I'm sure we'll all be delighted to see you at our next meeting. It's actually been rearranged for tomorrow evening – can you make it? 7.30pm is our usual start time."

"Yes. That will be fine," Mouland confirmed thinking how once, working as a busy active clergyman, such an arrangement at short notice would have been laughably impossible. Now his engagement diary was forlornly empty.

"So that will be three of you then?" Mary trembled but allowed no hint to betray her amicable response as she continued needlessly, "Yourself and your wife, Caroline, and Mr Devereux?"

"That's correct," Mouland confirmed. "Although there might be a possibility of one other – Mr Devereux's wife – I don't know yet. I presume if she did attend it would only be to observe at this stage."

"Oh, that's perfectly alright. The more the merrier." Mary giggled. "I look forward to seeing you all tomorrow." She replaced the telephone receiver in a highly satisfied state which was heightened by munching her way through a whole packet of chocolate biscuits. 'The tide is beginning to turn' she thought. MAD had three new members, one of whom had access to national radio. The vicar would surely bring her group to prominence. The next time he was asked to give an interview she would go instead – it was her right as MAD's leader. Yes, it was all coming together now!

At the same time, at a distance a little further into the city, Helen too was engrossed in thought. Hers, though, were less contented. She still alternated between confidence and direction and paralysing indecision. Today, she knew she was drifting. Drifting through her allocated slot in time, encased in her own bubble, observing more than participating – and she knew it was wrong. She had achieved nothing since resigning from her job and hiding away. She had reached no decision regarding how to use all the free time her father had purchased for her. All she had done was waste it. She had even withdrawn from her small circle

138

of close friends, including Anna after they had argued for the only time.

Anna had eventually fallen under the rejuvenation spell and could not fathom her friend's criticisms of the wonderful process. She thought that Helen should be grateful as 'in her position' as she put it, rejuvenation was guaranteed and at no cost. Others, like herself, had to scrimp and save to be ensured eternal life whilst Helen, who could receive everything, apparently did not want it! Anna was not good at budgeting.

'We used to agree on everything and have so much fun.' Helen thought shakily. 'Now even that has been taken from me. Rejuvenation has destroyed so much more than it has created.' She brooded constantly on the schism between herself and her former best friend which isolated her profoundly. Then she wondered at the tenuous nature of even the outwardly strongest of relationships which had been meticulously forged through common experience, time and chemistry. Even these could either be severed with one blow or gnawed at perpetually until they frayed and the last tie snapped and swung uselessly to one side. However estrangement happened, at least one of the parties would be left to ponder on the state of the human condition at rest, that is, completely alone. Helen and Anna's mutual laughter echoed backwards into time and all that remained were memories – even the sweet ones now stained and spoilt. Perhaps even she and Peter would have failed.

Helen's musings were distorted by the sound of mail falling through the letterbox. Picking the three envelopes from the floor and identifying them instantly as utility bills she noticed a fourth dangling from the flap which covered the opening – it was from her father. Recognising a lukewarm sense of foreboding she ripped open the envelope to reveal another cheque (for ten thousand pounds) to which was attached a small piece of yellow paper. Her father had scribbled a quick note: 'Here's another cheque to keep you going. Sorry I haven't been in touch – far too busy. Will ring when I get the chance.'

Helen held the cheque between her middle finger and thumb but did not look at it. It would have been easy to indulge her desire to crumple it and toss it away theatrically but she knew she could not. Now she depended on him financially – she depended on the fruition of his work – she was living off the proceeds of something she knew was wrong and it sickened her.

'Either I carry on like this or I have to make changes,' she consoled herself inwardly. 'Either I remain isolated and consumed with guilt or I move out into the world, interact and try to do something.' Helen decided at that moment to look for a job and join MAD. She telephoned Freddie for support. After the obligatory pleasantries, she came to the point:

"I've decided to join MAD," she confessed. "Have you thought any more about it?"

Freddie lowered his voice in reply, "I've thought of little else. Turning it over and over in my mind. Ada thinks I'm sickening for something – you know she worries. She's so much for rejuvenation, though, that I haven't said anything to her. I don't want an upset."

"No. No. Of course," Helen agreed hastily, an image of Anna presenting itself in her mind. "I wouldn't want to pressurise you and certainly would not want to cause an argument between you and Ada – it's not worth that."

"Well, it won't cause an argument if Ada doesn't know anything about it," Freddie replied surprisingly. "I really think I would like to go to one of their meetings – just to find out more. If I didn't like it I wouldn't have to go again. Ada doesn't have to be upset at this stage – nothing might come of it."

"That's a good idea!" Helen exclaimed, relieved at the thought of a 'get out clause' to bolster her typical indecision. "We don't have to commit to anything – just a little more investigation."

The pair agreed that Helen would contact Mary and inform Freddie of the outcome. Buoyed by the old man's support, Helen, slightly nervously, tapped out the telephone number printed at the bottom of one of MAD's leaflets. Mary, ever present, answered at once.

"Mary Fields – MAD," she announced formally.

"Hello. It's err Helen – I attended your open day."

Mary pretended not to remember; "Helen? Helen who?"

"Helen Day. I came to your open day with the elderly gentleman – Mr Meredith – perhaps you remember?" Helen's confidence tailed away.

"Let me see. We had so many people in that day and I've been quite overwhelmed with responses," she lied and then chided, "I can't possibly remember everyone."

Helen felt ridiculous but a wave of anger welled within. "Mr Meredith and myself were hoping to attend your next meeting but if you're overwhelmed perhaps there's no need – we wouldn't want to cause you any inconvenience."

"Not at all. I'm sure we can accommodate you both – you will be most welcome." Mary changed tack, afraid that she had pushed Helen too far and would lose two more, precious, potential members. "In fact, I'm beginning to remember – it was you and Mr Meredith who so kindly helped us clear up after that unfortunate incident. Some people are so brutal. I know it's not their fault really. I actually feel quite sorry for them – they're just unable to express themselves."

Helen rolled her eyes and frowned, taken aback by Mary's unexpected chatty candour.

"I'm sorry," Mary continued, "but I didn't catch your surname properly."

"Helen Day."

"Of course. For a moment I thought it was something else. I really am quite muddled today," Mary twittered falsely. Finally, the arrangements concerning MAD's forthcoming meeting were discussed and both women rang off.

Helen's sense of irritation nurtured the seeds of dislike towards Mary, whilst Mary herself, pondering again Helen's motives, prepared involuntarily, like a wary animal, for attack. She would have to be careful but she was ready. In any event, she would enjoy the preliminary stalking and teasing and when Helen finally made her move she would regret it. Mary would ensure that. She enjoyed her little secret and revisited it constantly, feeding off the thrilling sense of exhilaration it provided. Under other conditions, it would have been sensible to have discussed her suspicions and the possible threat with another trusted MAD member. Mary could not do that. She enjoyed the game and complete control too much.

In contrast, a few short miles away, Reverend Mouland felt that enjoyment was an emotion constantly racing further away from him. He had received a letter from the diocese office. Unexpected and merciless, the harsh message, embedded in thick, cream paper informed him that he was to be redundant from his post as vicar.

"We are able, however, to offer you a temporary post

decommissioning the few remaining churches in the vicinity," he read aloud to Caroline. "Unfortunately this post does not include habitation of St. Nonna's rectory and we therefore formally notify you that you will be required to quit the premises by the 30th June this year, at the latest."

"What are we going to do?" he almost whined. "No job. Nowhere to live. No reason to be."

"It is a nasty shock," his wife replied, slipping automatically into her role of supporter, "but not entirely unexpected. I was afraid that they would soon have no further use for us. At least they've offered you something to tide us over and we'll just have to find a place to rent. Presumably you're entitled to some kind of redundancy package?"

Philip was not listening. "How can they even think of suggesting that I should take on the job of decommissioning our places of worship. It's nothing short of sacrilege – it's pure desecration. I'm being asked to join hands with the Devil and undertake his work. I won't be a part of it!"

"Quite," Caroline replied gently. "I understand your feelings entirely, but perhaps you shouldn't dismiss it out of hand."

"What do you mean?" her husband snapped aggressively.

"If you accept the role," Caroline suggested with calm deliverance, "you will, at least, have some control over the contents of the buildings and perhaps be able to save the most precious (and by that I mean spiritually precious, the most steeped in prayer) for future use – when it's all over. Don't lose hope – if you do, you will lose your faith indirectly. Be strong. I know times are dark and it's very difficult to see the way ahead but it's happened before and probably will happen again, and there will be an end to this nightmare. When the time comes, you will be needed more than you have ever been."

Mouland sighed once, loudly, but otherwise stared at his wife silently. For one brief, inexplicable moment he suspected her of betrayal, of siding with the enemy, at the very least, of uncharacteristic naïvety. Eventually he summoned a lifeless reply:

"I have no response to make. I can't agree with you, yet. I need time. Time to think, time to pray." Then, giving his worried wife no chance to speak, he shuffled from the room. A few seconds later Caroline heard the familiar crunch of the gravel and watched her husband make his familiar journey across to St. Nonna's for

the last time. Tomorrow the sale would be completed and 'B –
Stored UK Ltd' would be the proud new owners of the ancient
building.

Caroline had witnessed her husband's descent into
hopelessness many times throughout their married life and knew
that he was equally capable of summoning great fortitude, energy
and optimism. Sometimes it seemed as though he needed to crash
into the depths of misery first, before he could find these reserves.
She hoped that this would be the case today but was worried. She
had witnessed an unfamiliar vacancy within the man who made
his way laboriously over to the church.

A tap on the door and Julian's voice roused her, gratefully.

"Anyone in?" he called needlessly, having opened the door,
poked his head round and peered into the kitchen.

"Yes, do come in Julian," Caroline replied hurrying towards
him, before automatically filling and switching on the kettle.

"I am pleased to see you," she emphasised the word 'you'.

"I don't usually elicit such enthusiasm," he remarked lightly,
before adding in a more serious tone, "What's happened?"

Caroline related the bad news and her concerns about Philip.

"Do you want me to go and speak to him?" Julian offered at
once.

"Later, perhaps. I think he should be left alone at the moment."

"Don't worry too much. I'm sure he'll rally – he always does."
Julian tried to sound much more positive than he actually felt.
"And we have the MAD meeting tomorrow evening, hopefully
we'll all be enthused by the end of it. That's partly why I called
round, by the way, not only to partake in one of your delicious
cups of coffee, but to let you know that Felicity won't be going."

"Oh, that's a pity." Caroline handed him a mug of the much
vaunted beverage. "Has she another engagement?"

"Well, no." Julian looked unusually embarrassed. "Actually
she's refusing to attend. I showed her the leaflets and gave her an
account of the 'Open Day' and she took a dislike to the whole
thing – became quite aggressive at one point."

Caroline pursed her lips in an attempt to hide a smile.
"Really?" she replied.

"Yes. You know what she can be like when she gets a bee in
her bonnet about something – takes an extreme view,
sometimes."

Caroline remained non-committal, Julian continued:

"She says that she can't reconcile MAD's ethos and practices with her own, as a Christian. She was particularly put off by the compulsory meditation. I told her that she could pray instead but she insists that she'll have nothing to do with it. The more I tried to persuade her, the more entrenched she became. Called them a load of loonies and me a heretic!"

"Oh dear. We can count her out, then. I can see her point of view but I wouldn't dismiss them all as loonies and you're far from a heretic. Some of their points are very valid – not only have we lost our way spiritually but we do seem to have lost our ability to work with nature, particularly when it comes to meditation. I'm sure more natural approaches can often be greatly beneficial. I'm no expert, but modern medicine so often seems to treat the symptoms rather than the causes."

"Sounds as though you'll soon be a fully paid up member of MAD," Julian joked. "Mary Fields had better watch out!"

Caroline gave a short, rueful laugh. "Mary's another kettle of fish completely." Then, remembering, she glanced anxiously out of the window.

Julian patted her arm. "Don't worry too much, Caroline," he insisted. "We both know how he reacts to things – feels them too deeply at times I suppose, but that's what makes him tick and makes him so suited to his job."

"That's why I'm so worried, this time – he has no job. His vocation has been taken away from him."

"But he always bounces back. Unfortunately, I'm not very surprised at the redundancy, the clergy has been decimated one way or another, you must both continue to believe that we're experiencing a temporary, aberrant situation."

"I tried to tell him that," Caroline replied with an air of failure, before adding sharply, "So you think we should have seen it coming?"

Julian shrugged his shoulders, embarrassed, but answered honestly, "Yes."

Caroline sighed. "You're right," she admitted, "I think we both did, but we did not dare speak its name. I know it crossed my mind sometimes but I buried it and did not voice my fears. Philip never mentioned it either. I think he hoped he would hang on until the last."

"He has, really. He's done very well. He's just been overtaken by this roller-coaster of events, which was bound to happen." Julian prepared to leave. "Thanks for the coffee," he added, tapping the mug with a long, lean finger. "I'll pick you up tomorrow at seven. And I'll pop over to St. Nonna's a bit later."

"Thank you, Julian," Caroline replied, grateful for his support. "He'll be there for some time, I'm sure."

g

Chapter Thirteen

The following evening, as MAD members, old and new, made their way to Mary's flat, she was preparing as usual, but this time nursing an aura of trembling excitement. Five new members! She would make her mark soon. Reverend Mouland would surely bring more exposure to the group and, of course, to herself. 'What about Helen, though?' she wondered. 'Was she dangerous or useful?' Mary decided that she would be useful.

Devereux, as promised, tapped the door of the rectory at exactly 7pm. A morose Mouland opened it and, leaving the duty of polite pleasantries to his wife, installed himself in the front passenger seat of Devereux's pristine, classic car. He could not prevent himself from staring at the now defunct priory, as he waited for Caroline to lock the front door and squeeze herself into the back of the vehicle. 'The new owners have wasted no time,' he thought bitterly, having witnessed several men in suits arrive at the building that afternoon. One had even driven into the small churchyard and parked his monstrous four-wheeled drive vehicle on several ancient graves. Another had disturbed the ex-vicar's brooding by coming to the rectory and asking whether he retained a key for St. Nonna's. Mouland had snapped, "No," and slammed the door in his face. Even at this time of the evening one of the new owners was still there. Mouland could see a light in what used to be the vestry. 'No doubt still revelling in getting their hands on it,' he thought miserably.

Julian slammed his car into gear and spurted down the drive, splashing shards of gravel into the air as he went. Mouland was jolted back in his seat and transported away from the source of his gloom and despair.

"Should be interesting, tonight," Julian remarked grimly, in an attempt to engage his friend. "I rather hope that Joe will not attend."

"We're trying to drum up support – not turn it away," Mouland replied argumentatively.

"True. I just find him rather irritating, that's all," Devereux responded lightly.

"At least we're doing something," Caroline joined in. "It shows we're not completely isolated."

Her husband, bored by the repetitious attempts at optimism, ignored her and stared unseeingly out the side window.

Rose, Sonja, Howard and Ricky all arrived at Mary's flat within minutes of each other and with plenty of time to spare, each having recalled Mary's wrath at the previous meeting.

"Have you any news concerning Joe?" Rose addressed Ricky, with concern.

"I don't know why you're asking me. It's not as if I'm his friend, I only had the misfortune to discover what he's been up to."

"What do you mean?" Rose looked vague.

"He's been arrested," Howard replied. "I saw it in the local rag."

"Whatever for?"

"Neglect or cruelty or something. I don't know the exact legal charge, but the gist of it is, he was starving his mother to death."

"Oh, my goodness!" Rose was aghast. "But why? There must have been a reason. Couldn't he afford to look after her or is he just not capable?"

"Stop trying to find an excuse for him or a reason to feel sorry for him," Ricky ordered impatiently. "You didn't see the distress she was in. I did. It was awful, you wouldn't treat an animal like it. He's a wicked, mercenary sod."

"Oh. . . perhaps I'll go and visit his mother then," Rose decided, pleased to have found someone in need.

Mouland's troupe caught the last part of the conversation, having been admitted to the flat by Sonja.

Mary had hidden herself in the small bedroom so that she could make a dramatic entrance, impose herself and signal the

147

start of the meeting. For the moment she listened attentively at the bedroom door.

"I could pay the unfortunate lady a visit myself," Mouland observed in automatic clergy mode, before remembering that it was no longer expected of him.

"Yes. You should," his wife encouraged before whispering, "There's no reason to give up your role entirely – you can still undertake the same works."

"I told you I didn't like him," Devereux hissed triumphantly.

"To be honest, he always got on my wick," Howard admitted with brutal candour. "He never seemed to actually do anything but liked to have a lot to say. Did you notice how he bottled out at the open day?"

"When the thugs arrived, do you mean, and he thought it was the boys with the football?" Ricky asked needlessly but determined that everyone would relive Joe's humiliation.

"Yeah," Howard grunted. "Never saw him move so fast in my life."

This time Rose took a turn to respond to a rap on the door (it was unclear as to whether the doorbell was working or not) and Helen and Freddie were ushered in.

Ricky glanced at his watch. "Twenty-five past," he announced. "Let's all find a seat and make ourselves ready for a prompt start." After a supportive wink in Sonja's direction, he added in a hushed voice, "Sorry it's a bit of a mess in here – with all you, welcome, new members it's quite crowded. Let me help you with that deckchair, Caroline."

"Where's Mary?" she whispered in reply. "She is coming, I presume?"

"She's here already," Ricky confirmed. "This is her flat, but she likes to make a big thing about starting the meeting sometimes, especially if there are new members – which there haven't been, for a long time," he added unnecessarily.

With everyone settled, a hush fell on the group. Helen, Caroline and Sonja cast their eyes round expectantly, Mouland slumped silently in his seat, his thoughts elsewhere, and Howard sighed a couple of times. The others seem to be prepared to wait patiently for Mary's appearance. At 7:59pm and fifty seconds precisely the sound of the bedroom door being tugged open and unceremoniously beaten closed again (the plimmed up timber catching at the foot of the frame) alerted everyone to the commencement of the meeting.

Mary made her much practised entrance, and adopting a variation of a slow march, moved her stiff, upright body to take its place in its usual chair. She had chosen to wear a long, flowing, cotton dress, in shimmering turquoise for the occasion, and had washed her hair and allowed it to fall loosely about her shoulders. She could almost have looked pretty were it not for the icy emptiness which emanated from her forget-me-not eyes.

"Good evening all," she said serenely. "Let us begin in our usual way, with a short meditation." Then, after pressing a switch on the cassette player at her side, she closed her eyes and tossed her head back regally. Devereux wrinkled his nose and remembering his wife's objections felt heretical. Howard's sighs became snorts and both Mouland and Caroline prayed fervently, urgently and desperately. Freddie and Helen, unsure as to what was expected of them, closed their eyes politely and after a few moments, involuntarily gave themselves to the pungent tone of the heady music. Ricky and Sonja, both believers, meditated assiduously whilst Rose tried hard, but was distracted by items to be added to her shopping list for the next morning, which, to her annoyance, kept popping into her mind.

At last Mary counted them back into the present and switched off the music.

"Welcome new members." She smiled at them sweetly. "Let me introduce, or perhaps it would be more accurate to say re-introduce, you all."

She then proceeded to bore everyone by reading out the constitution and reminding all members of their responsibilities to the group.

"Attendance at all meetings and events is compulsory, without a very good reason, and giving notice," she warned. Ricky gave Rose a knowing glance, who looked puzzled at hearing this piece of news. Devereux felt the seed of rebellion grow within.

"Do you know if Joe's coming back?" Rose enquired recklessly.

"I have no idea," Mary responded, making it clear that she did not care either way. "My concern is with those who are present tonight and our plans for the future."

"I must say the 'Open Day' went well," Howard commented "Look, we've got five new members. That's fantastic."

149

"Perhaps we should have another?" Sonja ventured.

"No!" Mary almost shouted. "The open day proved that there are people out there willing to support us but we need a bigger event in which to identify them. I propose a mass rally!"

"A mass rally?" Ricky sounded quizzical. "Wouldn't we need more people?"

"No!" Mary did shout this time. "It will be self perpetuating. People who sympathise, who come to watch, can join in."

"We'll need a good publicity campaign to make that happen," Ricky continued, still doubtful.

"That's where Reverend Mouland comes in," Mary replied gleefully as the vicar pulled himself upright. "He can give us publicity on the national radio – when's your next interview?"

"There isn't one planned. It doesn't work quite like that," Mouland mumbled.

"But surely you have connections – know people in the right places. Can't you pull some strings?"

"I'm afraid I can't. They've become progressively less interested in my views, to the extent that they're now not interested at all. I'm sorry, but I'm no use to you in that respect."

Mary clenched her teeth and observed the hapless man through half closed eyes but before she could further humiliate him Caroline spoke:

"There is a host of ways in which Philip will be useful – do not doubt that for one moment. He will be a great asset to MAD."

Devereux rocked and nodded in agreement. "Here, here," he said loudly.

"You're welcome in any capacity," Howard agreed whilst patting the vicar's arm. "We're pleased you've joined us."

"Oh yes," Ricky and Rose agreed in unison, afraid that Mary would alienate the precious new members.

"If you want publicity why don't you advertise on the radio?" asked Helen unexpectedly.

Mary gave her a look of contempt. "How do you think we would pay for that?" She demanded nastily.

"Well if your funds wouldn't stretch that far, I could help out," Helen ventured, surprising herself with her boldness.

"In what way exactly?" asked Ricky curiously. "Do you mean that you have 'connexions' and could get us a good deal? I'm afraid even that would be no good – our finances are rather parlous." Ricky's nerve held sufficiently for him to ignore Mary's venomous stare.

"No. No. I haven't any 'connexions'," Helen declared hurriedly, the one enormous connexion she did have, bearing down upon her. "I could finance it if you like."

The MAD members gawped at her in amazement until Rose spoke. "I don't think you realise, dear. It would cost an awful lot of money. We couldn't expect you to foot the bill. It's lovely of you to offer though."

Howard grunted in agreement whilst Ricky raised his eyebrows expectantly. "Yes. It's a very generous thought."

"Look, I'm not completely naïve," returned Helen who was beginning to feel patronised – a dangerous event which always caused a thunderous rush of anger to gush through her – "I can afford it – whatever the cost – and as far as I can see it's the only way the rally has a chance. Mary's right, we need publicity."

No one could think of a reply. Mary purposely remained silent, eager to encourage Helen to play her next card and to hopefully reveal a little more of herself. Helen, taking her cue from the blank faces which surrounded her continued:

"Let me explain. I came into a, how shall I put it, a handy sum of money quite recently and I've wanted to put it to good use. So far, I haven't thought of anything – the only thing people are interested in is rejuvenation. If I could use it to help MAD spread the word then I'd be delighted. I want to use it for the greater good."

Ricky shrugged. "It sounds good enough for me. Shall we vote on it? I'll propose it."

"I'll second it," Rose volunteered whilst wishing that she had an excess of cash too.

"I'm not sure. . . yet," Mary dithered, unprepared for the sudden acceptance of Helen's offer and being the only person to suspect that she had lied regarding the source of her income.

"Come on!" drawled Howard. "She's agreeing with your publicity plan – what more do you want? Let's vote on it."

The vote was taken and passed unanimously by MAD's sitting members (Philip, Caroline, Julian, Freddie and Helen not being 'sworn in' until the end of the meeting).

"Well done," Freddie whispered and grinned encouragingly.

Mary, harbouring a sense of annoyance that something had

slipped from her control, as a result of her preference for secrecy over collaboration, continued with the meeting.

"In that case I'll leave the publicity in your capable hands," she addressed Helen coolly, before adding quickly, "but you must allow me to confirm the exact wording etc. Next, we must identify the requirements and associated actions in order for the event to take place." Mary sounded as if she was reading from a particularly tiresome instruction manual.

"What d'ya mean?" asked Howard aggressively. "If you mean where and when, and who's going to make the banners etc, why don't you just say so?"

"There's more to it than that," Mary replied through clenched teeth. "I want everything to be perfect and if there's to be any chance of that, we have to think of everything and plan to the last detail."

"Where and when were you thinking of?" asked Rose casually, whilst a list of Scouts' activities, jumble sales and dancing lessons and, quite incongruously, a recipe for rhubarb crumble, ran through her mind.

"Four weeks on Saturday – the sixteenth – at eleven o'clock, when all the shoppers are about."

"Where exactly?" Ricky enquired.

"The High Street," Mary replied, thinking it was obvious.

"Do we have to inform the police?" Sonja asked. "I'm sure I read somewhere that you have to get permission."

"That's only if you need to close the road," Ricky replied, authoritatively. "I doubt if it will be necessary," he smiled apologetically at the new members before Mary snapped:

"What do you mean? Of course the rally will be big enough for that. You must all understand the nature and extent of the event. We must make our mark, bring our vision to the light, seek out those in doubt and bring them within our fold. We can't afford to be faint hearted, we must be ambitious and MAD will. . ."

"Quite," Reverend Mouland agreed, just in time to prevent Mary reaching her crescendo. "You are absolutely correct. I'm sure I speak for Julian and Caroline, when I say that we were attracted to MAD for its ambition and our belief that together we can bring about awareness and change. To do this, and to avoid being downtrodden we must aim high. We must oversee a seismic event."

"Thank God he spoke up," Howard whispered loudly to Sonja, who aware that Mary had heard, shifted in embarrassment at her guilt by association.

"Oh, yes. We're quite prepared to throw ourselves wholeheartedly into arranging a rally," confirmed Caroline, "aren't we, Julian?"

"Oh, yes," Devereux agreed uneasily.

"Right, Sonja – you can contact the police regarding the road closure," Mary ordered, "but don't give any specific details about us – just make a general enquiry."

"It might be on the net," Ricky volunteered helpfully as Mary continued listing and delegating tasks.

The final item on the agenda was the 'swearing in' of the new members. Mouland, Devereux and Caroline filled in their forms, took the oath self-consciously and handed Rose their annual subscriptions. Freddie and Helen looked at each other hesitantly as Sonja held out their forms.

"Is there a problem?" Mary demanded, at once.

"No. It's just that we hadn't definitely decided to become members, yet," Helen began to explain, before Freddie interrupted.

"We're very interested though. But we thought tonight we'd just dip a toe in the water."

"I'm afraid that's quite unacceptable," Mary replied tersely. "Either you're in or out. I don't see how Helen can think she can pay for advertising if she's not a bona fide member."

"I must say, I tend to agree with Mary, on that point," said Howard to general murmurs of assent and nodding of heads from the others. "I can't see why you would offer to put your own money into a 'good cause' – as you say – but not actually want to become part of that cause. If you believe in what we're trying to achieve, what's the problem?"

"Exactly!" Mary cried, only just managing to prevent herself from adding: "It's because she's Helen Deighton! Professor Deighton's daughter. She's an interloper – a spy sent to destroy us!" There was still pleasure to be extracted from the secret so Mary held her tongue.

Then Ricky joined in. "Whilst not wishing to pressurise you in any way, there seems to me to be no point in waiting or procrastinating. You've seen what the group stands for, from the Open

Day and here tonight. We're very transparent. Our general ethos is to respect and give the workings of nature a chance, which has culminated in our opposition to rejuvenation. It's that simple. If you feel the same way, then join us here and now and help us make the rally a success."

"I must admit, we all thought about it very carefully," Caroline revealed, "but we're very aware that the opposition to rejuvenation is so small that individuals will not make their voices heard. We need to forget our differences and misgivings and join together in one cause."

"Perhaps Helen and Freddie are not opposed to rejuvenation?" Mary could not help adding. All the MAD members recoiled in surprise.

"Surely you are?" Rose addressed them both. "Otherwise why are you here?"

"Exactly!" Mary cried again, while Helen studied her agitation, beginning to suspect that Mary knew her secret.

"No. No. You're right," Freddie confirmed hastily. "I think I can speak for both of us, we are against rejuvenation, it's just taking the plunge and joining the group," he continued whilst thinking of Ada.

"Well it's up to you," Ricky conceded before throwing himself back in his seat and crossing his legs, an indication of his sudden lack of interest and that he had nothing further to say.

Helen began to fill in the details on the registration form. Freddie watched her for a moment before muttering, "In for a penny, in for a pound." And dispelling Ada's shadow, which peered over his shoulder, became a member.

Reverend Mouland broke the uneasy silence. "Well done. You won't regret it! Now I've signed up, I feel renewed, reinvigorated, even rejuvenated!" Ricky and Howard both groaned loudly. Sonja glanced at Mary anxiously, who with an eerie look of satisfaction concentrated on Helen's evolving, spidery signature.

"It's all very encouraging," Mouland continued, "to meet with like-minded people and finally be able to begin the fight back. I'm sure the rally will prise out more support for ourselves. We only have to nurture and feed the flame."

Caroline recognised the signs. Her husband having reached his nadir, was now climbing out of the abyss. There was reason to feel hope, at least, on a personal level. She offered a short, mental prayer in thanks for her husband's ascent, before adding eagerly, "I couldn't agree more. The meeting's been very positive. Don't you agree, Julian?"

"Oh, yes. Quite," Devereux replied unenthusiastically before adding in an unfortunate monotone, "Can't wait to get started."

Mouland stared at his friend in puzzlement. "I'm certainly enthused and reinvigorated," he declared, "despite the unwelcome news we received yesterday – today's the time to move on, as they say."

"What was your unwelcome news?" Rose asked cautiously.

"I'm to be made redundant," the vicar replied. "And with effect from twelve noon this morning St. Nonna's, my church, has become the property of 'B Stored UK Ltd'."

"The tentacles of this monster are reaching everywhere," Mary declared solemnly.

No one was quite sure whether she was referring to 'B Stored UK Ltd' or the general concept of rejuvenation. "We must mount attacks on all fronts," she continued.

"Quite right," agreed Devereux who had been brought to life by the thought of the sacrilege done to St. Nonna's and Mary's military language.

"Oh, I am sorry to hear that," Rose commiserated with Philip. "These churches are such beautiful buildings too. They'll never be the same once they've been converted and used for storage."

"On the whole, I'd say it's been an excellent day," Howard enthused. "Five new members and a new project in hand. There's life in us yet!"

"What about Joe?" asked Rose. "Is he still a member?"

Everyone looked at Mary, wondering whether she would disassociate the group with him or defend him at all costs, if only to retain MAD's membership numbers.

"That remains to be seen," she answered curtly. "It depends on the outcome of his court case. There may be an opportunity there for publicity for us. We'll have to wait and see."

"We don't want any bad publicity, though," Sonja ventured anxiously.

"I said 'we'll wait and see'. Let me be the judge of it." Mary cut her down ruthlessly, a tactic she employed often, designed to thwart the young woman's confidence, 'put her in her place' and ensure that she would not develop leadership ambitions.

Sonja trembled and cast her eyes to the floor in silence. Rose tried to send an encouraging wink and smile. Mary rearranged the papers on her clipboard before bringing the meeting to a close.

"We'll adjourn until next week," she ordered, adding, "Same time and place," for the benefit of the new members, "and I expect there to be progress in our plans for the rally. Everyone must have got as far as possible with their remit. Some of you should have no problem in completing them. We'll have a review and assign tasks for the next stage."

Then, allowing no responses, she marched from the room and shut the bedroom door firmly behind her. Devereux was very surprised.

"Is that it?" he asked Ricky who was sitting next to him. "Do we just let ourselves out?"

"Yep," Ricky replied as a matter of fact, before continuing, "She doesn't always abandon us quite like that – only on special occasions, such as tonight, when she feels the need to flaunt her authority and – er – 'leadership skills'. She'll feed off this for days."

Devereux did not quite understand what Ricky meant.

"Strange woman," he muttered. Devereux was both used to leading and being led as a result of his officer duties during his career in the army. In some respects he had not quite managed to quell the inbuilt compunction to obey an order, if barked with adequate authority, in civilian life. Mary was certainly prepared to issue commands, he thought, but on whose authority? She seemed to have assumed the leadership role, she so coveted, with no opposition from the membership of MAD.

Howard opened the front door for Julian, Philip and Caroline. "See you next week. Don't be late." He grinned. "Or Mary'll have your guts for garters!"

"She does appear to be quite driven," Caroline replied diplomatically.

"How come she's in charge?" Julian asked, grabbing his chance.

"She was voted in," Howard answered simply.

"Who was her opponent?" Philip enquired.

"Joe."

"Oh."

There was an uneasy silence. Howard looked at the trio curiously.

156

"None of you have leadership ambitions, I hope? Mary would not be happy about that. We want to increase support not end up with factions or divisions."

"No. No," Philip replied to the general assent of his companions. "It's just that Mary can be very abrupt at times and I wonder how the other strong personalities in the group, such as yourself, react to that."

"I know Mary has her funny ways but that's what makes her a good leader – she's dedicated and extremely focused. MAD comes before everything else for her. She's kind of worn herself out with her intensity but she's got a vision and nothing will deflect her from it. You couldn't have found a better ally in your fight against rejuvenation, you know. We accept her bluntness and cajoling because she's on our side – sometimes it's the only way to get things done. So many people let you down. In any case, the rest of us are too busy to take on the role – Ricky's a deputy head, Rose's got about forty seven children and Sonja has her studying to do. We're quite happy with Mary really – sometimes we have a moan but it's not serious – we have to accept her idiosyncrasies as well as her drive."

"I see. What you say makes sense," Caroline confirmed. "Rest assured, we're not here to rock the boat – our ultimate aim is the same as yours."

Freddie and Helen parted at the end of the street and Helen made her way home in a state of nervous excitement. Although still twisting with guilt at her disloyalty to her father, deep down she knew that she was treading the path to whole-hearted opposition to his lifetime's work. It was no good pretending. She had chosen to take each step which lead inexorably to conflict. Yet she was unable to identify exactly what caused her to do so. It was just the feeling that she had. 'Perhaps this is how people used to feel when religion caught them and dragged them into its arms' she thought. 'Perhaps it's similar to finding a vocation.' She had found neither of these. Her lack of religious faith puzzled her at that moment – it would make more sense if she had some sort of conviction. It would make her opposition to her father more acceptable, more defendable and easier to explain. Yet all she had was a feeling. She could not identify its source but knew that it could not be contained or concealed within her conscience forever. To date, it had dripped constantly, turning gradually to an irritating leak. Soon it would burst out, take control of her and determine both her future and her relationship with all those around her.

Philip, Caroline and Julian arrived back at the rectory. The presence of St. Nonna's loomed, gloomily and largely at their side but each person averted their gaze, and without commenting or acknowledging the dying building, made for the sanctity of their respective homes. Once inside, Philip and Caroline discussed their roles within MAD and assigned tasks regarding the proposed rally. Caroline was relieved at her husband's animation and renewed enthusiasm and their conversation lasted until past midnight.

Eventually Caroline yawned excessively. "That's it! I'm off to bed!" she declared.

Philip agreed, "I'll be there too in a moment," as he failed to resist the temptation to adjust the curtains very slightly and stare, for a moment, through the chink at St. Nonna's. Then, with a sigh, more of finality and acceptance than distress, he followed his wife up the stairs.

Neither had slept for long before they were abruptly woken by the sound of blaring sirens, flashing blue lights and raised voices.

"What on earth's going on?" Philip mumbled as, stumbling to the window, he dragged himself from the depths of a dream to a very low level of alertness. Caroline crept from beneath the bedclothes and felt for the lamp switch beside the bed.

"What is it?" she asked, opening her eyes with reluctance. It took her husband a few moments to adjust his eyes to the mixture of darkness and artificial light. An orange haze glowed beyond the red, blue and white lights of the fire engine.

"Oh, no," he whispered, "it can't be. . ."

"What's happened?" Caroline repeated, urgently now sitting upright in the bed.

"It's St. Nonna's," Philip replied, desperately throwing on his clothes. "It's on fire!"

Caroline leaped from the bed and pulled the curtains widely apart, ignoring her husband's half-dressed state.

"Oh, my God!" she cried, watching two more fire engines and a police car arrive. "However did that happen?" There was no answer. Caroline looked round for a reply but Philip was already charging down the stairs; seconds later she followed.

Mouland took his usual shortcut and vaulted easily over the low stone boundary wall. The smell, sound and sense of destruction intensified as he neared: the chancel roof was ablaze. Realising that his presence was superfluous, Mouland could only stand and witness the event unfold. He could have been watching a film but for the physical assault on his senses. Acrid smoke, hissing heat and dirty water mingled with the roar of engines and shouts of the fire crews. A large, blackened, oak roofing timber, finally cracked and split downwards, followed by tumbling stone tiles, leaving a large hole, like a dark stain in the chancel roof.

At that moment, the building suddenly lost its sanctity for the vicar. He saw it only as a manmade heap of stone and wood – a building which had been constructed for a purpose but which had not become that purpose. Mouland understood the danger of attributing holiness to an object purely as a result of its antiquity and perhaps worshipping too much the layers of atmospheric energy cocooned within. It was a pity to witness any sort of destruction of an item of worth or beauty, he thought, but St. Nonna's had lost its soul at twelve noon, the previous day, when B Stored UK Ltd had assumed ownership.

Mouland began to feel uncomfortably glad at the physical destruction, perhaps God was relinquishing his claim on the building.

"There's nothing more for us to do," he stated calmly to Caroline who had appeared at his side. "Let's go."

"Excuse me, sir!" a voice called out, before they could retrace their steps through the churchyard. "This is a restricted area. What are you doing here?"

"I'm – was – the vicar," Mouland replied to the voice, which it transpired belonged to a policeman. "I live next door, over there," he indicated, "and this is my wife."

"You'd better get back over there. As I said, this is a restricted area. Looks like the roof's about to cave in completely."

Mouland and Caroline started to obey his instructions, only to be called back.

"Wait a minute, sir. You said you used to be the vicar – who's the current one? We'll need to contact him."

Mouland explained, wearily.

"I see." The policeman observed him suspiciously. "So you were dispensed with, really, only yesterday and the new owners have only just taken control. I'd better make a note of your full name and address – I expect someone will want to speak to you, in case you saw anything. We don't know how the fire started yet. I don't suppose you have a contact number for the new people?"

"No. I've had no direct contact with them. The sale was dealt with by the diocesan solicitors. My role was merely to vacate the building and arrange for the disposal of the contents," Mouland replied.

"OK, I've put a call through. That'll be as quick as anything. Thanks, vicar."

Philip and Caroline made their way back to the vicarage in shocked silence. To their surprise a slightly dishevelled Devereux was hovering in the porch.

"Oh, there you are!" he exclaimed, obviously relieved. "You know what's happened then? It looks pretty bad. I couldn't get near though." Julian, like almost everyone else in the street, had been awoken by the arrival of the emergency services and had joined the small crowd which turned out to watch the building burn and the efforts of the fire crews. Although a cordon was quickly in place, he had skirted around it, squeezed through a tiny gap in the hedge and begun to pad his way to the north side of the building. To his dismay he was intercepted almost at once and escorted humiliatingly back to the crowd on the pavement. For a moment, all eyes were on him rather than the fiery drama.

"Then I thought I'd better come round here to see if you'd heard," he continued.

"I wonder how it started?" Caroline mused.

"Haven't a clue," Devereux admitted. "I mean, everything else was safe and switched off when we left it."

"Oh, well. It's no longer our responsibility," Mouland declared, conveying a rare lack of concern and interest. "They've had people in there all day – probably a workman's fault."

"Not a very auspicious start for 'B Stored UK Ltd' is it?" Caroline remarked.

Her husband merely shrugged one shoulder in response. Suddenly the orange glow within the church disappeared, deflating like a punctured ball. The fire had been extinguished.

"Looks like it's under control now," Devereux observed authoritatively. "But they'll be here all night damping down."

"I'm off to bed," Mouland replied. "We've had too much

excitement for one evening." Without waiting for a reply, he let himself through the front door, closely followed by his wife. Devereux stayed for a while, still watching the fire fighters at work and marvelling at the swiftness and intensity of fire's destructive power.

Chapter Fourteen

The next day, as promised, the policemen arrived to question Philip and Caroline. The vicar opened the door to Inspector Roux and Sergeant Inch and at the same time admitted a strong stench of burnt timber, roasted stone, brickwork and tiles, and melted electrical wiring.

"How can I help you?" Mouland asked suspiciously, whilst observing the two sharply dressed men and wondering whether they were representatives of 'B Stored UK Ltd'. The inspector flashed his warrant card as he introduced himself and his colleague.

"We'd just like to ask you a few questions regarding the fire, sir," he said, nodding in the direction of St. Nonna's which stood naked and decayed in the pale morning sunshine.

"Oh, yes. Come in. The constable said to expect a visit – but not quite this early!" Mouland led them to the comfort of the living room and offered them seats. Caroline promptly offered tea or coffee which they both declined.

"If we can start with you first, vicar," Roux began. "Just run through what happened. When did you notice the fire?"

"I think it must have been about two o'clock – we went to bed late."

"And what brought your attention to it?"

"The sirens and general commotion, etc. I looked out of the window and saw the building ablaze."

"Then what did you do?"

"Dressed as quickly as I could and went to see what was happening."

"Apparently you were found inside the police cordon – how did that happen?"

"I took my usual shortcut from the rectory garden, across the churchyard. The cordon only really extended from the chancel to the tower on the south side. At first I didn't even know it was there."

"So you weren't inside the cordon for any particular reason?"

"No," Mouland sounded puzzled. "Obviously my reason was to see what had happened and by chance I happened to be inside the cordon."

"You're definitely sure about the time? You didn't perhaps go there before two o'clock and were returning back here when the emergency services arrived?"

"No," Mouland sounded even more puzzled. "What reason would I have to go there, earlier?"

Inspector Roux, ignoring the vicar's question continued, "Let's go through your movements prior to being awoken. How did you spend the evening?"

"I went to a meeting, came home, talked with Caroline and went to bed at some time after midnight. That's it. Very boring I'm afraid."

"What time did you leave for the meeting?"

"About seven o'clock."

"Did you go on your own?"

"No. I went with Caroline and a friend, who gave us a lift."

"What's the friend's name?"

"Julian Devereux – he's the churchwarden."

"Right. Where was the meeting?"

"At a flat in Livesy Street – can't remember the number."

"What was the meeting about?"

"It was about rejuvenation, if you must know – I'm rather concerned about it actually." Mouland was beginning to sound irritated.

"Who else was at the meeting?"

"I don't know all their surnames. The leader's called Mary Fields though."

"The leader?"

"Yes. It was a meeting of a group called M A D which opposes rejuvenation." Mouland could not disguise the mixture of irritation and embarrassment he felt as he spelt out the letters. The two detectives exchanged glances.

163

"You mentioned to the constable, last night, that you're no longer the incumbent here – is that correct?"

"Yes. St. Nonna's now belongs to a company called 'B Stored UK Ltd.'"

"When was it sold?"

"Yesterday. At least that's when the sale was completed."

"And what about yourself? Do you have another appointment within the church?"

"Of sorts," Mouland grimaced. "I've been offered the opportunity to clear and decommission a number of other churches in the vicinity."

"You don't sound very happy with that?" The sergeant probed.

"Of course I'm not!" Mouland snapped. "Would you be?"

"Not unhappy enough to set fire to it?"

Mouland, full of disbelief, could not respond at once but his wife interjected angrily, "Don't be ridiculous! Of course he didn't! Anyway, I was with him all the evening. I can vouch for his movements."

"OK, Mrs Mouland, we'll speak to you in a minute – if you can leave your husband to answer the questions."

Caroline snorted and folded her arms aggressively, her features pinched with anger. Then Mouland gave a rueful laugh and shaking his head answered, "No, not unhappy enough to set fire to it."

"Right." The inspector turned towards Caroline. "If you can run through your movements from when you left for the meeting last night?"

Caroline obliged with a sequence of events identical to her husband's. When she reached the point at which she was awoken by the sirens Roux questioned her carefully.

"So, when you awoke, what was your husband doing?"

"He was at the end of the bed by the window."

"Was he dressed?"

"No. He was in his pyjamas but he had just started to put something on, to go outside in."

"You're sure he wasn't undressing?"

"Of course, I'm sure. He'd been in bed for almost two hours."

"He could've nipped out though, while you were asleep."

"But he didn't. I would have known. Anyway, the whole idea's quite ridiculous, as if Philip would want to damage St. Nonna's!"

164

"Are you sure it's arson?" Mouland asked.

"Not yet, but it looks that way. The fire investigators are still going through it. Can you give me a contact address for, er, Mr Devereux and Miss, or is that Mrs, Fields? We'll need to corroborate your story."

"Story!" Caroline began angrily before being interrupted by her husband who, after searching through his diary for Mary's full address, gave the police officers the required details.

"Thank you, vicar." The sergeant rose from his chair. "You've been a great help. We'll be in touch."

"Good bye, vicar and Mrs Mouland," the inspector added politely as Mouland ushered them onto the driveway.

Caroline was livid.

"What a bloody cheek!" she cried. "Of all things, accusing you, of all people, of arson! Of setting fire to St. Nonna's! They're completely mad!"

To her surprise Philip merely chuckled.

"I find the whole idea rather amusing," he conceded. "Don't worry, we both know I didn't do it so there'll be no evidence. I suppose they have to investigate every possibility. It's interesting that they think it was deliberate. But me, an arsonist!" He laughed again before being struck with another thought, "I wonder how old Julian will get on with them?" he added with a huge grin.

Inch and Roux arrived at Devereux's quaint thatched cottage which nestled incongruously amongst the much more modern buildings that lined the street to the south of St. Nonna's. The cottage was the sole remaining link with the church and almost a millennium back in time had played an insignificant role among an array of dwellings which comprised the church close. Devereux was extremely proud of his grade one two star property which had somehow managed not only to evade the World War Two bombers but also the equally destructive hand of 1960s planners. When the remaining cottages had been razed, having been condemned conveniently as insanitary and thereby providing a ready excuse to build boxes of flats and 'The Close' shopping mall, Devereux's had escaped as a result of still being in the ownership of the diocese, being in an unarguable state of good repair and remaining the residence of the St. Nonna's incumbent.

The front garden, immaculately manicured, boasted beds of

roses of a range of varieties which Devereux obsessively tended, clipping their thorny fingers and lavishing them with affection. The gravel driveway swung round to the side of 'Priory Cottage' to reveal a large countryside garden filled to the seams with old fashioned flowers and shrubs. Inch and Roux were directed by Felicity to Devereux's shed at the far end.

"Quite a jungle, isn't it, sir?" Inch commented as he brushed past a clump of damp protruding hollyhock spikes.

"Yes," Roux replied, "I imagine it must be quite a picture in the summer."

The two men followed the narrow, winding pergola until they reached the shed at the bottom of the garden. The door was partially open and the electric light inside revealed Devereux bending over something in the corner, hard at work.

Roux tapped politely at the door, "Mr Devereux?" he enquired.

"Err. What?" Devereux responded with unintended rudeness, still being engrossed in his task and failing to be drawn from it.

"Your wife said we'd find you here," Roux continued. "We're from the local police station. I'm Inspector Roux and this is Sergeant Inch." Both men waved their warrant cards ineffectively at Devereux who at last looked up, withdrew his attention from his labours and, wiping his blackened palms on a soiled piece of cloth, took the few, short strides to the shed's entrance.

"Good morning officers," he replied whilst quickly scooping back an errant, thick strand of hair to its rightful place at the side of his strictly demarcated parting. "You've come about the fire, I suppose?"

The inspector and the sergeant replied simultaneously. Inch started to say "Yes" but conceded at once to his superior, who commented:

"That's a magnificent looking bird you've got there." Devereux stared guiltily at the brass eagle which, having been removed from its plinth, rested grandly and superciliously on the workbench.

"Oh, yes it is," he agreed cautiously. "Actually, I was just giving it a bit of attention. There's a stubborn black patch under one wing which won't shine up properly. I found a recipe for a special paste you can mix up, on the internet, and I was just having a go with that."

"Hmm. Right, back to business!" Roux declared brusquely, his interest in the object having evaporated. "You're correct, we are here concerning the fire down the street at St. Nonna's. Can you start at the beginning and run through the events of last night, please?"

Devereux obliged, beginning with when he was awoken and relating his version of the drama. He was purposefully vague regarding his vantage point and hoped the detectives would assume that he had merely taken his place with the crowd of onlookers. Subsequently he made no mention of squeezing through the hedge, breaching the cordon and being sent back by a police officer.

"Tell us about your movements earlier in the evening," Inch demanded to Devereux's surprise.

"Earlier?" he repeated, failing to see the relevance. "I went to a meeting with the vicar and his wife."

"Would that be a meeting of a group called MAD?" Inch continued.

"Well, yes," Devereux repeated whilst shaking his head, briefly.

"Can you confirm the time you left for the meeting and the time you returned?"

Devereux complied.

"Can anyone corroborate these movements?" Inch continued with undue aggression.

"Philip and Caroline, of course – and the other members."

"What about your wife? Was she still up when you got in?"

"No."

Roux took over. "So after you dropped off the vicar and his wife, you returned straight home and went to bed?"

"Yes."

"Did you see anyone during that time?"

"No!" Devereux began to sound exasperated. "Well, I saw a man on the other side of the street, taking his dog for a walk, but no one to talk to."

"And you definitely didn't pay St. Nonna's a visit at any time during the evening, either before or after the meeting?"

"Of course not! Why would I? The church was taken into 'B Stored UK's' ownership yesterday. I have no further role to play there."

"Quite," Roux replied.

"Doesn't that upset you, sir?" Inch enquired. "I mean, churchwarden is a very responsible post – isn't it? – and suddenly there's no more use for you and the building you've cared for and, may I say, become attached to, is no longer your responsibility. In fact, it's become a 'no go area'. And what's worse, it now belongs to a company actively involved with rejuvenation – something you oppose strongly."

"Of course I was upset!" Devereux retorted with anger. "Everyone was, but to counter your insinuations I can confirm quite definitely that I did not sneak back to St. Nonna's at any time last evening and I certainly did not use the 'window of opportunity' that you have so cleverly identified to go and set fire to it! There must be hundreds of people who had the opportunity at any time during the evening to do so, but it was definitely not me!"

Inspector Roux closed his notebook indicating that the interview was coming to an end: "Thank you, sir. Oh, what about your wife? Did she go over to the church too?"

"No. She slept right through it – always does. Sleeps like a log, you know. And I was in such a rush I didn't think to wake her."

"We may need to contact you again, depending on the outcome of our enquiries. We'll just catch up with your wife on the way out," Inch continued.

Devereux failed to reply but fixed a thoughtful gaze on the two policemen's backs until they disappeared near the entrance of the cottage.

Roux and Inch spoke briefly with Mrs Devereux, who confirmed that she knew nothing of the happenings of the previous evening, before they wandered across to the decayed priory.

"Interesting that the two men most likely to feel aggrieved by the sale of the church were both found inside the cordon, last night," Roux observed, drily.

"Both of them?" Inch responded in surprise. "It was only the vicar, wasn't it?"

"Only the vicar owned up to it but Mr Devereux was there too."

"Was he really. How do you know?"

"I saw him. Just as we arrived. Of course, I didn't know who he was then. I saw one of our officers direct him away from the building. Afterwards I asked the constable if he'd taken his name but he hadn't. I recognised him straight away this morning."

"So it's likely he's got something to hide. The thing is, if he's just started the fire why would he still be that close, still in the vicinity? Surely he would have had plenty of time to leave the scene, go home and even try to create an alibi?"

Roux gave Inch a sympathetic look. "You still have a lot to learn about psychology, Inch," he replied. "Time after time, perpetrators of crimes like this, and often worse, can't just do the deed and go home, they need to bask in the consequences of their crime. They like to witness the drama, the panic, the arrival of us and the other emergency services, etc. Either of them could have started the fire earlier and gone back to see how things were progressing."

"True," Inch admitted, "but in this case, neither of them are serial arsonists are they? Presumably this is a one-off. They'd say they were driven to it by extreme circumstances or something. Besides, we don't know if it was arson, yet."

"In answer to that, I'll bet my pension that it was arson and people who are 'driven' to committing a criminal act, as you say, are often the most dangerous, the most extreme and the most reckless. Devereux appears to be an obsessive type – look at that eagle, for example, and the vicar by his very nature and chosen occupation must hold deep convictions, especially as he's still clinging to them. Both of them are desperate men."

"The connection with that MAD group's interesting though, isn't it, sir, considering they've just come to light with the Whittleburgh case."

"Yes. It's amazing how often that happens, isn't it? Someone, or something, comes to our attention out of the blue and all of a sudden we find that they, or it, seem to have tentacles reaching everywhere. The name starts turning up over and over again like a bad penny."

Roux and Inch ambled their way through the Victorian lychgate and along the path through the churchyard to the charred remains of the chancel. The fire-fighters had performed well and apart from the dead chancel, little damage, except for the incursion of smoke, had been done to the remainder of the building. The north and south aisles, the west tower and even the vestry remained intact. The chancel was a different matter,

h

however, blackened, wet, full of rubble and with its roof open to the now blue sky, it invoked a peculiar absence of hope akin to that felt the day after a funeral. Even Roux and Inch, both keen adherents to rejuvenation, felt it.

Roux approached a young member of the fire investigation team who was delicately scraping a deposit from a charred stone block into a sample pot.

"Bob around?" he enquired.

The young woman stared at him blankly before replying cautiously, "Yes, I think he is somewhere. Who can I say is looking for him?"

"It's OK. I'm Inspector Roux. I'm leading the investigation. We haven't met before, have we? Are you new to the team?"

"Yes. It's my first post. Do you mind if I see your warrant cards?" she asked, mindful of official procedure and determined not to make a mistake at such a crucial stage in her career.

"Not at all." Roux smiled to himself, reached for his identification, and with a minute nod indicated to Inch that he should do the same.

"Mr Blacktop's outside, with the structural engineers – round there." She pointed helpfully.

"Thanks," Inch replied pleasantly, unable to prevent himself from desiring to make a particularly friendly impression on the woman.

The two detectives followed her directions and moments later spotted Bob Blacktop parting company with a man dressed in a suit, fluorescent jacket, wellington boots and a hard hat. As he turned to re-enter the building he noticed Inspector Roux and cried out warmly, "Christian! I'd guessed I would run into you sooner or later. I knew they'd set their best man on the case. Morning, Inch."

"So what can you tell me, Bob?" Roux asked at once.

"Nothing's official yet," Bob warned. "But it's got to be deliberate. We've found traces of petrol and are pretty certain the fire started over there, at the foot of what would have been some type of timber construction. Something like a screen perhaps. Come and look."

"That would be the reredos," Roux explained to a blank Inch.

"Oh, I forgot," continued Bob cheerfully. "You would know all the technical terms coming from a religious background."

"Lapsed religious," Roux countered with mock sternness. "I gave it all up a long time ago but holidays with my ordained uncle, as a boy, did give me a useful education in the finer points of ecclesiastical architecture!"

Inch gazed at his superior in surprise and grudging admiration. He seemed to know something about everything. Inch felt ignorant in comparison and resolved to study the list of adult education courses, which fell through his letterbox on a regular basis, in the hope of finding something which would improve his self perceived low level of education.

"Just here!" Bob crouched down and indicated a seemingly insignificant spot at ground level, behind where the altar had once been. "All the signs are that the combustion started here and the ignition was petrol."

"Hmm." Roux looked thoughtful. "How about accidental ignition – a carelessly discarded cigarette, for example?"

Mr Blacktop shrugged his shoulders. "As I said, nothing's official yet. There are all sorts of possibilities, we've got to complete our investigation, but between you and me – it was deliberate. I've seen too many of them and after a while you get a feeling, or maybe it's a smell – I don't know." He jerked his hand in the direction of the young woman who was still carefully engrossed in her task. "When young Lucy's been doing this job as long as I have, she'll know what I mean." Then he continued in a brisk, more businesslike tone, "But in the meantime we must go through the investigation process to the letter and, if possible, come up with some hard evidence."

"Thanks Bob," Roux replied, tapping his arm. "You've given me a head start." The inspector knew that although Bob already believed that an arsonist was at work he would not allow this conviction to cloud or compromise the investigation. If the accumulated evidence eventually pointed towards an accident Bob would not hesitate to admit that his initial 'gut reaction' had been wrong.

"Mouland and Devereux are definitely 'in the frame', as you say, but perhaps not exclusively – who else had access to the building?"

"The new owners, I suppose. Perhaps an estate agent? Do you think the vicar, and or that churchwarden, kept a key back – unofficially?"

"It's a possibility and not unlikely. It would have torn people like that apart to have this place taken away from them. I wonder if anyone from 'B Stored' is on site?"

The structural engineer roamed into view.

"Let's have a quick word with him," Roux declared, whilst hurrying away. Inch followed a few paces behind. Roux went through the monotonously rehearsed introductions before asking, "Can you tell me what the verdict is on the damage? Are they going to lose the building, do you think?"

"No." The engineer sounded pleasantly surprised. "It's amazing how the fire seems to have been contained. No serious structural damage has been done to the building, despite the chancel roof coming down. If there had been, you and I wouldn't be standing here now! They'll be able to rebuild it – if they want to."

"Thanks."

Roux and Inch wandered into the churchyard.

"Right, sergeant, what have we got?"

"Probable arson and two likely suspects, sir."

"The evidence, so far, is only circumstantial. There's nothing to connect either to the crime and they both have alibis of sorts."

"I suppose we need to know what time the fire actually started. If it was when they were at that MAD meeting it puts them both in the clear."

"Correct, Inch. Let's forget about Reverend Mouland and Mr Devereux, for a moment. Who else might have had an interest in the place burning down?"

"The new owners perhaps – for the insurance?"

"Well done! You can look into that when we get back to the station. I wonder if the MAD group knew about the storage proposals. Presumably they're a bunch of fanatics who wouldn't take kindly to 'B Stored's' expansion, whether it was into a church or any other building. It's going to be interesting talking to Mary Fields."

"I suppose there's another angle, sir," Inch said thoughtfully. "What if a pro-rejuvenation fanatic attacked the building not knowing it had changed hands? There seems to be a growing minority of people who are very anti churches and religion nowadays. I can't see why, religion's no threat, rejuvenation's not going to go away just because a few people, who can't move into

172

the twenty-first century, don't like it. Some people seem to get very upset because there are still a few churches around – even if they're empty."

"True. That's certainly another possibility, although if that's the case, I've a feeling we'll never know. No witnesses or anything. We need to talk to 'B Stored', find out who was here yesterday. They might even have started alteration works."

The detectives' deliberations were rudely and abruptly interrupted by the arrival of the large, shiny black four by four vehicle which had been parked on the graves yesterday. After stopping briefly at the taped off entrance and exchanging a few words with a constable, the driver revved the engine impatiently and the vehicle spun into the grounds, kicking up dirt and gravel and spraying the two policemen with tiny stones.

"Oi! Steady on there! What do you think you're doing?" Roux demanded, his face stinging from the assault.

The driver, a man in his late twenties, casually dressed in jeans and an open necked designer shirt, jumped from the vehicle, turned his back on the detectives and gabbled importantly into the mobile phone, clamped against his ear. Inch, trying unsuccessfully to brush specks of mud from his jacket, fought a desire to punch the man hard in the face. Roux, more experienced, and satisfyingly aware that one way or another he could have the last laugh, proceeded with calm professionalism:

"If you don't mind, sir, can I have your attention, for a moment?"

The man frowned and waved at him dismissively, indicating that his telephone conversation should not be interrupted. "No, I haven't made contact yet," he informed the unseen caller, "The police are supposed to be investigating it, but you know what they're like – more interested in persecuting innocent motorists. There's a plod guarding the entrance but that's about all. I'll get back to you."

Inch glared at Roux, greatly offended by the criticism. The inspector registered his colleague's irritation with a miniscule smile but otherwise ignored him. Inch rubbed at another speck of mud on his sleeve but only succeeded in transforming it into a long, narrow, more obvious blemish.

"Right. Now you've finished your very important discussion, can I have a word?" Roux persisted, patiently.

"Not really," the man replied, glancing around with the impression of looking for someone in particular. "Far too busy. Loads to sort out since the place went up. I suppose you're from the local rag? Well you'll have to find another story."

Inch spluttered as the man attempted to march away.

"We're from Greenborough Police Station, actually. I'm Inspector Roux and this is Sergeant Inch. As you can see, not all of us spend our time harassing motorists, but while we're on the subject a little more care taken with your driving wouldn't go amiss, would it, sir?"

The man stopped, turned round slowly, placed his right hand on his hip and stuck his left foot forward. Then sighing loudly, in exasperation and embarrassment, he raised his eyebrows and stared at the detectives as though they were at fault.

"Oh, and make sure you're not tempted to use that thing, while you're actually driving, sir," Inch added gleefully, nodding in the direction of the mobile phone.

"Right. So what have you found?" The man attempted to turn from defence to attack.

"Can you tell me who you are and what interest you have in St. Nonna's?" Roux continued, ignoring the man's question.

"I'm Adam St. John-Beauclerc, MD of 'B Stored UK Ltd'."

"Pleased to meet you," Roux stuck out his hand. "I was hoping to find someone from the firm here."

St. John-Beauclerc gave the proffered palm a glancing, disdainful pat. "So have you any news?" he demanded.

Inch, noticing that his head trembled in agitation, suddenly had a vision of a coconut shy.

"Presumably it was arson, I suppose? Bloody lunatics."

"We don't know for sure yet, sir. But it remains a strong possibility," Roux replied before asking, "Were you here yesterday?"

"Yes. As soon as the sale was completed I came here with a colleague and a builder to discuss the conversion."

"What time did you leave?"

"About four o'clock, I think."

"Everyone at the same time?"

"Yes."

"Did the builder start any work while he was here?"

St. John-Beauclerc looked incredulous. "Do you really think

174

so? Of course not! It's nothing short of a miracle to get a builder to even turn up and look at a job, let alone start work!"

"OK, sir," Inch took over, "so the building was empty and secure when you left and everything was switched off, etc?"

"Yes. As far as I know. I didn't go round checking every socket or switch but nothing appeared to be on. Can I get on now? I'd like a word with the fire investigation team."

After giving some contact details, St. John-Beauclerc was allowed to resume his very important, busy life.

"I think it's time we took a few precautions," Roux decided, aloud. "Forensics had better pick up the clothes both Devereux and Mouland were wearing yesterday and test for an accelerant – just in case. They both had windows of opportunity, with very weak alibis. I think Mouland's wife would back him to the hilt but I'm not so sure about Mrs Devereux."

"No. She's more feisty. At least, that's what you'd say if she was younger. Battleaxe is probably the word to use."

"Don't you think that's a little unfair, Inch?" the older man suggested.

"What? No," Inch replied at first, before realisation of his prejudice struck and he back-tracked with genuine regret. "Actually, you're right sir. It is unfair to call her that just because of her age. I hadn't thought of it like that before."

Roux studied his watch. "I think it would be a good time to visit Mary Fields. See what she has to say and find out a bit more about this MAD group."

The two men shortly arrived at Livesy Street and disturbed Mary who was investigating Helen via the internet. At first she ignored the doorbell but eventually curiosity won, abetted by the fact that she had not had a visitor for several years, and she responded to their persistent ringing. Roux made the introductions and asked if they might be invited in. Mary hesitated momentarily, until she realised that she would be the centre of their attention for at least a short while, so she led them into the squalid living room. Inch, breathing shallowly, perched the seat of his designer suit on the very edge of the shiny sofa. Roux, whose suit and psyche were made of sterner stuff, relaxed back into the voluptuous folds of the lumpy armchair.

"I hear you run a society called M A D," he began, spelling out the letters. "Could you tell us a little about it please?"

"I could, if I wanted to. There's nothing illegal about it though.

175

I have every right to run whatever type of society I choose," Mary retorted aggressively.

"Quite, quite. I didn't make myself clear," Roux apologised soothingly. "It's just some background information we're after and a list of members. We're investigating a fire at St. Nonna's which broke out yesterday evening, we have no concerns regarding MAD's activities."

"St. Nonna's," Mary murmured. "That's Reverend Mouland's church – or was. He told us it had just been sold."

Inch threw Roux a glance, who did not respond but continued to question Mary, "Yes, in fact the reverend was apparently here last night, at a meeting. Is that correct?"

"Yes," Mary replied simply.

"Can you confirm the time he arrived and departed and who he was with?"

"As far as I know he came with his wife and a man called Julian Devereux – some kind of friend. They were here at the start of the meeting and left when it finished. I can't give you the exact times as I was preoccupied."

"Who else attended?" Inch asked. "Was it all your members?"

"Yes. Well except perhaps one – we are not sure whether he is still with us."

"Who would that be?"

"Joe Whittleburgh."

"How come the reverend told you about St. Nonna's?"

"He seemed emotional. Very up and down. It was the final straw I think, which prompted him to join us."

"What did the other group members think? Were they equally outraged?"

"No. Although we abhor the rise of rejuvenation and welcome support from all quarters, we have no interest in saving buildings or any particular religion."

"What about Mr Devereux? What did he seem like?"

"Depressed and lacking in commitment. It was as though he didn't really want to be here."

"And Caroline Mouland?"

"Supportive of her husband. Trying to jolly him along."

"What did you do after the meeting?" Inch enquired. "Did you go anywhere?" Mary's eyes narrowed and her cold stare sent an eerie shiver through the young sergeant.

"I remained here in a state of meditation for several hours then I went to bed."

"I don't suppose anyone can verify that?"

"No."

"Could you sort out a list of names and addresses of members please?" Roux requested pleasantly. "And while we're here, can you tell me what sort of chap Joe Whittleburgh is, in your opinion?"

Mary opened the leaf of the rickety bureau and took out a notebook. "Perhaps the sergeant would like to copy from this?" she offered before continuing, "Joe Whittleburgh has been an ineffective member of MAD for many years – since its inception. His attendance at meetings and other occasions has been tardy and sporadic. His input consists of criticism and failure to complete the tasks he has been assigned and he has unrealistic leadership ambitions. Is there anything else you wish to know?"

"Why do you keep him?" Inch asked incredulously. Mary did not respond. Her interest in the two men had vanished and she began to resent their incursion into her world. Roux sensed that she was shutting down and stood up, indicating that the interview was at an end.

"Thank you very much Ms. Fields. You've been most helpful."

Mary merely gritted her teeth, unable to bear the close proximity with authority any further.

Inch sprang from the edge of the settee and striding ahead of his superior, made for the front door. As soon as he was outside, he stood gasping in large lung fulls of fresh air. Roux joined him. "Don't be so precious, Inch," he declared. "It wasn't that bad in there – Whittleburgh's place was much worse."

"I feel dirty," Inch complained. "I'll need a good shower and now I'll definitely have to get this suit cleaned again."

Roux tutted and shaking his head unsympathetically unlocked the car.

"Did you see the computer screen, sir?" Inch asked, indicating the return of his professionalism, as he took his place in the front passenger seat.

"No – what about it?" Roux replied.

"It was only on for a few seconds when we walked in and then it went blank, but it looked like she was Googling Helen

Deighton – you know, the professor's daughter. Why would she be doing that?"

"I've no idea. Perhaps we should do a bit of digging concerning MAD? See if they've been involved in anything."

"We can start by going through the list."

Roux and Inch spent the next few days tracking down each MAD member and interviewing them. The results were unenlightening. Everyone confirmed the time of the meeting and the names of the attendees and they could all account for their movements later in the evening.

"They're just a bunch of harmless loonies," Inch finally declared with disrespect. "They've never done anything good or bad and their membership is miniscule. We're wasting our time with them. I'd put my money on the vicar or the churchwarden – it's a sign of how desperate they are that they've joined MAD. It's not going to get them anywhere!"

"You're probably right," Roux agreed, "but we must leave no stone unturned – it's quite acceptable to spend time investigating and either drawing a blank or eliminating the suspect – basic police-work, Inch."

Roux's comment annoyed the sergeant, of course he knew it was basic police-work – sometimes he thought Roux treated him like a probationer. What had Roux brought to the case? Nothing.

Later that day Roux received a telephone call from Bob Blacktop. "Hi there, Christian," he began, "the results are through and I'm about to finalise my report but I thought I'd let you know first. It was definitely arson."

"As you thought," Roux replied. "Any idea what time it started?"

"Yes. Interestingly enough, it was much earlier than I would have guessed. The fire took a long time to take hold. I would say between 5pm and 7pm."

"Really? That eliminates several suspects. Thanks Bob."

Roux gave Inch the news.

"That only leaves Mouland and Devereux then, and there's absolutely no evidence against either of them."

The sergeant, who had been hoping for a result, replied morosely, "In that case we must assume that it was neither of them."

"Put it down to kids, I suppose. Found out the church was empty and got in there."

"Or someone completely random. There's obviously a percentage of people with arson tendencies about and there always has to be a first time. Unfortunately we'll have to add it to the ever growing list of unsolved crimes."

Inch was surprised at his superior's candid assessment, being more used to crime figures being carefully massaged and dressed in fantastic optimism, but secretly he agreed with his colleague.

Chapter Fifteen

Helen had left MAD's meeting nursing a bundle of emotions. In some ways she was angry at having allowed herself to have been cajoled into membership, but at the same time she felt relieved the decision had been made and the deed had been done. She wondered what Freddie's thoughts were.

Now that she had a task, Helen was prepared to devote a huge amount of energy to it and so she embarked at once on the publicity campaign. To her annoyance, she recognised a desire to please Mary. 'No! I'm doing it for myself. It's something I believe is right.' She told herself, sternly. Nonetheless, it would be nice to avoid Mary's cold stare and cutting criticism if at all possible. Helen had a knack of making things happen and her efforts made her aware precisely how powerful an unlimited budget could be, and within a very short time, MAD's message, promoted by Helen's very generous funding, slipped into a prominent slot on the radio just after an advertisement for 'B Stored UK Ltd'. She also arranged for several full page notices to be placed in the local newspaper.

Freddie too, was busy with his assignment and had surreptitiously been constructing a number of placards, away from Ada's prying eyes, in his garden shed. His wife, however, immediately detected the change in his routine.

"You've been spending a lot of time in the shed, lately. What are you up to?" she asked, on only the second day of his activities, as she stood at the back door, peering at the locked shed.

"Oh, nothing you need to concern yourself with," Freddie replied, before adding wildly, "It's a surprise." Then, wracked with guilt, he determined to reframe an old print Ada had much admired and picked up at a jumble sale several months ago. Despite his enthusiastic promise to undertake the restoration work, it had lain in the shed, gathering grease and dust since then. So, in between making placards, he began the careful restoration of the frame, having found himself unable to discard the battered but skilfully worked antique relic.

Helen had had little contact with her father in recent months, apart from the odd rushed telephone call. He was exceptionally busy, he explained unnecessarily, being required, not only to oversee rejuvenation training and undertake the procedure himself on occasions, but also constantly travelling the globe to lecture as a guest of honour, where he was fêted as a king. For once he had a spare date and Helen met him for lunch. After cataloguing his list of engagements, her father finally thought about enquiring after her own activities:

"Have you done anything of note, lately?" he enquired, half-heartedly, sub-consciously aware that nothing could match his endeavours.

"No. Not that I can think of," she replied feebly.

"A lady of leisure, eh?" Her father patted her knee patronisingly. "That's fine by me. You don't have to do anything – after all, I've done it all!"

Helen noticed a discomforting gleam in his eyes, which reminded her, in a way, of Mary.

"Don't you think you've done enough?" she stabbed the question unexpectedly at him.

"In some ways, yes. I've done more than enough for mankind. More than anyone before me and probably more than anyone ever will after. Don't worry, I won't overdo it, but it's given me immense satisfaction and given me great purpose in life."

"What about the implications though? Do they never concern you?"

"Implications? I can cope with those. Fame and riches beyond human imagination – no problem there." Then he stopped suddenly, leant forward and smiled with realisation. "If you want more money, you can have it," he declared, missing Helen's point entirely. "Anything's just a drop in the ocean to me. Sometimes I can hardly believe how well it's all worked out – a place in history – not only have I changed the world but I've changed the very nature of mankind and its entire future!" Helen noticed the far away look in his eyes again.

"As for money," he continued with a dismissive chuckle, "I've so much of it, I can barely keep track. Do you know what, I've set myself a little task, a little challenge – just out of interest (no pun intended) – I'm going to see by how much I can make it grow. A little dabble here and there – purely for my own amusement. In fact, I've invested in a company called 'B Stored UK Ltd'. You may have heard of them, they've recently launched a huge advertising campaign – funded by my investment I suppose!" The professor laughed again.

Helen recognised the name, of course, and also remembered her interview with Roux and Inch, following the fire at St. Nonna's.

"Why did you choose that company?" she asked. "Surely you could have found something more useful, I mean more generally beneficial. . ."

Her father interrupted her, "How can anything be more beneficial than storage for those awaiting the process! You do make me laugh sometimes, Helen!"

"Surely there must be other ways to help humanity," Helen continued. "Your process will cause huge energy and food problems in the future – why don't you use some of your wealth investigating solutions to those?"

Professor Deighton, never able to accept the slightest criticism and having become used to being the focus of fawning admiration, gritted his teeth and almost snarled, "You're not going to raise that old chestnut again, are you? Why can't you appreciate my achievement? Why does it have to be you who feels free to criticise when it should be you who is my greatest supporter? I should have thought it not too much to ask from my own flesh and blood!"

"That's exactly why!" Helen retorted. "I'm probably the only person who's not too much in awe of you to raise objections. All the other hangers-on just want your approval and a bit of deflected glory. They wouldn't dream of saying that something might be wrong."

"But you would!" Deighton snapped, as he stood up and indicated to the waiter that he was ready to settle the bill. "You are prepared to criticise – no, let me rephrase that – you delight in criticising me, yet you are happy to live off the proceeds of my achievement. Perhaps you should question your own moral stand in that case. I'm extremely disappointed in you." He looked at her in disgust, as though she was unworthy of him. The diners in the cubicle opposite, momentarily stopped eating and listened to the argument in silence. Deighton marched away leaving Helen seething.

She was more distressed by his personal attack than by his refusal to entertain even a modicum of objection to his achievements. 'How can he not know me at all, after all these years?' she thought angrily. 'How can he think my sole motivation is money? I've never been like that. He's judging me by his own standards.' Although they had never been particularly close, Helen now felt a stranger to him. Somehow it would not have been so upsetting if her father had merely been ignorant of the facets of her character, but to misjudge her so badly and unfairly sparked a desire for some kind of redress. Helen became entrenched in her opposition to rejuvenation or 'the awakening process' as he now preferred to call it. She would continue to take his money, if still offered, and use it against him.

Deighton stormed out the restaurant equally angry. His blinkered mind completely incapable of comprehending Helen's call for caution. At exactly the same moment that the switch flicked and hardened her resolve, her father decided to set her a test. 'I'll continue the payments into her account,' he thought grimly, 'in fact, I'll increase them. Let's see how easy it is for her to either accept it or maintain her, apparently rigid, principles and objections. I think I'll find that wealth will have the upper hand.' Then with a brief, nasty chuckle, he slid into the waiting car and forgot about his daughter; his next engagement, with people who appreciated him, far more important, filled his thoughts.

Helen threw herself into the planning and organisation of the rally with a level of commitment which surprised and invigorated the other MAD members, but which left Mary disturbed and puzzled. She could not fathom Helen's motives but was unable to extinguish a lingering feeling that somehow she would manifest a threat, either to the group or to Mary personally. Mary could not deny that Helen had fulfilled her promise and had funded and organised a comprehensive advertising campaign. Whilst the other members offered their thanks, Mary feared a twist in the tale, a future betrayal or undercover assault. She planned to allow Helen a little more time, enough so that MAD could extract all that was useful from her, and then she would launch her attack. Mary would confront her and reveal that she was aware of her true identity. The other, gullible, MAD members would not be so welcoming and appreciative then!

MAD's preparations were interrupted by Joe's trial, which naturally proved to be of great interest to his former associates. Ricky was to appear as a witness for the prosecution, as was Mary, to her glee, as a character witness. The case had taken a dramatic turn following the death of Mrs Whittleburgh a short while after she had been taken to hospital. Joe was facing a murder charge following his failure to act and ensure the care of his mother. The case attracted little public interest. Violent crimes went undetected and unpunished every day as far as the general public were concerned. What was significant about an old woman dying? She could be rejuvenated, couldn't she? Consequently, the public gallery was empty, apart from Howard, Rose and Sonja who was particularly nervous and afraid she would unwittingly commit contempt of court and find herself too, before the judge.

Joe was brought in, dressed uncharacteristically in a smart suit and tie, but red-faced and sweating profusely. His tiny eyes, almost invisible in the depths of his bloated face, squinted at first at the jury, then the public gallery where, resting them on the MAD members, he wondered whether they were there to support him or to witness his downfall. 'Probably delighted to see me put away.' he thought angrily. 'None of them bothered to visit me, to see how I was – yet apparently Rose found time to visit mother. They don't realise how pathetic they are!' After this internal outburst he turned his attention to the prosecuting barrister and gave him a venomous glare. 'It was alright for him – he must have plenty of money. Probably always had – he wouldn't know what it was like to have to work hard and struggle. They were all against him!'

The judge took his seat and the well-practised judicial

proceedings slid into action. Joe was charged with murder as a result of the duty of care towards, and special relationship with his mother. The prosecution outlined his failings and accused him of imprisoning and starving Mrs Whittleburgh for financial gain. Joe had pleaded not guilty. Ricky was called as the first witness for the prosecution. Being quite used to addressing an audience and communicating with all types of people in his professional life, he was undaunted and outlined succinctly the events of the evening during which he had stumbled across the dying woman.

"She was imprisoned in a small room," he explained, giving Joe a threatening look. "The door was locked, there was no light – the light bulb had purposely been removed – there was no heating. Mrs Whittleburgh was obviously very weak and malnourished. She was lying on a dirty bed and was barely able to move her head. It was a great effort for her to speak."

"Did she speak to you?" the prosecutor asked.

"Yes. She asked me to let her out. Then she said, 'He keeps me here. . . my son'."

"Are you sure those were her exact words?"

"Yes. Positive. I'll never forget them. She also said, 'he takes the bulb out'."

Joe emitted a loud snort and shook his shoulders dismissively as if to infer that Ricky was lying. Ricky's stare drilled itself from the front to the back of Joe's skull, taking with it the feeling of revulsion he felt for the accused man. Joe hunched his shoulders and swung to one side unable to face the challenge.

The paramedics were called to the witness stand and they confirmed Ricky's description of Mrs Whittleburgh's prison and also confirmed, in technical terms, her medical condition. Sergeant Inch then revealed how Joe, as primary carer had been in receipt of a carer's allowance, collected his mother's pension and how some time ago he had become a trustee with full control over her finances. As a result of this he had access to a considerable sum of money. The only item of worth which remained in his mother's name was the once well-kept house.

"Witness for the prosecution – Mary Fields," called the clerk. Howard elbowed Rose violently and Sonja felt a sense of foreboding. Mary, draped in black for the occasion, walked slowly and deliberately, in the manner of an official at a ceremonious function, her eyes fixed ahead and her back strictly perpendicular. Gorging herself on being the focus of attention, she briefly inwardly acknowledged that this was the best day of her life. Her time in the witness box was frustratingly short though.

"For how long have you known Mr Whittleburgh and in what capacity?" the prosecutor asked. Mary replied, avoiding naming MAD.

"Would you say Mr Whittleburgh is a trustworthy person?"

"No."

"Can you elaborate on that please? Why do you say he is untrustworthy?"

"He lies constantly," Mary revealed, not afraid to glare at Joe stonily, and revelling in the opportunity to destroy him. She had not forgotten his challenge. "He can never be trusted to do anything – even the simplest task. For a very short while he was our society's treasurer until some money went missing. . ."

"Objection!" called the counsel for the defence.

"Please confine yourself to the facts, Miss Fields," the judge leaned forward and warned her.

"Thank you Miss Fields," the prosecutor dismissed her abruptly, the trace of a smile about his eyes. She had performed as desired. Mary, surprised and disappointed, made her way as serenely and slowly as possible from the court room, determined to wring as much pleasure from her performance as possible. Howard suppressed a giggle. Rose gave him a knowing, warning look but remembering where she was, managed to remain silent.

Finally, Joe was called to be examined. Puffing and panting, whilst running his fat finger around the inside of his shirt collar, he lumbered towards the stand. After being allowed to confirm his personal details, he was subjected immediately to the prosecutor's attack:

"How long have you lived with your mother?"

"All my life – fifty-eight years."

Rose nodded at Howard quizzically, as if to indicate that she had thought him older. Sonja thought fifty-eight was old anyway.

"How long have you lived alone with her?"

Joe managed to beat down the impulse to blurt out 'too long' and instead explained that it had been almost eight years – since his father had died.

"Do you have any siblings?" the prosecutor continued. "Or any

186

other relatives who might take responsibility for her welfare?"

"No."

"So you assumed the care of your mother?"

"I suppose so."

"What was her health like?"

"Good – before she became ill," Joe responded enigmatically.

"What was the nature of her illness?"

"I don't know, I'm not a doctor and she refused to see one and she refused to eat." Joe glanced at the jury triumphantly believing that he had played a trump card.

"Don't you think it was your duty to call a doctor to the house, in that case. After all, a sick person may be unable to make a lucid judgement?"

"No. She was an adult and I respected her wishes. You don't know what she could be like."

The prosecutor pounced immediately on Joe's unguarded statement. "By all means Mr Whittleburgh, explain to us what she could be like."

Howard watched the defence counsel cringe and visibly deflate as Joe relished the opportunity to badmouth his mother, uninterrupted, to the large number of attentive listeners.

"She was difficult and wanted her own way – always had done. She was always telling me what to do and I didn't like it. Always saying 'get a job, get a job' and wanting me to pay rent or pay for food, or pay the electricity bill or something. She could never just leave me in peace."

"When did you last work, Mr Whittleburgh?"

"I had a very good job." Joe puffed his chest out importantly and pointed to himself. "I more or less ran Boxer & Co. – the paper wholesalers, you know, but I left when my father died. He wouldn't have let me give it up before but I'd had enough. I was the only one there any good at my job and all these incompetent youngsters just got on my nerves." He glanced again at the jury, this time suggesting that they shared a well known, but usually unspoken, secret. The members of the jury did not flicker.

"So you have been living in your mother's house for the last eight years without contributing financially to any of the costs?" the prosecutor asked.

"Objection!" called the defence counsel, desperately. "These personal details have no bearing on the case."

187

The judge peered over his glasses at the prosecutor who explained, "I wish the jury to be aware of the background of the relationship between the defendant and his mother, m'lud."

"Objection dismissed."

"At what point did you become a trustee of your mother's estate?"

"About six months ago. She wanted me to."

"Really?"

"Yes. She said she couldn't be bothered with dealing with money and wanted me to do it."

"Was this at the same time that she first became ill?"

"Yes – well, after she'd been unwell for a few weeks." Joe mopped his face with a brand new handkerchief.

"What happened after that?"

"Like I said, she wouldn't eat."

"Mr Trago is quite certain that you had deliberately removed the light bulb to keep your mother in the dark, is that correct?"

"No, no. Of course not. That's a misunderstanding. I took it out because it was broken and was going to replace it."

"How do you explain that Mr Trago found a used light bulb just outside the room which still worked perfectly?"

"I don't know," Joe replied, a note of anger slipping out. "It must be something wrong with the wiring. She would never spend anything to get things fixed – asked me to pay, yet again."

"I suggest that, as your mother confirmed to Mr Trago, you routinely removed the light bulb to purposefully keep her a prisoner in the dark."

"That's rubbish," Joe declared, raising his voice.

"Now, Mr Whittleburgh," the prosecutor continued calmly, ignoring Joe's reply, "Mr Trago also found the door to your mother's room locked. Why was that? Surely she was safe enough in her own home?"

"He's mistaken. It wasn't locked. I never locked it."

"Are you quite sure? Mr Trago has stated under oath that it was locked?"

"Of course I'm sure!" Joe snapped, a bead of sweat dribbling down the side of one cheek. "He's mistaken – or lying," he added viciously as an afterthought.

"I suggest that it is you who lies, Mr Whittleburgh. Can you confirm the ownership of the house?"

"Yes. It's, was, my mother's."

"Any mortgage outstanding or other interest in the property, for example equity release?"

"No. They paid off the mortgage years ago."

"Did your mother make a will?"

"Yes."

"Who was the beneficiary?"

"Me. As her only son, that's quite natural, isn't it?"

"So you were due to inherit the house and any capital, is that correct?"

"Yes."

"When was the will made?"

"I can't remember. A long time ago, I think."

"Let me remind you. There was indeed a will made following your father's death in which the main beneficiaries are named as a number of charities. You were to receive a sum of five thousand pounds only. About six months ago, at the same time your mother made you a trustee under her living will, she also changed her wishes regarding the distribution of her capital and property. You were named as the sole beneficiary. Have I jogged your memory?"

Joe did not reply.

"I suggest that you deliberately imprisoned your mother and when she was in a state of desperate weakness, you forced her to change her will and allow you to assume control of her affairs. Once this had been achieved you continued with your plan to bring her life to a premature close with the intention of claiming your inheritance. I recommend that the jury find you guilty!"

"That's rubbish!" Joe shouted again. "You're living in cloud cuckoo land! As if I would do that! It'd be impossible anyhow! Besides, you've no evidence!"

The prosecutor sat down, "No further questions."

Joe was escorted back to the dock.

"Call Doctor Swithin," ordered the clerk.

A stocky man in his late forties, wearing an expensive grey suit, which matched the colour of his hair, took his place in the witness box. He confirmed that he was Mrs Whittleburgh's physician.

"When did you last attend Mrs Whittleburgh?" asked the prosecuting counsel.

"16th July, last year."

"About nine months ago?"

"Yes."

"Did she come to your surgery or was it a home visit?"

"She came to the surgery."

"What was her reason?"

"She had a cough and complained of general lethargy. I was concerned that it might be the start of a chest infection so I prescribed an anti-biotic, told her to go home and rest but to come back if things did not improve."

"Generally, was she in good health?"

"Oh yes. As strong as an ox. I never saw her from one year to the next. I assumed that as she did not revisit the surgery she had made a complete recovery."

"Did she attend the surgery on her own?"

"No. She was accompanied by a friend – an elderly lady."

"Thank you, Doctor Swithin."

"Call Janet Flew," the clerk bellowed.

The usher directed a smartly dressed elderly lady to the witness stand, clutching her handbag tightly she confirmed her name and address.

"Mrs Flew, thank you for agreeing to help us today," began the prosecutor, pleasantly. "Can you please tell the jury your connection with Agnes Whittleburgh?"

"I'd known her for years. We used to go to the Women's Institute together."

"When did you last see her?"

"In the summer – in July. I took her to the doctor's because she had a nasty cough and hadn't been feeling too well. We collected her prescription and I took her home. Then I went back to visit her a few days later."

"How was she then?"

"She said she felt a bit better and thought the tablets had started to work. She was due to take one while I was there but couldn't find them. I said to let me know if she needed another lift to the doctor's."

"Was her son, Mr Joseph Whittleburgh, present?"

"Yes, he let me in then scuttled off somewhere."

"Why didn't he accompany his mother to the doctor, rather than yourself?"

190

Mrs Flew sniffed loudly. "Him? He's far too lazy. All he wants to do is sit in front of his computers all day. Agnes used to say sometimes how she worried about him and that he ought to stand on his own two feet someday. Besides, he'd never bothered to learn to drive."

"How come you didn't visit Mrs Whittleburgh again?"

"Oh, I did. Several times. At first there was no reply, then he said that his mother was sleeping and shouldn't be disturbed and the final time he said that she'd gone away. I was very surprised and asked where she'd gone. He said to be looked after by a distant relative somewhere in Devon or Dorset I think. I didn't know that she had any living relatives apart from Joe but you don't know everybody's business, do you? Anyway, I asked him for her address and he said that he'd sort it out but he never did. I called back at the bungalow two or three more times but there was never any answer. I feel terrible now," Mrs Flew's voice faltered. "If only I'd known she was in there, I could have done something but now it's too late."

Joe, avoiding her saddened expression remained hunched and motionless in the dock. 'Stupid, interfering old hag' he thought.

"Thank you Mrs Flew," the prosecutor dismissed Mrs Whittleburgh's friend. "That concludes the case for the prosecution."

The defence counsel began his difficult task, arguing that Joe had not failed in his duty of care because he was incapable of undertaking a duty of care.

"Let's be in no doubt, Mr Whittleburgh is an inadequate individual," he admitted, as Joe squirmed in a mixture of anger and embarrassment. "He has been unable to hold down a job for many years, has never left the family home and has limited social skills. A man of this level of intelligence could not be expected to provide the standard of nursing and social care that Mrs Whittleburgh, as an elderly and infirm lady, required. What we have here is an unfortunate series of events, Mrs Whittleburgh became ill and subsequently infirm and her son was incapable of looking after her. As for the suggestion that he kept her as a prisoner, manipulated her and finally withdrew sustenance from her, that is the stuff of fantasy. There is no evidence, merely conjecture. The missing light bulb, the locked door, both have perfectly reasonable explanations. With due respect, Mrs Flew is an elderly lady herself, could she not have become confused regarding the whereabouts of her friend – quite a natural response from someone under pressure and concerned? Is the amending of her will by a grateful mother, nearing the end of her days, not wholly reasonable? Remember that this took place a good six months before Mrs Whittleburgh's demise, at a time when she probably treasured the companionship of her only son and close relative. I suggest that there is nothing sinister about the change of mind. Furthermore, I would suggest that Mr Whittleburgh did his best in circumstances which were well beyond him. There was no malice or motive for personal gain behind his tragic shortcomings."

Joe could not help extending one side of his mouth into a sneer. He did not enjoy hearing himself described as inadequate and socially backward. He was better than all of them! As for Mary calling him untrustworthy, he would show her – he'd force a leadership challenge as soon as this was over. This time he would be successful and she could enjoy taking orders from him. Mrs Flew was just a wicked old witch – like his mother – and Trago was too big for his boots, showing off with his fancy clothes and expensive sports car! Joe's internal rant was brought to an abrupt halt as he was called, once again, to the witness stand,

"Just one last question, Mr Whittleburgh," the prosecutor went on. "Can you tell us where your mother is now?"

'Hell, I hope,' Joe thought, but restricted himself to saying with feigned puzzlement, "She's deceased."

"She hasn't been through the rejuvenation process?"

"No."

"She's not in storage, awaiting the procedure?"

"No."

"Can you explain why that is?"

"She didn't want it. She made it clear in her living will – she didn't agree with it and I don't either. I'm a member of MAD – Mary Field's group that opposes it and I would never sign the necessary papers."

"Quite."

"She didn't want it!" Joe almost shrieked.

"Thank you."

The prosecuting counsel summed up the case against Joe: "Ladies and gentlemen of the jury, we have before you a man who took advantage at the first opportunity; a chink in his mother's health leading to active involvement in her decline and eventual death, purely for financial gain. He took advantage of her weakened state during which time she suffered from a chest infection and exacerbated this by removing her medication. At this time he persuaded her (perhaps even using force – we'll never know) to change her will for his benefit. He then, keeping her prisoner, systematically withdrew food, water and care to the extent that caused her death. Although rejuvenation is nowadays a possibility, Mr Whittleburgh ensured that it was not an option for his mother by refusing to release funds for it or to give his consent. I suggest that when taking all the evidence into account you will be unable to reach a verdict other than guilty."

The counsel for defence briefly reiterated the view that Joe was innocent, having not purposefully withdrawn his duty of care towards his mother, and suggested that whether or not she was a candidate for rejuvenation was irrelevant. The jury retired to consider the verdict. Howard, Rose and Sonja took advantage of the recess to drink herbal tea and discuss the case.

"The jury won't take long. He's definitely guilty," Howard declared confidently.

"It certainly looks that way," Rose agreed.

"Do you really think so?" Sonja ventured. "The defence may be correct, perhaps Joe isn't capable to providing care, etc?"

"The only way in which he's incapable of providing help to anyone is due to his personality, his selfishness, rather than any sort of psychological backwardness. He knows perfectly well what he should or should not do, it's just that he only wants to benefit himself," Howard retorted.

"And then there was the money," Rose reminded her. "His motivation was to get his hands on the house and everything else, as soon as possible."

"I wonder why he wanted so much money?" Sonja asked, dreamily, unable to comprehend the pursuit of wealth purely for its own end. "It doesn't sound as if he had much to show for it."

"Some people just like to accumulate money. It gives them great satisfaction to count it, or at least calculate how much they have in the bank," Rose tried to explain.

"I've heard that he had thousands of pounds worth of electrical equipment; you know, computers, DVD players, things like that

j

– all state of the art, all in pristine condition locked away in an attic room. They only searched the place properly after Mrs Whittleburgh passed away," Howard revealed.

"How do you know that?" Rose asked in astonishment.

Howard winked and tapped one nostril secretively, "I've got my contacts." He grinned.

"I must admit that I never really clicked with him," Rose confessed. "But I thought he was just a harmless sort of buffoon – you know, full of self importance but never delivered. I'm surprised Mary let him stay in MAD for so long, especially after he stood against her in the leadership challenge."

"He was never going to win that!" Howard laughed briefly, thinking the possibility quite ridiculous. "Mary knew. She knew she could control him and that he was no threat to her and she liked to keep the numbers up, especially after Will and Carly jumped ship."

"I suppose you're right," Rose agreed, in between munching her way through a large chocolate éclair. Sonja gazed at it with envious temptation but reminded herself how bad it was nutritionally and instead attacked her little packet of raisins.

"Mary enjoyed herself, though, didn't she?" Rose added, licking a lump of cream from her forefinger. Howard laughed again.

"Yes, quite a performance – pity it was cut short. I've never actually seen anyone do a slow march quite like that!"

Rose almost laughed but instead felt a pang of guilt. 'Why are we sitting here so ready to criticise and poke fun at others?' she suddenly asked herself. The trial was not meant to be a form of entertainment and for a moment she recognised Mary as being a tragic, isolated figure. 'Just because I have a family and friends does that make me any better than her?' she wondered. She should try to be more like Sonja who always tried to find something good in people. And to be fair, where would MAD be without Mary? It was unlikely that it would exist at all. It was Mary who had given them a chance to actively oppose rejuvenation etc. She should be grateful for that. Then Rose's eye caught Sonja nibbling at her raisins and she felt ashamed. She had even, in her sub-conscience, considered the younger woman to be naïve and weak, now she was not so sure. Sonja was probably a better, stronger person than herself.

Howard interrupted her musings by announcing that he intended to 'stretch his legs' before the jury was due to be recalled. Rose quickly reverted back to her usual self, slightly embarrassed by her sudden, secret guilt, and threw herself into compiling her weekly shopping list. Sonja, examining her watch and doing a quick mental calculation decided to use the time visiting a nearby health food shop. An hour later, the trio were seated expectantly in the public gallery again. The court was ordered to stand and the judge took his place. Sonja was immediately overcome with a strong sense of history which permeated the atmosphere like a physical presence. She felt as though she was floating in space and time as the rituals which had survived centuries of use were played out and strengthened once again. 'How many times have these words and motions been repeated before and in the exact tone?' she wondered. Time had imbued them with respect in a way similar to the pervading sense of spirituality which used to be present in St. Nonna's. For the briefest of moments she understood the nature of time, history and humanity but then it was gone and however much she tried she could not claw it back. Instead, she felt the harsh reality of the present and listened as the foreman of the jury was asked whether they had been able to reach a verdict.

"Yes," the woman replied, loudly in an attempt to cover her nervousness.

"Do you find the defendant Joseph Whittleburgh guilty or not guilty of the murder of Agnes Whittleburgh?"

"Guilty."

An eerie yelp momentarily froze the courtroom. Joe was on his feet in the dock and pointing at the public gallery, he shrieked, "It was them! All of them from MAD! They made me do it! They made me get the money – for them! It wasn't me! They made me do it!"

Two security guards dragged him away as the judge called for an adjournment prior to sentencing. Howard, Rose and Sonja were all in a state of shock. "What on earth did he mean?" asked Rose nervously. " 'We made him do it!' I've never heard so much nonsense in all my life – and don't forget I've got three teenagers."

"Do you think they'll believe him and re-open the case?" asked Sonja, dreading the prospect.

"Oh, no." Howard tried to sound unconcerned and authoritative. "They'll know it's just the ravings of a madman. He didn't mention it before, did he? The defence would have latched onto it if they had thought it would strengthen their case. Anyway, it's not true is it? They couldn't prove it because it didn't happen."

"If it was true, why would Ricky have reported him and drop us all in it?" Rose added logically. "Don't worry Sonja."

"I'm going home," Howard decided. "We've heard the verdict and I expect if I scour the paper hard enough I'll find out the sentence. See you at the next meeting." With a flick of a wave he disappeared down the stairs.

"I must be off too," Rose agreed. "Are you going to wait for the sentencing?"

"Oh, no," Sonja replied, horrified at the thought of sitting there alone and possibly being the subject of Joe's vile wrath. "There's no need, I'll be going too, now."

Joe was sentenced to ten years imprisonment and an order was made to confiscate the proceeds of his mother's wealth in order that he would not benefit from his crime.

"What do you think of the sentence, sir?" Sergeant Inch asked his superior. "About right?"

"No. Not really," Inspector Roux replied. "He'll serve less than half of that and I was hoping they'd make an example of him. For once, we've got a result and a definite motive rather than yet another completely mindless crime of the sort which seems to be swamping us at the moment. It's more than satisfying to see someone put away at last."

"I suppose you're right, sir," Inch conceded. "If Whittleburgh hadn't already been banged up I would have put him in the frame for the arson attack on St. Nonna's, considering he was part of that weird MAD group."

"Frustrating, isn't it?"

Inch thought he detected a note of sarcasm in the older man's reply.

"Had to be one of them though, didn't it?" He continued regardless.

"Not necessarily, Inch, you mustn't let your prejudices get the better of you," Roux warned. "We couldn't find a scrap of evidence – ultimately it could have been anyone. I hate to say it but another motiveless crime – someone getting their kicks from destruction, with no point to it other than that – a kind of fleeting, warped satisfaction."

Chapter Sixteen

Devereux awoke early on the day of the demonstration and observed the clear, fresh, morning, from his bedroom window, with a sense of foreboding. He was far more used to enforcing authority than playing the inferior role of a minority protester. He wondered at the outcome and whether the gathering would attract any attention at all. The police authority had displayed disappointing disinterest when Sonja had provided the requisite seven days' notice and had merely replied with the shortest note of assent dependant on no conditions, regarding location, numbers present or the length of time involved. The authorities obviously did not expect 'serious disruption to the life of the community'. 'At least it's a nice day,' Devereux thought, not entirely without bitterness, as he wrenched the curtains apart. His wife groaned, invisible under the bedcovers.

It was Mouland's turn to drive, so at ten o'clock precisely, Devereux, feeling rather foolish and attempting to carry his placard so that the slogan on it could not be seen, hurried the short distance towards the vicarage. 'I should have put a sack over it,' he reprimanded himself sharply, before deciding to take the short cut across the grounds of St. Nonna's. Philip was waiting eagerly.

"At last we're doing something," the vicar enthused before continuing dreamily, "It takes me back to my student days – always protesting about something or another, then. Disillusionment follows, of course, some would call it increased awareness and a certain loss of naïvety – I never thought I'd be demonstrating on the streets again at my age. It just goes to show how unpredictable life can be."

Devereux slid his placard into the boot with the others.

"What did you decide on, in the end?" asked Philip.

"Err 'Give Peace a Chance'," Julian replied uncomfortably, hoping that the double entendre would be obvious to all.

"Oh, I see – that's rather good," Philip mused. "Ours aren't anything like as clever as that. I've got 'Salvation not Rejuvenation' and Caroline's says, 'Wake up to Life'."

"I hope our esteemed leader doesn't object," observed Devereux, dryly.

"Why on earth should she?" Mouland was astonished.

"She might object to the overtly religious tone," Devereux explained patiently. "And, after all, MAD's raison d'etre is not a religious one."

"Well I don't care." Philip shrugged off the suggestion physically by swaying the top half of his body from side to side. "Mary knows quite well 'where we're coming from', as people like to say. She knows that our faith underpins our motivation – the other members can wave more secular signs if they wish. Where's Caroline got to? Oh, here she is."

Caroline appeared at the front door, flustered and carrying a handbag and a large hessian shopping bag.

"Hello Julian," she called distractedly as she fumbled to lock the door.

"What on earth have you got there?" her husband enquired, looking inquisitively at the bulging bag.

"Just some food. I've made some sandwiches and brought a couple of flasks of tea and coffee. I thought we might feel hungry after standing around for a long time. There's plenty for you too, Julian."

"Err, thanks."

"Caroline, it's only up the road, for God's sake! We're hardly likely to starve."

"It's far better to be safe than sorry. Now are we all ready?"

"Yes. We've been waiting for you, actually."

"Right. I'm here now, so let's go."

Howard, Rose, Sonja and Ricky were waiting for them in a corner of the small market square, as arranged. Their placards were leant casually against a low stone wall and Howard was pouring himself a cup of coffee from a thermos flask. Caroline elbowed her husband triumphantly:

"See, I'm not the only one."

Philip failed to reply, instead he asked, "Where's Mary?"

"Goodness knows," replied Howard between sips.

"Don't worry, she'll be here – on the dot," Ricky added. "It will be another of her dramatic entrances."

Philip nodded, reminding himself that he should accept Mary's idiosyncrasies, unquestionably, as the others seemed able to do for the greater good.

"Ready for the off then?" Howard turned encouragingly to Sonja, half expecting her to decide to go home. Instead she surprised him with her reply:

"Oh, yes. I'm looking forward to some action at last. It's been fun planning it but I'm ready to make my voice heard." For a moment, something about her reminded him of Mary and he stared at her in an attempt to identify it. She smiled and the allusion faded.

"Here she is!" Rose announced, peering down the High Street. Everyone looked at the portly figure moving slowly towards them. She was dressed entirely in black and, as far as the others could see, appeared to be carrying a partly filled but bulging, black dustbin bag.

"This one's hers," Howard announced whilst prodding one of the placards with his toe, "I offered to make it for her – knowing that she's not much good at that sort of thing."

"What's the slogan?" Caroline could not help asking.

Howard twisted the handle of the sign round so that the wording faced outwards. " 'Drop Dead'," he read, unnecessarily. "It's what she wanted."

"I hope ours are alright," Caroline replied lamely.

"What have you got?" Howard asked before confirming their suitability. "They're fine – it's just to draw attention to ourselves."

Helen and Freddie arrived from the opposite direction.

"Hi – you're just in time," Ricky welcomed them motioning towards Mary's approach.

Mary joined the group and cast her eyes round quickly. "Good, everyone's here." She untwisted the top of the dustbin bag. "I've brought some things," she said and pulled out a large megaphone.

Howard whistled in surprise.

Mary stopped for a moment, still bent over the bag, and stared at him. "We'll need to attract their attention in some way. It's no good standing here in silence drinking coffee – we've got to make a noise. I've brought some whistles as well. . ." She fished deeper into the bottom of the bag and produced a handful of them. "But I don't know if you'll be able to use them because I want you to wear these."

To Devereux's, Ricky's and Caroline's horror, in particular, she pulled out a large, rubber mask of the variety which covers the wearer's full head.

"I've obtained three designs," she continued aware of, but deliberately ignoring, the atmosphere of horror which had enveloped the party. "One skull, one corpse-like and one Frankenstein's monster – you'll have to fight over them. I think I'll wear a skull."

"You are joking," Devereux announced, leaving no doubt that he was making a statement rather than posing a question.

Mary stared at him through cold, half closed eyes for a full five seconds before snapping, "You're either in or out. Do this whole-heartedly or get lost!"

Devereux, unused to being challenged in this way, struck his placard hard down onto the top of the small wall, splitting its face and prepared to storm off.

"Wait a minute, wait a minute!" Freddie intervened as peace maker before Rose got the chance. "I think Mary's right – we've got to draw attention to ourselves, but perhaps some of us could wear masks and the others have whistles. It'll be very difficult to blow a whistle and march with one of those on. I'd willingly wear a mask but my breathing's not so good so I'd rather have a go with a whistle. Who else will wear a mask?"

Julian, Caroline, Philip and Ricky remained silent.

"I would, really," ventured Rose, "but I'd get too hot and bothered – perhaps the younger ones. . ." She tailed off hopefully.

"I'll wear one," Sonja announced unexpectedly. "Any one of them. I don't care. If we're going to do this let's do it properly."

"Well done!" Rose nudged her encouragingly.

"And me," Helen volunteered.

"I thought I could rely on you," Mary replied sweetly, wondering whether both Helen and Sonja were more keen to hide their identities than to support the cause.

201

"Go on. I'll have one too – as long as it's the monster one – and no funny remarks!" Howard assented.

Mary pulled the various masks from the bag and the eventual wearers examined them closely in an attempt to delay having to put them on. One or two shoppers gave the group bemused stares but most hurried past, oblivious to them, wrapped tightly in their own busy worlds. An exception was a woman, probably in her late twenties, with an eight-year-old boy tugging at her sleeve.

"Go on, ask," he urged.

"How much are the masks?" the woman asked Mary.

"What?"

"How much are they?"

"What do you mean?"

"You're selling them, aren't you? After all, this is a market," the woman indicated the square. "How much are they? Kane wants one."

"They're not for sale." Mary sounded angry at first but then had an idea and softened her tone, "They're not really for sale," she repeated, "but Kane could have one for fifteen pounds."

"Fifteen pounds! You're joking. I wouldn't pay more than a couple of quid! Come on!" She pulled the disappointed child away and moved on, reiterating to him in a loud voice how outrageously expensive Mary's wares were. Kane, who allowed himself to be dragged off extremely unwillingly, turned his head and stuck his tongue out at Mary.

"Stupid brat," she muttered. "Once more my decision to remain childless has been vindicated."

Howard glanced at Ricky and was forced to bite his lower lip until it hurt while suppressing a grin which seemed uncompromisingly determined to expel itself. The others looked on in silence, except Rose who began hotly:

"Well I must say, I've never regretted having any of mine. . ." before Mouland interrupted, unexpectedly:

"What have you got left in the bag, Mary? I'd like a skull mask, if possible, please."

Caroline's mouth fell open with surprise and she stared at her husband, wide eyed. Devereux responded by giving the vicar a stern look whilst worrying that he too would be expected to relent and choose one of the awful objects.

Mary handed the vicar his requested mask which he donned at

once and thrusting his face close to his wife's emitted a loud growl.

"Really, Philip!" she responded, not knowing whether to laugh or whether to be alarmed at his enthusiasm. "People are looking." It was true. In addition to the passing shoppers who were taking a more surreptitious interest in the group, now the occupants of two hired vans which had just parked across the road were watching Philip's antics.

"Take it off for a moment," she urged. "Even those men are looking."

Philip obeyed. "What men?" he asked.

"The ones getting out of the van, over there. I don't know – football supporters or something. You're making yourself look ridiculous."

Philip glanced across to the vehicles. "Good," he retorted. "I'm glad I've attracted their attention. That's the whole idea, isn't it? We want to reach as many people as possible."

"Right everyone. It's time." Mary called them to attention. The words seemed to echo in her brain and a thrill of excitement made her shudder. "We'll form a group, initially at the entrance to the market place so people who are entering will have to walk past us and people on the pavement will have to pass next to us on the other side. If we get the chance later, we'll move into the road and march down it, which will interrupt the traffic and make them listen to us, too."

The rest of the group, with the exception of Sonja, felt a mixture of fear, excitement and foolishness. Helen thought of her father and stretched the mask in her hands. Devereux felt as he had many times before as he was about to go into action. Freddie thought of Ada but immediately obliterated her from his mind, and Rose hoped the rally would not go on for too long as there was an enormous pile of ironing waiting for her at home. Philip, Caroline, Ricky and Howard recognised a fatalistic sense of calm conviction which settled itself over them. It was, and there was, no time for doubt. Mary was right, it was time. It was the point at which everything was right for their voices to be heard. The right place, the right moment and the right state of mind. The vicar felt, for an instant, that he understood the workings of the mind of a martyr. Supremely conscious of the warmth emanating from his wife beside him, he uttered a quiet prayer.

Sonja surprised them all. Displaying no fear or reticence but instead indefatigable drive and conviction, she appeared in front of them, raised one fist into the air and yelled:

"What do we hate? Rejuvenates!"

"I didn't know we were going to have to shout that," Caroline whispered uneasily.

"Rejuvenation is not salvation!" Sonja continued shouting into space, now oblivious to all social convention and the society which surrounded her.

"That's better," Caroline added, obviously relieved.

Mary was wise enough to let the young woman have her moment and galvanise the potentially unsteady group into action. They marched loosely to the chosen spot, lead by Sonja and responding to her chants. Then Mary took over, using her megaphone, and the group raised their placards, blew their whistles and cried out in unison.

Some of the passers-by ignored them completely and went about their business as if MAD did not exist, or at least as if the antics of a protest group was a normal, wearisome occurrence. Others glanced at them suspiciously and took a detour round them anxious to avoid confrontation. Kane and his mother approached, having completed their circular tour of the market stalls. Kane could not take his eyes off the group and their masks in particular.

"It's not fair," he simpered. "Why can't I have one?"

"Don't look," his mother commanded. "They're just a bunch of weirdos."

A few people stopped for a moment and watched the protest curiously unsure as to what it was about. Some decided that it was a fundraising stunt and several asked which charity they were collecting for. Mary broke off from her megaphone and explained impatiently:

"We're not! We're just protesting against rejuvenation – can't you read?"

A group of teenagers perched themselves on the adjacent wall, swigging from bottles of lager and alcopops and sniggering at the group. One of them pointed at Ricky, made a rude gesture and laughed even more loudly. On occasion they joined in MAD's chants substituting obscenities where possible. The men from the hired vans leant against their vehicles and watched, mostly silently, save for passing a few remarks amongst themselves.

After less than an hour, two police community support officers, who happened to be passing, approached Mary and asked if she had police clearance to protest.

"Sorry to disappoint you – but yes," she replied, fumbling through her bag for the letter.

"Funny sort of free country we've got, haven't we?" Sonja shouted aggressively. "It's OK to protest as long as we have the state's permission – long live freedom and democracy!"

"What's your name, madam?" one of the officers enquired.

"I don't have to tell you that! I'm not breaking the law, big brother."

"They've got permission," the first officer confirmed after scanning the letter. "Let's move on."

"Just the usual Saturday morning nutters," he mouthed to his colleague when they were a few safe paces away.

"Do you think we're having any effect?" Howard asked, pulling off his mask to reveal his perspiring face and matted hair.

"Not really," Ricky replied mournfully.

"I can't blow this whistle any more," Freddie announced, breathlessly.

"You have a rest then, dear," Rose replied at once.

"It's a bit of an anti-climax, so far," Mouland agreed, his words muffled from behind his mask.

"I don't know what I expected, really," Caroline confessed. "Perhaps all we can hope to do is to make people think – we won't see the results of that today. It's a long term thing – we must plant a seed of doubt and hope that it will take root."

Mouland moved his mask temporarily. "Aren't you hot in that?" he asked Helen. "Why don't you take it off for a breather?"

"Yes, you're right," she replied, glancing around through the misplaced eyeholes and then tearing it off.

Sonja was the only MAD member to continue to wear her mask and keep her placard fully raised throughout the lull in the proceedings. Mary took control, once again; "Attention everyone. We're going to march. Line up, three abreast, behind me and prepare to move into the road."

Julian and Caroline exchanged uneasy glances. Sonja almost

leapt to the front, immediately behind Mary, and pulled Helen, who happened to be standing nearest, in line next to her.

"Come on!" she urged, her wide pupils just visible behind her mask and a tremble about her body which Helen detected through her brief touch. Freddie filed obediently into place on her left side.

"Caroline, you'd better stand between myself and Julian," Philip decided as he assumed his position behind Helen. Finally, Ricky, Rose and Howard formed the last row. Mary observed them critically, in the manner of a sergeant major inspecting his men before a grand parade.

"Spread out a bit, sideways and between rows. We want it to look like there are more of us."

Mary's troops complied with her command and soon she was satisfied, and gave her final orders, "We'll do a few chants here, in this position, just to get warmed up again, then we'll move out of the entrance to the pavement and as soon as the lights change we'll set off down the High Street. Any questions?"

"Yes," Julian called out. "Are we going to turn left or right out of the market place into the road?"

"I said, we'll march down the High Street. So that will be left, won't it?"

Sonja jumped up and down on the spot a couple of times, in the manner of a boxer getting ready for a fight. Mary, catching the action from the corner of one eye, declared, "Right. Let's do it!" Then she bellowed into her megaphone, "Who do we hate?"

"Rejuvenates!" Sonja's voice shrieked above the others. After about thirty seconds Mary began to lead her group through the entrance to the market place, where she purposefully stopped and blocked it to the annoyance of several shoppers. Passing cars slowed down out of curiosity and their occupants stared in puzzlement at MAD's members. One vehicle, a saloon car, packed with men, stopped completely, sounded its horn and the front seat passenger wound down his window and called out a quiet but venomous obscenity. The car only moved on as a result of impatient hooting from the vehicles pulling up behind. Then the driver screeched away and sped into the car park opposite, where he parked next to the hired vans, whose occupants he appeared to know.

After blocking the entrance effectively for a good ten minutes,

Mary directed the group into the road and began to lead them at a snail's pace down the High Street. Her sense of supreme enjoyment was interrupted abruptly by the sound of a baying crowd, which far outnumbered MAD and easily drowned their chants with crude insults. The men from the hired vans had formed an unruly mob on the pavement opposite and seemed to be orchestrated, albeit loosely, by the aggressive driver of the saloon car. Everyone in MAD's group felt varying degrees of fear – except for Mary and Sonja. Sonja merely shouted more loudly and performed something akin to a strange, grotesque dance, rather than a march, as she moved down the road. Mary, predictably, felt a surge of annoyance which rapidly morphed into extreme rage. 'How dare these people try to ruin her demonstration. She would not let them. She would make them sorry.'

"Do you think we ought to stop?" Caroline addressed her husband nervously, just making herself heard amongst the din after several attempts to slip in her question, while Philip took an intake of breath. He did not reply but instead responded with gusto to Mary's cry.

Ricky felt a volley of thuds against his placard and a handful of nails rained down onto him. This was quickly followed by a deluge of penny washers which hurtled from above onto the MAD members. For a while they struggled successfully to keep in formation and continue chanting. Then their opposition became more aggressive. Helen was struck in the face by a small piece of broken concrete which had been deliberately aimed at her. Yelping with pain, she stumbled backwards into the vicar who, seeing at once what had happened, drew level with the mob and addressed them angrily:

"What do you think you're doing? There's no need for that!"

The perpetrator identified himself immediately by laughing loudly and hurling another stone at the group,

"There's plenty more where that came from. Come on lads!"

This time a glass bottle struck the face of Mary's placard.

"Bastard!" she cried, and with a huge swipe whacked the nearest protestor on the side of his head with her board. The man crumpled, unconscious. As he fell, a strange expression in his eyes, Mary experienced a great surge of pleasure. Then she recognised him: it was Will, the former member of MAD.

"That's enough! Run for it!" Devereux yelled, taking charge and trying to shield both Caroline and Rose. "Make for the market place!"

Most of the MAD members obeyed at once, flinging down their placards and attempting to run back to the market place. Luckily for them, several police cars and a police riot van, sirens screaming, arrived at that moment and launched themselves at the protestors.

Devereux manhandled Caroline to the relative safety of a spot behind the market place wall and then made as if to go to the aid of his friend before being restrained by Howard and Ricky.

Mary was using her placard as a weapon to good effect, lashing out at anyone who ventured near, ignoring the detritus which continued to fall on her.

Mouland was scuffling with the protestors' leader and had managed to land at least one good punch to his face, causing the man to rock and reel lifelessly for a few seconds before regaining his composure. A policeman dragged Mouland away from behind before he could deliver a second blow. The vicar, fearing an attack from an enemy protestor, twisted himself from the policeman's grip and punched him hard in the stomach. Immediately, three of the policeman's colleagues pounced on the vicar and brought him to the ground.

Mouland lay there, face down, legs kicked roughly apart and his hands handcuffed behind his back. His sense of reality vanished and he felt as though he had hijacked the body of another person, his cheek taking in the unfamiliar sensation of the rough road surface and his nostrils inhaling the odour of damp tarmac. During these moments he gradually transformed back to his normal self and felt fear. His overriding concern was not at the consequence of his actions; he still, almost, did not regret them, but terror at this exposure of a side of his personality which hitherto had been unknown and unrevealed, even to himself. 'Is that me?' he thought, 'Am I really like that?' Shame and shock enveloped him. 'I'm a hypocrite,' he despaired, 'How can I expound the word of God and oppose humanity's baseness and rail against the death of spirituality when I'm as bad, perhaps worse, myself? Yes worse. Worse to be a hypocrite in the name of the Lord. I am the false prophet.' Another thought and persistent image prodded at his mind until he gave in, declaring to himself that despite this image he did not seek justification of his behaviour. The image was one first implanted and retained since his days in the infant class at school – that of Jesus' anger in the temple, his overturning of trestles and chairs and his expulsion of the moneylenders. 'Rage is justified at times' his inner dialogue told him. 'It's right to fight for your beliefs and for what is right. But I shouldn't have used violence. I was unrecognisable, I was inhuman. Besides, those protestors were fighting for their beliefs. Who am I to judge? Perhaps the essence of humanity is to be inhuman? The veneer of civilisation is painfully thin – little more than an illusion.'

"Forgive me, Father," he cried loudly, "for I have sinned in your name!" One of his captors observed him critically, preparing for an attempt to escape or, at the very least, an incoherent outburst.

"We'll leave him a minute. See if he calms down before we get him into the van," the policeman ordered. "Keep an eye on him though. If he shows any sign of distress get him up and call the medics over. I don't want anyone keeling over under my watch – even if he is off his head already."

Mouland, at that moment, was experiencing forgiveness in a way he had never felt throughout his years of faith and commitment to his God. A sensation of endless peace stretched out before him and his guilt and anxiety withered to nothing. He searched fruitlessly for them until he knew that they had, indeed, been washed away. 'Seek and ye shall find, ask and ye shall receive' he thought 'Heal me O Lord, and I shall be healed; save me, and I shall be saved; for thou art my praise.' Mouland, overcome with serenity, knew that he had experienced true forgiveness.

It had taken three police officers to bring Mary down. She had, somehow, turned herself into a demon – a bundle of pure malevolent energy with a power far above her usual capabilities. The police officers struggled with her, unable to take grip, her energy seemed to consume their attempted grasps and for a while it was as though they were grappling with a ghost. As the crowd was dispersed and the High Street became uncomfortably silent, like a wet Good Friday, Mary's demonic possession waned, her incoherent babbling reduced to a dribble, her senses returned and finally, her body collapsed.

"What was all that about?" one exhausted officer cried, breathlessly, wiping the perspiration from his forehead, with his sleeve. "I've taken on some big blokes before – but never like that. She was like an animal."

"Get the cuffs on her," his superior replied. "I'm not taking any chances. Then get the ambulance over here, quick."

The MAD members were looking on anxiously, hemmed in by a small number of police officers. Sonja, having been ordered to cease chanting and having had her placard taken from her, leaned against the wall crying softly. Rose put a comforting arm around her, "Don't worry, dear. It's all over now and you did very well."

"Yes. Quite an inspiration," Ricky agreed kindly.

Caroline, meanwhile, was arguing with a policeman; "Let me go to my husband." She demanded, her eyes never averting themselves from Philip's prostrate body. "How do you know he's alright? Why have you left him there so long? Surely he must be allowed to get up? He's no threat to you, it was extreme provocation. He's not a young man, you know, forcing him to lie there in the middle of this dirty road could bring on a heart attack or something. Let me make sure he's alright!"

"Just stay where you are, madam. We'll allow your husband to move, shortly, when we're sure he's calmed down. You'll need to come down to the station with the others, anyhow."

"But that's not good enough!" Caroline continued. "I've heard about police brutality before but never really believed it – now I know it's true."

The police officer interrupted her sternly, "I've told you several times, madam and this is my final warning – anymore from you and you'll be arrested, handcuffed and put in the van, and you'll be separated from your husband for a lot longer than is necessary."

"I'm separated now," Caroline muttered with childish petulance.

"Shh," Devereux urged. "You'll only make it worse. Look, they're allowing him to get up. He seems fine." Caroline's attention transferred solely to her husband and as she watched him being escorted, unceremoniously, but without aggression, to a police car, she forgot to argue.

Helen was also leaning against the low wall and having been ordered to remove her mask was allowing Freddie, Howard and Julian to examine her cheek, where the stone had struck.

210

"The blow's coming out now," Howard confirmed as a blue, egg-sized lump appeared. "It does look quite nasty – you might have broken something."

"Yes. You really should have it checked," Ricky urged, "Let me ask one of these policemen if you can go to A & E."

"No. It's not that bad," Helen lied, wincing with pain as she spoke. "Rose, do you have a mirror?"

"Yes, of course." Rose broke from comforting Sonja and fished in her bag amongst an array of essential cosmetics before producing the required item.

"I really think it needs looking at," Freddie agreed. "You ought to just have an x-ray, just to make sure it's alright."

Helen nervously prepared herself to look in the mirror. Her left eye was beginning to close and pain throbbed through her cheekbone and radiated to her ear.

"Can you move your jaw OK?" Howard enquired.

Helen replied affirmatively.

"I don't like the look of it," Freddie muttered within Helen's hearing. "I reckon she's got a cracked cheekbone."

"It's alright!" Helen insisted, an edge of annoyance in her tone. "Stop making a fuss. We should be more concerned with Reverend Mouland and Mary."

The three men exchanged silent, defeated looks. Howard shrugged his shoulders but could not help noticing that Helen's left eye had now closed completely and her right one was watering with pain.

The MAD members had watched Mouland and Mary's battles unfold with horror and disbelief. Mary had by now been escorted to the police riot van by six police officers and been driven away to an unknown destination. Reverend Mouland had followed soon after.

"What on earth happened?" Ricky sounded completely deflated. Realising that both his hands were still quivering he shoved them quickly into his trouser pockets in the hope that the others would not notice.

"Rent-a-mob turned up – that's what happened," Devereux replied. "It was a bit of a trap, really, I suppose. Our advertising campaign paid dividends – but not in the way we had hoped."

"So do you think it was planned?" Rose asked in surprise, having assumed that the protestors were reacting on the spur of the moment, taking advantage of an unexpected opportunity to cause mayhem and indulge in violence.

"Of course it was!" Ricky declared. "Where do you think they got the nails and washers from? I'm sure they didn't just pop across to the market for them."

"Oh." Rose became even more subdued.

"They didn't have any placards though," Sonja added.

"They were using the element of surprise," Devereux explained patiently. "And quite successfully too, I might add."

"Ironic though, isn't it?" Howard chimed. "We, or should I say Helen, spends all that money on an advertising campaign and the only people to turn up are those hell-bent against us. Who would have thought of that?"

"It isn't your fault, Helen," Rose responded at once.

"Actually, I didn't think it was," Helen replied coldly, her voice unfamiliar and strained with pain.

"No, no. Of course not. I didn't mean that anyone thought it was."

"I'm still worried about you, love." Freddie studied her intensely.

"I'm alright." Helen tried to sound strong and resilient but had begun to sound listless and was fighting a dreaded sense of nausea and giddiness. Her features had become drained to a porcelain hue, her face tightly drawn and her wet, matted hair had begun to settle in its natural waves and kinks, accentuating the undyed roots. Her companions continued to observe her closely with growing concern, each of them aware that she needed medical attention but equally anxious to abide by her wishes. At the moment that she slid, almost silently, to the ground and propped her back against the stone wall, Ricky recognised her. His eyes widened and jaw dropped momentarily, before he clamped his lower lip between his teeth.

"Excuse me, officer," Sonja called out briskly using a tone which somehow prompted instant obedience, "we need an ambulance. Quick."

Helen rolled over to one side in faint and was only prevented from causing further damage to her injury by Rose, who by now was kneeling at her side and allowed her to rest against her plump body.

"We'd better put her in the recovery position," Caroline decided. "These policemen should be trained in first aid. . ."

"We are, madam," the policeman who had called for an ambulance on his radio, intervened. "I'll take over. Stand back and give her some air."

The MAD members complied willingly and Ricky sidled up to Howard. "I think I've discovered something," he whispered.

"So have I," Howard replied seriously, "and I think I know what you're going to tell me."

"It is her – isn't it?" Ricky continued, unsure as to whether Howard's discovery was the same as his own.

"Yep, I reckon it is. Her name's not Helen Day – she's Deighton's daughter."

"What's her game then? Why has she joined us?"

"Haven't a clue – though she seems pretty genuine. She turned up for the rally, after all, and funded the advertising, which must have taken a big wad of cash."

"Yes. But look how it's turned out. Do you think she's really in league with those thugs?"

"I really don't know." Howard shook his head and sounded almost too tired to be bothered with yet another problem. "I suppose we'll find out in due course – perhaps it doesn't matter."

"It will matter if today's events signal the end of MAD. We really are the only ones left. Rejuvenation, to everyone else, seems as natural as drinking water or giving birth. In the few, short years since Deighton developed it, it's buried itself in the psyche of the entire Western World. We're seen as little more than killers."

By now, Helen was being transferred to an ambulance, where an oxygen mask was gently clamped to her swollen face and within seconds she was driven away. Rose had asked to go with her but permission was refused, instead the police officer had taken her place.

"Are you a relative?" he asked, before adding without waiting for a reply, "You're all going to be questioned down at the station. We're just waiting for some transport."

Howard turned to Caroline. "I must say I was impressed with your husband – he got stuck in there, no messing, it was quite a surprise to me – a man of the cloth and all that."

Caroline was torn between admiration for Philip's willingness to fight, as it turned out, even physically, for his beliefs and the nagging sense that he should not have done so.

"He's not a man of violence, you know, but he is a man of deep conviction," she replied. "I wonder how Mary is and where they've taken her?" She continued, partly as a result of genuine concern and partly in an attempt to deflect the conversation from her husband's actions.

"She'll be alright," Howard affirmed confidently. "She's very strong – stronger than any of us. You don't know her as well as we do." He motioned to Ricky, Rose and Sonja. "Nothing will break her – she'll thrive on it and come out the other end even more determined and full of schemes and ideas for revenge."

"Oh," Caroline sounded startled, uncomfortable with the notion of vengeance.

Devereux had remained mostly silent throughout the group's exchanges. He was annoyed with himself, as an ex-military man, for not having gone to Philip's immediate assistance although he also knew that he had acted on the instantaneous, correct decision to ensure Caroline's and Rose's safety first, thus limiting the potential number of casualties. 'If only Howard and Ricky hadn't held him back,' he thought angrily.

Another police van drew up. One of the guarding police officers waved his thumb at it.

"Right you lot. In you get. You're required to answer a few questions at the station."

The MAD members obediently trooped towards the van and formed a queue behind the rear doors.

"I don't know what my Ada will say," Freddie moaned as Ricky and a police officer helped him inside. "I've never been in trouble with the police and I've certainly not been arrested before. Ada's going to give me a right earful."

"Are we actually being arrested?" Rose asked. "I thought we were just helping them with their enquiries."

"No, we're not being arrested," Ricky replied with impatience. "They have to read our rights otherwise it's illegal. We actually haven't done anything wrong – we had permission for the rally – Mary's got your letter, hasn't she Sonja? And we didn't retaliate against that mob – none of us can be accused of violence."

Caroline squirmed uncomfortably but remained silent.

"He's right," Howard agreed. "They'll just want to question us generally. It will give us a chance to tell them exactly what happened and to point the finger directly at the mob that turned

214

up organised, armed and determined to cause trouble. We were acting within the law."

"That's a relief," Rose said emphatically before sighing heavily and resting her back heavily against the worn, sticky seat.

"I don't care if I'm being arrested!" Sonja declared loudly, the fire recombusting within her. "I'm not afraid to stand up for what I believe in! I won't be silenced by that mob or the police!"

"Well, you're not being arrested," Devereux countered through gritted teeth, tempted to add 'you silly little girl' but managed not to. Nevertheless, his unspoken words somehow conveyed themselves through the ether and each person fell silent, engrossed in their own thoughts. Rose was hoping that her husband would remember to put the previously prepared casserole in the oven at the correct temperature and not forget about it. Sonja, Ricky and Howard rehearsed what they would say whilst being questioned. Caroline's mind was filled with anxiety regarding her husband. Freddie's thoughts were filled with anxiety regarding his wife. He hoped she was not worried that he had been absent for so long and that she would manage to prepare her lunch without his help. Devereux was still angry. Embarrassment at his failure to act during the battle gnawed at him until it created a hollow, sinking feeling deep inside.

Chapter Seventeen

Mary, writhing, muttering and shrieking, was quickly transferred to the local hospital where she was sedated and placed in the most secure ward. The police were informed that she would not be fit for questioning for some time. Mouland was taken to the police station, where, after being assessed by a doctor, he co-operated fully with the authorities.

"I admit that I succumbed to a violent response," he declared with candour. "I am extremely ashamed of myself and agree that this kind of behaviour is completely unacceptable, especially from a man of my position. The only thing I can say in mitigation is that we were attacked first and I acted under provocation. I had not set out with the intention of violence – none of us had, we had planned a small, peaceful demonstration. Unfortunately, it got out of hand – which I think was the intention of our opponents. As for striking the police officer, I truly believed that I was being attacked from behind by one of the mob and responded automatically in, what I believed, was self defence. I should like to offer my sincere apologies to the officer in question and hope that I have not caused him too much pain or injury. I will plead guilty to whatever you wish to charge me with."

Inspector Roux and Sergeant Inch who were both seated opposite at a small rectangular table, allowed Mouland to complete his speech without interruption. They remained silent for a few moments after he had finished, then Roux sighed:

"You really should have a solicitor present, you know,

Reverend. It is your right. We can arrange to get hold of someone if you like."

"There's no need," Mouland replied defiantly, determined to be punished for his misdeeds and unknowingly searching for redemption, "I have done wrong and I will accept the consequences."

"Well, if you're sure, we will continue with the interview but you can change your mind at any time," Roux acceded, somehow intrinsically understanding the vicar's need to be punished as a way of making amends and resetting his moral equilibrium.

"If you wouldn't mind starting at the beginning, sir, and run through everything that happened," Inch commanded politely.

Mouland complied and related a detailed and accurate account of the morning's events.

"What was MAD's intention?" Roux probed. "What did you all hope to achieve today?"

Mouland could not prevent himself from shaking his head ruefully; "At the very least we hoped to awaken people to the arguments against rejuvenation – to deter them from the path they have so mistakenly chosen and at best win some converts."

"Would you say each one of you limited yourselves to that aim? No one was spoiling for a fight?" Inch began to perform his mildly aggressive role.

"Of course not!" Mouland replied incredulously, and at the same time wondered whether Inch had taken leave of his senses. "Look at our membership – a bunch of geriatrics and a couple of younger women. That's just a hilarious suggestion!"

"Nevertheless Mary, and yourself, I might add, weren't afraid to get stuck in," Inch teased.

"I told you, we were provoked and physically attacked. Helen was struck in the face by a brick or something – she could have been killed. We couldn't just stand there and let them do it."

"So you made a conscious decision to attack one of the perpetrators?"

"No! No!" Mouland experienced a mixture of rising anger and concern – 'Why are they twisting my account,' he thought, 'I've made it easy for them, I've admitted assault, why is that not enough?' "I did not launch an attack," he continued. "It wasn't even a counter attack. I acted in self defence of my associates."

"Why didn't you just run away?"

217

k

"There wasn't time. . ."

"The others (except Mary) managed to," Inch interrupted.

"But that was only because you arrived. For all we knew we were at the mercy of that mob – they would have made mincemeat of us. Why aren't you questioning them?" Mouland replied hotly.

Inch ignored his question and continued to rile the vicar, "So you decided that the best form of defence was to attack?"

"Yes. Well, no. I didn't consciously decide anything. I just reacted. You know, the fight or flight response, I suppose."

"Exactly," Inch pounced and Mouland felt like kicking himself, beginning to realise that it would be better to say as little as possible. "I really have nothing to add," he declared testily, "I have recounted the series of events, honestly and in detail. There's nothing to be gained by your twisting of my words."

"Would you say that you're a hot-tempered man?" Roux intervened.

"No," Mouland replied with obvious hostility.

"You have a reputation for your forthright views. You're not afraid to champion unpopular causes, in fact, wouldn't you agree that you quite enjoy a metaphorical fight?"

"Metaphorical – yes. Physical – no," Mouland replied between gritted teeth.

"But you are a passionate man – someone wholly committed to defending right from wrong?"

"Of course I am. Why do you think that I am – or rather was – a clergyman?"

"I suppose being made redundant fired you up? Was that why you decided to join MAD?"

"Not exactly."

"And then there was the arson attack on St. Nonna's. We haven't closed the file on that you know but it's unlikely it was a prank. My gut feeling is that the building was targeted because of what it stood for or what it had become."

"Why are you bringing that up? You know it wasn't me. I have an alibi and since I didn't do it, you can't possibly have any evidence against me. Just charge me with assault, if you want to, and let me go. I've explained the circumstances. There's nothing more."

Roux stood up and switched off the tape recorder which had

been silently running throughout the interview. "Thank you, Reverend Mouland. You can go for now while we continue with our enquiries. I must remind you, that even in this day and age, assaulting a police officer is still taken very seriously. We'll need to speak to you again, no doubt, so don't plan a trip away from home."

Mouland was led from the room feeling like a naughty schoolboy.

"Can I phone my wife now?"

"Yeah." Inch sounded uninterested.

Mouland waited in the car park for about thirty minutes, relief at being set free competing with heavy depression as he pondered the rally's spectacular failure. A jittery Caroline drew the car to a halt beside his loan figure and pushed the passenger door open.

"Are you alright?" she asked, unable to contain a tremor in her voice. Her husband did not reply but slid into the car where he remained silent until they had almost reached the Rectory. Caroline snatched several sideways glances at him, knowing that it would be counter-productive to press him further. At last Philip spoke:

"Sometimes I feel that I am Septimus Smith," he said, with a wretchedness that chilled his wife to the bone.

Helen came round from her faint in the ambulance to find an oxygen mask clamped to her face and a paramedic watching her closely and feeling her pulse. The swinging motion of the vehicle added to her sense of nausea and for a while she struggled to recall the morning's events. 'Am I in hospital? What's happened?' she thought, opening her eyes widely, but very briefly, before the effort became too much and they fell shut again. For now she was only able to concentrate on the throbbing pain which had started in her cheek but had spread like a stain to her eyes, ear, jaw and brain. Somehow it seemed that this was all she was – a sensation of pain and conscience, no other part of her existed.

On arrival at St. Imelda's her stretcher was pulled from the ambulance and trundled into the Accident and Emergency department. If she felt being swung, matter of factly, onto a trolley she did not remember, but the paramedic's conversation with the nurse, who took the scant known details, drifted through her pain.

"Sorry love – got to leave you here." The paramedic apologised automatically as she was wheeled to a space amongst a line of waiting trolleys in the corridor. "They'll get to you as soon as they can."

Helen lay there for several hours, unattended and untouched except for when a cleaner accidently jabbed her with the handle of the mop which he was flicking down the centre of the corridor, his mind on his next task at another location several miles away. Eventually, Helen began to take notice of her surroundings; whether or not her pain had subsided or she had become used to it she could not tell.

"How long have I been here?" she asked a passing nurse, forcing her words out in the manner of a ventriloquist.

"Not long, just wait your turn, we'll see you as soon as possible," the nurse replied brusquely without slowing her stride.

Helen obeyed, gradually remembering what had happened. Her memory returned chronologically but beginning with the most recent event. Eventually, after reliving the entire morning as a series of discrete instances, she became angry. Determined not to wait any longer, she sat up carefully, imploring herself to take her time and rest after her movement. Then she slowly swung her legs round so they dangled at the side of the trolley. Pain pulsed through her right temple. Finally, she pushed herself lightly to the ground and made her way feebly along the corridor, leaning heavily against the grimy wall. Through the flashing pain, which intermittently blinded her eye, she discerned a figure coming towards her.

"Is this the way out?" she called breathlessly.

"Yes. Down the corridor and turn right," the man replied helpfully, with no flicker of concern or even curiosity.

Helen continued her laborious journey until she reached the glare of the glass entrance doors. There she hesitated, wondering what to do next until she spied a 'freephone' taxi handset next to the lift opposite. She had just taken hold of the receiver when the lift doors opened and a porter, pushing an empty wheelchair, emerged.

"Can I help you madam?" he enquired, sizing up the situation at once.

"No. It's alright. I'm just about to go home."

"That's a nasty mark on your face, have they looked at it for you?" he continued, aware that they had not.

"No. That's why I'm leaving. I can't wait anymore." Helen winced.

"I could take you back there and have a word, make sure they haven't forgotten about you."

Helen gazed at the inviting wheelchair.

"I'm going that way," the porter continued.

Helen remained silent and motionless.

"I'll tell you what," the man persisted kindly, "I'll take you up there, ask how long you'll have to wait and if you still want to go home, I'll bring you back here. You've nothing to lose that way."

"Alright," Helen mumbled listlessly, the throbs having converted themselves into lightning flashes. The porter, whose name was Terry it transpired, upheld his side of the bargain.

"I'll have a word with Sister Muller – she's alright, I've known her for years." He confided before disappearing further into the department and returning with a student nurse.

"Where's your notes?" she asked.

"Dunno," Helen replied with effort, her eyes closed.

"Probably on one of those trolleys," Terry pointed out logically. "Try looking on that empty one."

The student did as instructed and retrieved the clipboard. "What's her name?" she asked Terry.

"I don't know. . ." he began impatiently, before Helen responded automatically:

"Helen Deighton."

"It's got Helen something else, I think, on here. I can't read the writing very well. It says she has a contusion to the right cheek. It must be her."

"When was she admitted?"

"Twelve-thirty."

"Crikey! That's five hours ago! No wonder she was on her way out."

Sister Muller appeared.

"She's been waiting five hours!" Terry cried in his cockney twang.

"Thank you Terry. Bring her in now, please, nurse."

Helen was wheeled awkwardly into a consulting bay and Terry

221

sauntered back the way he had come, hands in his pockets and whistling softly.

After examination it was diagnosed that Helen had suffered a fractured cheekbone and severe bruising to her jaw, with suspected concussion. She was given painkillers and told to go home and rest.

"There's some confusion as to your identity," Sister Muller told her. "We had you down originally as Helen Day but you have since told us your name is Helen Deighton. You are Helen Deighton, aren't you?"

"Yes," Helen replied with resignation, "but I sometimes use my mother's maiden name."

"Pity your father hasn't found a miracle cure for broken bones, but never mind, it'll heal again soon enough!"

Then the senior nurse changed her tone and stole a quizzical glance into Helen's dull eyes, "There will be someone at home with you, I suppose?" she commanded rather than enquired.

"Yes," Helen lied.

"Good. We'd like to keep you in for twenty-four hours for observation, as a precaution, but there's no chance of a bed. How are you going to get home?"

"I'll ring someone."

"OK. Here's a letter for your GP. Drop it in as soon as possible. I'll ask someone to ring for a porter to take you down to the pick up point."

Sister Muller hurried on to her next patient, to be replaced, after a short wait, by Terry who reappeared with a friendly smile.

"Got you sorted out at last, have they? About time – I don't know what the place is coming to. . ."

They had not gone far when a man, dressed in an expensive waterproof jacket and aged about thirty-five, almost leaped from the hard plastic seat on which he had been sitting, in front of the wheelchair.

"Watch it, mate. What's the rush?" The man ignored Terry's reprimand and addressed Helen, whilst simultaneously thrusting a small tape recorder at her.

"Miss Deighton?" He shot the words at her, confidently aware of the identity of his prey.

Helen stared at him blankly.

222

"What have you got to say about your attendance at this morning's protest?"

Helen remained silent.

"What does your father think about it?"

Terry tried to manoeuvre the wheelchair round the inquisitor but he positioned himself in front of it again and even grabbed hold of one of the arm rests.

"Surely your father isn't happy – don't you think you've made him look ridiculous?"

"That's enough! Get out of here or I'll call security," Terry yelled.

"OK. I've got what I wanted." The newspaper reporter grinned smugly and backed away. Terry pushed Helen a few more paces along the corridor whilst muttering something under his breath about 'bloody reporters'. Helen was not safe yet, the reporter having given them a short start, quickened his pace, overtook them and then turned and flashed a camera at Helen's face. Then, very pleased with his day's work, he scuttled down the corridor before disappearing through a convenient side exit.

"I don't know who these people think they are," Terry grumbled. Although he had known the identity of his patient since taking her back to the Accident and Emergency department and had, in the meantime, gleaned some details regarding the rally through gossip in the 'Porters' Room', he prided himself on his professionalism and ability to always put his patients first. He was able to completely sever his work in the hospital from his personal views or life outside and although he was an ardent supporter of rejuvenation, under no circumstances would he let Helen's dignity or well being be compromised whilst she was his responsibility.

Helen's fear that she would be recognised at the rally had come true and, no doubt, her father would soon be aware of her outright opposition to his treasured achievement – if he was not already. 'It couldn't be worse.' she thought. She would have preferred to have told him face to face, at a time when both she and he were ready. As sometimes happens when all is lost, Helen was able to push the thought of the inevitable conflict and recriminations to a point somewhere far away in an inaccessible recess in her mind leaving only a feeling of emptiness rather than concern. 'It will happen and there's nothing I can do to stop it,' she thought.

Terry was saying something to her, "If you take a seat there, hopefully your lift will be along soon. Bye, love."

Helen sat down as instructed and wondered who to call. For a moment or two, thoughts of Anna lodged themselves uneasily in her mind and she almost felt it possible to dial her number. Almost immediately, the scene of their row replayed itself in front of her and she recalled the cold emptiness which had struck on realisation that Anna was not the unflinching, loyal friend that she had once appeared to be. Helen slowly rose from her seat and moved gingerly to the free taxi phone.

Mouland and his wife had driven home in silence and had remained uncommunicative on their arrival. By the following morning, although still shaken, Philip felt able to answer Caroline's questions (which, unknown to him, she was desperately trying to contain). She made little comment as he ran through the previous day's events except to sigh, loudly and angrily, through closed lips as he recounted the accusation that he had planned violence.

"That's about it," he finished at last, "but tell me what happened to you and the others."

"Oh, we were carted off to Jubilee Street Police Station," Caroline replied, almost cheerfully. "I fail to see why they separated us from you and Mary. Anyway, we weren't there long – they had no excuse to keep us. They even managed to find a copy of the paperwork giving permission for the rally. I think they were disheartened after that and let us go."

Philip's still pale face reminded her. "Did you know Helen was taken to hospital? We think that the rock or stone or whatever it was, may have broken a bone or worse. She turned deathly white. Oh, and there's something else – she's not Helen Day but Helen Deighton, the professor's daughter – what do you make of that?"

Her husband, whose replies had consisted of monosyllabic grunts, came alive at this piece of information: "Really? How bizarre! What on earth is she doing with MAD?"

"Exactly! Is she an imposter?"

"What about her friend Freddie, did he know?"

"Apparently not and I think I believe him. If anything, he seemed more surprised than the rest of us."

"We mustn't jump to conclusions. It's perfectly reasonable for a daughter to hold opposing views to her father."

224

"But the subject is rather important, currently," Caroline argued, "and with ninety-nine-point-nine percent of the population being in favour what is the realistic chance of his one and only daughter coming out against him – especially to the point of joining MAD?"

"The one thing we've found, which I think we can all agree on, is that views for or against rejuvenation are polarised – there's no common ground. If Helen genuinely disagrees with the process then I feel that it is quite natural that she would seek out others who hold similar views. We did exactly that."

"But we are no closer to knowing what she really thinks," Caroline persisted.

"True – but we shouldn't make a judgement yet. If she is an 'imposter' as you say, now that her identity has been revealed, she'll have to give it up. In any case, she's done MAD no harm, on the contrary, without her financial input the rally could not have taken place."

"What if she did more than that?" Caroline demanded excitedly and Philip caught sight of a gleam in her eye:

'She's scheming,' he thought, before asking wearily, "Did what, exactly?"

"Set us up! What if she funded the rally for MAD but also engaged those protestors to start a fight in the hope that we'd be discredited? Whether we were the perpetrators or not won't matter at all, as soon as the press gets hold of it. You can be sure that they'll paint a very poor picture of us and it will give all the pro-rejuvenates yet another excuse to discredit our views."

"I'm sure that's not the case," her husband replied dismissively, successfully concealing the feeling of concern that he had felt rising inside. If his wife's allegations were correct, he knew that it would be the final blow and rejuvenation would win. The handful of opponents which would remain would no longer be treated with contempt and would no longer give rise to vehement opposition from the victors, they would have lost the power to do even that. They would be ignored. Worse than that, people would feel sorry for them because they were unable to accept progress. They would be classed as mentally deficient.

"No. I'm sure Helen's genuine," he reiterated, more intent to convince himself than his wife.

"No doubt we'll find out soon enough," Caroline continued grimly, her mind firmly made up.

"I suppose someone ought to organise something," Philip suggested. "A MAD meeting – we need to draw our troops together, agree our next move. I wonder what has happened to Mary?"

Mary had been 'sectioned' under the Mental Health Act. Although she had not helped herself by destroying her bed clothes and wrecking several items in her room as soon as the sedative had worn off and then by attacking the police officer, by spitting in his face and kicking his shins, who attempted to question her, those in charge were pro-rejuvenates who considered her mad anyway. Mary was the figurehead and the ringleader and she deserved to be punished. Interestingly, not one of the baying mob of protestors was detained for more than an hour at the Police Station. Even the man who had purportedly hurled the missile at Helen was allowed to go, following one or two derisory questions.

Caroline's fears fulfilled themselves in most respects; the rally turned out to be a disaster for MAD and for Helen in particular. Pictures of her bruised and swollen face were splashed on the front page of all the newspapers and description and analysis of her brutal betrayal of her esteemed father seemed to fill the news bulletins on television and radio for days. Professor Deighton could not resist the further attention of the media and publicly denounced his daughter whilst only admonishing himself for 'somehow having failed as a parent'. His popularity reached new heights.

Opposition to rejuvenation became an irrelevance. The populace, devoid of meaningful concerns, managed to effect mass horror at what it considered to be Helen's gross disloyalty to her father. Somehow it managed to transfer all its guilt and sin to her, and in its opinion she symbolised the growing defects in current society. The outpouring was similar to scenes past when mass hysteria followed the death of a person in the public eye. This time collective grief was replaced by contempt and indignation. Helen, although hounded, called upon a strength that only she knew was hidden in her core, and determined to use the opportunity which the hitherto unwelcome publicity brought with it, she expounded the anti-rejuvenation view mercilessly.

As is usual, the general public eventually became bored with her and the media turned its attention elsewhere, desperately seeking a new scandal with which to tantalise the masses. In some quarters, it was even feared that Helen's constant exposure and subsequent airing of anti-rejuvenation might even win new converts. It did not. When the frenzied boiling pot had died down, slowly at first and then reduced to the odd bubble passing to the surface until finally there was no movement at all, Helen was forced to accept that MAD was beaten.

Shortly after the rally, Mouland and Devereux had decided to call a meeting at the vicarage. All the MAD members turned up with anxious expectation, with the exception of Mary who was still incarcerated. Mouland welcomed them and explained his reasons for summoning them.

"I'm sure most of you are aware of this, but for those who are not, the news regarding Mary is not good – currently she is to remain held in a secure unit for an indefinite period – until she is deemed to be no longer a risk to society. This leaves us with a dilemma – do we wait for her or do we carry on with MAD as usual? The question also remains whether we wish to continue with MAD at all, following the aftermath of the rally?"

"I'm continuing," Sonja confirmed brusquely, her eyes flashing. Everyone understood that she would resume the battle alone if necessary.

"I definitely think we should continue, in some way," Ricky drawled slowly, still in thought. "Just because Mary's temporarily unavailable that's no reason to fold."

"Mary'd never get over it if we did," Howard observed pertinently, before adding tactlessly, "She'd end up a right basket case."

"What do you think, Helen?" Devereux asked pointly. All eyes turned towards her, Caroline's a little guiltily. Helen, used to public scrutiny, did not flinch.

"I'm sure you can guess my reply. Although I haven't welcomed the attention I have received I've tried to use every opportunity to put our message across. If we gave up now, everything will have been pointless – my dispute with my father, Mary's and Philip's arrest."

Mouland cleared his throat and took an interest in his highly polished shoes, hardly aware of Freddie's croaked, "Here, here," in support.

Devereux looked at Rose quizzically. "You're uncharacteristically quiet – if you don't mind me saying. What are your thoughts?"

Rose hesitated and gave a gentle sigh before replying, "Obviously, I haven't changed my opinion regarding rejuvenation – if I had been going to fall on the wayside, it would have been long before now and I think that's true of all of us." She turned her head and swept each person with her gaze. "I still support MAD generally but I don't want to become involved in any more violence. I'm too old to 'man the barricades' and besides, I have my children to think about. It's not a good example to them and they've suffered from dreadful teasing at school. . ."

"I don't think another rally's on the cards," Howard declared, before aiming a question at Caroline in a deliberate attempt to draw her opinion. "What do you think?"

"Well, no," Caroline replied. "The last one did turn out to be counter productive. I see ourselves continuing in a low key way, enough to keep the flame alight to be fanned when the future opportunity arises."

"I don't mind that," Rose sounded relieved.

"Here, here," Freddie called out again and then, having gained everyone's attention, felt obliged to add a further comment. "To tell the truth, I'm far too old to get involved in skirmishes and suchlike and what was worse – a lot more frightening and dangerous – was my Ada! She was furious! I didn't get any dinner for a week!"

Helen smiled amongst the others' chuckles, knowing that Freddie was embellishing his story and aware that he undertook all the cooking in his household. Ricky, having surreptitiously consulted his watch, called for a vote:

"I propose that MAD continues – any seconders?"

Sonja's arm shot up. "Yes, me."

"For?" Ricky called.

Everyone else raised their hands.

"Against?"

"Abstentions?"

"Right. It's passed then."

228

"I think we need a temporary or acting leader," Sonja suggested hopefully. "Someone to at least co-ordinate things or act as a spokesman just while Mary's unavailable."

"You're right," Howard agreed. "Any volunteers?"

No one spoke for several seconds. Sonja fidgeted desperately, hoping that someone would suggest her. The idea did not occur to any of her associates who were all considering whether they would stand as a last resort. Finally, Rose broke the silence at the exact moment that Sonja was taking an intake of breath prior to putting her name forward.

"Why not Helen?" she asked logically. "She's the one most in demand and the one with the most opportunity to get our point across. Also, she's proved to be an incredibly loyal member as well as helping financially. She's sacrificed more than the rest of us put together."

Sonja slumped in her seat. Helen turned red and fought the familiar sensation of embarrassment.

"Here, here!" Freddie repeated severely, more loudly this time.

"Helen – if willing – is an eminent choice," Mouland agreed at once. "I'm quite prepared to second your proposal, Rose."

Howard turned to Helen, "What about it? Do you want to go for it?"

Helen knew she had little choice but was becoming increasingly aware of the attraction of the position so she agreed without feigning reluctance. "Yes. I'll do it," she replied simply, "but on the understanding that the moment Mary returns I'll step down. MAD belongs to her."

"For?" Ricky cried out again. All hands were raised.

"Great. That's decided. I'm sorry but I have to rush off," he continued, jingling his car keys. "I'll see you all next meeting."

"Well done, Helen," Caroline congratulated her warmly. "You really are the best person to take over – you're in a unique position to keep our message alive."

"I suppose it will give the newspapers another story – if they're desperate. It's strange though, isn't it, how you can become used to anything. Their jibes and apparent disgust don't bother me at all. If anything my belief has become even more entrenched – I've nothing left to lose."

Caroline stared at her – not quite understanding – but aware that Helen was speaking her most internal thoughts.

"Can we hold the next meeting here, please?" Helen asked, back in organisation mode. "My place is too small."

"Yes, of course."

"In the meantime, someone ought to keep in touch with Mary – let her know that MAD hasn't finished and we're waiting for her return."

"Philip will do that. He has been trying to arrange a visit and I think it's possible in the next two or three weeks."

"Good. Let me know when a date has been finalised and I'll arrange the next MAD meeting for after that – so we can all have an update on Mary's progress."

Chapter Eighteen

Reverend Mouland's visit to Mary was confirmed shortly after MAD's meeting and on the appointed day he and his wife arrived at the 'Sunny Days Clinic'. Caroline clutched a bag of fruit in one hand and a large bouquet of flowers nestled in the crook of her other arm.

"I suppose it's alright to bring these. . ." she began uncertainly.

"Of course it is!" her husband reassured her. "Mary will be delighted with them."

They were directed to a small, austere lounge, which, although an attempt had been made to make it appear homely, still emanated a clinical atmosphere. The plain blue carpet bore a multitude of unidentifiable stains and the chairs and settee were of the type often found in the public areas of municipal offices. On entry to the building, to Caroline's horror, a nurse had grabbed the bouquet and bag of fruit and examined them thoroughly.

"We have to make sure that any items brought in by visitors do not contain anything which could present a danger to either patients or staff," she explained as if reading from an official edict and finally confirming that the gifts were acceptable. "A member of staff – probably myself – will be present for the duration of your visit. It's still an early stage in Mary's programme and you're her first visitors so we don't know how it will go. As I say, there's been no one else – she hasn't any relatives. Please be aware that we may have to end your stay prematurely if she shows any signs of distress."

Mouland nodded and took his place next to his wife on the

settee. They waited in silence while the nurse disappeared to bring Mary from an unidentified location somewhere in the depths of the building. Eventually, Caroline spoke:

"Why are they taking so long? You'd think they'd be ready for us. Do you think there's a problem?"

"I hope not. Shh!"

The nurse's now familiar voice could be heard in the corridor: "This way please, Mary – your friends are in here." She held the door open and Mary entered obediently, walked to the centre of the room and waited to be told what to do next.

"Take a seat, Mary," the nurse instructed.

Mary obeyed, sat opposite her visitors and stared at them silently. The nurse seated herself by the door and made no attempt to disguise her scrutiny of her patient and the two uncomfortable visitors. Caroline was sure she was making mental notes which she would record the minute the visit was over.

"Hello, Mary." Philip rose and embraced her stiff body warmly.

Caroline proffered the presents. "How are you?" she asked.

Mary cast a glance at the nurse. "I'm doing very well – so they tell me."

The nurse nodded encouragingly.

"In fact, they're quite pleased with my progress. I'm no longer a danger to myself, apparently, and soon I will no longer be a danger to the public. I do everything they command because I want to get well. I take all the medication and I have a CD of calming sounds, like the sea or grasshoppers, which I listen to every day, until she takes it away from me." Mary stared harshly at the nurse for a second. "I know it's doing me good. They're also pleased with me because I've taken an interest in charitable work."

Philip swallowed hard and Caroline's eyes widened. The nurse's encouraging expression remained fixed.

"What sort of charitable work?" Caroline asked, wondering what Mary could possibly do in the confines of the institution.

"Oh, I make little dolls – don't I, nurse? For the children's wing here, and if I make enough they are going to send them to the local hospital as well. The children like them because I make them look like little people – one of them looks just like the nurse here."

"That sounds very commendable," Philip replied. "Everyone should have a hobby – something which takes them out of themselves."

"Yes," Mary agreed. "It makes one less egocentric and more able to empathise with others. I understand, now, that that has been one of my weaknesses."

This time she did not seek confirmation from the nurse but kept her eyes fixed firmly on Philip and Caroline.

"Well, I'm glad things are going well. How is it here, generally, do you like the food, etc. and what about the other patients?" The vicar just stopped himself from referring to 'inmates'.

Mary sniggered and revealed a flash of her old self. "They're all mad!" She laughed and, without realising, rocked to and fro a couple of times. The nurse's expression changed from benign to intent. Then Mary became serious; "Speaking of which – how is MAD doing at the moment. No one will tell me anything in here. I hope you have not all abandoned me?"

"No! No! Of course not!" Caroline began and at the same time noticed her husband glancing at the nurse for tacit approval, who gave it with a raising of her eyebrows. "We had a short meeting about a fortnight ago and everyone is determined to carry on. We've thought it best to put public events on the back-burner, though, for the time-being. Helen was quite badly injured, you know."

"Was she?" Mary murmured. "I don't remember. I remember hardly anything about the rally or the days afterwards. I know that there was a rally, and what I did, because the police told me. All these tablets and potions are designed to make me forget. They want to change me into someone else – a better person. So I must take my medication and when I'm better I'll be allowed out."

"That reminds me. Do you think your flat is secure? Would you like us to go round and pick up the post and make sure everything's alright?" Caroline offered brightly, expecting Mary to agree gratefully.

"No."

"We don't mind. It wouldn't be any trouble."

"No." Mary's face hardened and her raised voice contained a note of aggression.

"That's fine then," Philip intervened hurriedly and, desperate to change the subject, added rashly, "Did the police tell you that I was arrested at the rally and ended up with a caution?"

"No, they didn't. They said that the rally had been a waste of time. I think they meant ours rather than theirs. So you attacked someone as well, did you?"

"Well, no – not exactly," the vicar replied, wishing he had not mentioned his involvement.

"Not at all!" Caroline retorted. "You acted, quite rightly, in self-defence. You did not intend to punch that policeman."

"So you attacked a policeman, did you?" Mary continued thoughtfully. "I didn't attack a policeman. Why did they let you go and keep me here?"

The nurse in the corner stood up. "I'm sure it's been very nice for you to see your friends, Mary, but now it's time for them to go. I'm sure they'll be able to come again but it's time for your medication, now." She opened the door and motioned Mary out.

"Goodbye, Mary. We will come again," Caroline called to the departing figure.

"Goodbye," Philip echoed cheerfully.

"Yes. It's because you are a better person than me," was Mary's muttered response, which floated along the corridor.

"What did you make of that?" Philip asked his wife, as they drove away.

"I'm not entirely sure," she replied doubtfully. "Mary certainly seems confused – not her normal self – but I can't help thinking she's playing with them. At times she's too compliant."

"Don't forget she's on medication, something fairly hefty, I suspect."

"Oh yes. It's bound to have an effect but underneath it all I caught very strong glimpses of the old Mary, as we know her."

"It must be very difficult to treat someone like that, out of the blue as it were. Someone who you don't know at all and, presumably, have no previous knowledge of. I didn't realise that she has no family to consult. Still, I'm sure they know what they're doing. They've probably treated hundreds, if not thousands, of cases like Mary's."

"Don't you think it's ironic, though? Remember what MAD stands for? We tend to just concentrate on the opposition to rejuvenation but Mary's been opposed, rightly or wrongly, to chemical intervention for years and now look at her."

234

"Hmm," Philip agreed. "But it's very difficult to know where to draw the line, isn't it? They considered, and perhaps still consider, her to be a danger to herself and others."

"But are they correct? Yes, she's definitely a bit odd and a fanatic and all that, but is she really such a threat or are they just punishing her for her opinions?"

Philip looked at his wife with mock surprise. "Really, dear, you're beginning to sound most militant! I hope you're not right, though. I think what happened was that the rally pushed her over the edge and brought out her frustrations."

Caroline folded her arms and stared, unseeingly at the road ahead. "Pushed them over the edge, more like. People commit much worse crimes and get away with it. You were lucky you didn't end up in there with Mary."

Philip felt a surge of embarrassment. "I hope I'm not that bad," he muttered.

Caroline pounced at once, "There you are! You've admitted it! You agree with them that Mary's a bad person. That's what she was saying, something about having to be a better person."

"Caroline! What's got into you? You're trying to put words into my mouth. You're my rock – you know that – don't crumble. Don't let them put a wedge between us!"

"I'm sorry. I didn't mean it." Caroline was surprised at herself. "It's just that I found the clinic and Mary's behaviour unsettling. It's like seeing a wild animal caged up in a zoo. She shouldn't really be there."

"Don't worry. She's a very strong character – I've a feeling she'll be alright."

Helen subsequently called the first MAD meeting under her acting leadership, as promised. Freddie sent his apologies, being unable to attend as a result of a downturn in Ada's health. The other members were all present but brought with them a depressed, downbeat attitude. It was not improved by Mouland's account of the visit to Mary.

"Oh dear, poor thing," said Rose at once, with genuine concern. "I wonder if I could send her something? Do you think she'd like one of my cakes?"

"The point is – is it enough to just 'tick over' for the time-being?" Howard asked, completely ignoring Rose's question.

"I don't think anyone's quite up to another rally at the moment

235

– are they?" Ricky replied, taking a sweeping glance at everyone present.

"Philip certainly can't take part in one," Caroline declared.

Mouland cleared his throat.

"It's a pity we can't do something just to make our presence felt," Devereux suggested. "The furore caused by the rally's died down but it would be nice to build on the impetus. We certainly earned the publicity, we don't want to have to start all over again from nothing."

"Don't forget that the publicity was all negative," Rose reminded him.

"You know what they say – there's no such thing as bad publicity," Howard countered.

"Perhaps Helen is the best judge of that," Rose replied, pointedly.

Helen gave a wry laugh. "I'm quite resigned to it – used to it, even – now. I agree with Julian, we mustn't mothball MAD, we must find a way of keeping the momentum going."

"What about leaking something to the papers?" Sonja suggested, eagerly. All heads turned towards her and she did not shrink away as she once would have done.

"What do you have in mind?" Ricky enquired, unable to hide the surprise in his voice.

"Why don't we let it slip out that Helen is our new leader? Surely that's newsworthy – Helen raising the stakes in direct opposition to her father?"

"You're right there." Howard scratched his beard thoughtfully, then added hastily, "If you don't object, Helen?"

Everyone looked at her. Although initially a little taken aback by the proposal, Helen had almost instantly regained her composure. "Actually, I think it's a very good idea," she agreed, "but we must emphasise that I'm only the acting leader. As soon as Mary is released I'll step down."

"The newspapers'll gloss over that," Howard whispered in Ricky's ear.

"Presumably you will undertake the leak?" Devereux addressed Sonja dryly as if expecting her to shy away from her bold suggestion.

"Of course. It won't be a problem."

"Are you sure, Helen?" Rose asked again, anxiously. "Do you really want to have to put up with the attention yet again?"

236

"As Sonja so succinctly put it – it won't be a problem." Helen grinned at the younger woman. "I'm used to it now – it hasn't diminished my commitment to the cause – probably the opposite."

"What about the personal grief – there's bound to be some fallout from your father?" Ricky joined in.

"Relations between us couldn't get any worse," Helen replied, shortly. "Let's vote on it."

The vote, predictably, was carried unanimously. Rose considered abstaining but with a shrug of her shoulders raised a hand. Sonja fulfilled her part of the plan and for a day or two the media howled its outrage at this ultimate act of betrayal. Helen was labelled a 'Judas', the irony of which was lost to her detractors but not to herself. Professor Deighton managed to assume fake humility in his ensuing television appearances and despaired loudly at his perceived failings as a parent. Nevertheless, this did not prevent him from declaring at every opportunity that he had 'washed his hands' of his daughter. He had already ceased making payments into Helen's bank account, as soon as the news of the rally had broken. Helen was unperturbed having made wise investments whilst she had the chance. 'I'll just find some work, eventually.' She thought, whilst remaining determined to eschew the myriad of offers to appear on celebrity game shows and reality television, aware that her pre-determined role would be that of a villain.

The months trundled by and MAD merely ticked over, its members unable to seize the initiative or attract further support. Ricky overhauled the website and sifted through the batches of emails which if not junk, were usually abusive. There were one or two messages of support from abroad but nothing to encourage the group. Philip and Caroline had been obliged to vacate the vicarage and were living in a small rented flat. Philip had overseen the decommissioning of more redundant churches than he could bear to count and now even this work was becoming scarce. It would not be long before his employment with the diocese would cease completely.

Freddie's appearances at MAD meetings had been sporadic and even when there he seemed to lack interest and Helen often noticed him daydreaming. She knew that he was pre-occupied with his wife and having remained a frequent visitor to the elderly couple's home, could see that Ada faded between each visit. Finally, one evening her telephone rang and Freddie blurted out the news:

"My wife's died!" he told her. "I thought you'd like to know. She couldn't eat anything for a week. I tried to tempt her with her favourite things, you know, some of our marmalade, but she only took a couple of mouthfuls. Eventually she just didn't want anything at all. They took her into St. Margaret's and said that it would be best if she slipped away. They took it for granted that she would be rejuvenated."

Helen offered the usual, inadequate condolences to the bereaved, lost man. Then she sat for a while, shaken by the finality of death's power, despite having witnessed it so many times before. A germ of doubt, which she knew had always been present somewhere in a deep recess in her mind, grew and uncoiled itself attempting to wend its way to the surface. 'What if the rejuvenates are right?' she thought, 'and I am wrong? How much easier wouldn't it be to abolish this fear of the unknown and cling to physical existence for eternity?' Then she remembered Reverend Mouland and his unwavering faith in the order of birth, life and death – 'as given by nature, if not by God' she thought, and an overwhelming sense that rejuvenation was not the answer, not the elixir of life, wrapped itself around her.

Freddie obviously dazed and, Helen suspected, unable to finally let go of his life-long companion, seemed vague regarding the funeral arrangements.

"I'll let you know as soon as I know," he insisted and Helen thought it best to withdraw and give him time to accept the reality of his loss and the huge change to his life that had taken place in the matter of a nano second. Helen brooded miserably. She could not help pondering the instant which separates life from death. If time can be divided infinitely at what point does it end for an individual? How can so great a change in being take place in such a short time, in an instant? Where does the vitality go? Only questions, leading to yet more questions, never the answer. . .'

A few days later Freddie called her again.

"I just thought I'd let you know – I've made my mind up – Ada's going to be rejuvenated – when I've got the money."

He waited for Helen's response which did not come, she was

busy processing thoughts and controlling her first reaction which was one of astonishment. She had not expected this.

"Are you there?" Freddie called anxiously, hoping that he would not have to repeat his admission.

"Yes. Yes," Helen stuttered.

"Just thought I'd better let you know. I'll resign from MAD obviously."

"Are you alright?"

"Yes. No. Well, as well as can be expected. I'm a lot more at ease with myself now I've decided to go ahead with it."

"What made you decide?" Helen asked tentatively.

"I've been thinking about it for a long time – before she passed away – and I've been torn between knowing it's what she really wanted (and it's in my power to give it to her) and a deep down feeling that somehow it isn't right. But I don't think that I should deny her. I haven't the right – besides, I miss her."

"How will you raise the money?" Helen was aware that Freddie and Ada had not been able to afford an insurance policy and their only income was Freddie's pension.

"That's the thing," Freddie sounded more cheerful. "Ada thought we could never afford it, that's why she didn't insist. She thought it was a dream only available to others, not the likes of her, but I've worked it all out. I've enough money to pay for storage with one of these companies – 'B-Stored UK' I think it is. They've made me a special offer if I do some publicity work – previously being against it all. In the meantime, I'll put my house on the market and rent something small. As soon as it's sold Ada can have the process done and we'll be back together again."

It all sounded so simple. Although disappointed by Freddie's conversion, Helen recognised his desperation and wondered how she would react in his position.

"I'm sorry that you'll be leaving MAD. We'll miss you but you must keep in touch. Let me know if you need anything or any help to move."

"Thank you, Helen. I'm sorry to have turned out to be a disappointment."

"You're not a disappointment, Freddie! I know that you've been faced with a very difficult decision and no one can blame you for your loyalty being to your wife. No one else in MAD has been tested as you have and I think we will all need something more than a moral stance or gut-feeling to overcome the instinct to survive."

"It's nice of you to try to understand. I will phone you again, soon. Thank you for all your support. Goodbye."

Helen busied herself by making an unwanted cup of tea whilst constantly turning over thoughts of Freddie and his dilemma. She wondered who would pass the test. Mouland and Mary definitely would, though for different reasons, and probably Caroline and Julian. As for the others, she was less certain. Howard would perhaps, if he could maintain a sense of belligerence and defiance against authority. Ricky would fail, as would Rose who would be unable to countenance the tearing apart of her family. Sonja's level of commitment was still unknown. She was becoming more intense by the day and if this were to continue and develop into obsessive fanaticism, similar to that which controlled Mary, then she too would pass. Perhaps there will be no test, hopefully society will have come to its senses and the truth, whatever that is, will have been revealed, Helen hoped unrealistically.

Mary had been making steady progress. Philip and Caroline, who remained her only visitors, had been to see her at the clinic regularly and it had reached the stage in Mary's recovery when it was deemed beneficial that she should be allowed out with them for a few hours at a time. Sometimes they wandered round the shops or walked in the parks and when the weather was less kind they drank copious cups of tea and coffee in one of the small cafés nearby. Once or twice, Mary spent the whole day with them in their cramped flat.

The outings were always strained. Mary only undertook them, apparently willingly, in order to complete a further stage in her treatment programme. Mouland and Caroline had little in common with her, who even when on her best, most affected behaviour, could not help slipping into blinkered, monosyllabic mode from time to time. The vicar and his wife took great care to avoid any topics of conversation which they thought might antagonise her. However, one day Mary surprised them.

"I hear that Helen has taken over MAD," she announced.

Caroline spluttered over her cup: "Not taken over. She's just acting leader until you're fully fit again – she's been very insistent on that, in fact, we all are."

"How did you hear?" Mouland asked, trying to sound casual.

"I read it in a newspaper weeks ago. I wasn't supposed to have access to newspapers or anything on the television which might upset me but someone left it lying around – rather fortuitous, don't you think? I suspect it was my nurse in an attempt to sabotage my recovery."

"It's not a secret as far as we are concerned."

"But you failed to inform me."

Mouland sighed but decided to be honest: "Look, Mary, we didn't know how you'd take it and it's true that we didn't want to upset you or do or say anything which might jeopardise your recovery, which is our primary concern and yours too, presumably."

"Helen only agreed to it on the understanding that it's a temporary, stop-gap measure," Caroline repeated. "We needed someone to take the reins in your absence – to ensure that the group doesn't fade away. As it is we're not doing very much – just keeping MAD running, really. The last little push we made was to leak Helen's temporary position to the press, and that was purely to keep our opposition to rejuvenation in the public eye – to let them know that we haven't gone away. We're waiting for you to return, take charge again and propel us forward."

"You needn't have worried. I am not upset by it," Mary lied, having lain awake night after night examining Helen's, and indeed all the other MAD members', possible motives for this act of treachery and planning a range of possible schemes in vengeance. "I quite understand and believe that you have made a very good choice in the best interests of MAD. It won't be long now, until I am ready to return."

Philip and Caroline sighed with relief, simultaneously, both believing that they had successfully navigated this particularly dangerous obstacle.

"Erm, there is one piece of slightly unwelcome news we must give you," Mouland revealed with obvious unease. "Freddie's left."

"Oh," Mary sounded uninterested.

"It was following his wife's death," Philip continued, assuming incorrectly that Mary would wish to know the details,

241

l

"She was very pro-rejuvenation, apparently, and he's decided that he shouldn't go against her wishes."

Mary failed to respond.

"I think he found the choice very difficult," Caroline added, in an attempt to soften what she considered to be bad news.

"As I said," Mary repeated, "I'll soon be freed and able to continue my work. At my next review they're due to decide whether I'm ready to be allowed out on my own."

"That's wonderful!" Philip exclaimed, genuinely pleased, "We'll keep our fingers crossed for you but I'm sure it won't be necessary."

Mary was duly returned to the sanctity of the clinic, where, as far as the staff knew, she continued to take her medication and endeavoured to become a model patient. Unsurprisingly, she had quickly developed a technique to conceal her tablets on a ridge, high up, on her right, upper gum. Once the nurse was satisfied that she had swallowed them she flushed them down the lavatory. Mary knew that the pills were useless, their only function being to contain her personality soporifically rather than to alter it. 'I have the right to think as I believe' she thought, whilst watching the little blue capsules disappear in a swirl of water. The medical team's main concern was her staunch refusal to end her opposition to rejuvenation which they believed was a sign that her progress was limited. Eventually Mary realised this and very gradually softened her attitude and, after a realistic period of time had passed, began to voice gentle doubts.

Consequently, at the review it was decided that she could now be allowed out unaccompanied between the hours of ten o'clock in the morning and five o'clock in the afternoon, once a week to be extended to up to three times a week if all proved satisfactory. Mary feigned gratitude and demonstrated just the right level of happy satisfaction. Inside the pleasure of her 'progress' burned like a white-hot rod and once in the confines of her room, she assumed what she considered to be a wide smile. There was no need to plan how she would spend her outings – this had already been done weeks ago. As leader of MAD she knew Helen's address, now it was merely a matter of locating it.

For several weeks Mary spent the whole of each of her free days watching Helen's home and following her, undetected. Sometimes Helen did not appear and Mary was unsure whether she was at home or not, but gradually she was able to identify tiny clues and gain an uncannily accurate sense of Helen's movements. One cold, wet and miserable winter's day found Mary in her usual vantage point, a bench seat in a little wooden shelter in the park opposite, awaiting Helen's return home. Mary knew she was out. The time edged nearer to 4.30pm when Mary would have to start making her way back to the clinic if she were to return on time, but today she felt an undeniable reluctance. For some reason she needed to set eyes on her prey, perhaps even to follow her. Today, watching and waiting would not be enough. 'It won't matter if I'm late back, just this once.' She thought. 'I've been very good until now and they probably won't even notice.' She continued to wait. A sixth, hunter's, sense prompted her to move to the seclusion of a large, ferocious holly bush which spread its prickly leaves at the side of the small iron park gate. Within seconds Mary shook in anticipation – Helen had returned.

Mary watched her unlock the front door and disappear inside. Then she witnessed the switching on and off of lights and the drawing of curtains in exactly the order she had predicted. She squinted at her watch face, which was by now speckled with minute raindrops, and decided that at 5.10pm it was time to go. As she left her hiding place, still in full view of her quarry's home, all the lights were extinguished and Mary knew that Helen must be going out again. With surprising nimbleness, she darted back behind the bush and did not even try to ignore the welling impulse to follow the unsuspecting woman.

Helen hurried down the street, the wind tugging annoyingly at her umbrella which did very little to protect her from the incessant rain. Finally, after it had blown inside out several times, she roughly snapped the useless device to closed position, deliberately bent the stem against her knee (with evident satisfaction) and stuffed it into the nearest bin. She had spent the day helping Freddie pack prior to his move which was due to take place the following day. At first he had been embarrassed at seeing her and felt sure that she would resent his change of allegiance. Even Helen was surprised that she harboured no anger or even annoyance or disappointment towards him. Instead, she experienced an unusual sense of calm understanding. Freddie, in his awkwardness, had tried to broach the subject and explain again, "I'm ever so grateful for your help," he began and then, standing with his hands on his hips and surveying the jumble of half-filled boxes, continued, "It's surprising all the things you accumulate when you've lived in the same house for so long. Let's see. . . me and Ada's been here for fifty-four years now. I'm going to have to try to get rid of more of it though, it will never fit into our new place. It's hard to know what Ada will want to keep."

"All we can do for now is to get it packed in time for tomorrow. You'll have to do some more sorting when you unpack," Helen suggested.

"I'm sorry that I've let you down," Freddie said, suddenly. "It's just that it's been so hard, you see. Life's too short, if you know what I mean. Mark my words, you must hang on to what you've got."

"I've told you before – you haven't let me down," Helen repeated, "and I do understand."

'Probably more than he realises,' she thought, sealing a large carton. Whether or not Freddie's actions had created the doubt inside her or whether it had always been there, in need of nourishment, she did not know. The explosive change in the nature of society had led her to question everything and then to question her questions. A recurring thought was that of her rift with her father. 'What was the point of living an extended life if it was to be one of conflict and pain? It was not a case of quality versus quantity – merely one of quality, whether a lifespan was a century or an eternity.' She could do nothing about society's growing ills but she could seek reconciliation with her father.

The desire nagged at her throughout the day and by the time she reached her home, still deep in thought, she had decided that she would arrange to visit the professor within the next few days. She tried to deflect her morose mood by settling into her usual routine and flitted around the rooms, making tea and switching the television on in time for the news. Before the kettle had had time to boil she glanced at the television screen unseeingly, for her attention was drawn to the faded photograph of her parents on their wedding day which stood next to it. This token from the past, a tiny slice of time preserved in two dimensions forever, made her tremble with hope, decision and a desire for action. 'Why wait?' She thought. She would go now. Her father was bound to still be at work, feeding from the opulence of his new, gleaming laboratory.

Chapter Nineteen

At 5.30pm that day, Reverend Mouland received a telephone call from the 'Sunny Days' clinic.

"Hello," called an anxious voice through the receiver, "I've been asked to contact you to see if Mary Fields is with you."

"No, she isn't," the vicar replied with an immediate sense of foreboding. "I haven't seen her for a while and certainly not today. Is there a problem?"

"Hopefully not," the voice continued. "She's just a little late back from her day out. That's all. She'll probably turn up soon – I expect she's sheltering from the rain somewhere." The voice attempted unsuccessfully to sound casual.

"Is there anything I can do to help?"

"No. It's quite alright – unless, of course, you could let us know if she does come round to you or makes contact?"

"Yes, of course I will."

Philip turned to Caroline thoughtfully, "I don't quite like the sound of that. The woman sounded extremely jittery, although she tried to hide it," he said, before repeating the contents of the conversation.

"Where do you think she would go?" Caroline asked. "I assume they've checked her flat?"

"I don't know. I didn't think to ask. Let's try ringing."

The vicar punched in the number and listened in frustration for several minutes to the cold tone of the unanswered telephone.

"She might not answer, even if she is there," Caroline observed. "Perhaps we should try all the MAD members?"

"Yes, I'll start with Helen."

There was no reply. Mouland had more success as he worked his way through the list – everyone else answered but confirmed with surprise that they had not seen Mary.

"We had better go round to her flat. We can keep trying Helen at the same time," Caroline suggested. It was obvious that Mary's home was deserted as they approached along the road. The curtains were half-drawn as they had been for months, there were no lights visible and a large weed had grown from under the threshold to the front door undisturbed.

"I'd better make sure," Philip muttered as he hurried from the vehicle into the rain, which was by now turning into a stationary mist. Caroline watched as he hammered unproductively on the front door and then stood back from the building and aimed a handful of gravel at the first floor living-room window.

"No good," he confirmed unnecessarily as he flopped, heavily, back into the driver's seat.

"There's still no response from Helen," Caroline said, waving her mobile phone in his face.

"Just keep trying – I'd like to be sure there's no problem. Better still, phone the clinic again – Mary might have turned up." Caroline did as she was told. Mary was still absent and it was soon apparent that Helen was not at home.

"I must admit I'm worried," Philip confessed. "Mary's always followed the clinic's programme and rules to the tee until now. Either something's happened to her or she's up to no good. You have tried Helen's mobile, haven't you?"

"Yes, of course, but it's switched off – I just get the answering machine – I've left a message."

"I'm not entirely convinced Mary's happy with Helen's acting leadership, you know, despite her positive reaction. In fact, she may have accepted it too easily – she could be pulling the wool over our eyes."

"She could easily be harbouring a grudge," Caroline agreed. "And she's intelligent and devious enough to bide her time – she would actually enjoy brooding on it. What's that saying 'revenge is a dish best served cold' – or is it hot? I can't remember but in Mary's case the longer she waits the more determined she becomes."

"Let"s try and think clearly," Mouland commanded, taking

246

control. "We don't know that Mary's with Helen but neither can we discount the possibility because we haven't been able to contact either of them. If Mary's up to no good we suspect that she might be upset with MAD having elected a new, temporary leader."

"In that case, she could take it out on any one of us."

"True, but no one's seen or heard anything of her. Helen would be her most likely target."

"Let's forget about MAD for a moment – who else could she have it in for?"

"God knows!" The vicar blasphemed in an unguarded moment. "I'm sure there's a list as long as my arm."

"What about the medical staff at the clinic?"

"She doesn't have to go missing to exact some kind of revenge on them – she could easily do that from within."

"Or the police officers who arrested her?"

"They're a possibility but probably not at the top of her list."

Then Caroline made a connection: "Oh! We've been so stupid! Who do you think's at the top of her list, always has been – Professor Deighton, of course!"

Mouland grimaced; "You're right – she could be after him, especially following all the recent publicity about the state of the art new laboratory he's just had commissioned, and the other connection is Helen, herself, of course. It could be nothing, and I sincerely hope it is, but her failure to respond to any of our calls makes me uneasy – it's uncharacteristic of her. Perhaps they're all together somewhere."

"Do you mean that she might be in league with Mary, that they've hatched some sort of plan against him and perhaps his new premises?"

Mouland sighed and rubbed a weary hand over his thinning hair. "I really don't know. Anything's possible. Don't forget Helen's steely determination – she's put up with more than anyone and sacrificed so much as a result of her beliefs and throughout it all she's never wavered. There's a touch of fanaticism about her too, you know."

"We'd better get over there," Caroline decided immediately, convinced and perturbed by her husband's thoughts.

"I'll go," Mouland replied. "It'll take hours in the car at this time of day. Drop me off at the nearest tube station and I'll make my way from there. You go home, give Julian a ring and tell him what we suspect and keep in touch with the clinic – if Mary or Helen turn up let me know." They departed on their respective journeys and Mouland joined the airless, frenzy of the rush-hour underground.

Mary had, with difficulty, kept track of Helen as she, too, boarded the tube-train.

Gradually, Mary realised her destination and she unknowingly assumed a wry smile as she clung to the overhead support in the packed, jolting carriage. After several stops the two women reached Imperial Street and made their way independently along the wide, straight road. In the distance, a good mile ahead, Deighton's gleaming, new, laboratory glowed in front of them. Helen strode purposefully, if not hurriedly, still engrossed in her thoughts, fears and hopes but determinedly eschewing the possibility that her father would reject her attempt at reconciliation or even refuse, with characteristic aggression, to meet her.

Mary followed at a safe distance, lumbering along in the shadows of the large, red-brick, Victorian warehouses which lined the pavements. They had covered almost half a mile when Mouland burst out of the tube station, breathless and perspiring, and joined the strange procession. Running as fast as his age and physical condition would allow – which was by now little more than a trot – and peering hard ahead into the gloom, he at last discerned the bat-like figure which was unmistakeably Mary.

The vicar relaxed, sure that he could catch up with her before she reached Deighton"s laboratory. Then she disappeared.

"Damn! Damn! Damn!" he cried. "Where can she have gone?"

Mary had decided to slip down one of the numerous, small, side streets which were inter-connected with tiny, rubbish-filled alleys. 'Then I will be able to approach her directly.' She thought. 'I will be able to step in front of her with no warning, no sense that she'd being followed and no give-away sound of the rustle of clothes or heavy footsteps.'

When Mouland reached the spot at which Mary had vanished he guessed her intention at once and, without thinking, started off once again in pursuit. It would have been more sensible to have hurried along the pavement towards the other silhouette which he had recognised as being Helen. He would have reached her before Mary and would have been able to warn her. Instead, he took a wrong turn and found himself in a dead-end. Swearing and praying simultaneously, he retraced his steps.

Helen had been oblivious to the person who sprang out in front of her. She immediately recognised, with puzzlement, the familiar, white face, which by now wore an impassionate, rictus grin, and the watery blue, expressionless eyes.

"What do you want?" she began, before feeling the harsh blow of steel between her ribs. Moments later, Mouland reappeared from the maze to find Helen lying in a crouched, child-like position, her forehead pressed against the damp, smelly pavement and Mary staring at her quizzically.

"My God! What have you done!" he yelled in horror, before rolling Helen gently to one side. The curved handle of some kind of knife, which Mouland was unable to recognise, protruded from the left side of Helen's chest.

"I did nothing. I saw nothing," Mary repeated mechanically over and over again.

Mouland, applying pressure to Helen's wound with one hand, fumbled with his other for his phone and rang the emergency services.

The door closed and Professor Deighton sighed loudly and contentedly. For a moment or two, he allowed himself to relax back comfortably in his leather, executive chair, close his eyes and wallow in the pleasant daydreams of his undoubted success. He had just completed an examination of his most treasured patient, John Chert, the forty-six-year-old man who had been his first successful rejuvenate. 'The man's a medical miracle.' Deighton mused without modesty, referring to the patient, although he would have felt no reluctance or embarrassment had he been describing himself. He mentally ran through the tests and examinations that Chert had passed with such flying colours.

Physically, he seemed at least ten years younger with the strength and energy of a typical, healthy thirty-year-old. Lung function – excellent, liver function – excellent, no sign of heart disease, cholesterol low. . . Deighton ticked off each test on his fingers before rubbing his chin thoughtfully. Interestingly, Chert's IQ had risen too, even allowing for improvement with increased frequency of testing. 'There might be something in that,' the professor thought hopefully, 'I wonder how I could exploit it – my next big discovery!'

Fame and fortune had become a drug to him. His desire for it was insatiable. His fear that one day it would wane, that the public would become indifferent to his discovery and uninterested in himself, was the only spot to blight his supreme self-satisfaction. The thought niggled him constantly. Deighton knew that, if left untreated, the blight would grow and eventually weaken and destroy him – perhaps Chert would provide the antidote. The professor smiled benignly as his patient's name formed in his mind. 'What a success!' He thought again. The whole process had given Chert more than, literally, a new lease of life and with it physical prowess – not only had the man achieved more in his working life than he had ever previously dreamed, he had increased his opportunities and become a rich man as a result of his celebrity status. The end result had been that he was more focused, more energised and more ruthless.

Deighton roused himself and glanced at his watch – 6.30pm. Should he examine Chert's data once more, or should he go home? Peering into the vacuum of a cold, damp, December evening, through the panoramic window which overlooked the city, he decided to leave. His decision was bolstered by the familiar scream of sirens and flashing blue and red lights of emergency service vehicles as an ambulance and several police cars halted awkwardly two or three hundred yards down the road. 'Damn!' He thought, peering into the darkened street, 'I'd better go before they close the road or I'll be here forever – I suppose someone's been mugged again.'

After hurriedly grabbing his coat and briefcase, he slipped quickly down to the underground car park. The plump, leather upholstery of his newly purchased, top of the range, Jaguar, wrapped itself round him, cushioning him from the reality of the depressing weather. The heater provided instant warmth and the oddly comforting sound of strangers' voices which babbled from the radio pushed the great scientist further into the recesses of his own world. Deighton swung his vehicle confidently out of the car park and up the, now quiet, street which was deserted apart from the drama being performed further along. The professor frowned, praying that he would be allowed to pass by. A policeman who had begun to erect warning and diversion signs gestured to

Deighton to stop. "You'll have to go that way, sir," he ordered, pointing to one of the narrow side streets on the right, "there's been an incident."

"Is there no way that I can be allowed through, officer?"

Deighton smiled as he enquired politely. "There's only me at the moment and the area's not cordoned off yet."

The police officer looked as if he was about to issue a short, hostile, rebuff when something stopped him. Instead, he peered at Deighton with an air of unplaced recognition.

"Would you switch on the interior light, sir?" he demanded, before staring into the Professor's face again. "Are you that reporter off the telly, the one that does the science news?"

"No. I'm Professor Marcus Deighton. You may have seen me on television – I'm often featured. . ." he began smugly before the officer interjected excitedly:

"I've got it! I know who you are – you're the bloke they call Mr Frankenstein – the one who invented rejuvenation!"

Deighton glanced in his rear view mirror and touched his grey hair unconsciously. "Yes. You're quite right – that is indeed who I am."

Someone shouted and the young police officer stepped back. "Nip through quick, sir – you've just got time."

Deighton flicked his head in an almost imperceptible gesture of thanks. As he accelerated away from the flashing lights, he caught a glimpse of the unfortunate victim but could not decipher whether it was male or female. Paramedics bent over the body, their green suits shielding it from prying eyes, whilst a blood-stained priest leaned wearily against the wall watching a woman being led to a waiting police car.

The professor instantly erased these images from his mind with minimal effort.

Feeling very pleased that his fame had, once again, afforded him special treatment, and smiling contentedly at the mirror, he turned up the radio and sped home.

Mary and Mouland found themselves, once again, being questioned by Roux and Inch at Greenborough Street Police Station. Mary, having been examined by a doctor and declared fit to be interviewed, was taken into a small room accompanied by the duty solicitor. "Remember, you are not obliged to say anything but if you've nothing to hide it shouldn't do any harm to answer their questions with care."

Mary merely pursed her lips and folded her arms in reply.

Mouland languished in a waiting area trying to decipher what he had witnessed. However hard he tried, he could not prevent himself from returning to the same conclusion over and over again – he was sure that Mary had done it. Roux and Inch assumed their well-rehearsed roles. Roux opened the conversation efficiently, but not unkindly:

"Right then, Miss Fields, if you could just run through what happened, please?"

Mary, who had regained her composure and had stopped repeating her mantra during the journey to the station, replied, "Well, it's exactly as I told Reverend Mouland – I saw nothing. I stumbled across her and saw that she had been stabbed. Then he appeared from down a side street."

The solicitor visibly relaxed. Roux looked at him swiftly and disdainfully from the corner of one eye before asking, "By 'he' you mean the reverend?"

"Yes. I have no idea what he was doing there." Mary stared into Inch's eyes until he felt uncomfortable and, annoyed with himself, eventually had to glance away.

"What were you doing there?"

"Minding my own business."

The solicitor coughed.

"Come on, Mary," Roux adopted an even kinder, fatherly tone, "you know that's no good. If you want to put yourself in the clear you have to answer our questions seriously and help us find who did do it."

"Alright." Mary shrugged in the manner of a sulky teenager. "If you must know, I was on my way to see Professor Deighton. I wanted to make a direct appeal to him to make him see sense and cease his meddling and put an end to his evil rejuvenation process. I suddenly realised, only today, that we had never interacted with him on a personal level and perhaps that was what was needed. I'm sure that I could convince him."

'Fat chance.' thought Inch.

"You reached that conclusion on your own, did you?" Roux continued.

"Yes."

"And you resolved to undertake the meeting alone?"

"Yes."

"So you hadn't made your way there with Helen Deighton?"

"No. She knew nothing of it. Anyway, she would be the last person I would consult – I'm sure you've heard about her fall-out with the professor."

"How did you get there?"

"Walked, tube, walked."

"What time did you set off?"

"Must have been about 5.00pm. I was due to return to 'Sunny Days' but that's when I had the idea and it couldn't wait – I had to go straightaway before it was too late."

"Are you usually impulsive?" Inch joined in at last.

"Not particularly."

"You'd been on one of your days out – hadn't you?" Roux assumed the lead again. "How had you spent the day?"

"Walking, sitting in the parks."

"Not very nice weather for that, eh?"

"No. As you can see, I'm very wet."

"Which parks and at what times?" Inch demanded.

Mary reeled off a short list of local parks and gardens in a bored voice, careful to omit the one opposite Helen's house.

"Have you still got your ticket?"

Mary retrieved it from her lumpy shoulder bag and slapped it onto the table. Inch began to examine it.

"I'll need it to get back to 'Sunny Days'." She warned him.

"Don't worry about that – we'll give you a lift," Roux replied gently. "So you set off to visit Professor Deighton, quite alone, and on your way stumbled across Miss Deighton?"

"Yes. That's exactly right. Apart from the fact that Reverend Mouland was there for some reason. He stepped out of the shadows and said something like, 'For Christ's sake look what you've done.' I didn't think Christians were allowed to say things like that – isn't it 'taking the Lord's name in vain?' "

Roux, ignoring her last remark, continued: "So, you think he thought you might have had something to do with the assault?"

"Obviously – as I am aware that you do, too. I can assure you that I did not, although I don't suppose that you will believe me.

You will find no evidence, though. Perhaps you should ask Reverend Mouland what he was doing there?"

"Oh, we will, in due course."

"Just for the record," Inch sneered. "Did you stab her?"

"No."

Roux sat upright, signalling the end of the interview. "I think we can let you go, for now – back to 'Sunny Days' – while we carry out the rest of our investigations."

"Thank you." Mary smiled sweetly at the inspector in a way that she had not done for many years. Inch escorted her to a police car where a nurse from the clinic was waiting.

'Why does everything go wrong?' Mary asked herself as she was ushered into the back seat.

"What do you think?" Inch asked his superior on his return.

"As mad as a hatter which means she's dangerous. Let's get Mouland in."

The vicar carefully described the evening's events and his and Caroline's concern for both Mary and Helen and even Deighton.

"So Miss Fields and Miss Deighton definitely weren't together?" Roux asked.

"No. Mary was following – I'm sure of that – that's how I came to get lost down a side street. I was trying to keep her in sight and following her."

"And when you came across the pair, what exactly did you see?"

"Helen was lying on the ground – curled up to be precise – with the handle of a knife protruding from her chest and Mary was standing over her."

"So you didn't actually see Mary stab her?"

"No," Mouland raised both hands helplessly as though he was about to bless the two men, "but there was no one else there. No one at all. I didn't see a single soul and I'm sure I would have. . ."

"Do you think she did it?"

The vicar cast both eyes to the ground before replying with reluctance, "If you wish to know what I really think – then, yes, but I may be wrong. Based on what I actually saw, or didn't see, it's the only logical explanation."

"OK. You can go now but we'd like to speak to your wife in the morning. Hopefully our forensic tests will throw more light on what actually took place – one way or another."

Roux waited for a few moments after Mouland had closed the door and padded down the corridor.

"I'm not at all happy about that chap," he revealed, thoughtfully, whilst stroking his chin. "We'd better keep a watch on him for the time being. First he turns up as a suspect in an arson case, then he assaults a police officer and now he's the first on the scene of, what could turn out to be, a fatal stabbing. Also, he's pretty determined to pin it on Mary, despite her efforts to make it look otherwise. It's his word against hers."

"It's a pity – or perhaps lucky for one of them – that there are no other witnesses. That's a bit unusual," Inch observed.

"We don't know for sure that there are no other witnesses – just that neither of those two saw anyone. It was that funny time, just after the rush hour when most people have just got in and on a night like tonight probably had no desire to go out again. Someone might turn up, though."

"Did you notice Mary's implication that it could have been him?"

Roux nodded before allowing Inch to continue:

"After all, he could have been lurking around somewhere and contrived to make it appear that he only just turned up."

"His wife should be able to throw some light on that – unless he hoodwinked her. Would you really get into such a panic just because Fields was missing and Miss Deighton didn't answer her phone?"

"Any news about Miss Deighton, sir?"

"Still critical. Hopefully she'll remember something if she pulls through."

"Oh well, if she doesn't her dad will have her rejuvenated, won't he?"

"Not necessarily. Don't forget she's been hell-bent against him and his precious process and if she's made a living will they won't be able to go against her wishes."

"Surely the state can over-ride the wishes of the individual in cases like this?" Inch asked in genuine surprise.

"I'm sure they will be able to – in due course – but the legislation's not out yet."

"What about motives?"

"Fields is a fanatic and is probably jealous of Miss Deighton – remember that fuss in the newspapers a few weeks ago about her becoming the new leader of that crazy little society – MADNESS or whatever they call themselves? That was her baby and she's led it for a long time. Besides, I don't think she would need a real motive, just something imaginary in her head."

"And Mouland?"

"Like I said, I think he could be a nasty piece of work, deep down. He's an extremist as well, of course, but why he would attack Helen Deighton I have no idea."

"Unless she'd had a change of mind about her opposition to the rejuvenation process? Why was she in Imperial Street? She must have been on her way to the professor's lab. Perhaps she was on her way to make it up with him and Mouland got wind of it? That sort of gross betrayal, in his eyes, could be enough to tip him over the edge."

"She could have been spoiling for another fight with her father over the new lab or something. We'll find out more soon enough, I suppose. I want to arrange a reconstruction for next week and let's hope this hasn't turned into a murder investigation by then."

"Murder's a funny thing now, isn't it?" Inch mused. It used to be the worst crime you could commit but now that people can be rejuvenated – as long as they've got the money or insurance cover – it doesn't really exist anymore. It's almost as if there's no point in doing it."

"Not everyone can be rejuvenated straightaway, don't forget." Roux pointed out. "Some, depending on the actual cause of death, can only be stored awaiting the medical advances to repair or cure their bodies."

"Yeah, but it's not the same as it was. It's not such a big thing, not such a crime. You can't really take a life anymore."

"Don't sound so disappointed!" Roux joked. "I think you'll find that the law will change in due course to take account of that. It's being discussed and thrashed out in high places and there's the suggestion of a new offence – 'interruption to life'. As you quite rightly say, though, it won't be considered as serious as the old murder charge."

"Do you think that's what accounts for the increase in attacks and murders that we've seen lately? People undertake it more lightly knowing that they haven't actually taken a life permanently, if you know what I mean?"

"It's certainly been a headache for the legal system – that's why so many cases have been adjourned or charges deferred. Of course, the prickly issue concerns those with no means for rejuvenation – should there be a separate offence for that?

Inch groaned. "That would be a complete minefield. They'd probably have to prove that the assailant knew the victim couldn't afford the procedure."

"I rather think they'll come up with a blanket offence based on the fact that rejuvenation is possible and therefore the permanent taking of a life is impossible. You know how these lawyers twist things!"

"And make a lot of money out of it. Well, it won't help us – there'll be more muggings, robberies and burglaries on an even bigger scale. People are even more desperate for money now. I'm glad I've got the force's insurance plan." Inch noticed, with irritation, a sliver of black ink on his stiff, white, shirt cuff. He dabbed at it with his dampened handkerchief, ineffectively.

"It's early days yet but as firms see the benefit of continuity of employment, I think more and more will offer schemes as a matter of course and then there's the government plan to increase National Insurance contributions and make it an extension of the welfare state but they're dragging their feet because they haven't the funds for people who want it now," Roux continued, before warning the dapper detective: "You'll only make it worse."

"It's one investment everyone's guaranteed to want a return on – which is why the premiums are so expensive." Inch swore quietly to himself; the ink stain now resembled an insect with a long thin body and a multitude of tentacles and legs.

Roux resisted the temptation to say, 'I told you so' and, instead, continued professionally, "The costs are bound to reduce as Professor Deighton expands his clinics and trains more operatives. Apparently, the procedure's quite simple, when you know how. Full medical training isn't necessary – technicians are doing it."

"Perhaps I missed my vocation, sir!"

Professor Deighton was just about to sit down to his evening meal when his housekeeper informed him that two police officers were at the door and wished to speak to him urgently. Puzzled and hoping that there had not been a security breach at the laboratory, the professor ordered that they be shown in.

"You are Professor Deighton, sir – the father of Miss Helen Deighton?" the senior officer confirmed, unnecessarily.

"Yes," he answered shortly whilst a bubble of anger formed within. 'What the hell's she done now?' he thought.

"I'm sorry to inform you that your daughter has been involved in a serious incident."

"Oh, Christ! I suppose she's been causing yet more trouble! Let me make it clear, I washed my hands of her a long time ago. I cannot take responsibility for, and am not interested in, her actions!" Deighton turned back towards his rapidly cooling meal in indication that the conversation was at an end.

"No, that's not it, sir – you don't understand. Miss Deighton suffered a serious assault earlier this evening and is in a critical condition at St. Imelda's."

"What kind of assault?" The bubble of annoyance burst instantaneously, Deighton's features had turned grey and an unfamiliar, empty chill gushed through him instead.

"A knife attack, sir. Just down the road from your new premises."

"I don't understand – what was she doing there?" The professor's arrogance was seeping away rapidly. "Do you know who did it?" he continued uncertainly.

"A couple of people are helping with our enquiries but obviously it's early days yet. Is there anyone who can drive you to St. Imelda's, sir?" The officer had noticed the half-empty wine glass.

"Yes. Yes." Deighton's confidence had shrivelled to nothing.

"We can give you an escort, if you like."

As the two vehicles screamed their way to the hospital, the professor, slumped in the back of his car, realised that he could not give up his daughter completely. 'If she doesn't pull through, I'll rejuvenate her, whatever her previous wishes. No one can stop me and I'm sure she expected to live a natural term rather than her life being snuffed out violently and prematurely.'

Helen remained unconscious for several weeks, although her condition changed from critical to stable. She had suffered serious internal bleeding which made her father's undisclosed plan to 'artificially close down life function' and rejuvenate her impractical. He still planned to put her in storage, pending medical advances in treatment, should she pass away naturally.

The police had made little progress with their investigation – Mouland and Mary had proved correct in their assertions that there were no witnesses. A reconstruction and huge publicity had produced no useful information. The forensic tests had revealed both Mary's and Mouland's DNA, amongst a small number of others' on the knife and Helen's clothes. Roux and Inch remained perplexed and frustrated.

"Between you and me – and don't let this go any further," Roux warned. "I'm being pressurised from above to get a conviction – any conviction. Deighton moves in high places and he's been bending the Chief's ear. The Chief's annoyed by all the negative publicity and the public grumbling about the rising crime rate and falling number of arrests."

"So it's got to be either Mouland or Fields, then?"

"Yes. The Chief wants us to go with Fields. His line of thought is that she's a nutter anyhow and she's got no friends or family to make a fuss. He thinks we should be able to persuade Mouland that he actually saw her put the knife in." Roux waited for Inch's response but the young man remained silent, still naïve enough to be shocked at the suggestion.

"I'm not at all happy about it," Roux finally declared. "I didn't join the police force, all those years ago, to frame people, so I'm going to hang it out as long as possible. We can't do anything, anyway, until Miss Deighton either recovers or otherwise. If she comes round, hopefully she'll be able to provide us with some evidence – she might even know who did it."

"Hmm," was the only reply that Inch felt able to make at that moment.

Helen regained consciousness shortly after and, on hearing the news, Roux and Inch rushed to her bedside.

"You can only speak to her very briefly – she's very weak," the attendant nurse warned.

Roux nodded impatiently.

"Did you recognise your assailant?" he asked the listless, pale figure who lay propped and breathless in the hospital bed.

"Yes," she whispered.

"Who was it?"

Helen made a huge effort, "John Chert."

Roux and Inch had not expected this. Inch stared at his superior vacantly.

"John Chert?" Roux repeated incredulously. "Are you absolutely sure?"

Helen, whose eyes had fallen shut as a result of her effort, nodded. Then after a huge and visible summoning of strength added, "He had no eyes. There was no light in his eyes."

The detectives exchanged puzzled glances and the nurse examined her patient's features anxiously. Helen sank back into the pillows. "It is done," she breathed.

The nurse who had been monitoring the bank of machines surrounding the bed, sprang into action, "That's enough! She must rest now."

Roux was already calling his colleagues and ordering them to track down Chert.

The arrest of Professor Deighton's first and most celebrated rejuvenation success signalled the end of his fêted discovery. DNA linked Chert to the crime and finally he, almost nonchalantly, admitted it confirming that it was a random attack carried out 'because he felt like it'.

"I often feel like it," he admitted casually.

It was true. Chert's admissions and further investigations linked him with a number of crimes ranging from assault to murder for which he showed no remorse, merely indifference. There were never any witnesses. He had never been seen. It was as though his presence could not be felt, seen or detected in any form. It was as if he had never been there. Psychiatric tests revealed that Chert's ruthlessness and aggression was increasing whilst his ability to empathise had reduced to nothing. He had become a shell – a human being devoid of a soul. Consequently, all rejuvenates were called in for comprehensive assessment and the public's worst fears were realised – every one of them was exhibiting signs of deterioration and at an exponential rate. Rejuvenation was banned.

Professor Deighton's devastation was compounded by the sudden news of his daughter's death. Having made slow, but genuine, steps towards recovery from her wound, Helen succumbed to one of the ubiquitous and invasive super-bug infections. The professor removed himself from the intrusion of publicity, which he now felt so painful but had once so desired, and locked himself into his palatial home, alone. There he remained for months subjecting himself to introspection and wishing that instead of devising a method of prolonging time, he could turn the clock back. Finally, typifying his lack of imagination, he took himself off to a Tibetan monastery where he attempted to cleanse his soul through meditation and self-denial. It was not greatly successful. In due course, he came to believe that it had been revealed to him that he could still serve society by dedicating his scientific knowledge and great resources to seeking an antidote to counter the march of the super-bug army. The thought flickered in the back of his mind that success in this field would replace his notoriety with fame and fortune, once again.

All the MAD members, unsurprisingly, rejoiced at the ban, whilst at the same time mourning Helen. Mary was freed from the 'Sunny Days Clinic' only after considerable pressure from Reverend Mouland, despite the fact that the authorities had little reason to keep her incarcerated. Mouland, Caroline and Devereux left MAD feeling that they had accomplished their mission and Mouland was reinstated as a member of the extremely busy and growing clergy. He was, once again, invited to be interviewed at the radio station. This time the presenter was to be Tara Golesworthy who, having used her talents to their full extent and shown almost insane determination, had been rewarded with several stages of promotion. She greeted Mouland in her usual manner:

"You must be feeling very smug, having been right all along?" she began.

"Well, I hope not smug, but I do have renewed faith in my convictions and am pleased that we managed to keep the alternative option alive. I take no pleasure, however, from the turmoil and distress that the rejuvenation debacle has caused."

"Although you may have proved your point, in that rejuvenation has turned out to have drawbacks, that does not necessarily mean that all your other mumbo jumbo is correct, though – does it?"

Mouland wondered why he had agreed to the interview.

"True. One cannot extrapolate directly from the folly of rejuvenation technique to the existence of God, for example, but I think that our failed attempt at creation – or re-creation if you like – has shown that there is definitely another component to the equation. Rejuvenation produced 'empty' people, as it were, and

I would argue that emptiness signifies a lack of spirit – a lack of a soul."

"You've shown yourself to be a bit of a rebel, haven't you, Reverend Moundland? Are you going to miss not having something to complain about?"

Mouland laughed. "I wouldn't describe myself as a rebel but my experiences during the last few years have brought something else to my attention. I feel that there is a very worrying tendency towards the stifling of freedom of speech and even freedom of thought. The authorities proved themselves very keen to lock away one of our MAD members for a very long time, purely on the basis of her beliefs, using the pretext of an isolated, minor offence whilst at the same time much worse offenders were having little, or no, action taken against them."

"Belief can be a very dangerous thing but thank you Reverend Moundland. We've reached the end of a chapter in your life, for sure, but I think we all agree that the worst thing about it all is that people had spent a lot of money on rejuvenation, for nothing."